THE WINNER

ALSO BY TEDDY WAYNE

THE GREAT MAN THEORY

APARTMENT

LONER

THE LOVE SONG OF JONNY VALENTINE

KAPITOIL

HARPER

An Imprint of HarperCollins*Publishers*

THE
WINNER

A NOVEL

TEDDY WAYNE

HarperCollins books may be purchased for educational, business, or sales promotional use. For information, please email the Special Markets Department at SPsales@harpercollins.com.

FIRST EDITION

Designed by Elina Cohen

Library of Congress Cataloging-in-Publication Data
Names: Wayne, Teddy, author.
Title: The winner: a novel / Teddy Wayne.
Description: First edition. | New York, NY: Harper, 2024. |
Identifiers: LCCN 2023043501 (print) | LCCN 2023043502 (ebook) |
    ISBN 9780063353596 (hardcover) | ISBN 9780063353626 (e-book)
Subjects: LCGFT: Novels.
Classification: LCC PS3623.A98 W56 2024 (print) | LCC PS3623.A98 (ebook) |
    DDC 813/.6—dc23/eng/20231201
LC record available at https://lccn.loc.gov/2023043501
LC ebook record available at https://lccn.loc.gov/2023043502

24 25 26 27 28 LBC 5 4 3 2 1

For Phoebe, Angus, and Kate

A little water clears us of this deed.

—*Macbeth*

The true defensive player (or "dinker," as he is unaffectionately called in recreational circles) is prepared to hit ten, twenty, or more balls in the court per point. . . . Dinkers understand the facts of life at the recreational level of tennis.

—Allen Fox, *Think to Win: The Strategic Dimension of Tennis*

I

CHAPTER 1

The road beyond the white security gate, fringed by the rich green foliage of June, curved gently out of sight.

"The code?" Conor couldn't remember anything from John Price about a gate code. "That's not an intercom?"

The cabdriver shook his head. "You need a code to get in," he said.

Conor tried calling John, but the connection immediately failed— just a lonely bar of finicky service. The driver's phone wasn't picking up a signal, either.

"Maybe you can walk," the man suggested as his flimsy mask slipped down his nose, as it had many times throughout the ride. Conor was glad his mother was safely cocooned in their apartment back in Yonkers, where nearly everyone was still covering up in public spaces.

The map on his phone wasn't loading, so he didn't know where exactly to find John's house on this two-mile pinkie of land jutting from the southern shores of Massachusetts. He had to transport an overstuffed backpack, a rolling suitcase with one wonky wheel, his three-racquet tennis bag, and, most cumbersome of all, his twenty-five-pound tabletop stringing machine in another bag. Each leg of the journey he'd taken on foot since that morning—from his mother's apartment to her Mitsubishi, the car to the Metro-North train, out of Grand Central to hail a taxi to Port Authority, boarding the bus to Providence, Rhode Island, exiting the station to this cab—had required him to shuffle along like a caterpillar.

But it was either walk or wait, with the meter running, for another car to open the gate. Conor paid, collected his bags from the trunk, and passed through an opening for pedestrians. A wooden sign nailed to a tree greeted him in cursive:

Private Property
No Trespassing, Please
CUTTERS NECK ASSOCIATION

Single-lane Cutters Neck Road, bisecting and snaking down the peninsula, was quiet except for birdsong and the metallic chirr of insects. Roadside honeysuckle sweetened the tangy ocean air. To his left, a sailboat drowsed in the calm bay. The Atlantic was visible on the other side of the stiletto-shaped neck, too.

Conor had seen aerial photography of the place from real estate sites, but he hadn't been quite prepared for the essentially unspoiled beauty of what he was now walking through—for what, incredibly, he was about to live in (on?) for the summer. He snapped a picture of the ocean to send to his mother once he had service.

He passed the first driveway, a gravel arc before a house studded with porthole windows, its slate-gray shingles blackened in spots like overripe bananas. The porch reassuringly featured a BLACK LIVES MAT-TER sign; he'd had no idea what to expect politically from a gated community in deep-blue New England.

The next few houses shared the same architectural style, though there were no more adornments except for one porch flying a massive American flag that twitched in the breeze.

Conor set down the stringing machine and rubbed his sore arm. He regretted bringing it; he might not even have any use for it over the summer. A sporting goods store in town was still restringing racquets, but he couldn't tolerate paying for anything he could do himself.

The first sign of human life in this idyllic landscape came from a golf cart whizzing by, captained by a preteen blond girl, with two younger and even more towheaded children next to her. Conor smiled and waved in neighborly fashion, hoping they might offer him a lift on the back, but the trio only stared at him as they passed, deadpan as child actors in a horror movie.

He finally reached the mailbox for John's address, whose number he'd fortunately remembered. Midway up the grassy driveway through a stand of trees was a short perpendicular path into more woods. There, tucked away in a clearing within sight of John's house, hid a squat cabin, Conor's free living quarters until Labor Day.

Or not quite free, but paid in kind. Having no luck on the job market and panicked about repaying his $144,000 in law school loans once the pandemic-triggered federal freeze was lifted, Conor had reached out in May to the Upper East Side tennis club where he'd worked summers in college. The lockdown had forced the place to close, but his old boss passed along an opportunity that had just come in: a member would put someone up in his waterfront guesthouse over the summer in exchange for lessons six days a week, and the instructor could turn a profit by charging other willing residents in the area.

And now he was here. The door was ajar; when he'd asked about getting the keys, John had told him no one locked their doors on the neck, unnerving the native New Yorker used to the nightly ritual of deadbolts and chains. Inside the one-room cabin were a twin bed and a desk, a kitchenette, and a small bathroom with a shower. John had stocked the fridge and cupboards and provided a bicycle with a basket for the twenty-minute ride to the village market.

Few frills, but also few distractions: an ideal headquarters for hunkering down for eight-hour days of studying for the bar exam in between tennis lessons.

Conor's phone was picking up service now, though still just one bar, and its seven-year-old battery was nearly dead. He sent the ocean picture to his mother and texted John that he'd arrived.

A few minutes later there was a knock at the door. When he opened it, a lean man in his sixties was standing a dozen feet back. He wore a dark jacket and tie paired with salmon-colored shorts and sockless loafers.

"Welcome to Cutters," John said.

"Nice to meet you, Mr. Price." Though they were at a safe distance, Conor fished his mask out of his pocket and strapped it on as a show of respect.

"It's John, please. And no need for the mask if we're outside."

"Of course," Conor said. "My mom has diabetes, so I wear a mask everywhere."

His eyes drifted down again to John's lower body. He'd never seen a man in pink shorts before.

John evidently noticed. "I've been in Zoom meetings all day, hence the Bermuda businessman look. I suppose the pandemic is the new casual Fridays."

"I've been on a bus from Port Authority all day. Hence . . ." Conor gestured at his wrinkled attire.

"That Providence station isn't much better," John said with a chuckle. "Someone here once parked his car around there, broad daylight—stolen in fifteen minutes. Did I not recommend you take Amtrak?"

He had, but the cheapest train ticket was one hundred and nineteen dollars versus thirty-four for the bus.

"I've always been a bus guy," Conor said.

John ran through the cabin's quirks and said he'd walk over with him to the tennis court in the morning.

"Oh," he said after taking two steps. "There's a party on the neck tonight. Outdoors, obviously. Please consider yourself my guest for any social events here."

"Thank you very much," Conor said. "I'm pretty beat, so I'll probably stay in."

"You sure? I know standing around with a bunch of stiff Wasps may not be the most exciting night, but you might meet some new clients. Assuming you don't mind mixing business and pleasure."

Conor had only three tennis lessons lined up in addition to John's unpaid sessions. Even if all of them turned into weekly appointments, he'd need to make much more money this summer.

"As long as the Wasps don't sting," he said.

After a harrowing couple of seconds in which Conor worried he'd offended him with his bad joke, John smiled.

"If we do, we're numb to it ourselves," he said. "God's frozen people."

. . .

JOHN HAD TOLD HIM THE CABIN ALSO HAD AN OUTDOOR SHOWER IN THE back, so Conor decided to try it out. He'd never taken a real shower outside before. Wind channeled through the wooden stall's eye-level window, which showed the blue-green water in the distance. His mom's windowless bathroom in Yonkers was cramped to begin with, and they'd been too afraid of Covid to have someone come in and repair the exhaust fan that had malfunctioned in April; every shower now produced a claustrophobic sauna. .

He couldn't believe his good fortune—not only to have a desperately needed job but for it to include an open-air shower with an ocean view.

A few minutes before six, he tucked a button-down into his lone pair of khakis and headed over to the party. He felt himself growing nervous as he approached, uncertain if he was dressed appropriately. (Should he have packed his blazer? Where did you even buy pink shorts?) His work as a tennis pro had thrown him together with plenty of well-off older people in his life, and he knew how to act around them: be exceedingly polite, good humored, and deferential, like a waiter at a high-end restaurant. Cutters Neck, however, was the most rarefied stratum he'd encountered, and more to the point, he'd never lived among them on their home turf.

A few dozen guests milled about behind the party house by an infinity pool that appeared superfluous, surrounded as they were by near-infinite ocean. The crowd was composed predominantly of boomers who, like John, had sought refuge from the virus here, along with a clique of college-aged or high-school kids and several gaggles of frolicking children and their parents.

Conor immediately noticed that there wasn't a mask in sight. Even if the recent George Floyd protests had suggested that outdoor gatherings might be safe, a crowded party was risky enough to make him consider turning around. If he contracted Covid, no one would take a lesson from him for two weeks, minimum.

But he also needed to rustle up more work. Not wanting to draw attention as either a hypochondriac or as someone who might have symptoms himself, he kept his mask pocketed and beelined for the hors d'oeuvres, as he hadn't eaten anything substantial since breakfast. When the two people before him plucked deviled eggs from a tray with their bare hands, though, he pivoted away from the food and fixed a gin and tonic.

John found him and led him into the fray. The men, a couple of whom also wore pink shorts, with one in tomato-red pants, all gave their first and last names as they shook hands, so Conor adopted the custom. He met John's friendly wife—who said she got her exercise in not by playing tennis but by cutting invasive plants on the neck—and the three people who had already signed up for lessons. To everyone else John introduced him as the exceptional tennis pro from Westchester (not Yonkers, Conor noted) whose slots were filling up rapidly. Most of them commented, discouragingly, that they didn't play or hadn't in years. Many residents bore a family resemblance to one another, save for one rumpled, wild-haired eccentric who spoke at length about the dangers of toxins in water.

Other than him, the Cutters residents were gregarious and welcoming, and Conor began to relax. Very rich people were still people.

"Good God, you're handsome!" gushed their hostess, the gray streaks in her hair betraying a recent disruption of regular salon appointments. "Are you sure you're a tennis pro and not a movie star?"

"My last acting role was in second grade," he said with a self-conscious lowering of his head. The embarrassment was real, even if the abashed smile and deflective modesty were effectively habit by now. He knew, from experience, this was the only acceptable response, because to dismiss the compliment altogether was almost more egotistical than embracing it.

His effect on women was the one area of life where he'd never had to put in much effort. It was pure genetic luck, absolutely a perk, but, on occasion, it gave him a partial understanding of the drawbacks that he imagined beautiful women felt more often: being desired and objectified at once, ogled yet not seen at all. Some people—his professors, especially—assumed he was an idiot until he disproved them.

He certainly wasn't complaining, but if he could have chosen a natural-born advantage, he would have taken money. So many things, from his mother's health to his career prospects to the basic convenience of not having to haul his luggage across four states by bus, would have been much easier.

"Then how about politics?" the woman, whose name Conor didn't catch, was saying. "You look like you could be the president. Doesn't he look like a president, John?"

"He does have a certain Kennedy-esque air," John said. "Before I give you my vote, you got any skeletons in your closet? Drive anyone off a bridge?"

"No one they've found yet," Conor said, even more uncomfortable now under John's scrutiny. "You have a beautiful pool, by the way," he added, hoping to change the topic.

"Thank you," she said. "You know, Suzanne Estabrook actually *stayed* at the same hotel with Teddy Kennedy on Martha's Vineyard the weekend of Chappaquiddick?"

The conversation naturally swung around to the presidential election. "Tom Becker's voting for him," she confided.

"You're kidding me—*again*?" John asked. "He hasn't learned his lesson?"

"He wouldn't admit it at first. Sally had to practically pry it out of him."

"Don't worry," John told Conor. "There are only five or six Trump voters on the entire neck. We'd love to get rid of them, if you have any ideas."

After some discussion of Covid (the hostess: "I hate to say it, but it's a class thing more than anything else. I'd be absolutely shocked if anyone on Cutters dies from it. I don't even think anyone here will *get* it"; John: "Oh, we'll all get it. Eventually we'll all get it. The only question is when") and gossip about a postponed wedding on the neck and the couple's extravagant registry (a Tiffany fork—a single fork, the hostess clarified, not a set—cost three hundred and sixty dollars), John left to say hello to someone. The hostess peeled off, telling Conor that she and her husband were going out of town on Monday for two weeks but that he was welcome to use the pool in their absence.

"Thank you," he said. "Though I'm not much of a swimmer."

The young girl he'd seen driving the golf cart skipped by in a floral dress and joined a group of similarly attired children. Amid the snowy tundra of white skin at the party was a single Black family, the popular-looking father and son in near-matching polo shirts.

The event had been a bust for drumming up business. He should slip out now, while John was occupied, but the cocktail he'd been nursing had only emphasized how empty his stomach was. He returned to the hors d'oeuvres when no one was around and, prudence chipped away by his gin and tonic, gobbled four of the creamy halved eggs in succession. Then he picked up the bottle of top-shelf gin to wash it down but, before tilting it into his glass, held it deliberatively with both hands. He had to make up for the day of exam prep lost to the bus ride, and one drink was his limit for retention of his books.

The college kids chatted in a circle by the pool. Though few of them looked old enough to drink legally, they all held tumblers or wine-glasses with body language that suggested a lifelong familiarity with seaside cocktail parties. They laughed the carefree laughter of young people who don't have to study for anything, who don't have jobs they have to wake up for in the morning, who can drink as much as they want without consequence. Conor couldn't imagine ever feeling the way they did. There had always been a morning tennis practice or a workplace to punch into, money to earn to help with rent, a looming test or paper or thick book. Although that was mostly all right by him. He felt best when he was working hard. Downtime made him restless.

But his alienation from his peers wasn't just from the gap in responsibilities. Nor was it the fact that he was always a little lost when they gossiped, in slang he was behind the curve on, about a new TV show or song or celebrity or something trending on the internet. It was how they spoke about themselves, what they freely divulged to anyone who would listen, flaunting frailty as a show of strength, taking pride in wounds and weaknesses that had once been shameful. Good for them, Conor supposed, but broadcasting one's vulnerability to the world was unfathomable to him. In a tennis match, you never revealed an injury to your opponent if you could help it.

An unsettling image flashed into his head of himself barreling into the group, like a bowling ball into a cluster of blond wood pins, and knocking the rich kids into the pool.

As he was about to set down the gin in favor of sparkling water, a voice behind him, low but distinctly feminine, asked, "Are you going to pour that bottle or cradle it to sleep?"

The woman was tall, close to Conor's height. Oversize sunglasses reflected the setting sun, and the wide brim of a straw hat shaded a bloodlessly pale face whose pointed features carved the air before her like the prow of a ship. Her medium-length hair was almost as yellow as that of the ubiquitous children. A network of blue veins peeked through the nearly translucent skin of her sinewy arms.

"Sorry," he said. "Did you want— May I pour you some?"

She held out her quarter-full glass as if he were a caterer. "Don't be shy," she said, crooking her finger after he made a modest pour. "I'm not driving."

He obliged and topped her off with a splash of tonic, then, when she nodded at the ice bucket, plunked in two cubes with a pair of tongs.

"So," she said. "I don't recognize you. Are you a bastard?"

"Excuse me?" He was thrown off enough by the obscenity that he wasn't sure if he'd misheard her.

"A bastard is someone's illegitimate son. I'm asking if that's the reason I don't recognize you."

Her odd question, delivered without the inflection of a joke, made him momentarily forget why he was there. "No, I . . . I'm the tennis . . . pro." Technically, he was certified only as a recreational coach, not a pro, but his former boss had recommended he stretch the truth to get this job.

"The tennis . . . pro," she repeated robotically. "Do you go by your vocation, or do you also have a name?"

"Conor. O'Toole."

"Oh, yes. There was an email about lessons." She cocked her chin up; behind her sunglasses she was probably squinting with suspicion. "You're not trying to con us all, are you, Conor O'Toole? You're not a con man impersonating a tennis pro for some nefarious purpose?"

The woman said this without a smile and took a drink, training her sunglasses on him the whole time. Women rarely made Conor self-conscious, but within a minute of talking to her he felt fidgety and diffident, as though a clutch of pedestrians were watching him parallel park.

"Just here to give lessons," he said.

"Quite utilitarian. Well, then, how does one receive a lesson from the very serious Conor O'Toole?"

"All my info's in the email John sent around." When she didn't respond, he added, "It's a hundred and fifty dollars for an hour-long lesson." (Conor had initially proposed a hundred dollars per lesson, the going rate at his old tennis club, but John had said he would attract more takers if he charged a hundred and fifty, as "no one here will think you're worth it if you don't cost enough.")

"It's gauche to talk money," said the woman.

This line was spoken more cuttingly than the rest of her teasing. He'd always believed transparency was for the benefit of the customer, but at the moment it was apparent that he'd grossly overstepped one of this world's unspoken lines of conduct, exposing himself as every bit the impostor she'd labeled him.

"I'm so—rry," he said.

A few weeks into eighth grade, Conor had developed a stammer, seemingly overnight. It began innocuously, a brief pause inserted into words here and there. But within a couple of months it invariably appeared if he spoke more than a few sentences, the delay extending tortuously; his mind would know what the next sound was, yet his tongue and lungs refused to cooperate.

His mother assured him that it would eventually go away on its own, but he was terrified it wouldn't. He'd heard that Joe Biden, then soon to become vice president, had overcome a childhood stutter by reciting Irish poetry for hours in front of the mirror. Conor decided to do the same, but with the medical journals his mother brought home from the gastroenterologist's office where she worked. He figured if he could negotiate the arcane jargon, then he could handle everyday speech.

It was almost comic in hindsight, a thirteen-year-old boy studiously enunciating until bedtime *upper endoscopy* and *management of anal fissures* from back issues of *Diseases of the Colon & Rectum*, but it had worked. By the time he entered high school, he'd conquered it—almost completely. The key was to stop thinking about it as soon as it happened, because if you didn't, if you kept worrying it was coming back at full strength, it had a chance of taking root.

The woman's sunglasses remained locked on him, as if privately documenting the existence of a defect, a marker of some innate inferiority. His body's thermostat spiked, his hairline prickling with sweat.

"I'm available Tuesday at five o'clock." It sounded like she was setting the time, not asking if he were free.

"Sure," he said, keeping his syllables to a minimum.

"I'll see you then, Conor O'Toole," she said and walked away.

Only later, when he was brushing his teeth at home, did he realize he hadn't gotten her name.

"Con man with some nefarious purpose," he said to himself in the mirror.

He would be making six hundred dollars off these people his first week. If he was a con man, then he was a low-rent one.

CHAPTER 2

Conor began his first morning of employment on the Cutters tennis court under a cloudless sky. John was a good player and in superb condition for his age. If they ever played a real match, he might scratch out the occasional point against Conor. After hitting for an hour, they recuperated courtside in the shade by a one-room clubhouse with a battered Ping-Pong table inside. ("It's called 'the yacht club,'" John said. "No actual yachts.") Past that was a pier terminating in a wooden platform over the ocean, where, John told him, everyone went swimming.

Conor identified the areas of John's game he wanted to improve over the summer. Then they gulped water in silence.

"You've had a place here for a while?" Conor asked to make conversation.

John gave him an abbreviated history of the neck: three siblings, one his grandfather, had bought the land in the 1920s and built houses. Their families had multiplied and erected more properties over the years, and Cutters was now on its fourth generation, with over twenty homes.

"A few outsiders bought in over the years, but I'm pretty sure all their ancestors came over on the *Mayflower*, too," John said. "Not all, actually. I knew Wesley Patterson from the Harvard Club, and I was the one who told him when the Stillwells' house was up for sale. He's a terrific guy, more a golfer than a tennis player, but they're a wonderful family—you should meet them, if you haven't." From John's conspicuous pride and praise, Conor could guess which family he meant. "And then a few women from my generation married Jews. And the younger people now don't care about that sort of thing like they used to.

"Which is great," he quickly added. "With the name Conor O'Toole, you must have some Irish blood going back a ways."

"My dad was born in Ireland and immigrated here to work in construction."

John nodded. "I'm a lawyer, by the way. Can't remember if I told you."

He hadn't, but Conor had done his due diligence. He'd been on the fence about abandoning his mother for the summer, but the decision was clinched when he'd learned that John was a partner at one of the city's most reputable firms. When they'd spoken in May about this job, he hadn't revealed that he was finishing law school, not wanting to scare his prospective employer with the idea that he might bail on the summer if he landed a real position. Now that they'd had a lesson together, Conor felt comfortable telling the truth.

"I actually just graduated law school myself," he said.

"Really? Where from?"

"Um"—Conor swallowed the next words—"New York Law School?"

"NYU's terrific. We have a lot of people from there."

Conor hesitated, reluctant to correct him, but didn't want to lie. "Actually, not NYU—New York Law School."

"Oh, of course. That's a fine school, too." John did his best to conceal his dip in esteem. Conor had been accepted into a few higher-ranked schools, but none gave him the same funding, so he hadn't had much choice in the matter. He'd ended up graduating near the top of his class, but that still hadn't helped him attract any job offers, especially with the hiring freezes that had begun after the pandemic hit.

"I'm studying for the bar and applying to jobs," Conor said. "I obviously wouldn't start anything until after the summer."

"What're you interested in?"

"I'm open to a number of fields, but I'm focused on corporate law."

"I'm in corporate litigation myself." John cleared his throat, likely eager to move on from the topic; his firm would never consider hiring someone with Conor's middling pedigree. "So, did your dad introduce you to tennis? I wouldn't think it was very big in Ireland."

Conor shook his head and took a long drink of water. "It was all luck," he explained, relaying a truncated version of his origin story. One April afternoon in eighth grade, as he was walking home from school past a park with public courts, he came across a racquet with a broken frame sticking out of a garbage can. Staring down yet another dull, quiet afternoon in their empty apartment, he found a nearly dead ball and hit by himself against a handball wall. He liked the soothing repetition, the mindless sense of accomplishment every time the racquet made solid contact.

He began to stop by the wall every day, sometimes studying the strokes of the accomplished players on the courts, until an older man who played there frequently invited him to rally. Richard Wotten ended up teaching Conor the game the rest of that spring and summer. None of the public schools in Yonkers even fielded a tennis team, but, thanks to Richard's interventions, Conor received special dispensation to try out for the one in nearby Hastings-on-Hudson, and he cracked second doubles on the JV roster in ninth grade.

The handball wall remained a fixture in Conor's life the rest of high school. Outside of tennis season and his after-school jobs (CVS cashier, Baskin-Robbins ice cream scooper, CTown supermarket bagger), when he couldn't find a partner or was simply feeling restless, he'd go and practice, sometimes until it was too dark to see, challenging himself to land twenty consecutive shots inside a small circle he chalked up, to sprint side to side hitting running forehands and backhands for a minute straight, to deflect reflex volleys from five feet away, all against a tireless, relentless, unbeatable opponent who only got better the harder he swung.

But he got better, too, and he'd found it exhilarating to chart his progress, to jump from a seemingly static plateau one day to a higher plane the next, to direct the ball with a level of control that was unavailable to him in the rest of his life. The drop shot that barely cleared the net and died the quietest of deaths on the bounce, a slice serve that tailed away into the doubles alley like a comet for an ace, a lob that arced just beyond your opponent's outstretched racquet before plummeting from heavy topspin—these were feats of beauty, geometry blended with fine art. And unlike the contact sports his friends were into whose outcomes were largely predicated on the sizes of the players, on the court, skillful and strategic Davids had a fighting chance against brute-force Goliaths. (Conor, topping out at five-ten-and-a-half in college, was in the underdog class among the throngs of power-serving six-footers.)

His solo training against the wall prepared him in ways beyond the physical for competition. Singles tennis was the biggest sport in which you competed fully alone, with coaching strictly prohibited during pro men's matches (golfers, at least, enjoyed the strategic and motivational company of a caddy). A solitary game, made for the lone wolves of the athletic world, lonely even when you won; there was no one else with whom to immediately celebrate.

"Sounds like some luck, but mostly hard work," John said. "I learned here from my dad, on this very court. Though it was grass back then. We got rid of it a while ago. Not the easiest thing to tend." He paused, perhaps noticing too late the discrepancy between a manicured oceanfront rectangle for lawn tennis and a dilapidated public court in Yonkers. "Your mentor must be very proud of what you've made of yourself."

"He was always very supportive," Conor said, and left it at that. Richard had been a retired real estate lawyer and recent widower when they'd met. On top of refining Conor's game and waxing poetic on the finer points of the sport—he liked to draw an equivalence between a men's Grand Slam match and the dramatic structure of a Shakespeare play, not that the teen had ever seen one—Richard had funded Conor's supply of racquets and sneakers and bought him his trusty stringing machine. (This last gift had saved him hundreds, perhaps thousands of dollars over the years—and when he'd popped a string within the first ten minutes of hitting with John, Conor was glad he'd brought it with him.) Most generous of all, he'd invested ten grand for his education in a 529 account, which had fractionally defrayed the cost of his law school tuition, and had, more than anyone else, influenced Conor's decision to pursue a legal career.

Before Richard died, of pancreatic cancer, Conor had been able to tell him he'd made first singles as an eleventh grader on the varsity team, but not that his ultimate dream for his protégé had come to fruition: the receipt of a full-ride athletic scholarship to college. (Albeit to a school with a lackluster academic reputation whose tennis team was the cellar dweller of its Division II conference, but, as would happen with law school, he'd had to jump at the chance.)

"With your work ethic and talent," Richard had told him more than once, "if you'd had more of a head start, you probably could've gone pro."

Conor occasionally thought of that remark over the years when he caught a match on TV—not that he truly flattered himself with the ability, in an alternate life, to sprout four more inches and compete with the Federers and Nadals of the world. But still, what if he'd started at six instead of thirteen; if he'd grown up in sunny, tennis-court-rich Florida or Southern California like most American professionals and hadn't needed to rely on a cracked racquet and a Yonkers handball wall for an opponent; if he'd benefited from veteran coaches in high school and tennis camps and not a bio teacher who'd been conscripted for the job?

Of course, there was also the other, off-the-court head start he sometimes wondered about missing out on, and if, having had it, he might now be a graduate of NYU and not New York Law School.

But whenever Conor sank into the quicksand of self-pity he quickly pulled himself out. The chance discovery of a tossed-out tennis racquet had, alongside the altruistic efforts of a senior citizen with time on his hands, led to his earning a law degree. With limited resources and no outside help, his mother had always provided shelter and food, ensured they were zoned for the best elementary school in Yonkers and then moved so he'd attend the top middle and high school, shuttled him to and from countless tennis practices, made him feel like he never had to go it alone, that they were doubles partners in the truest sense. Not everyone had a mom like that. Conor knew he was lucky in the ways that mattered most.

John drained his water bottle. "I'm going to take a dip before my glorious Zoom workday starts. I should've told you to bring along your swim trunks."

"I've got to start studying, anyway," Conor said.

HIS FIRST PAID SESSION WAS THAT AFTERNOON WITH A CRAGGY, STOOP-shouldered septuagenarian named Dick Garrison. After he wrote Conor a check for a hundred and fifty dollars, Dick committed to a standing lesson Thursdays at five thirty, "provided I see continued improvement."

Well, it was a start.

In his cabin, Conor devoted himself to bar prep until dinnertime. As he stirred a pot of pasta, he called his mother. This was the longest they'd gone without speaking for a while, having spent nearly every minute in the apartment together since March.

"I wish you could see it," he said after failing to do justice to the picturesque backdrop of the neck. "I feel bad you're stuck at home."

"Don't worry about me—I'm happy you get to enjoy it," she said. "Just send me more pictures."

"How's the job search going?" he asked. The elderly gastroenterologist who'd employed her for nearly four decades had decided to retire once it became obvious that Covid wasn't going away. Their monthly margins, narrow before the pandemic, were now in the red. His mother's unemployment benefits were half her previous salary and would expire within a year; she'd been rejected for disability benefits because her diabetes was controlled; and she still had about twenty thousand dollars in credit card debt that she periodically transferred from one card to another like a hot potato.

As Conor had fallen asleep the past few jobless months, his final thoughts were typically about their precarious finances and the daunting fact that their future livelihood would be almost entirely up to him.

"Same as before. No one wants a sixty-year-old receptionist with a preexisting condition who can only work remotely," she said. "Do you think John will offer you a job?"

He explained why that would never happen.

"I don't believe that. You were near the top of your class, you're an incredibly hard worker, you—"

"Mom, stop, please. It's not in the realm of possibility." His mother was savvy as a single parent, had adroitly navigated bureaucratic mazes, could whip up a pretty good dinner out of whatever she found in the fridge. But she'd been content as a medical receptionist in one office her entire working life and had never had to learn the implicit rules and value systems of the white-collar world he was trying to break into. There were some things that hard work and even talent couldn't always get you.

Her intercom rang.

"Who's that?" he asked. "You're not having anyone over, are you?"

"Relax. It's my overpriced groceries."

As hard as it was to stomach paying a surcharge for delivered groceries, he'd made his mother promise not to shop for herself while he was gone.

"I put a note in the app telling them to leave everything outside the door," he said. "Wait a few minutes after the guy leaves and wear a mask when you bring them in."

"*Wait a few minutes* and wear a mask *when I'm alone*?" she asked. "You're completely paranoid, Conor. And I'm perfectly capable of going to the supermarket myself. It's no different from when you went for us."

"Mom, I'm much more careful than you. I double-mask and I stay six feet from other people in the store, and if anyone comes near me, I move away."

"Exactly—you're paranoid. It's ridiculous. I'm not going to wear a mask for the twenty seconds I spend outside my own door." She made this infuriating pronouncement with the air of a judge handing down a sentence.

"You have type one diabetes," he said. "All it takes is one careless mistake to get it, and then what? Your life's over. Is that what you want? To die from going out in the stupid hallway to get your groceries? Just put on a fucking mask."

He had begun calmly but was certainly not composed by the end, and they both fell silent after his eruption. This outburst was an unpenning of months of frustration over her minimizing the threat and calling him a worrywart—even though she was the one in the most danger. Every time he held his breath in their building's elevator or swerved from a barefaced pedestrian, it was solely for her.

"I'm sorry," he finally said. "Look, if you're not going to wear it for your sake, please put it on for mine."

"I will," she said quietly.

AFTER TWO HOURS OF TREKKING THROUGH ONE OF HIS FOUR PREP BOOKS, each weighing several pounds, Conor stepped outside into the cool evening air. Giving the main house a wide berth in case John was on the back porch—he still felt out of place making conversation with his employer-landlord—he ambled toward the ocean.

The back lawn connected to a path that wound down toward the rocky, western shoreline, where Conor sat on a boulder large enough for two people. The water lapped pleasantly near his feet as red seaweed floated nearby. The sky was a rich spectrum of peach, tangerine, and, lining the ocean horizon, blood orange. What was one of the most dramatic sunsets he'd seen in his life was probably a daily occurrence here.

Aside from an eggy smell, he found himself thinking that this would be a nice place to bring a girl—not that he had time for that kind of distraction this summer. Takers for the bar exam, which had been postponed by Covid until September, were advised to study for five hundred hours total. To play it safe, he'd exceed that while wedging in lessons and job applications whenever he could. His law school classmates all dreaded the prep work, but Conor didn't mind it. He liked the law for some of the same reasons he liked tennis: it rewarded those who figured out the unlikely angles, could spin and slice an argument with logic and rhetoric, and were always two steps ahead of the competition.

He still hadn't seen much beyond the yacht club, so to get the lay of the land before he resumed studying, he retraced his steps and went back to Cutters Neck Road. No one else was out in the dimming light as he walked south past houses generously segregated by woods.

After fifteen minutes he reached the end of the road, where a grand lawn spread out before a house bigger than any he'd ever seen in person. Three chimneys sprouted from its roof, and white columns supported a porch that wrapped around the entire facade. As it was at the tail end of the peninsula and was thus the only house that could be situated in the middle of the land, it had unobstructed views of the ocean in not just two but three cardinal directions. A couple hundred feet to the side, and apparently part of the property, was another, more modestly sized cottage with its own attached garage. A golf cart was parked inside an open shed. What looked to be a private pier extended out over the ocean.

The other houses on Cutters were impressive but well within the bounds of his conception of a luxurious lifestyle. This one was preposterous, a caricature of mansions fit for helicopter landings on a reality show. He couldn't picture a human being actually living here.

Maybe none did; there weren't any cars parked outside, though perhaps they were in the closed garage, and he couldn't see any lights on. A gravel footpath to the right curled around the perimeter of the property. Conor was tempted to follow it. He could likely sneak a peek of the back and, if he were stopped, claim he thought it was a public path. But he couldn't risk a misdemeanor on one of his first nights here; if the owner caught him trespassing, he'd have to ask John to vouch for him and embarrass them both.

He had about two hours until bed—two hours he should be dedicating to exam prep, not gawking at the sunset and real estate. After a day at a construction site, resting prone on the living room carpet with an ice pack strapped to his achy back, his father had liked to remind him, "Better work your mind now or someone'll make you work your body later." Conor turned back.

In his cabin, he read until his eyelids drooped. Before he turned off the light, he looked up the address of the gigantic house. It had ten bedrooms and fourteen bathrooms and covered an astounding twenty-two thousand square feet. There was no sales history, but the owner, as best he could find out, was named Thomas Remsen, and the home was valued at more than $26 million.

Hard to believe that someone thought he needed that much space, that many bedrooms, that many *toilets*, and for a summer home, no less. It put him in mind of Richard again. His tennis teacher had preached conservative consistency over flash in all arenas. "Don't have to hit a winner to be the winner," he'd say whenever the boy gambled on a statistically improbable shot, successful or not. He taught Conor a mantra to mentally recite between points: *steady strokes, no big shots*. Don't go for a big shot—and don't *be* a "big shot," an epithet to the old man.

"That guy thinks he's ranked number one in the world," Richard told him one day in the park, after a Porsche with a thumping stereo screeched past the court. "He thinks money is happiness."

When Conor nodded from the baseline and picked up a ball, eager to get back to hitting, Richard beckoned him to the net.

"Listen to me—put down the ball," he said. "Happiness is security. Feeling safe, taken care of. If you don't have enough money, it's hard to be secure, because you're always looking over your shoulder—'Am I gonna lose my house, lose my job?' But these big shots with their sports cars, they're looking over their shoulder just the same. They're terrified of losing what they have, too—not because they're gonna be homeless or anything like that, but because being a big shot is how they value their lives. So they become obsessed with getting fancier cars, bigger houses, more women. More, more, more."

After revving its engine at a red light, the car roared off.

"The sweet spot," Richard went on, "is being ranked a rung or two *below* the big shots and not caring about being on top. Because it's not about getting everything you want, but being satisfied with what you do have. *That's* real security."

Richard's doctrine of temperance had stuck with him all these years. Conor hadn't gotten a job yet, but he had only to keep playing the game of life as he played tennis—steady strokes, no big shots—and there was little doubt he'd remain on the winning path to security, for him and his mom.

CHAPTER 3

On Tuesday afternoon he had a lesson with Suzanne Estabrook, the woman who had been around Ted ("Teddy"?) Kennedy before Chappaquiddick. When they were done, she apologized for the dozen or two balls she'd launched over the fence, asked for another lesson the next week, and took off without paying.

"I can take a check, cash, or Venmo, whatever's easiest," Conor was forced to call to her back.

"Oh, I'm *so* sorry!" Suzanne said, spinning around and theatrically clapping her hand over her mouth. "I completely, *completely* forgot. I didn't even bring my pocketbook. Could I pay you double next time?"

She seemed a little scatterbrained, and he didn't trust her to remember next time, either, unless he nudged her beforehand with a reminder. Alternatively, he could walk home with her and wait outside while she got the money, but that felt like crossing a line of propriety.

"No problem," he said, as cheerfully as he could. His tennis club had always invisibly handled transactions in the past, and he knew better than to personally press these clients (even Dick Garrison's handing over a check after their lesson felt, well, *gauche*). Only the poor were accustomed to being hounded for their debts. He'd have to hope she paid up before his credit card bill was due in nine days.

He'd brought his swimsuit and a towel this time, and his lesson with the nameless woman from the party wasn't for another couple of hours. He changed in one of the stalls connected to the yacht club and padded barefoot down the pier over boulders to the platform, enclosed by wooden rails with a metal staircase descending into the water. Fifty feet out, an anchored wooden swim raft swayed in the waves.

When Conor had told the pool owner he wasn't much of a swimmer, he was drastically downplaying it; he could only dog-paddle. His parents hadn't been capable of even that, and he'd had precious few opportunities to improve growing up in Yonkers. After a certain age, he'd decided it was a lost cause. But he could at least cool off for a few minutes.

The platform and the surrounding water were empty, otherwise he wouldn't dare go in. He never swam in front of others, and he'd spent many an afternoon standing in the shallow end of hotel pools on team trips, pretending he didn't feel like getting fully wet, to spare himself judgment. No one would have believed that Conor O'Toole, the prelaw tennis star who seemed to master anything he set his mind to, could barely stay afloat.

Now he proceeded cautiously down the steps into the swelling waves, the water pricking goose bumps on his calves. John had warned him that the ocean didn't warm up until well into July. Finally, he cast off from the staircase and thrashed furiously to warm up—and because it was close to his natural, helter-skelter swimming motion. He paddled parallel to the shore with the current, intending to venture out briefly and come straight back, if only to prove to himself that he could do it.

The thought of unseen creatures with teeth or claws or stingers lurking below the surface made him paranoid. He windmilled his arms and kicked harder to scare off any predators as he bounced along the chop.

He turned his head for a moment just as a wavelet caught him in the face. To cope with the salty sting and the piercing angle of the sun, he shut his eyes as he swam. When he reopened them to get his bearings, he was alarmed to find himself much farther from the shore than before; his chaotic strokes had veered him off course.

Still half-blind, he headed back to the platform but was now against the current and spent from his wasteful paddling. The muscles that were indefatigable on the tennis court were like a child's in the water.

He looked over at the horizon, and another swell sucker punched him. As he gagged and sputtered on the saltwater in his nose and throat, the first real terror for his life stabbed him, along with self-loathing: how pathetic this would be, to drown on his very first swim, here in this coastal paradise. They'd eventually figure out what had happened to him, once John noticed he was missing and they saw his bike and clothes, but they'd never recover his body from the Atlantic. His mother would have to hold a casketless Zoom funeral.

He hadn't come this far to die at the bottom of some rich people's ocean.

With his head down, he pawed and kicked as hard as he could, holding his breath to keep the water out, powered less by his limbs than the implacable determination to prevail that had served him for years on courts and in classrooms, a resolve that only strengthened when the tide against him was stronger.

Steady strokes, no big shots, he told himself when he felt his body overreaching in panic.

Just when he started to doubt his capacity to go on, a beautiful glint through his inflamed, half-lidded eyes: the metal staircase. He grabbed it, heaving and gasping, as drained as if he'd played five sets, though the whole ordeal had probably lasted only a minute or two.

The sound of snickering. Out on the raft, four of the college kids were sunning themselves like sea lions. They must have gone out there during the first half of his own swim. When Conor looked at them, they turned their heads and resumed their inaudible conversation.

As he hastily mounted the staircase, grabbed his stuff, and left, he felt more ashamed of himself than angry at them for not having tried to help. Though, if they had, he would have felt even more shame. Worse than the crack it showed in his manhood, the ineptitude of nearly drowning had exposed a deeper layer of disgrace: now it was clearer than ever that he wasn't one of them. The fancy tennis pro from Westchester was really just a Yonkers kid too poor to have learned to swim.

CONOR WAS READY A FEW MINUTES EARLY, AS USUAL, BEFORE HIS LESSON with the woman from the party. By a quarter after five she had still neither shown up nor texted—she would have had his number from John's original email. He should've brought along one of his prep books to make use of the time. He'd give her till half past before leaving.

A few minutes before his deadline he heard gravel crunching behind him. His student was in a golf cart careering down the driveway.

The woman stopped at the bottom of the hill without bothering to park on the grassy periphery. She wore her sunglasses from before and tennis whites: a visor, a V-necked top, and a mid-thigh skirt. Contrails of mineral sunscreen over her arms and sternum enhanced her blinding aura. It looked as though she'd never allowed the sun to touch her body.

"Hello, Conor O'Toole," she said as she approached, a strange calmness in her voice. She offered no apology or explanation.

Normally when a client was this late, he'd ask if they'd had any problems getting there or whether he'd gotten the start time wrong—he didn't want to establish a permissive pattern—but the notion of receiving another withering remark from this woman made him hold his tongue.

"As much as I enjoy standing here in silence, I was hoping you'd teach me to play tennis," she said.

"Of course," Conor said. "What's your history with the sport?"

"My history with the sport," she said. "You're very formal, aren't you? Let's see. I played a bit when I was growing up, but I haven't picked up a racquet in some time."

He took the hopper to the far side of the net. "We'll start off nice and easy, then."

"Will you be gentle with me? Even though it's not my first time, you'll still be gentle?" There was the barest insinuation of a smile.

"Yes."

"Yes," she mimicked him, as she had at the party, with a cartoonishly furrowed brow. "We must train. Let's not have any fun out here."

Not sure how to respond, he directed her to stand on the T of the service boxes, where he fed her soft lobs for a few minutes. Most of the balls she didn't whiff she slammed into the net or to the fence. When they'd burned through their supply, he told her they'd work first on her form. He gobbled up the errant balls with the hopper on his side of the court and did the same by the net in her territory, feeling her eyes on him the entire time. As he crossed the net post, he spotted a stray ball he'd missed against the fence and doubled back for it.

"I'll get it," she said. She walked ahead of him and, rather than kneeling in ladylike fashion, bent over to retrieve the ball. The hem of her skirt rose, exposing her hamstrings and a glimpse of her scarlet underwear.

Conor respectfully turned away, but there was no ignoring that she looked good, for any age. He'd guess hers at around forty-two.

Instead of tossing the ball, she handed it to him, her fingertips grazing his palm. Hurrying to the other side of the net, he showed her the Semi-Western grip and the ready position and told her to imitate him. With his back turned so she could replicate him, he demonstrated the footwork and basic movements for a forehand. She tried copying him but didn't bend her knees or swing properly. Conor verbally directed her a few times, but she seemed unable to alter her natural mechanics.

"It'll be easier if you show me over here," she said. "The net's blocking my view of your legs."

He joined her on her side and, standing a few feet away, ran through the correct form again. She still failed to execute it.

"Can you just come closer and show me what to do?" she asked. "I'm not going to give you Covid. I haven't left the neck once since I've gotten here."

That had better be true. He moved nearer. She was wearing perfume, a subtle vanilla.

"You need to bring your right arm higher up on the backswing. Just think 'up' every time, and after you do it enough, you won't need to think it anymore—it'll be in your muscle memory."

"Move my arm for me," she said. "I can't tell how high to do it."

This was an uncommon request; the only students he ever physically manipulated were young children. Standing as far back behind her as possible, he braceleted her wrist with one hand and guided her arm in a loop. He did that twice and retreated a few steps. "Now try on your own."

"Keep doing it," she said. "I need to get it in my *muscle memory*."

He returned to his spot, but she shuffled her feet so that they were a little closer than before. If he heard anyone coming down the driveway on the gravel, he'd immediately back off.

"When do I bend my knees?" she asked as he assisted her swing.

"You do it as you pull the racquet back, then you straighten up as you swing."

"Like this?" She bent at the knees, but instead of simply lowering her body, she pushed out her ass. Because they were close to the same height, her skirt brushed against his crotch. He stepped back a few inches, hoping she hadn't noticed.

They continued swinging in tandem. After about ten more loops it happened again, with more palpable contact.

Twenty seconds later, a third time—still softly enough that he wasn't sure if it was just the material of the skirt or her body, too, and in either case whether she was aware of it. But the thought that she might be conscious of what she was doing, as much as the touch itself, jolted awake something inside him that had been dormant the past several months of lockdown. It was a primal response, despite their age difference, the public location, the transactional nature of their situation. Or perhaps all those variables magnified it.

He was in mesh shorts and boxer briefs; an erection would be impossible to hide.

"I think you've got it," he said and abruptly let go. He returned to his side. The woman didn't speak until he was back on the T of the service box.

"You think I'm ready for you to give me some balls?" she asked.

There was no sly smile or winking note this time to suggest a double entendre. He knew how to gently redirect unwanted advances in bars, but he'd never been flirted with this aggressively on the court at the Upper East Side club, having taught only children, men, and women either older or more discreet than she was.

He nodded and hit to her. She was marginally better than before, though her figure-eight loop still needed tweaking. He didn't want to be recalled to her side of the court for more hands-on coaching, so he let it go without comment. When his phone alarm signaled the end of the lesson, he courteously asked if she wanted extra time, as they'd started late.

"That won't be necessary." She drank a bottle of water and watched Conor pick up the balls.

"You don't have to stick around while I do this," he told her.

"I'm hydrating. You can never have too much water." She held out the bottle. "Want some?"

"Thanks, I've got my own." No client of his had ever offered to share a bottle, let alone in these hygiene-conscious times.

Conor finished gathering the balls. He didn't see any means for her to render payment—not even a phone. "Well," he said, even more apprehensive about asking for money from this woman, "that does it, then."

She tilted her head all the way back, finished off the bottle with a gulp that traveled down her long neck, wiped her fingers on the water that streaked her chin, and spread the residue over her throat and breastbone, leaving a glistening trail that disappeared into her cleavage.

"You need to be paid, don't you," she said.

"Check or cash is great. Or Venmo, if you have it."

"It's at the house. Meet me there in an hour."

He would have much preferred she get his money immediately, but after Suzanne's missed payment, he didn't want to strike out on collecting for the entire day.

"Sure," he said. "Which address?"

"The house at the end of the neck," she said as she walked off.

He wasn't sure what shocked him more—that she was the one who lived there, or that someone really did inhabit that gargantuan house. He still didn't know what to call her, though her surname, presumably, was Remsen.

. . .

AN HOUR LATER, CONOR RODE TO THE END OF THE NECK, WONDERING IF, as a reward for the inconvenience, he might at least get a glimpse inside the outrageous mansion. He kickstanded his bike on the circular driveway and rang the doorbell. There was no response. After two minutes he tried again. An intercom crackled with the woman's voice: "Go around back."

Tall wooden fencing with a closed door blocked the eastern side, so he went around the garage to the west until he reached the rear, where a stone patio stretched the length of the house, offering several rocking chairs and wooden chaise longues with thick green cushions. On a table between two chairs was a tray with bottles of gin and tonic water chilling in an ice bucket and two tumblers that looked like wineglasses garnished with lime wedges. The Remsens were apparently getting ready for cocktail hour. At least this meant there wouldn't be any awkward flirting in front of the husband. On the far side of the house was the border of a pool; that must have been what the wooden fence was enclosing. Before him was more lawn, then the ocean, where waves smashed against boulders buttressing the tip of the neck—the "skull," he supposed.

"You should be drinking by now," the woman said when she came out of a sliding glass door. She was in another dress, this one floral patterned, that exposed a good swath of leg.

"Oh—was this for me?" he asked.

"Conor," she said, as if lecturing a simpleton, "when you see two gin balloons set out, and you're meeting one other person, it's safe to assume it's for you."

Thomas Remsen must have been off working somewhere, then, but Conor certainly didn't want the guy coming home to find his wife having drinks with the young tennis pro. And the last thing he needed was alcohol with hours of studying to go.

"Well, go on, then," she said. "Pour mine, too."

She was insistent, and he was still curious about this extraordinary house. And this woman. One drink wouldn't ruin him; he'd make coffee as soon as he got home. He mixed two cocktails, diluting his with more tonic, and handed her the other.

"I believe you were having gin at the party, and you didn't strike me as a wine drinker," she said. "Nor a dark-and-stormy type."

"Dark and stormy?"

"Rum and ginger beer. What the effete men here drink when they want to feel like heroic sailors. Overcompensation for being in the shadow of their forefathers."

He couldn't think of a response to that. She took one of the rocking chairs, and he followed.

"So, Conor O'Toole," she said, putting an elbow on the arm of her chair and curling her fist under her chin in a parody of inquisitiveness. "How have you been?"

Conor smiled politely. "I don't believe I ever got your name."

"Catherine." She switched to a Southern belle's drawl: "But folks 'round heah just call me Cathy."

Conor again felt excluded from the joke, even if he got it. Catherine wasn't wearing a wedding ring, he now noticed. It was a feature he'd only lately learned to look for after a few female classmates had become engaged during law school. It was possible she'd taken it off to play tennis and hadn't replaced it yet.

"You have a very nice house," he said.

"You have such a lovely home. I simply *must* get this recipe," she said in another put-on voice. "Aren't you a well-mannered boy."

There was no winning with this woman. No matter what he said or how he said it, she could find a way to mock him. But if this was what it took to keep one of his few paying clients, he could handle it.

"Have you been here throughout the pandemic?" he asked.

She nodded as she drank.

"By yourself, or . . ."

"If you're inquiring whether I'm a divorcée, the answer is yes," she said. "And no, I don't plan on remarrying, not for all the tea in China, so don't even *think* about proposing."

If she were in her twenties, he would already have been flirting. But he didn't want this to be anything but business and to be back in his cabin soon with his hundred and fifty dollars and exam book and coffee.

"So," he said, unable to come up with an artful segue, "where do you live? Normally?"

"I don't live anywhere normally," she said. "Only abnormally. In a gilded turret on Fifth Avenue. Where do *you* live—very normally, it appears?"

"West—" He couldn't say it, it sounded too phony. "Yonkers."

"*West* Yonkers? I wasn't aware it was segregated."

"No, just . . . Yonkers."

"Ah," she said. "The most beautiful place-name in the English language. *Yong-kers.* It just glides trippingly on the tongue."

Conor again smiled, less politely this time, looked at the ocean to avoid her unrelenting eye contact, and swigged his gin and tonic to hasten the end of this meeting. "And you've been working from here?"

"Oh, yes," she said. "Work, work, work. Meetings and conference calls and spreadsheets."

"What do you do?"

She finished off her drink and held out the glass for Conor to refill. "I'm a rentier," she said as he poured. "It's a very demanding time of year for me. You're lucky I could carve out a moment for this social call."

"A . . . rentier?" He'd studied Spanish, not French.

She didn't define it for him. "And you're a tennis pro. Is that the sum of your earthly ambitions?"

"No," he said, feeling a need, despite his desire to get out of there, to prove his merits. "I just graduated from law school. I'm giving lessons while I study for the bar and apply for jobs."

She reached for his glass. "Your drink needs refreshing."

"Unfortunately"—he retracted his hand—"I have to cut myself off. I need to study for a few hours after this."

"You're no fun. One more drink won't kill you."

He stood. "Thank you, but I really do have to go."

She remained seated and casually drank.

"So," he said, "did you say cash or check was easier for you?"

She didn't answer as she took a long draft of her cocktail. Then she went into the house and returned with a short stack of bills that she handed over, with a crisp fifty on top.

"I'll take my next lesson Thursday at five," she said.

He was once more knocked off-balance by her presumptuousness. "Can you do it any earlier? I have another lesson then."

"Who's it with?"

"Dick Garrison."

"You've got Dick at five o'clock?"

"Well, five thirty, but if you can come at four fifteen, that would give me enough time."

"I don't like being out in direct sun—I have very fair skin," she said. "Hmm. How can we arrange this so that your Dick appointment is free for me?"

He remained stone-faced.

"Reschedule with him," she said, waving her hand as if it were nothing. "I'll pay extra for your trouble."

"It's a standing weekly lesson," Conor said. "And it's only our second meeting, so I don't want to get off on the wrong foot."

She nodded understandingly, and he thought the matter was closed, until she spoke again.

"Everything has a price," said Catherine. "What's yours?"

He tried to think of a diplomatic way to turn her down.

"I'll pay you double," she said.

Three hundred dollars for an hour of work was more than he'd ever made in his life, more than he could expect to earn even as a lawyer for a long time. He could give Dick a discount to meet at another time and still come out ahead.

"Okay," he said.

Catherine gave him her first smile that didn't seem taunting.

"That wasn't too hard, was it?" she said.

. . .

CATHERINE HAD GIVEN HIM TWO HUNDRED DOLLARS DESPITE JOHN'S INI-
tial email stressing that gratuities were not expected.

Conor drank coffee with his dinner of two tuna sandwiches but found it hard to read his prep book. He searched Catherine's name. All he found was a *New York Times* announcement from June 1996 documenting the wedding of Thomas Remsen and Catherine Havemeyer, which took place at the groom's family's summer estate on Cutters Neck. The bride, whose ancestors included a titan of the insurance industry on her father's side and a shipping magnate on her mother's, was twenty-five at the time, which would make her forty-nine now.

She didn't look it—or act it. Her behavior—the innuendo-laden speech and the almost certainly intentional physical contact during their lesson—struck him as an idle game, an escape valve for a cooped-up pandemic. He was a new toy she wanted to play with, nothing more. Yet it felt good, now that he was comfortably back in his cabin, to have been audaciously flirted with like that. Out of concern for his mother's health, the last time he'd hooked up with a girl had been back in February. His longest dry spell since he'd lost his virginity.

He wouldn't be falling asleep anytime soon, not with two cups of coffee sloshing inside him and sex on the brain. He could easily take care of the urge himself.

But there was a bar and grill on the main drag in town that advertised its outdoor seating, and Conor could use a break from the rich people of Cutters Neck.

CHAPTER 4

Conor locked his bike to a post on the sidewalk, strapped his helmet around a belt loop, and secured his mask before traversing the nearly empty, nautically themed interior of the Porthole. Though it was a Tuesday, stir-crazy patrons jammed the tables and bar of the back garden, where three middle-aged men in baseball hats played a passable cover of "Beast of Burden."

Conor had expected the locals to be more concerned about safety than the sequestered Cutters residents in their gated community, but here, too, all the masks, if they existed, were at chins or hanging off an ear.

Then again, he wasn't living with his at-risk mother anymore. And the party on the neck had given him a taste of freedom. As long as he steered clear of anyone coughing, he'd be fine.

He ordered a beer by the end of the bar. Halfway through it, he received a tap on his shoulder. "Excuse me," said a girl around his age, her bangs dyed a shade of purple so bright he could see it vividly in the dim outdoor lighting. "You look so familiar. Do you go to Kayak Coffee?"

He recognized the pickup line. "No, I don't," he said, smiling kindly to soften the rejection. "Sorry."

"Oh, okay." She caught the hint and turned to leave. The bottom of her shirt didn't reach her low-slung jeans, and the band of uncovered skin revealed part of a tattoo, centered between two dimples, above a flash of fuchsia thong that nearly matched her bangs.

He felt a sudden, sharp throb of libido, a more recognizable sensation than what he'd experienced on the tennis court with Catherine.

"I'm actually a movie star," Conor said. "That's why I look familiar."

The girl turned back around. "Is that so? Because I don't recognize you from anything." She grinned, showing teeth that had never had braces. A similarly snaggled look inherited from his father had been in Conor's own mirror until Richard paid for his orthodontics the summer after eighth grade.

"I'm in disguise." He gave her an ironic wink. "Doing research for a role."

"You look pretty normal to me."

"I'm impersonating a normal person," he said. "I'm a con man. Pretending to be one of you for a nefarious purpose."

The girl covered her mouth. She had a nice, musical laugh. Catherine hadn't laughed once, just smirked at her own jokes, if you could even call them that. It was fun to be flirting again, with someone his age, in an appropriate setting—to sink back into the easy rhythms of regular, prepandemic life.

"Well, movie star, or con man, whatever you are, you don't sound like you're from around here."

"No, New York. I'm staying in—or on—a place called Cutters Neck."

"Wait—you're from *Cutters*?"

"No—not *from* there," he clarified. "Just staying in a cabin on someone's property for the summer. In exchange for tennis lessons."

"Shit," she said. "I've always wanted to see that place. Is it as cool as it sounds?"

"It's all right," he said. Her outsize reaction made him uncomfortable.

Another girl joined her. The first introduced herself as Georgia ("Like the state?" Conor asked, making sure he'd heard right; "No, like the country," she retorted)—and her friend as Amber. "He's staying on Cutters," Georgia told her.

"Mister High Fuckin' Roller over here," Amber said.

"I'm not from there," he said again, reexplaining his arrangement.

The two of them were originally from the small city nearby and now shared an apartment in town. Georgia worked at the aforementioned coffee shop, Amber at a clothing boutique. Conor didn't mention law school.

Soon two young guys came over: stocky Charlie, with a bright blur of orange stubble and red acne peppering his thick neck, and Kyle, his dim-looking sidekick, gaunt and goateed. It wasn't clear if they had romantic claims on or interest in the girls.

"Tennis," Charlie sneered when they told him about Conor's setup. He had a thicker New England accent than the girls. "The only thing pussier than tennis is golf. A baseball player's got to hit a little ball going a hundred miles an hour while a whole stadium's yelling at him, but if you fucking sneeze during a tennis game, they throw a hissy fit."

"I learned to play in a park on the street, so noise doesn't really bother me," Conor said.

Charlie was not appeased. "Any game where there's no contact is bullshit," he insisted. "You can't even touch the fucking *net.*"

Charlie was confrontational and surly, likely annoyed that the girls had flocked to this handsome stranger, and gym-built muscles broadened his short frame. Conor was more athletic-looking than both of them, but he was in their territory, and certain men—especially yappy terriers like Charlie—rather than backing down in the face of a challenge, were more motivated to prove their mettle.

"I got the next round," Conor said preemptively. He was flush with Catherine's cash—until his credit card bill was due, at least—and, given the value of the expected payoff (going back to Georgia's apartment) if he kept the peace, it was a worthwhile investment. Charlie held up his beer bottle sulkily as Conor asked for their orders.

As they worked on their new round of drinks and the subject circled back to Cutters Neck, Charlie's contempt rose again. "Those motherfuckers," he said. "I catered a party there last summer, and this rich dick who threw it stiffed us."

"He didn't pay you at all?" Conor asked, indulging him but also dubious.

"He paid a deposit for the alcohol, but some drunk asshole fell into the drinks table and knocked a bunch of bottles over, and when my boss told the guy how much he owed the next day for the shit we lost, he wouldn't pay up. Said it was our fault we didn't have a sturdier table." Charlie shook his head. "The richer you are, the more you steal—I'm not even fucking kidding."

"We should go there tonight," said Kyle. "Fuck up his house, yo."

Conor's spine stiffened.

"Wasn't at his house. It was next to a tennis court." Charlie eyed Conor as if he were responsible.

"That's the yacht club." Conor flushed with a self-awareness that was unfamiliar to him. "It's just called that. There aren't any yachts. People play tennis and swim there."

"Word? Swimming?" Kyle said. "Let's go."

"I got that handle of Jack in the trunk," said Charlie.

Conor didn't like where this was going.

"It's not that cool," he said, but his words were drowned out by the band's belting the chorus of "Take the Money and Run."

"I don't want to go back for my suit," said Amber.

"Then skinny-dip. It's not like I haven't seen your little tit-tays before." Charlie pantomimed squeezing her breasts with his tongue lolling out.

"Fuck off," she said as she pushed him away. "You're driving."

Conor hadn't even envisioned bringing Georgia back to Cutters—he'd hoped they would just hop over to her apartment—let alone the two jackasses. "The ocean's still really cold now," he said, louder this time. "It's not great for swimming until August."

"We could just dip our feet in," Georgia suggested, giving him a meaningful look. "I'd love to see where you live."

Charlie polished off his beer and burped. "Let's bounce," he said.

The group was already in motion. Georgia was clearly game for whatever the night held with him, which meant he could bow out and get her number for another time, but now that they had the idea in their heads, there wasn't anything to stop the others from simply parking outside and walking past the gate. If they got busted for causing a ruckus on their own, they'd tag him as the responsible party, and there went his summer job. At this point, his best bet was to stay on their good side and try to stop them—namely Charlie—from doing anything too stupid.

HE WAS THE ONLY ONE WHO WORE HIS MASK WHEN THEY WALKED BACK through the bar. Out on the sidewalk, the others split for Charlie's car. This was Conor's last opportunity to deter them.

"It'll take me about twenty-five minutes to get there on my bike," he said, exaggerating the amount of time they'd have to wait.

They ignored him.

It might not be so bad. They'd find the water too cold, everyone but Georgia would leave from boredom, and he'd take her back to his cabin.

He unlocked his bike and started off. Within a minute a tan, decades-old Buick nearly sideswiped him.

"Bitch!" heckled a deep voice.

If Conor had a rock in his hands, he might've thrown it at Charlie's taillights.

He hoped the drawbridge out of the village would be up as a final disincentive, but it wasn't, so he took his time biking to Cutters; maybe they'd turn around at the gate out of impatience. At this point, he was ready to forfeit his night with Georgia.

Half an hour later he pedaled downhill to the gate. The Buick was parked on the side of the road near the security box, and the four of them were leaning against the hood, sharing a bottle of whiskey.

"What's the code, chode?" Charlie asked as he coasted up to them. Every word out of this fucking guy's mouth made Conor want to punch him.

John had indeed neglected to mention the gate code before his arrival, though he'd written it on a paper in Conor's cabin. Even if various delivery trucks and grocery shoppers had access to it, giving it to these people would be frowned on. "I'll do it," Conor said, walking his bike up to the box.

"You afraid we'll come back and fuck shit up?"

That was precisely what Conor was afraid of. But if he offended Georgia, it might nullify the purpose of this whole outing. Nor did he want to be lumped in as an ally of the robber barons on the neck.

Conor told him the code; surely these guys wouldn't be so idiotic as to commit a real crime against people with this much influence over local law enforcement. Charlie smugly typed in the digits, and the gate opened with a slow, rusty yawn. The foursome hopped back into the car.

"Follow me to the yacht— the swimming place," Conor said. "And watch out for the speed bumps." He didn't want Charlie chasing his heels.

He biked ahead, dismounted at the top of the yacht club driveway, and told them to park on the side of the road. The visitors jounced downhill, Charlie taking slugs of Jack Daniel's. At least no residents would be swimming at this late hour.

"This shit is *noice*," said Kyle, sniffing the air. "Smells like clean laundry."

"I've worked nicer places," Charlie said.

"C'mon, bro. Nicer than *this*? With the ocean right up in your grill?"

"I been to places on the Cape that make this look ghetto," Charlie said. "Huge new mansions with big-ass swimming pools. These houses are old as fuck."

When they reached the pier there was noise in the distance, but it might have been the ocean and the wind. It grew louder as they approached the platform, and Conor leaned over the side. Treading water below were three of the college kids. They looked up at Conor as Charlie continued to yammer obliviously.

Conor didn't want the townies seeing him as one of the Cutters residents, but he *really* didn't want anyone from Cutters seeing him with these guys. And he could easily imagine Charlie picking a fight here that ultimately led to his firing.

"I just remembered," he said. "There's a pool we can use instead of this."

"Fuck it, we already here," Charlie said.

"The pool's way better. A lot warmer and no fish that bite. They get really bad here at night."

The threat of lower-body danger was persuasive. "Aight," Charlie said.

With relief Conor led them back up the driveway and over to the house that had hosted the pool party. It was certainly dicey to be on private property, but he'd take his chances at an unoccupied house over mixing the Cutters kids with these two Massholes.

"No one's home?" Charlie asked as they headed to the back of the dark house.

"They're here," Conor lied. "They just told me I can use the pool at night, as long as I'm quiet."

The girls raved over the setup of the pool and the view of the ocean, brushstroked with dabs of moonlight, and they all stripped in the darkness.

After initially swimming the length of the pool, the others were content to stand in the shallow end, thankfully, and drink whiskey.

"Which house are you staying at?" Georgia asked Conor.

"It's not a house. It's a small guest cabin. Kind of a long walk from here," he said, in case Charlie got any ideas about moving the party.

"Who's the guy that owns the house?"

"He's a lawyer."

"Lawyers," Charlie said, "are the biggest scumbags in the world, bar none."

"He's actually a pretty nice guy," said Conor.

"I bet a million bucks he didn't get a place here by being a nice guy."

"Well, no, his family owned it. Most of the people here, their families have had the houses for a few generations—"

"Ex*actly*—the only way into a place like this is being born into it. And their families didn't buy them by being nice, either. No one gets *this* rich by playing nice. It's because someone in their family way back in the day fucked someone over or did something illegal. Or barely legal."

"Barely legal," Kyle tittered like a teenager.

"Or maybe they just made something of themselves," Conor said quietly, surprising himself with his defense of the Cutters Neck "forefathers."

"Starting with the land," Charlie said, ignoring him. "Property is theft."

"What's that mean?" Kyle asked.

"It means, like . . . property is theft," Charlie reiterated. "These people"—he circled a finger overhead—"think they're clean because their ancestors didn't own slaves. But they own all this property, which they got by killing Indians. Straight-up genocide. You saw that Black Lives Matter sign? I bet they're all into that shit. As long as they don't have to matter anywhere near *them*."

Conor didn't argue further with him, in part because he suspected Charlie had a point, mostly because he wanted them gone as soon as possible.

"Being rich doesn't automatically make someone a terrible person," Georgia said to Charlie. "And just because *you're* cynical and racist doesn't mean everyone else is."

"I'm not racist," Charlie muttered, but she succeeded in shutting him up on the topic.

After talk shifted to the delayed start of the baseball season and the quality of the Red Sox' starting pitchers, Georgia softly asked Conor if she could see his place. The other three showed no sign of tiring.

"Maybe we should get out of here," he announced to the group.

"Nah, we good," Charlie said.

"In case the owners wake up," Conor said. "They told me I shouldn't swim past midnight. They might call the cops."

"So we'll go when they wake up."

He couldn't stay up supervising them till who knew when, destroying himself for his morning lesson with John and a day of studying.

He wasn't even that excited anymore by getting Georgia into his cabin, but he'd invested too much now to pass it up.

"I'd leave before then," he said. "The cops don't mess around when people from here call."

Hoping his warning was sufficiently ominous, he left with Georgia.

HAVING DONE THEIR BEST TO DRY OFF WITHOUT ANY TOWELS, CONOR pushed his bike home alongside Georgia.

"Sorry about Charlie," she said. "He's Amber's ex from high school. He picks fights with guys he doesn't know, like, all the time, but he's a sweetheart when you get to know him."

"Yeah, he seems like a very gentle soul," Conor said.

Even in the dark she covered her mouth when she laughed. Despite the self-consciousness, it struck Conor, in conjunction with her excellent laugh, as an endearing tic. What had begun as a strictly one-off mission at the bar had been transforming over the last half hour. Georgia was refreshingly grounded compared with the Cutters people, pretty in her own way, smart and assertive enough to cut Charlie down to size. Even the purple bangs were growing on him. Maybe they'd continue to see each other over the summer.

"Okay, maybe not a sweetheart, but he's incredibly loyal," Georgia said. "This guy Amber once . . . never mind."

"What?"

"Well, Amber was seeing this asshole. He got her pregnant and refused to help pay for the abortion. So Charlie gave her the money, and then he showed up at the guy's house one day and beat the shit out of him."

"Really," Conor said, much more worried now about leaving Charlie alone.

"Yeah. The guy didn't press charges, because he didn't want the abortion stuff coming out. But I bet he never weaseled out of paying for one again," she said. "Also, to show you I'm not blindly defending my friends, Kyle's a total moron. And not even a nice guy."

They reached John's tree-framed grass driveway. "Holy shit," Georgia said. "It's like a fairy tale tunnel into the woods. My room looks out over an alleyway with garbage cans and rats."

"Yeah, it's nice," he said.

"You're so lucky," Georgia said. "I'll *never* live in a place like this."

He knew the feeling, having had a similar reaction to the place just a few days earlier. But he was slightly embarrassed to hear her verbalize it, even if no one else was around. In high school he'd attended a Yankees game with some friends. They'd bought the cheapest tickets possible but sneaked into the field seats along the third-base line by the seventh inning. The rest of his group couldn't stop giggling over the giddy threat of being struck by a foul ball. Conor was the only one who'd kept his cool, instinctively aware that their behavior would not only tip off the ushers but was also simply . . . gauche. He'd understood the idea then even if he hadn't known the word.

And now he wished Georgia hadn't acted the same way. It punctured his little fantasy of dating her. They may have come from similar backgrounds, and Conor was indeed here only by luck and would never again live in a place like Cutters Neck, either, but they were too different, even for a summer fling. He was certain that all his hard work was leading him toward a better destination. It was depressingly apparent that Georgia would remain stuck in this town or one like it.

Conor told her she could go into the cabin while he parked his bike under an overhang.

"Want to give me the keys?" she asked.

"No one locks their doors here," he said. "It's a pretty casual place."

They wasted no time getting into bed. He'd packed condoms for the summer and had, with optimistic foresight, slipped a couple into his pocket before heading out that evening. The sex was fine—better than not having sex, but probably not worth all the work he'd put into making it happen and the trouble Charlie might still cause. He was sure it was more his fault than hers. He attributed his response by turns to the alcohol, his fatigue, that comment from Georgia that had killed his mood, and, ultimately, the hollowness of the activity itself. Conor had had far more than his share of casual sex—he'd lost count of his partners after sophomore year of college—but at this point it was more a hunger that needed satiation rather than something he savored. Even the anticipatory excitement before the first time with a new girl was starting to fade.

He'd had just one serious relationship, starting his junior year of college, with Ally, a freshman on the women's team. His friends wouldn't shut up about how she was the hottest girl in school, but he had learned by then that he cared less than the average guy about female appearance, not viewing it as a referendum on his own. Besides, he appreciated Ally for many other reasons: she was good-hearted, fun, spearheaded community service projects with her sorority, got along with his mother, came from a tight-knit family in Albany that embraced him, took her schoolwork seriously. She'd been worshipful of Conor, the dashing captain of the men's team, and when he ended the relationship as he started law school, citing his upcoming workload and the six-hour drive between them, she was devastated.

For Conor, on the other hand, it barely made a dent in his daily emotional life. He'd genuinely liked Ally, but he'd never felt anything close to the kind of overwhelming love he'd seen in the movies. Secretly, he suspected he was incapable of it. It was just a hormonal rush, anyway, chemicals that got you high and fooled you into thinking there was a spiritual component behind your evolutionary lust. It did worry him, though, and he wondered if something inside him was broken, if a few switches were pointing the wrong way in his circuitry. Richard had once given him some pointers on nuptials well before he had his first girlfriend.

"Don't marry someone just because she's pretty and you can't believe you got her," he told Conor. "Beauty fades. Infatuation fades. Marry someone you respect, who's going to be a good partner, who's going to take care of you when you need it. That's what Linda and I had. Those things don't fade. And when you finally find the girl you want to marry, don't blow it—they don't come around often."

He'd kept these criteria in mind all these years, though the idea of being with somebody for life whom he respected but wasn't initially crazy about didn't sound terribly appealing.

His mind drifted as he pumped away numbly. Catherine's little tease on the tennis court had to have been on purpose, factored in with all her suggestive talk. Same with bending over for the ball. Daring him to catch a peek of her underwear. Wanting to feel his dick against her ass. Right in the middle of the tennis court by the Cutters Neck yacht club, where any of these stiff Wasps could see them all but dry humping.

"How about from behind?" he said.

He and Georgia parted and shifted and clumsily rejoined. Her lower-back tattoo looked like a stalk of wheat, a curious choice. He continued with his eyes closed, gripping the softness of her hips, re-membering how Catherine had bumped into him, then imagining her underwear slipping down her legs to the court, his shorts doing the same, banging into her as they rhythmically stroked together until she pushed her ass out so far that he slid inside her.

He came in a rapid surge.

"Sorry," he told Georgia when it was over. "I thought I could hold off longer."

"'Sokay," she said. "Fun while it lasted."

She smiled at him in the darkness, then snuggled into the shared pillow. Conor didn't sleep that well with another person next to him, especially not in a twin bed on a warm night. It might not be too late to hail an Uber.

"Just so you know, I have to be out of here by seven a.m. to give a tennis lesson," he said.

"That's so romantic of you, the first thing to say after fucking me." She switched to a lunkheaded baritone: "'Um, just so you know, I have to be up really early, so maybe you can get the fuck out of here.'"

"No, I want you to stay," he told her. "It was only so you knew my alarm was going to go off."

"I've got work in the morning, too, you know."

"Okay. Forget I said anything."

An owl hooted twice. Conor hadn't ever heard one in real life before. Though he'd been on Cutters for a few days, he suddenly felt, with the unease of a foreign exchange student on his first night in a new country, that he was far from home, surrounded by strangers, and that it would be a long time until he returned to anything familiar.

"What's your tattoo of?" he asked to break the silence.

"It's a reed."

"Any reason?"

"There's an Aesop's fable about the oak and the reed. The oak thinks it's strong because it's big and solid, but then a storm blows it over. The reed looks weak, but it bends in the wind and doesn't break."

"Oh, yeah. I've heard that one before." His college coach had invoked it once, before a match against a giant with a fearsome serve and a big forehand, comparing Conor's adaptable game to the properties of the flexible reed. Whatever inspiration it stirred had been insufficient; he'd been trounced in straight sets.

They were quiet again.

"I don't usually sleep with someone the first night I meet them," Georgia said.

"I don't, either," Conor lied.

"I don't know your reasons, but I . . ." She sighed. "Forget it."

"No, go on," he said, mostly to disprove her dim view of his chivalry.

"Well, I don't really feel like going into all the details, but, basically, my stepdad abused me and my sister for years, and my mom was in denial and looked the other way, and it fucked me up for a long time and made me not trust anyone."

Conor felt an uncomfortable blend of compassion and a desire for this line of conversation to end as soon as possible.

"I'm really sorry," he said. "That's horrible."

"It was. But I've gotten a lot healthier about my intentions and my relationships the last couple years, ever since I began processing everything."

Though he was inclined to cut Georgia plenty of slack, he found this use of *processing* annoying. People who were hung up on bad things that had happened to them, who thought the only way to deal with what made them unhappy was to endlessly think and talk about it, were asking to remain endlessly miserable. If you really wanted to put something behind you, you were better off just letting the past be past and moving forward.

"Good," Conor said. "You seem healthy to me, for what it's worth."

"Most of the time I feel okay," Georgia said. "But some days, all it takes is one comment from someone, and I'm nine years old and terrified and ashamed again." She paused. "I know that's some heavy shit to dump on you right after having sex. But this book I'm reading about trauma says you should tell people as soon as you feel the urge, because hiding it becomes its own separate shame, and if you bury something, it always comes out in some other form. Sorry if I made things weird."

"No, not at all," he said. "It's totally fine."

His vacuous words and tone were unconvincing and disappointing—*he* was disappointing—but he didn't have it in him to be otherwise, not right now. He almost felt like apologizing. Georgia deserved to be with a different kind of guy, someone who didn't instinctively recoil from "heavy shit."

"So," Georgia said, "that's *my* fucked-up childhood. What was yours like?"

"I'm an only child, which I guess was a little lonely," he said, offering the blandest of tidbits while estimating how many hours he had until his alarm went off.

She murmured that she was grateful she at least had her sister by her side through her childhood, he didn't volunteer any more information, and those were the last, forgettable words they spoke for the night.

HE STARTLED AWAKE IN THE SMALL HOURS, TERRIFIED THAT CHARLIE and Kyle had burned down the house with the swimming pool, and didn't fall back asleep until shortly before his phone alarm pestered him. As he dressed in his tennis gear and guzzled water from the kitchen tap, Georgia remained in bed with her back to him.

"Hey," he croaked, hesitantly tapping her bare shoulder. Strange, still, after all the one-night stands he'd had, that you could blithely insert your genitalia inside another person's in the darkness of night and then be ill at ease touching her shoulder in the morning. "I've got to go."

"I don't have to be at work till ten," she mumbled.

He didn't want her there when he returned, and he especially didn't want John to run into her. Having company wasn't against any stated house rules, but he could imagine his formal boss reacting poorly to Georgia's purple hair, notwithstanding his own pink shorts. "The owner doesn't want me having people over. It's a Covid thing."

Georgia didn't move.

"I'll get you an Uber." She still didn't respond. "Sound good?"

"Fine," she said.

He ordered a car, included the gate code, and relayed its arrival time to Georgia. "It'll be right out on the road here." He waited for her to acknowledge what he'd said. "You'll be there?"

"Yes," she said, her back still to him.

His wallet was in the jeans he'd worn the previous night and thrown on the floor, and his laptop was out on the desk. Georgia wasn't the type to steal—but he'd just met her, didn't even know her last name. He zipped up his valuables in his backpack. "So just go back out and down the driveway in about fifteen minutes," he reiterated at the door. "Or ten, to be safe."

Georgia finally turned over. "Do you not even want my number?"

"I do," he said. "I thought you'd maybe leave it here for me."

She made a *tch* sound at his flimsy excuse but traded numbers with him.

"Thanks," he said as he opened the door. "Have a good d—ay."

He left before she could comment on his stammer.

CHAPTER 5

That afternoon, having bicycled past all the houses to confirm they were still standing, he devoted twenty minutes to crafting a text to Georgia. He gently expressed that he'd had a great time with her, but he had to make studying for the bar and applying to jobs his priority this summer, and he wished all the best for her. It was a variation of texts he'd sent in the past—he didn't believe in ghosting anyone—and perhaps overboard for a one-night stand in a place to which he'd never return. But even if they obviously had no future together, she needed to be handled with care.

Three hours later he received her reply: *I bet you think of yourself as a nice guy. But you're actually an asshole.*

The comment stung, especially after he'd taken pains to protect her feelings. *I'm sorry*, he wrote and, not wanting to deal with any further insults, blocked her number.

In bed that night, after he turned off the light, he remembered telling Georgia that no one locked their doors on Cutters. Why had he done that? To show that this place, despite the gate, wasn't fixated on keeping out the barbarians? Leaving doors unlocked meant no one had a security system, either. Even if Charlie and Kyle hadn't stirred up trouble last night, they might in the future, when they had more time to prepare. They had the gate code, and they'd probably figured out that the party hosts were, in fact, out of town.

And they now knew where he lived, too. His treatment of Georgia wasn't on the level of shirking payment for an abortion, but Charlie wouldn't need any excuses.

He secured the hook and eye latch on his door.

. . .

CATHERINE WAS PUNCTUAL FOR HER SECOND LESSON ON THURSDAY. SHE wore the same outfit as before.

"Hello, Conor," she said as she sauntered onto the court.

She'd left off the *O'Toole* for once. He grabbed a few balls out of the hopper. "Ready to begin?"

"Well, you're all business. Aren't you going to buy me dinner first?"

He still didn't know how to respond to these remarks. If she were his age he could come up with some banter, but with a woman who had a quarter century on him, it seemed almost disrespectful, even if she were the instigator.

"Yes, I'm ready to begin," she said when he didn't come up with a reply. "I've been practicing my forehand motion."

Catherine was a little improved, though she still hit most shots into the net or over Conor's head. "I want to try my backhand," she announced when they were halfway through the hopper. She did, swatting recklessly with a one-hander.

"How do you feel about switching to a two-handed backhand?" he asked.

"You'll have to show me what that looks like," she said.

He demonstrated the form.

"You can't expect me to learn anything when you're over there."

He couldn't really imagine she'd pull anything again, not after he'd backed off last time. He crossed over to her side and got into the ready position next to her.

"Show me like you did last time," Catherine said. "Move my arms for me."

She was going to do it again.

And maybe he wanted her to.

"Okay," he said.

The backhand required him to place both hands on her forearms. As he enfolded her, he talked her through the movement. After they slowly swung in unison several times—there was no contact beyond his hands on her arms—he let go, stepped back, and told her to keep going.

"Make sure you rotate your hips." He showed her how, isolating his motion to his trunk. She mimicked him but didn't twist enough. "You rotate your hips backward, like you're cocking a gun—that's how you generate your power—then explode forward."

"I don't think I'm going to get it until you show me yourself," she said, taking his hand and placing it on her hip.

There was a tingle in his balls at the intimate and bold contact. He delicately laid his hands on either side of her skirt, directed her hips a few times, and told her to add a half-speed swing and a pause after the downswing. Once she'd done it three more times, he retreated a couple of steps.

"Don't stop," she said. "I'm still getting the hang of it."

She stepped back within an inch of him, rotated, and swung. When she turned in slow motion for another swing, she knocked against him—and this time she froze upon contact, with just the four thin layers of his boxer briefs and mesh shorts and her skirt and underwear separating her ass from his dick.

"Just like this?" she asked.

"Yeah," Conor said quietly.

"And then I explode?"

He tried not to think about what was happening, but it was impossible.

"Uh-huh," he said.

Catherine swung, their bodies cleaving, and when she went for another backswing, now at regular speed, she banged against him with more force. On the downswing hold, she subtly pushed up against him, as if they were grinding on a dance floor. She uncoiled, making some distance, and didn't wait to repeat the motion. Another backswing, another bump, and, during the pause, sustained pressure. Then another, his underwear and shorts tented, his embarrassment eclipsed by the stimulation.

He couldn't believe she was doing this, right out in the open for anyone who might be coming down to swim. Unless that was why she was doing it in the first place.

She collided once more with his erection. This time, instead of another touch-and-go swing, she stayed on him.

For what seemed like minutes but was probably five seconds, neither of them moved.

Conor had never been more uncomfortable and aroused at once in his life.

She swung, then broke free from his light grip and stepped forward. He pivoted to hide his lurid silhouette.

"I think I've got it," she announced cheerily. "You can go back to your side."

He walked away with his back to her. "Let's take a water break," he suggested.

"I don't need any."

He pretended to need to tie his shoes and tried to will his hard-on to subside with memories of his dead grandmother, but it refused to comply.

"C'mon," Catherine said. "Time's a-wasting."

Once he turned, there'd be no hiding. But she knew it was there. If this was what she wanted, then so be it.

He strode to midcourt. When he faced Catherine, she was smirking. "All set?" she asked. "Everything good?"

"Yes," said Conor.

"Good," she said. "Very good."

WHEN THE LESSON WAS OVER, CATHERINE AGAIN TOLD HIM HER CHECK-book was at the house.

"It's pretty easy to sign up for online payments," he said. "I can walk you through it and you can pay me later."

"I don't do things like that on my phone," she said, as though apps, too, were gauche. "Meet me on my patio in an hour and I'll pay you there."

Their little game on the court had been relatively harmless fun, but he felt more at ease, counterintuitively, engaging in this decidedly physical tango in public than with her acid tongue at her home. "You can just pay me double after the next lesson," he said.

"I'm not certain I want another lesson yet. So it's best if you come today."

She walked off to her golf cart; the discussion was over.

He could just write this one off. But he needed the cash now, especially after he'd bought that round of drinks the other night and then Georgia's Uber.

Conor showered, biked to Catherine's house, and went around to the patio, where she'd again set out the tray with gin and tonic and two glasses—or "gin balloons." He poured weaker drinks this time for both of them, started in on his, and tried to check his email but couldn't pick up a signal. He was halfway through his drink when Catherine emerged in another revealing dress.

"You're learning," she said when she saw her prepared drink.

He handed it to her. "Cheers."

"God, please don't say that," she told him. "It's middle class. Just drink."

Once he was finished, he'd politely but firmly say he had to get back to studying, ask for the check, and be on his way.

"The architecture here is quite impressive," he said, a more sophisticated compliment than he'd paid her house the first time.

"The proper word is 'gaudy,'" she said. "Most of this used to be woods. My ex-husband cut down all the trees, razed the beautiful house that had been in his family for about eighty years, and constructed this . . . monstrosity." She wrinkled her nose, as if smelling sewage. "There's a *bowling alley* here."

"Where is he now?"

"I imagine he's in his place in the Hamptons, which is even more garishly modern than this one. I believe he can control the entire house from his phone. He's quite comfortable around the trappings of new money. Very American that way."

"You don't share this house with him?"

"No," she said. "I do not."

He couldn't believe that Thomas Remsen, a seemingly savvy businessman (Conor had looked him up; he held a leadership post at a major bank), would completely lose his ancestral summer property in a divorce.

"So, tell me about the industrious Conor O'Toole," she said. "Skip over the boring parts—Yonkers, law school, bar exam, blah blah blah. Only the juicy bits."

He deliberated, then said, "My dad died when I was eleven."

Odd how much more readily this had come out with her than the more sympathetic Georgia. Though he'd mostly said it now to defuse Catherine's mockery. Let her find a way to spin this one into a joke at his expense.

But she didn't. After a moment, she asked, "Was it a long illness?"

"Heart attack," he said. "He was a construction worker. Happened on the job."

For once Catherine was speechless as she looked into her glass. Her phone, on the arm of her chair, buzzed with a text. She entered the passcode—the last two digits, Conor saw, were both zeros—and wrote something out of his view. The phone vibrated several more times. She stood and spilled more gin into her glass.

"Excuse me for a moment," she said.

"Do you know the Wi-Fi here?" he asked, setting himself up for an excuse to leave when she came back. "I have an email I'm waiting on and I'm not getting a signal."

She told him—it was the street address—and took the phone into the house, sliding the door shut behind her. Conor entered the Wi-Fi password, figuring he may as well check his email, and nursed his drink so that she wouldn't have an excuse to "refresh" it. Catherine didn't come out again for ten minutes, however, by which time he'd finished it.

"Where were we?" she asked, immediately refilling her glass. When she poised the gin bottle over his, Conor pulled away.

"I should stop at one," he said.

"Oh, don't be such a Puritan. We've barely started chatting."

He needed the work—especially if she kept tipping him fifty bucks—but he couldn't go on letting this woman order him around and derail his studying.

"I'm enjoying talking with you," he said, setting his glass down with a declarative thunk, "but I really can't drink any more tonight. I have a lot of reading ahead of me."

He couldn't tell if the movement of her eyebrows indicated irritation with or respect for his defiance.

"Have you been anyplace off the neck the last few days besides a supermarket?" she asked. "Or been inside with anyone who has been?"

He didn't want to give her a Covid-related reason to stop taking lessons with him, if that's what she was getting at. "No," he answered. Surely Georgia wasn't sick.

"Then I'll give you a tour of the house, since you seem so curious about it." She stood. "Follow me."

If this was an attempted seduction, he didn't want any part of it. Fantasies aside, the real thing would complicate his business arrangement with one of his only, and so far best, clients. He'd much rather she continued paying for lessons and tantalizing him—while preserving plausible deniability—than force him to turn her down outright.

"I actually have to get back home," he said. "I've got to deal with that email."

Catherine considered this tactful demurral.

"You did such a good job on my ground strokes that I was considering paying you three hundred dollars per lesson from now on. There are other areas of my game I'd like help with. Like my serve."

"Sure," he said, corralling his excitement. He hadn't intended for his rejection to be received as a negotiating tactic, but that seemed to have been the profitable result. Maybe she'd pay extra all summer just to keep him around. "Text or email, and we'll set it up."

"You could show me the proper form right now, and I'll consider it a lesson," she said. "I believe my racquet's upstairs."

Conor's muscles tensed. The atmosphere, already fraught with sexual tension, was suddenly charged with illicitness. This was no longer
just a seduction; it was a carefully worded proposition. What did she
expect for her three hundred dollars—what they'd done on the court,
a little clothed rubbing, or, more likely, something that required him to
accompany her to the vaguely defined "upstairs"?

"Why don't we save that for the tennis court next time," he said.
"It won't be that helpful unless you're hitting. And I really do have to
get back home."

She remained standing and silent, eyeing him from her vantage.

"I'll get my checkbook." She went into the house and came back in
a few minutes with a check for three hundred dollars. Conor thanked
her.

"See you later," he said as he took off, though he was certain this
was their last meeting; she wouldn't ask for another lesson after his
clear refusal, and he took her overpayment as a kind of severance
package.

Catherine sat in her chair with a dignified posture and raised her
drink.

"Cheers," she said.

HIS LEGS CHURNED ON HIS BIKE PEDALS, AS IF HE WERE TRYING TO OUT-
run Catherine's proposal.

When he deposited her check on his phone, he was greeted with a
notification that his mother's ninety-day insulin supply had been automatically refilled, at a cost of $672.78. Almost two Tiffany forks. It had
been $25 on her employer's plan. Afraid she might dangerously lower
her dosage if she knew how exorbitant it was on her health insurance
marketplace plan, Conor had stealthily switched the charges for her
refills to one of his credit cards.

He ate two cans of split pea soup with a baked potato—his cheap,
nutritious, and filling go-to meal—and tried to study, but it was hard to
learn about intentional torts after what had just happened. Unless he'd

grossly misread the situation, she'd all but openly offered him money for sex. It was unsettling.

But also flattering. Catherine was beautiful, though Conor had had no shortage of attractive girls coming on to him. But none of them was the owner of a $26 million mansion overlooking the ocean that supplemented a Fifth Avenue "turret."

He'd been on the same page for ten minutes. He needed a distraction, then he'd get back to work. Taking his laptop into the bathroom, he watched one of the first videos that came up on a porn site, but the enterprise felt deadening and obligatory.

Thumbnails of other videos were to the side. One was labeled "MILF Fucks Neighbor Boy." It was a category he'd never sought out before, and on the occasions he'd run across it, it hadn't done much for him. He clicked.

As the titular character seduced a guy who looked younger than Conor, an elemental id unlocked within him. He closed his eyes and pictured the tennis court sequence again. He could have done that the rest of the summer. Why'd she have to ruin things? All the excitement without crossing an unseemly threshold, a nearly innocent game by comparison. It was like Richard said: the big shots always wanted more, more, more.

A woman two and half decades his senior, bluntly propositioning him with three hundred dollars. Paying him after they were done like he was an escort. In one of her ten bedrooms.

The image of her writing him a satisfied postcoital check pushed him over some psychological cliff he hadn't known existed.

After he cleaned up, he spoke the word *rentier* into his phone. It provided a succinct definition: "A person living on passive income from property or investments."

Three hundred bucks was pennies to her. And it was about six weeks of insulin for his mother.

He didn't have Catherine's number. Before he could rethink the wisdom of what he was doing, he left the cabin, remembered the condoms, went back for one, and jumped on his bike. He rode to the end of the neck, his mesh shorts and boxer briefs rubbing him as he ped-aled, the foreplay-like friction overpowering both his refractory period and his nerves.

What would Richard say? He'd be appalled, of course. But put-ting aside the moral objections, he'd tell Conor he was reaching for a low-percentage shot down the line when he could be staying in the game with a safe topspin up the middle and continuing his well-compensated lessons with Catherine. But she wouldn't want those les-sons if he didn't go through with this. And it was appalling only if he let himself think of it like that. No different, really, from women who went out with rich men for the expensive dinners and presents. At least this would be for lifesaving medicine. And it wasn't like he was signing a long-term contract. If this episode made him squeamish, he simply wouldn't do it again.

After hiding the bike behind some bushes in case anyone came by, he marched up to the front door, rang the bell, and waited in his con-fusing state of jittery arousal. There was no sound from the intercom. She'd probably gone to bed. He should go, too.

He didn't even know what his dad would have said. He recollected a piece of fatherly wisdom delivered not long before he died. "Don't ever trow the first punch," he'd said to Conor one day, apropos of nothing, in his brogue. "But if your man hits you, you hit him back harder."

He might understand Conor's predicament here. The pandemic had hit them; he had to hit back harder. Though he'd certainly be shocked. Fathers were traditionally horrified if their daughters re-sorted to this, but most would be disturbed to learn their sons were doing it, too.

Well, Conor had $144,000 in loans and a diabetic mother to take care of. If they were going to survive—literally, in his mother's case—it was all on him.

He rang again.

"Conor O'Toole," Catherine said as she opened the door. "To what do I owe the pleasure?"

He grew even more nervous in her presence; if he wanted, it would really happen now. But he could still put a stop to it. Claim she'd overpaid him for the lesson and he wanted to return the money, get back on the bike, go home.

But three hundred dollars was on the line.

"I was seeing if you want to practice your serving form now," Conor said.

If she understood his code word, her face wasn't giving it away. "My serving form?"

"Yes," he said.

"How in the world could we play tennis at night?"

She understood it, but she'd thought better of her invitation, as he should have. And now he was creating an awkward situation by making her turn him away.

"I'm sorry. You're right." Mortified, he walked off.

"Oh, serving *form*," she said. "I suppose we don't need the court for that. Come in."

He stopped short, came back, and entered the foyer as she stepped aside with a pleased look and told him to wait there. She disappeared through a door.

It wasn't just in his head anymore. He was here—not on a tennis court, not on her patio, but inside her house, about to do something that few people ever did directly for money.

Above him was a high ceiling, beneath his feet burnished hardwood, and pillars stood by love seats on either side of the front door. The hallways were museum wide, with still lifes and pastoral paintings on the walls; he was no art historian, and he couldn't make out the signatures, but they appeared to be old. To one side was a wooden trunk that seemed to double as a bench, though a panel on top had a large crack. If Thomas's efforts at building his home were gaudy, then Catherine's taste, from his scant expertise with interior decoration, was classic and restrained. He hadn't ever been inside a house like this. Even the air, chilled from an overhead vent, smelled like it had been imported from somewhere expensive.

By the time she returned with two glasses—gin balloons again—and handed him one, he was thinking more clearly. He could still back out.

Catherine headed to a staircase over a stone wall, the outline of her ass shifting in her pants.

He didn't want to back out.

Upstairs was a hallway with more doors than he could quickly count. She led him through one at the end and turned on a dim floor lamp in a large bedroom. Behind an ajar door was a bathroom. One of those sofas with elaborate rounded armrests and two chairs, all in gold and burgundy velvet, sat by a bank of windows facing the ocean. The king bed was normal-looking; he'd imagined it might have one of those four-poster canopies.

Her tennis racquet really was there, against a wall. "So, you want to pick up the racquet and I'll show you how to serve?" he asked.

"No," she said. "Stand over there." She directed him to the foot of the bed as she stood by the coffee table.

"Take off your shirt and shorts." He set his drink on the floor, slipped out of his flip-flops, and removed both articles of clothing.

"You've got a real athlete's physique, don't you?" Catherine observed in the dispassionate voice of an appraiser anatomizing a Thoroughbred. "Take off your underwear."

He stepped out of his boxer briefs. She looked pleased with his swelling presentation. "Now lie down on your back." Catherine went over to the nightstand and took a jar out of the drawer. She sat next to his supine body, unscrewed the jar, and dipped in her fingers.

"Close your eyes and spread your legs," she said. He obeyed her instructions. In all his sexual adventures, he'd never had his partner dictate everything like this. He shivered at the cold touch of lavender-scented cream as she ran her hand up and down the length of his erection, rotating her wrist around his girth. She paused, for long enough that he wondered if she were stopping or transitioning to something else, before resuming.

Conor had received numerous hand jobs in his life and wasn't much of a fan; even if they weren't too rough and wrenching, as was often the case, he'd always thought he could do better himself. But he'd been missing out. He'd just never had one like this.

Back and forth Catherine's nimble fingers and lotioned palm traveled, sometimes squeezing delicately, occasionally refueling with more cream. He held off from coming, assuming this was just a prologue. The pleasure was exquisitely agonizing, the blood frothing in his veins like water shrieking in a kettle.

She brought her head close to his. "You liked today's lesson, on the tennis court?" she asked, her breath hot in his ear, her vanilla perfume like an entire garden.

"Yes," he said.

"When I put my ass on your cock." She switched hands, one maintaining the stroking while the other massaged behind his balls. "On your hard cock. You liked that?"

The repetition of the word did something to him. He never used it, only *dick*, as much a term for a jerk as for male anatomy. But *cock* indisputably meant sex.

"Yes," he answered between shuddering inhalations.

Without warning, one of Catherine's lubricated fingers found his anus and pressed lightly, tiptoeing up to a sex act Conor had never tried.

"I know you want to stick your stiff, hard cock in my ass for real," she said, tonguing the inside of his ear and probing him somewhere past her first knuckle, the taboo sensation amplified by the free association his mind came up with: stiff cock in the ass of a stiff Wasp.

Sometimes he wistfully recalled the life-changing phenomenon of the first orgasm he'd ever had, self-induced at thirteen: his body was capable of *that*? Due to the law of diminishing returns, nothing had matched it since. But despite his having ejaculated less than half an hour earlier, this one was up there, a seismic undamming of the desire that had been rising in him since their initial lesson.

"Stay where you are." She went to the bathroom and returned with a damp hand towel, with which she dabbed his abdomen. "You're a very messy boy."

"I can go again in a few minutes, if you wanted to . . ." He made it sound like it was an offer to an unsatisfied customer, but it was as much for himself: he wanted the complete experience.

"I don't doubt you can," said Catherine. "But that's enough for now. I'm going to give you the name of a doctor in town. Call him first thing tomorrow and make an appointment for a full panel of STD tests. I'll give you money to cover it."

She retreated a foot and folded the damp towel in half. "You can let yourself out," she said, as coolly as if he were a repairman who'd just fixed her boiler.

Conor felt vulnerable reclining on the bed in the low light, flaccid and naked, with her fully clothed. He scrambled to dress himself. "Would you want another . . . lesson then?" he asked.

"Once you get the test results. Five o'clock that day, on the court."

He'd used the word as a euphemism and was puzzled that she apparently wanted an actual tennis lesson. Maybe it was a way to justify what she expected afterward. He had to make his own expectations clear.

"And you said you don't use Venmo, right?" he asked.

Catherine didn't answer but walked over to a closet with double doors. She opened one; it was immense, a walk-in the size of his entire bedroom in Yonkers, with a table near the front cluttered with items, including her bag. She rooted through it to the sound of jangling keys and pulled out a checkbook and a pen. Then she picked up a pair of reading glasses from her nightstand, turned away from Conor as she put them on, scribbled on a check, and removed the glasses.

"Confirm the lesson when you get the test results," she said as she handed him a check for six hundred dollars.

II

CHAPTER 6

Conor sailed home on his bike, check safely folded in pocket, a zephyr at his back shushing through the roadside foliage, nearly all the houses dark as the moon lit his way.

More money than he'd ever made in one day, and one of the most gratifying sexual encounters in memory. He still felt dirty about what he'd just done. But another emotion, one mostly foreign to him, chased it: arousal because of the dirtiness. He'd been well behaved his entire life, hadn't done any drugs harder than pot, never stolen so much as a candy bar. They'd not only smashed various taboos just then, they'd even, depending on how one interpreted the payment, committed a misdemeanor. A lawyer breaking the law. It was enough to get him disbarred.

Only he hadn't taken the bar yet.

After he got to his cabin, he remembered he still didn't have her number to send the results. But when he deposited the check on his phone, a text from a new number was waiting for him with the name of a doctor.

A doctor who would give him the all-clear for paid sexual intercourse. Had she done this before with other men—other young men—or was she simply directing him to the best doctor in town? Regardless, there was no getting around it: what he'd just done was prostitution. Though he'd been into it, too, and the pleasure had been all his, so did it really count? Knowing now how good it was, he would've done it for free—the money was a bonus. In college everyone had called it "sex work," presumably to remove the stigma; he could think of it in those terms, simply as a job. And an enviable one at that. The guys on his team would think it was the height of studliness, getting lavishly compensated by an attractive older woman to let her give him a hand job in her mansion by the ocean.

Not that he'd ever tell a soul.

THE NEXT DAY HE CALLED THE DOCTOR AND SNAGGED AN APPOINTMENT for that afternoon. He biked into the village, submitted to urine and blood tests, a cheek swab, and a physical examination, and was told it would take a few days for all the results.

There was a beach on the neck that Conor had been bringing a prep book to on hot afternoons. Due to the pointy shells and rocks that covered most of it, no one used it besides the occasional dog walker from off the neck, which made it preferable to him for swimming, though after his near-drowning incident he never paddled beyond shallow waters. Half a mile to the right was the platform of the yacht club.

He was there, lying on his stomach facing the ocean, reading about trusts and future interests, distracted by the dipping sun that glazed the beach and marsh in a brassy cast, when he heard a rustling behind him. Coming out of the path between swaying beach grass was a barefoot girl around his age in cutoff jeans, a T-shirt, and glasses, carrying a towel.

"Hey," Conor said.

"Hi," she said.

He pretended to read, watching out of the corner of his eye as she walked past him, set down her towel, and removed her cutoffs and shirt to reveal a forest-green two-piece. She placed her glasses onto the towel, stepped gingerly over the band of sharp stuff by the shoreline, and waded into the seaweedy water.

The girl swam out a ways to the right until it became clear she was going all the way to the yacht club. He resumed reading but periodically lifted his head to measure her progress. When she reached the platform fifteen minutes later, she turned back. He focused on his book until her wet figure briefly appeared in his peripheral vision. The smell of cigarette smoke soon wafted over.

Something about this girl compelled him to keep sneaking looks at her.

"Sorry about the smoke," she said. "Is it bothering you?"

"No," he said. "I'm Conor."

"Emily."

"I'm the tennis pro here for the summer. Staying in John Price's cabin. Don't think I've seen you around before."

"I just drove up today from Brooklyn."

"Going crazy stuck in your apartment?" he asked.

"Something like that." She craned her head to see the prep book he'd set down. "Hefty book you've got there."

He held up the cover for her. "It's a study guide for the New York bar exam."

"Sounds like a great beach read." She had very nice teeth.

"Yeah," he said. "This section on trusts and future interests is riveting."

She didn't give him a courtesy laugh for the obvious joke, and the smile she'd been wearing dropped. "I've got to go," she said. She flapped the sand out of her towel as she walked away.

"Nice meeting you," Conor called, thinking he must have said something wrong, though he couldn't imagine what.

THE NEXT DAY, AS CONOR RESTRUNG ANOTHER POPPED RACQUET, JOHN knocked on his door and introduced a man named Lawrence Newcomb, who looked to be his junior by at least a decade.

"I'm sorry to interrupt you," Lawrence said. "Do you have a few minutes?"

"Of course," Conor said. "Just stringing a racquet."

He had a feeling in his stomach he'd hated on the rare occasions it had surfaced in his obedient childhood: that he'd done something bad and was being called to account for it by an authority figure. Had they somehow learned about him and Catherine? There wasn't anything wrong with it—they were two consenting, single adults—nor was there any way to prove the money exchanged wasn't for tennis services.

"It appears a house on the neck was broken into this week," Lawrence said. "We're not sure when, because the owners just came back today. Some jewelry was stolen. So we're asking around, trying to figure out what we can, since the police here are fairly incompetent and lazy. And we were wondering if you had any ideas."

"I'm sorry, I don't," Conor said, at first relieved that it had nothing to do with Catherine. But it likely *did* have something to do with Charlie. If so, then he was an unwitting accessory to the crime—and there went his newly lucrative summer job. "Which house was it?"

"The Bakers'. Fourth one as you come onto the neck."

Not the house with the pool, then. But even that degenerate wouldn't have been so stupid, especially if he thought the owners were home. He would have hit another house—especially one on the way out. Or come back another night. It still could be a coincidence, though.

"And all that was taken was jewelry?" Conor asked.

"All that was taken, yes. But they scribbled 'BLM' with a marker over the walls. For Black Lives Matter."

It was no coincidence. How stupid he was to give away the gate code. Not just stupid: weak willed, scared of Charlie's condemnation. He could have pretended that, as an outsider himself without a car, he simply didn't know it. Even if the gate blocked only vehicles, it was still a deterrent, and Charlie probably wouldn't have robbed a home if it meant making a long getaway on foot.

But unless there was a camera at the gate, there was nothing connecting him with Charlie. As long as he didn't say anything foolish, he was still safe. "Well, if I somehow hear of anything, I'll let you know," he said.

Lawrence paused. "This is a somewhat delicate subject. But you were seen, briefly, around ten or eleven p.m., with a group of young people on Tuesday night at the yacht club. Is that correct?"

A python wrapped itself around his chest. "It is," he said. "We only stayed for a minute because it was sort of crowded."

"Where'd you go after that?"

A white lie would make him look guilty, and the honest answer might even help him out. "To the house that had the pool party. The owner—I'm forgetting her name—she told me that I could use the pool while they were out of town. I hope that was okay."

"How long did you stay there?"

"Not that long. I went home after half an hour or so."

"And your friends?"

"They stuck around for a bit," he admitted. "I'm not sure how long."

"And who . . ." Lawrence fumbled for the right words. "Who are they, exactly?"

He was asking not for their names but their socioeconomic standing. Telling the truth, that the two guys in the group were rough-around-the-edges townies he'd met at a bar that night, wouldn't go over well.

"Law school friends who were stopping by on their way up to the Cape," Conor said.

"Stopping by . . . at ten at night?"

"I'd met them earlier for drinks in town," he said. "At a bar. The . . . Porthole. Then we came here for a quick swim before they went on their way."

It sounded just plausible enough, that a group of vacationing twentysomethings would make a pit stop to see their friend's swank summer digs, even late at night.

"But they drove onto the neck?" Lawrence asked. "They had the gate code?"

The college kids had likely taken note of Charlie's vintage Buick by the yacht club driveway. Better again not to lie by saying he'd forced them to park outside the gate.

"Yes, they—we used it to come in. But don't a lot of people have it? Uber drivers, delivery trucks, repairmen?"

"They do. Though we change it every two weeks, for that reason.

We're changing it now, of course, and we're making it weekly from here on in."

That made him feel a little better. At least Charlie couldn't easily commit another burglary. "And there's no security camera at the gate?"

"Unfortunately not. I've been trying to get one installed for years, but too many people in the association don't like the idea," Lawrence said. "Why do you ask about the camera?"

Lawrence had detected something evasive in his answers. If he'd just confessed to his mistake in bringing outsiders onto the neck and offered to make amends to the Bakers, it would have been okay. But it was too late now to come clean.

"Lawrence, what do you want out of this?" John interrupted. "You want Conor to ask his friends from law school if they broke into the Bakers' house and vandalized it?"

Conor felt a welling up of fondness for John. Lawrence seemed shamed, finally, by this remark.

"No, of course not," he said. "I'm sure it was a stranger. Sorry to have disturbed you, again."

Lawrence told John he'd see him and his wife for cocktails the next night, and they both left. In a minute there was another knock at the door. John was there alone. "Sorry about all that," he said.

"Not at all," Conor said. "I hope I didn't cause any problems inviting friends over."

"Absolutely not. Lawrence is just very . . . territorial. And he secretly loves that it happened, because it gives him an excuse to try to ban all visitors during the pandemic unless residents get permission ahead of time from the association, which is insane. He's like our Trump." He made a mock angry first. "'Build the wall.'"

"Is he one of the Trump supporters you told me about?"

"Lawrence?" John grimaced. "God, no. Huge Democrat. Laura's grandfather was an adviser to JFK, and they're still close with the family." He thought about it some more. "The Trumpers here are quite generous, actually, at least on a personal level—go figure," he said. "I didn't realize you had your own stringing machine. Can I drop a couple broken racquets off and pay whatever's appropriate for the string and labor?"

Conor told him he'd be happy to do it. His machine was now even helping him turn a little profit.

"I was thinking of taking the boat out for a cruise after dinner tonight," John said before he left. "Nancy is having one of her vertigo spells, so she's staying in. Would you care to join me?"

Conor began to say no, worried about yet another night of studying lost, but sailing with John would be a good opportunity to put this break-in business behind them quickly. And even if John's firm would never hire him, the rich conducted informal business on exclusive grounds: golf courses, Michelin-starred restaurants, boats. Maybe something else would come of this.

"I KNOW A MOTORBOAT ISN'T QUITE THE AUTHENTIC NEW ENGLAND SAILing experience," John said as they maneuvered out of the neck's congested marina, "but I figured you'd rather relax with some wine than spend the whole ride ducking the boom." He pronounced it *rah-ther*. "Wouldn't be very fun if you got conked on the head your first time out."

"I wouldn't be much use to you as a first mate, anyway," Conor said. "I haven't been on many boats in my life."

"I've got a little yawl, but I'm buying a thirty-eight-foot sloop with two guys here for longer trips. We were supposed to have it by now, but there's been a shortage during the pandemic."

Conor was surprised someone of his means would be sharing ownership of a boat. John invited him to open the bottle of wine and dig into the crackers and cheese from the cooler he'd brought. Under yet another staggering, pink-cheeked sunset, Conor leaned back on a bench and sipped his wine out of a plastic cup as they picked up speed on the open water.

"Feel like taking a turn?" John yelled above the wind.

"I've never done it before!" Conor shouted.

"It's easy! Just like driving a car!"

Conor joined him at the wheel at the rear of the boat. He got the hang of the throttle within a minute, keeping the speed low, and John left to get himself a glass of wine.

Conor allowed himself a sip as he steered solo. The wine tasted good rolling down his throat. The wind felt good combing back his hair. The ocean smelled good. It was a good life John had, an extremely good life. A nice house here, a boat, a cooler full of excellent wine and cheese, the bountiful blue sky and green ocean. Not a life spent on steaming subway platforms, eating split pea soup in tiny apartments.

Before this, Conor had known about John's kind of lifestyle only in the abstract, and, from that distance, he hadn't given it all that much consideration; he'd grown used to and comfortable with the grind and expected little more from becoming a lawyer than the stability that Richard had promised him. To take care of his mother, to pay off his debts, to own a modest home someday, to provide for a family well down the road: that was all he'd really striven for, a life that was a rung or two (if not three or four) below the top rank.

But now he'd seen this up close. Now he'd had a taste of what he'd been missing all these years, what a select few enjoyed. He didn't care about the cultural trappings of John's world—he could do without the starchy etiquette, the fetishization of sailing, those ludicrous pink shorts—but he'd take the money and the real estate and the bone-deep confidence that this country was made, from the very beginning, for your interests.

"Feel free to give it a little speed," John said when he returned.

Conor nudged the throttle forward, then again at John's encouragement. The motor growled as the boat accelerated, seesawing on the waves, poised to go airborne.

"Is it okay that we're bouncing like this?" he asked.

"Absolutely. This boat can handle anything."

Even if the boat could, it felt like he might be thrown overboard at any moment, and he wasn't wearing a life jacket; he questioned his ability to swim if he were stunned by the impact. It seemed unmanly to request one.

"I can take over," John said. "If you want to enjoy your wine."

Conor handed over the wheel, as relieved as if he'd stepped off a roller coaster, and John slowed them to a cruise. Once they motored to a secluded marsh off the bay, he killed the engine and joined Conor on the opposite bench as they drifted.

"I'm sorry you're not getting more business," he said, swirling his wine. "When I sent the email out asking who was interested, I had a lot of responses."

"That's all right. I'm sure things'll get busier in July and August."

"Well, the market's rebounding, so people may decide to start treating themselves," John said. "Not me, unfortunately. Two of my daughters decided to buy houses last winter, right before everything crashed. That's on top of tuition for ten—excuse me, eleven—grandchildren."

"Eleven—wow," Conor said. "How many kids do you have?"

John flashed his outstretched palm. "All daughters. After three, we tried one more time for a son and ended up with twin girls. My wife says my Y chromosomes must be X'd out."

Conor politely chuckled. That explained why he was buying only a one-third share of a boat.

"How's the job hunt going?"

"Still nothing yet," Conor said. "Luckily, I only have four daughters to support."

John laughed. Then he turned sober. "I do feel responsible for your situation here. Please allow me to pay you a few hundred bucks a week to cover my lessons."

"That's very generous, but I can't accept it," said Conor. "You're giving me a place to stay, and I came here without any guarantees. I don't generally like amending articles of incorporation." Proudly refusing assistance while couching it in legal terms would please John.

"Well, look, send me your résumé. My firm has a hiring freeze now, as do a lot of others, but if I hear of anything, maybe I can pass it along."

"Thank you," Conor said. "That's also extremely generous."

His small mission accomplished, he reclined and swirled his wine the way John had. His instincts were validated. The only way to do business with the rich was to get invited onto their home field.

John's phone rang. "I'm very sorry," he said, "I have to take this." He spoke quietly as he took the call, though Conor could hear as he pretended to gaze out at the water. It was about a case, the context of which eluded Conor as John talked with characteristic gentility. Then his tone instantly sharpened.

"Hold on," he said, lowering his voice as he spoke in a manner that was all the more menacing for its methodical precision, shaking his finger at the invisible listener. "It took a hell of a lot to get my client on board with this settlement, and now you're telling me your client wants to walk away at the eleventh hour? Do they think this is a game? Tell them to think hard about this one, because things are going to get ugly if that's how they want to play, and they'll wish they took this deal when they had the chance."

He hung up. "I'm sorry about that."

"No need to apologize."

"I try to be as diplomatic as possible when it comes to this pretrial lit shit," John said, his rare turn to coarse language signifying that this was now a confidential, man-to-man talk about business. "But at this level, with these stakes, if you're not somewhat . . . ruthless, let's say, then the other guy's going to be, and you're essentially asking to lose."

Conor nodded.

John broke into a smile. "Between you and me, I was bluffing. If this deal collapses and we go to trial, we stand a very good chance of losing."

"Really," Conor said. "You had me convinced."

"It's actually a tennis strategy my dad taught me," John said. "When you're down forty-love, your opponent expects you to play defensively. So you switch things up and play as aggressively as if you were *up* forty-love. Throws them off their game plan."

He'd liked John before this, if placing him somewhat in Catherine's category of effete Cutters men in the shadow of their forefathers. But behind the genial facade of an old-school Wasp, behind the sailing and rum cocktails and pink shorts, was a litigator who wasn't afraid to be ruthless—and to go on the offense when he was losing. Conor was taking notes.

CHAPTER 7

After Conor received his clean bill of health by email, he texted Catherine that he could meet for their lesson. She responded with a thumbs-up.

She was no-nonsense when she met him on Friday, greeting him without coyness or allusion to what they'd done last time. He didn't know if she'd still ask for full-contact instruction on the court, now that they'd gone much further in the bedroom. The neck was filling up, raising the odds someone might see them behaving inappropriately. She stood only to become the subject of gossip, but he could lose his job.

Within ten minutes of their lesson, a few residents passed the court on their way to the swimming platform. Catherine kept a professional distance, even as he tried to improve the mechanics of her serve, which might have genuinely benefited from physical correction.

A couple of senior citizens waved to Catherine as they strolled by, wearing scraggly terry cloth robes that apparently doubled as towels.

"It's hot today," she remarked to Conor.

"Uh-huh," he said, though it wasn't that hot, especially this late.

"Aren't you uncomfortable?"

"I'm fine."

"You should take off your shirt," she told him. "You'll overheat."

She'd phrased it as a suggestion, but her voice made it clear that this was an order, part of her three hundred dollars' worth. He wondered if this was for her visual benefit, or if she was trying to show him off. Or if she was simply proving that he had to do her bidding.

Fine, whatever. He pulled off his shirt and tossed it aside.

"Much better," Catherine said with a smile. "Right?"

He nodded.

The older couple returned in half an hour. Conor could feel their eyes on his bare back as they passed. They looked a few years older than his mom. He felt a hot surge of shame for what he'd done, for what he was going to do again. But he'd done it for her.

Mostly for her.

After the lesson, Catherine asked to see his medical report. He showed her the email on his phone, and she told him to come to her house at nine o'clock but to avoid the main road. There was a footpath along the western shore of Cutters that people never used, which he could take to the end of the neck, where he'd find another path that led up to her house. He was not to go to the front door, but should knock on the glass door on the patio.

A few hours later, he took the narrow, rock-strewn footpath to the end of the neck and knocked on Catherine's patio door. She opened it for him clutching two gin balloons.

"No one saw you?" she confirmed.

Beyond the purpose of their meeting, he wasn't sure why she was suddenly so concerned about his going unseen; she hadn't seemed to mind his ringing the front door when he'd been over for drinks. "No. I used the path."

"And you haven't gone anywhere without a mask or been inside with anyone?"

He told her no and started in on his drink as he climbed the stairs behind her. He'd hoped she might have eased them into it this time around, perhaps given him the tour of the house she'd offered earlier; he was especially curious to see the bowling alley.

But this time she was even more businesslike. In her lamplit bedroom, Catherine directed Conor to strip, item by item. Though he'd been through this before, his heart was still palpitating. Then she told him to lie on the bed.

"Should I get a condom?" he asked. He'd brought three with him.

"Your tests were clean, right?"

"Yes. You saw them all."

"Then we don't need it," she said.

She turned off the lamp. Other than some moonlight slanting in, the room was dark. Catherine shimmied out of her clothes before she straddled Conor. She placed his hands on her breasts, which were far firmer than he would have expected for her age, and brought her mouthwash-scented mouth against his. It felt good, soft and slippery.

Catherine stopped, pulled back a few inches, and stroked the contours of his face. "Such a handsome boy," she said. She took his cock into her hand and rubbed it against herself, lubricating it as his nerve endings tingled.

"I want you deep inside me," she told him, and plunged it in.

An annihilating bliss of immersion. He'd nearly forgotten how much better sex was without a condom. Catherine curled over his torso like a supplicant, biting his shoulder, haunches rising and falling, impaling herself again and again. As before, she was in the driver's seat. He felt a deep and unfamiliar pleasure over his own helplessness.

Catherine elevated her upper body and touched herself. She moaned, at first quietly then louder, the sounds alone bringing Conor closer to orgasm, until her free hand, which had been on his sternum for balance, abruptly gripped the base of his throat, briefly choking him, as she climaxed.

He'd been diligently holding off for her benefit and was on the verge of joining her when, without warning, she dismounted. He thought she was going to change positions or try something new, but she simply walked to the bathroom and shut the door.

He remained on the bed, baffled and still engorged, having fallen from the precipice of ecstasy to frustration within seconds.

He couldn't let this go without comment. When she returned, he said, "I didn't finish, you know."

"Next time," she said firmly, as if dangling a treat to a child for good behavior.

As the anticlimactic disappointment sank in, she did a curious thing. She lay next to him on the bed and lifted his head so that it rested on one of her breasts. With one arm cradling him, the fingertips of her other hand moved in small circles through his hair.

It was an odd position to be in. Not physically uncomfortable, but it felt off. They lay quietly for a minute or two. Whereas he normally didn't like to talk after sex, the silence now felt oppressive.

"I heard there was a break-in on the neck," he said. "The Bakers' house."

She didn't respond.

"Did you hear about it?"

"No."

"It happened sometime this week. Lawrence Newcomb—"

"Can you just . . . not talk?" she asked.

Her brusqueness felt excessive, more than a little hurtful. He was just a sex machine to turn off immediately after use.

Hurtful—but also hot. Girls often fell over themselves for him, but this was different. An attractive, improbably rich woman desired his body so much that she was willing to pay for it, to quantify its value, and wanted nothing else. Even this position was starting to reinvigorate him. But before he could signal his intent to make "next time" happen right then, Catherine said, "Use the back entrance and the footpath again when you go," and wriggled out from under him.

"You want to set up another lesson?" Conor asked as he dressed.

This time she didn't need to be reminded of the check; it was ready to go in her nightstand drawer. When Catherine gave it to him, her free hand fondled the thin barrier of his shorts as he stiffened.

"I'll be in touch," she said, then promptly let go and turned her back.

SIX MORE TIMES OVER THE NEXT TWO WEEKS THEY WENT THROUGH THE same paces. Catherine would initiate each meeting with a text demanding a lesson, during which she more or less behaved herself (the heavier stream of foot traffic as the summer deepened may have had something to do with this). Then she'd issue a nighttime invitation to her house, at which he arrived via the footpath and patio.

He hadn't been this fixated on sex since he was a teenager. A whiff of her perfume could get his blood going, and he was usually whipped into a frenzy by the time he followed her upstairs. (Likewise, he made a point of not showering afterward so that he could awaken and smell the heavy aroma of sex that clung to him.) It was as though his brain were laced with an aphrodisiac. Even the most mundane moments were tinged with eros, with the promise that, after the drudgery of cooking dinner and studying legal arcana and doing dishes, he'd be rewarded with—from a biological perspective, and maybe others, too—the fundamental purpose of life.

He was concerned, once it became clear he was as into it as she was, that she might withhold payment. But the opposite happened: she began using the checks as a marital aid of sorts, usually leaving one out on the nightstand before they commenced, once holding it above his head as a prize as he (happily) ate her out.

He'd never made so much money in his life.

"MY LAST INSULIN REFILL DIDN'T SHOW UP ON MY CREDIT CARD," HIS mother informed him over the phone one day. "The pharmacy said it was switched to your card. I told them it was an accident and changed it back. So look out for a big charge next time, and I'll find some way to repay you."

"It wasn't an accident," he said. "I put it on my card. Tell them to change it back."

"Conor, you can't afford that."

"It's fine."

"I'll let you help with the rent and my groceries, but I can't let you pay for my insulin."

"A lot of people here just started signing up for weekly lessons," he said. "It'll cover your insulin and then some. Everything's gonna be okay."

She was quiet.

"You're a very good son," she said.

ON ONE OF THEIR ENCOUNTERS, CATHERINE LED HIM NOT TO HER BED-room but the attached, unlit two-car garage, where a black Mercedes sedan was parked.

"Have you ever had sex in a car?" she asked.

Conor nodded. Several times, going back to when he'd lost his virginity in ninth grade to a junior in her Camry.

"Well, I haven't. So I want to do it in the back seat like a teenager." Catherine unlocked the car and gestured for him to take the driver's seat. She got in on the other side and handed him the key. "Turn it on."

"I don't have my license on me," he said after starting the car.

"We're not going anywhere. Keep it in park." Catherine cranked up the air-conditioning and hunted for a signal on the radio, but all she got was static or commercials. "Just use your phone. Put on . . . the Cars."

Conor was confused. "Put the phone . . . on the car?" he asked, holding his phone over the dashboard.

"The *Cars*," she repeated. "The band. Play 'Just What I Needed.'"

He found it on the internet. As the song kicked in, his beat-up phone, acquired in high school and never upgraded, began to crackle, the song coming out garbled.

"What's wrong with your phone?" Catherine asked sharply.

"The speaker's broken," he said, ashamed. Every time he'd considered buying a new one, he'd put it off—the phone still worked fine otherwise. "I'll plug it in." She nodded permission, and he connected it to the car's charger. In a moment the superior sound system of the Mercedes took over.

"I'm only a freshman," Catherine said, her voice an octave higher. "And I'm a virgin. Can we start off slow?"

She reached across him and reclined his seat. Then she unbuttoned his shorts and gave him a blow job. The whole scene—the role-play, the fellatio, the leather interior of the luxury car, and the brooding, decades-old song—conjured an adolescence he'd never had, the kind of cinematic youth he suspected the Cutters kids (and their parents) enjoyed, one of freewheeling decadence.

Catherine lifted her head. "It won't hurt, will it?" she asked in the same voice as she caressed him. "You won't hurt me, will you?"

He couldn't stop himself. She sensed his orgasm approaching and pulled her head away before it spurted up and behind him in a staccato rope. There was no telling in the dark where it landed, but it had to have gotten all over the back seat—even the roof.

"I can go again in a few minutes," he told her. "And I'll clean it up later."

"Don't—I like it there," she said. "And I never even drive now."

She was stuck there, imprisoned by the virus, which meant more money—and more sex—for as long as John would let Conor stay on the neck. He intended to get as much of both as he could while he had the opportunity.

WHENEVER HE LAY MOTIONLESS IN THE DARK WITH HIS HEAD ON HER breast and her fingers in his hair, the strangeness of the situation struck him anew. A much-older woman was paying him three hundred dollars for a perfunctory tennis lesson chased by anything-but-perfunctory sex and absolutely silent cuddling.

They knew hardly anything about each other. The only prologue to sex was his continued confirmation that he'd been following Covid-safe protocols. He'd tried to strike up postcoital conversation a couple of times, but she never responded. It was equal parts turn-on and alienating. But it would end after the summer, so he should just take the cash—and the fun—while he could. Then again, she lived in Manhattan; after they left Cutters, they could theoretically continue. He'd have a hard time passing it up if he still didn't have a job.

Even if he got a job.

Was this what he was supposed to have felt with Ally, with all the others? To be utterly consumed with another person, even if a normal relationship was so obviously out of the question? Or was its very abnormality the source of these emotions, because something about *him* was abnormal, and only through an arrangement like this—imbalanced in every way, financial at its core, devoid of any nonsexual closeness—could he feel some semblance of what normal people felt?

"When do you think you're going back to New York?" he finally asked the next time they were in bed together.

"I don't know."

"But after Labor Day, or do you think you'll wait until—"

"You know I don't like talking after sex," she said.

He shut up. She was paying him—very well—and the customer was always right. But this wasn't a patron sending an undercooked steak back to the kitchen. Despite the money changing hands, they were engaging in the most intimate of acts, and she was muzzling him in a voice of unchallengeable authority.

"Maybe *I'd* like to talk," he said.

There was a silence, one long enough for every fragment of self-doubt to explode outward like shrapnel from a grenade; he'd ruined everything. But then she exhaled, her warm breath tickling his neck. "And what do *you* want to talk about?"

He deliberated, then asked a banal question he'd wondered about. "Do you dye your hair?"

She laughed. "*That's* what you want to know? Obviously I do. Every woman who isn't gray does."

"How do you do it, if you never go off the neck?"

"I pay a hairstylist from town to come here and do it outside," she said. "But I shave my legs all by myself. Do you have more grooming questions?"

He paused before bringing up a more delicate subject. "Do you have kids?"

He could feel her body tighten almost imperceptibly. "No," she said.

He knew better than to ask why that was the case.

"Why did your marriage end?" he asked after a moment.

"Because we got along so well," said Catherine. "That's why all marriages end, isn't it? The people are just too much in love with each other, they can't bear it."

He let her sarcasm go without comment. There was more he wanted to know: how she spent her days as a rentier without any responsibilities, whether she'd ever had a career, and, perhaps most of all, whether what they were doing was new for her, too, or had she paid other men—other young men, other young men on Cutters—before him, and if not, was this as significant to her as it was to him. But she was clearly never going to let him get that close.

"What happened to your finger?" she asked.

He'd accidentally sliced his pointer finger earlier and, lacking any first aid supplies and not wanting to bother John, had fashioned a crude tourniquet out of toilet paper and tape, which she was only now noticing in the dark.

"Cut it with a knife," he said. "I didn't have any bandages."

Catherine shifted their bodies as her hand crawled down his abdomen and played with him until he was erect again.

The doorbell rang. Catherine's fingers froze and her breathing halted. "Shit," she said when it rang again.

"Who is it?" Conor asked.

"Stay here," she told him as she threw on her robe from the bathroom. "No, get in the closet and take your clothes with you."

She was leaving before he could state the obvious objection, that no neighbor ringing her bell at ten at night would ever wander up to her bedroom. She closed the door behind her, and he obligingly hid himself with his clothes in the closet. He couldn't hear anything downstairs. After five minutes, Catherine came back and opened the closet doors. His check was in her hand.

"Who was it?" he asked.

"Neighbor. Wait here a few minutes before you leave."

Catherine went to the bathroom and returned with a box of bandages and a tube of antibiotic ointment. She unpeeled the toilet paper, dabbed ointment onto the wound, and covered it with a bandage, pressing firmly to affix it.

"Keep it," she said, handing him the box and the tube along with her check. "And be more careful with yourself, okay?"

CHAPTER 8

The only problem with his nights with Catherine was that he was falling behind on his studies, unable to log all the hours he'd promised himself he would. He needed to buckle down.

A few afternoons later on the beach, as Conor bushwhacked through the thickets of secured transactions in one of his prep books, he heard someone walking in the sand behind him. It was the girl he'd somehow offended a few days earlier—Emily.

He waved, and she returned it. She dropped her towel fifteen feet away and stripped to her bikini—a little shyly this time, it seemed. When she returned from her swim to the yacht club, she wrapped herself in her towel and put her glasses back on. Conor found himself studying her face. Unlike the movie trope in which the bespectacled girl removes her eyewear and is transformed, Emily's glasses suited her perfectly, made her more striking, even if they were the trendy tortoise-shell ones worn by every other woman in New York.

She caught him watching her as she dressed.

"That's a long swim," he said.

"It's not that hard," she said. "If you go slowly."

She flopped down onto her towel and lit a cigarette. In the past seven years, having associated almost exclusively with athletes and law students, he hadn't encountered many people his age who smoked anything other than vapes.

"Do you find this disgusting?" she asked, reading his mind. "You don't have to answer that. I find it disgusting. And I don't smoke nearly as much as it looks like. You just keep seeing me during my late-afternoon break."

"What's the break from?"

"Writing a novel," she said. "Another good exercise in self-disgust."

"That's your job? You're a professional writer?"

"You mean . . . you *don't* know who I am?" She looked and sounded serious.

"I only know your first name," he said.

"Usually people just recognize me by sight," she said. "I'm not offended. This is actually great. It's so refreshing for me to meet someone who has no idea who I am."

"I can't tell if you're serious or not," he said.

She broke into laughter. "Sorry. That went on longer than I expected. I'm not a professional. I'm barely an amateur. I've only published two stories in the lit mag at Bard. And one of them was flash fiction, so it doesn't really count."

"Well," he said, "then I'm barely a lawyer. So we're in the same boat."

"The same Beetle Cat," she said.

"What's that?"

She pointed at a small sailboat off in the distance. "The kind of boat we have here. Don't worry, I don't even know how to fucking sail," she said. "I've had a real job, by the way. I graduated college last year, and I was the personal assistant to this woman on the Upper East Side until March."

"My mom was let go when Covid started, too," Conor said in commiseration.

"Mine wasn't because of Covid," she said. "It was incompetence. I should never be anyone's personal assistant. I screwed something up every day. Then two weeks before everything shut down, I booked her a flight and told her it was from JFK when it was actually LaGuardia. The next week she had another flight, and I was so determined not to mess it up again that I somehow did, only in reverse." After Conor laughed, she said, "When she fired me, she told me, 'I need someone who can anticipate what I'll want before *I* know.' As if that's a healthy way to live, thinking all the time about what someone who has power over you may want in the future. Good thing I don't want to spend my life as a secretary."

"My mom's been a secretary her whole life," he said.

"Oh, fuck me," Emily said. "I'm such an asshole."

"It's okay. I get it."

"No, it's gross," she said. "I wouldn't normally say something like that to someone I just met. It's being here. This place brings out the snob in me that I normally do a good job suppressing."

"Honestly, don't worry about it."

She looked at him with another solemn expression. "I want you to know that I'm listening to the communities who have been offended by my careless words, and I want to thank them for calling me out," she said. "While I can't promise I'll be perfect in the future, please know that I'm doing the work to educate myself so that I can do better next time."

She made this speech with such unblinking sobriety that, had she not tried to fool him once already, Conor might not have been sure she was joking.

As Emily laughed again, her phone alarm went off. "See you later," she said.

Conor said goodbye, and she started off.

He didn't have plans with Catherine for the night. It would just be him and his bar book until bedtime. He still had a lot of catching up to do, but he'd put in eight hours already since breakfast.

"Hey," he said. "You want to meet up here later tonight for a drink?"

She stopped before the path. "What's your name again?"

"Conor."

"You got a last name, so I can look you up and make sure you're not gonna murder me?"

"O'Toole."

"'Conor O'Toole.' Well, *that* sounds completely made-up. You're obviously a murderer." She waited a moment. "And you're not even denying it." She continued walking.

"Wait," he called after her. "What about tonight?"

She stopped and looked over her shoulder.

"I'll be here at eight," she said. "Or not. We'll see."

OPERATING UNDER THE ASSUMPTION THAT SHE WOULD SHOW UP, CONOR biked into the village later planning to buy some midpriced beer before opting for a six-pack from a microbrewery. On the way home his phone buzzed with a text. *Lesson at 10*, Catherine wrote. *Meet at your cabin.*

He'd nearly forgotten about her in his excitement over his date with Emily, and felt a pinprick of guilt over two-timing Catherine. But of course he wasn't: they weren't in a real relationship, and he was free to have a drink with other girls, especially age-appropriate ones.

She meant ten tonight, surely, not ten in the morning. Why would she want to do it at his place, for the first time—had the neighbor's visit the other day spooked her? Or was it just to mix things up, for the thrill of fucking him on John Price's property? And why no actual lesson? Had she decided that keeping up appearances was no longer necessary?

He could feasibly pull double duty, seeing Emily for a couple of beers at eight and getting home in time for Catherine. But if things were going well with the former, he didn't want to have to cut the night short. And knowing he was about to see Catherine right after, to dash back for paid sex, would probably put him on edge as they hung out. *Can you do it tomorrow?* he responded by the side of the road. *Have a lot of work.*

When he reached home, she wrote back, *10 or never again.*

Jesus—the *one* time he asked for a say in their timing, and she was apparently threatening to pull the plug altogether. Catherine now constituted the bulk of his income stream for him and his mother, which was otherwise down to his two weekly lessons with Dick and Suzanne and the unemployment checks. He'd have to reschedule with Emily instead—except he hadn't asked for her number and didn't know her last name or where she lived on the neck. She seemed mercurial, and showing up at the beach only to tell her he couldn't hang out could sink his prospects for another date.

He'd scramble to see them both and make it work that night.

CONOR ARRIVED AT THE BEACH EARLY, HOPING EMILY WOULD ALSO BE ahead of schedule and that he could shift the whole night up to give himself breathing room between rendezvous. But she came well after the appointed time, when the beach was already dark.

"Sorry I'm late," she called out behind him. "I was on a writing jag and I lost track of time."

Her voice gave him an unexpected little leap in his chest.

He told her it was no problem—if anything, he was impressed with her work ethic—and fished out a bottle of beer for her from his make-shift cooler, a shopping bag rattling with melting ice cubes. They sat side by side on the sand, looking out at the ocean.

"I know a girl from Bard who went to NYU last year for law school," she said after he told her where he'd graduated from.

He nodded.

"Sarah Parkhurst," she said. "Do you know her?"

"I actually went to New York Law School," he said. "Not NYU."

"Oh. Is that not as prestigious?"

"No," he admitted.

"Well"—she stood abruptly—"this was a colossal waste of my time." She promptly sat again. "Kidding, sorry, bad joke. I would never get into any law school."

"So what's your book about?" he asked to get off the subject. "What's the plot?"

"I'm not really into plots," she said. "When I see a book jacket that's, like, 'Emily can't believe her luck when she lands a job at a new company, but she soon discovers that not all is as it seems at her mys-terious workplace'—or if it's set on three continents or, like, present-day *and* World War Two, and you don't find out what the connection is until the last chapter—I just check out. Also, I couldn't come up with a real plot if I tried. It's part of my general ethos of ineptitude. If I were capable of any other job with a social purpose, I'd do it in a heartbeat."

"Then what do you like? In books?"

She thought about it. "Just small moments from real life without anything . . . happening."

Conor hadn't read a novel since sophomore year of college and was confused as to what this might entail. "So there's . . . no story at all?"

She described her novel as vignettes that mostly followed a girl with her exact background from childhood through high school.

"It's everything the world is demanding to read now," she said. "Plotless autofiction that's not about the trauma of racism or sexual abuse but the inherited trauma of family money. My blurbs are gonna say it's so urgent and necessary. I'll be an inspiration to all the poor little rich girls of the ruling class."

"What's going on with the ocean?" he asked, uncomfortable discussing both money and literature (if that line about blurbs was a joke, he didn't completely get it). The surface of the waves crashing on the shore was neon blue. "Is that the reflection of the moon?"

"It's the bioluminescence. Algae and other organisms light up when they get disturbed." She rolled up the legs of her jeans. "It doesn't happen often here—usually it's later in the summer. Let's look at it up close."

He followed her to the shoreline, anxious that she'd suggest they go for a dip, but they just stood at the edge of the tide. The water glowed almost magically as it pooled around their bare feet. It was mesmerizing, like nothing Conor had seen in his life; his best analogue was the gridded lights of New York City from an airplane window. But this wasn't an electrified city. It was unpolluted nature. It was a private, secluded beach. It was Cutters Neck.

How much else had he not seen, not experienced, landlocked all these years in Yonkers?

He glanced over at Emily. She was gazing at the shimmering water with an unguarded wonder that made her look younger. The moon and the light from the ocean cast a faint incandescence over her face. In profile she resembled a classical statue, or maybe a noblewoman sitting for an oil painting from centuries ago. Unlike Ally, she'd never stop anyone in their tracks at a frat party, but there was no question about it—Emily was beautiful. And she'd never go to a frat party in the first place. She'd be at home, working hard on her novel.

He took a step closer, and she turned to face him. But before he could lean in, she walked back up the beach to the shopping bag.

Conor followed her slowly. Neither of them commented on what had just failed to happen.

"My cousins are hanging out at the yacht club," she said. "I haven't seen them all yet and I should probably make an appearance. You want to stop by for a couple minutes?"

She'd deflected his kiss but wasn't ending the date. It was 9:17, just forty-three minutes until he had to be in his cabin. He really should go home now.

But he wanted to kiss Emily first.

SEVEN OF THE YOUNGER KIDS HE'D BEEN SEEING FROM A DISTANCE ALL summer—a few had probably been on the raft that time he'd nearly drowned—were drinking beer and passing a vape around a bonfire by the yacht club. Emily introduced them all, their names going in and out of his head except for that of a girl called—he was pretty sure he heard right—Beebee. One boy appeared to be gay; otherwise, it was hard to distinguish them amid the blur of light hair and skin and interchangeable bone structure.

Conor stayed quiet. They were all at various stages of college, with two heading off to school in the fall—surprisingly, nowhere particularly name-brand. He'd expected Ivy League preppies, but everyone was in T-shirts and shorts, flip-flops or sneakers or bare feet. He evidently needed to revise his stereotypes of young old money.

"Bobby, you hated your internship with Douglas Atherton, right?" asked Beebee. "I saw him on the road today, and he told me he'll hire me when I graduate if I don't have a job."

"Super, super boring," said the shaggy-haired boy who seemed gay. "But you can do whatever you want. I spent, like, eight hours a day on TikTok, and no one ever noticed."

The rest of them chimed in with anecdotes of how much fucking around they'd gotten away with at their respective internships and how much easier it was now when working remotely. Two girls spoke of an extended European trip they planned to take together upon graduation and traded notes on the best party cities. ("It's the four Bs," a boy advised them. "Berlin, Barcelona, Budapest, Belgrade, in that order.")

Conor should have expected this lack of ambition. They had massive safety nets of money and nepotism, a tribe to take care of them when they couldn't make it on their own. He'd been laser focused on becoming a lawyer ever since high school and, aside from Richard's help, had engineered it all on his own. It had required becoming so proficient at tennis that a college was willing to let him attend for free, nonstop studying to maintain a high GPA so he could get into a law school and win a few, very modest scholarships, summer and after-school jobs to cobble together living expenses, topped off by loans he'd be repaying for a decade or more—and even after all that, a full dozen years after he met Richard and began his preprofessional journey, he was still officially unemployed. These kids slacked off at their unpaid internships and literally bumped into job offers on the road.

He looked around at the untroubled faces in the firelight. All this because someone deep in their families' past—one of their shadow-casting forefathers—had been so remarkably successful that he could bankroll generation upon generation to come, each underperforming relative to the previous one, until they'd arrived at this set of passive-income loafers who partied away their summers on land seized so long ago that they never even considered it stolen.

And he was certain—though they surely would never admit it, even among themselves—that they believed, on a cellular level, that their privilege was proof of their innate superiority, while Conor's strenuous climb up the social ladder was in compensation for his inferior heritage.

These were Emily's family, the people she grew up with, the cushy world she took for granted. Intriguing and self-deprecating as she was, whether she'd admit to it or not, this was her heritage, too. As she'd said, Cutters brought out the snob in her.

"I should get going," he said to her, and stood.

"I'll leave with you," she said.

"WELL," EMILY SAID AS THEY CLIMBED THE DRIVEWAY OUT OF THE YACHT club, "sorry you had to sit through that. Not sure what I was thinking."

"They were fine," Conor said.

She gave him a look. "It's not even their fault. They don't know any better. They're completely undisturbed by being rich. Plus they all live in the whitest suburbs and come from these picture-perfect families, where everyone's so smiley all the time. And they're *genuinely* happy— it's not a facade. It's creepy. It's like inverted John Cheever."

He was greatly relieved by her reaction, and additionally identified with this last point (even if he didn't understand the Cheever reference). Ally always used to unintentionally alienate him by talking about her scores of relatives who cheerfully congregated for holidays and reunions.

They reached the road. "You want to be a proper gentleman and walk me home?" she asked, starting off down the neck.

Chaperoning her in the opposite direction from his cabin was a bad idea. Not only might he not get home in time, he might also run into Catherine on the way. But Emily's renouncement of her cousins had renewed his interest, and if she was too skittish to let him kiss her on the beach, she certainly wouldn't do it right here by the yacht club. Walking her home would be his only opportunity.

"Maybe they'll get better when they enter the real world," she went on as they strolled together. "But they might not even enter it. They're all pretty insulated."

"They do seem kind of . . . relaxed about their future," Conor observed. *Secure* was another word that came to mind.

"That's a direct function of their . . ."

"Of their what?"

Emily's footsteps picked up the pace. "So the other day, you said something about trusts? It was the name of a chapter or something in your book."

"Oh—trusts and future interests."

"Well, I knew you were just making a joke, but . . . I've got a trust fund. I just wanted to get that out there, in case you asked how I make a living."

Conor feigned nonchalance, though he'd never wittingly met someone with a trust. He was very curious how exactly it worked and, more important, how big it was. The rule of thumb was that retirees could safely withdraw 4 percent a year from their retirement accounts; an unemployed trust-fund kid probably lived within similar means. Someone recently out of college, with a car in Brooklyn, first on a low-paying job and then without that for several months (would someone in her position even apply for unemployment?), and expecting even a fraction of the lifestyle that people here were accustomed to, had to be taking out, at minimum, a hundred thousand a year to cover expenses and taxes. That was 4 percent of $2.5 million.

"I give away twenty percent of what I get each year to charity," she continued. "At least. It'll be way more this year, 'cause I just donated to a bunch of Black Lives Matter bail funds. And my political contributions will be a lot higher."

More than a hundred grand, then.

The wind shivered the trees and accentuated their silence.

"Should I keep prattling on about my unearned pile of cash that keeps growing on its own as you say nothing?" she asked. "It's obviously a comfortable topic for both of us."

That broke the tension, and she asked him instead about his tennis background. He tried to impress her by highlighting the aesthetics of the sport and the tactics and brainpower behind his game.

The unabridged edition was that, in his playing days, Conor's best weapon was essentially invisible. His college coach claimed that at their level, about one-tenth of points were lost due to inattention, tight nerves, or lack of will. For Conor, this metric was close to zero; his concentration seldom strayed on mundane rallies, at critical junctures he maintained a preternatural cool that bordered on the robotic, and he never surrendered a single point, even when he was getting creamed.

"Mental toughness," sports people liked to call this resilient, unflappable sangfroid. On the tennis court, once your confidence faltered, once you started thinking you couldn't get your serve in or hit a backhand to save your life, or you figured you were going to lose anyway so why bother chasing down that drop shot, it was all but over.

(The only time when self-doubt did plague Conor in a matchup of sorts, it occurred to him as he explained some of this to Emily, was in his one-on-ones with Catherine.)

As a result, he often beat more naturally gifted players he had no right keeping up with. "The human backboard," he was nicknamed by his high school teammates (or, by opponents, slurred as a "pusher," the lowest form of tennis life). He never pummeled opponents into submission, as nearly all dominant players did; he simply waited for them to make an unforced error. Eventually they almost all became frustrated by his stubborn, endlessly patient consistency and started slamming chancy shots or prematurely rushing the net.

In this expensive, gentlemanly sport, Conor had developed a vision of himself as a scrappy grinder who had blazed an unheralded path to success. The rich boys he'd squared off against in college, like the suburbanites he'd played in high school from Bronxville and Scarsdale, were soft and entitled, and if victory didn't come easily, if they saw they couldn't close out points within four shots, if they thought they were getting screwed by the umpire, or balls skimming the net kept unluckily dropping on their side, or they were simply worn out from three arduous sets against a guy who hustled to return every goddamn shot and they just wanted to go back to the frat house and pound beers, they either waved a subconscious white flag or very consciously tanked the match (while hurling their $250 racquets in disgust at losing to a fucking pusher from *Yonkers*).

By contrast, no matter how much Conor was down, he believed a comeback was still possible. Like baseball, tennis was a sport without a clock. Winning might require perfection and exceptional luck from then on out, but you had all the time in the world; even against the steepest of odds, there was always a chance.

Though Conor's stoic expression as he shook hands after a match was the same regardless of the outcome or opponent, he most enjoyed beating the boys who had conspicuously come from money.

"So you don't take any chances and just safely hit the ball back every time," Emily said, astutely summing up his special talent. "In other words, you're the most boring player in history to watch."

"Yes," he said. "I'm the tennis equivalent of having no plot."

"It must be nice knowing you're actually *good* at something," she reflected.

"We all have our thing," Conor said. "Yours is writing."

"I don't know." The mischief in her voice was suddenly gone. "I haven't shown this novel to anyone. It might be bad. *I* might be bad. Or even just . . . average. Which would be really depressing, if I turned out to be *just okay* at the only thing I've ever wanted to do with my life."

Brash confidence would have been sexy, but her vulnerability did something to him he couldn't quite articulate, other than that he felt a strong urge to protect her.

"Oh, shit!" She snapped her fingers. "Now I know what it reminds me of. You play *exactly* like David Foster Wallace."

Conor was surprised she knew of a player he didn't. "He's on the tour now?"

"*Definitely* not on a book tour."

"Book tour? No, the ATP."

"You mean A*WP*?"

"What's AWP? Aren't we talking about a pro tennis player?"

She giggled. "No, a pro writer. And he's dead. But he has an essay about playing tennis as a teenager. I'll send you a link."

When he texted her to exchange numbers, it was 9:42. Emily was still dawdling. "Your place is nearby?" he asked, trying to speed her up.

"Up here on the left."

He'd been immersed enough in the conversation that he hadn't noticed where they were on the dark road: coming up on two houses on opposite sides, a hundred feet beyond which was the driveway to Catherine's. If she left on time and was using the road, she'd cross paths with them in the next few minutes.

He sped up a little and stopped at the driveway to the house on the left side of the road, but Emily continued past him. Was there another house he hadn't noticed between this and Catherine's, a hidden driveway he'd thought was a path into the woods?

A horrible premonition seeped through his body.

"You don't live in that big house, do you?" he asked as he followed her.

"*No*," she said, as though the idea were preposterous, and he relaxed again, but only until her next sentence: "There's a guesthouse I stay in."

Conor stopped walking.

"What's wrong?" she asked.

"Do you . . . rent it, or something?"

"Rent? No."

"So you own it?"

"Me, personally? Of course not," she said. "Why?"

There went his kissing her. There went his seeing her again.

"I just remembered I forgot to call my mom back," he said. "She's going to sleep soon. I should head home."

Emily took a moment to adjust to his change of mood. "Of course," she said. "Gotta call Mom before bedtime."

Conor couldn't afford more banter. He said a quick goodnight, turned, and, when she was out of sight, sprinted home.

. . .

WHAT A MESS HE'D GOTTEN HIMSELF INTO.

If only he'd asked Emily her last name at any point, this all could have been avoided. But Catherine didn't have children, and they didn't resemble each other all that much. Maybe she was Emily's aunt. Or an older cousin. That degree of relation wasn't so terrible, at least for the short term, especially since Catherine had married into Cutters.

But even if they were third cousins-in-law once removed, what a fucking mess.

He made it back to his cabin with a few minutes to spare, which he used for a quick indoor shower to rinse off his newly acquired perspiration. When he came out of the bathroom with a towel around his waist, Catherine was sitting on his bed. The bedside lamp provided the only light.

"How'd you get here?" he asked, worried she'd run into Emily on the road.

"The path along the shore," she said. "No one saw me. Take off your towel."

This woman didn't miss a beat. He dropped the towel. Catherine put an index finger on her lips, mulling her next order.

"My kitchen sink is broken," she said. "Can you fix it?"

"I don't know anything about sinks," he said. "Can't you call a plumber? Or are you worried about Covid?"

"Jesus, Conor. I'm *role-playing*."

"Oh. So you want me to . . . pretend to be a plumber or something?"

She rolled her eyes. "My God, do I have to spell it out for you? Yes, go over to the sink and fix it."

He walked over to his kitchenette sink in the nude.

"Get on all fours," she said, "and look inside the cabinet."

He did it, feeling defenseless from behind.

"What seems to be the problem?" she asked.

"It's . . . broken." He didn't like doing this. It felt contrived and odd, more so than their high school reenactment in the Mercedes. He wouldn't be a good con man, after all.

"Are the pipes clogged?" she asked, helping him along. The floorboards creaked in back of him.

"Yes. It'll be expensive to fix."

"Oh, dear," Catherine said right behind him. "My husband will be so upset. I don't suppose we can work something out?"

"Maybe," Conor said, and as soon as the words were out, Catherine's hand was between his legs.

"Good," she said. "Because we can't have any pipes clogged around here."

It felt good to be back in her hands, and he temporarily forgot about the stressors of the past fifteen minutes.

"So you can unclog it?"

"I'll try my best," he said.

Her loosely caressing hand squeezed tight.

"You won't *try*—you'll *do* it." In an instant she switched from damsel in distress to haughty employer. "It's absolutely unacceptable if you don't."

Though spoken in character, the words *absolutely unacceptable*, along with her fingers' constriction, had a tangible effect on Conor. It was as though the full force of her authority, of her social position—of, ultimately, her oceans of money compared with his dirty puddles—were knocking him backward, like a cop's baton jabbing a protester in the ribs. Were this a real exchange, were he actually a plumber coming to service a rich woman with a clogged sink, he would have meekly offered to fix it at a discount. It was as demeaning as it was titillating.

"Why'd you want to do this here tonight?" he asked later, as they were having their strange, mute cuddle. It had to be because of the interruption the other night, which he now suspected to have been Emily, but he didn't know if she'd tell the truth about who had rung her bell.

"I have someone staying in the guesthouse for the foreseeable future," she admitted. "We won't be interrupted here."

"Who?"

After a pause she said, "My daughter."

Not third cousins, not even aunt and niece, but mother and daughter. *Mother* and *daughter*. Good thing Emily hadn't let him kiss her.

"You told me you didn't have kids."

"I don't. I have one child."

"That's not how people usually answer that question."

"Well," she said, "it's how I answer it."

If there had been any doubt over how he might proceed, this snuffed it out. He hadn't done anything wrong, hadn't known who Emily was when he'd asked her out. He'd nip it in the bud with her tomorrow.

"So you want to meet here from now on?" he asked.

"Yes," Catherine said. "I won't take tennis lessons anymore, so when I text you about having a lesson, it means I'll meet you here at the time that I say. You'll respond only about that. Don't initiate any texts or calls to me."

Though Emily had been on the neck for a couple of weeks—hence, in hindsight, the requirement that he enter the main house from the shoreline path, out of sight from the guesthouse—her ringing the bell that time had clearly made Catherine decide her place was unsafe for them, and he presumed these regulations were in case her daughter ever saw her phone. She wanted to keep this from her, as would be expected. Not that it would matter for him, anyway; if Emily learned about them, it would be Catherine's problem.

Catherine dressed without further discussion, took a check out of her pocket, placed it on his bedside table, and departed by way of the rocky shoreline.

CHAPTER 9

The next morning, Conor started a text to Emily similar to the one he'd sent to Georgia. But that message had backfired, and, besides, it would be even more excessive for a single date that had ended without a kiss. Emily lived all the way at the end of the neck. He'd just stay off the beach in the late afternoons, and if he ever ran into her on the road, he'd explain then that he was focusing on his studies.

He went all day without a text from her, either, so this could be easier than he thought. When he returned from a late-afternoon grocery shop, however, a paperback was lying outside his cabin door, with a handwritten note tucked inside:

I remembered there was another essay on tennis in this, so I went to the bookstore in town (curbside pickup!) and flagged the two tennis essays.

—E

P.S. Please don't start wearing a bandana (sp?).

Conor didn't really read books outside of those assigned in school; his little extracurricular reading was usually just the news. Touched as he was by Emily's thoughtfulness, he now felt obligated, even if he wasn't going to see her again, to take a look at her present. He had reams of legal data to memorize and didn't have time for this. But he opened it to the first dog-eared essay anyway.

It was the one she'd talked about, how the author had learned, in his teenage heyday on the junior circuit, to exploit his knowledge of geometry, volatile midwestern winds, and the decaying, sloped tennis courts of Illinois. Conor nearly shivered with identification at Wallace's description of how, to make up for a shortfall of God-given physical ability, he had become the consummate pusher.

The other tennis essay was a profile of a young player, ranked deep in the double digits, whose monomaniacal pursuit of athletic excellence had, in the writer's view, stunted him in other areas; he seemed to have no additional interests, few friends outside the game, no romances. A small, cloistered life, despite traveling the world as a minor sports star. In the light of this essay, it seemed tragic: to devote your existence to a game at which you were better than all but eighty or ninety people on the planet but still be deemed somewhat marginal.

Was Conor also stunted? Not from tennis—he hadn't invested nearly the number of hours as anyone on the pro tour—but from his dogged efforts at carving out a better life for himself? Like the player in the essay, he didn't have any passions or hobbies. He'd been accepted by his teammates but had never truly felt like one of them, and now they'd drifted apart. Same with his law school classmates. And just the one real romance, with Ally, which felt less meaningful the more it receded in the rearview mirror. There was a whole world out there he hadn't seen beyond the tennis court and the court of law. Literally—he'd never been out of the country except for a few college road trips to Montreal and Toronto.

Most of the girls he'd been with had been athletes, sorority girls, the kind who showed up in big, boisterous groups at bars and college parties. Artistic girls had never shown much interest in him, and he, in turn, had always been intimidated by them, their indifference to what he had to offer—even his looks. But Emily seemed to enjoy his company.

He reread her note. He liked that *E* she'd signed with. He couldn't recall Ally's ever sending him a note or a present outside of birthdays and Christmas. And no one had bought him a book since he was a child.

Want to get together tonight? he texted Emily.

I was going to make curry if you want to come over, she wrote back.

Forgetting for a moment where she lived, he almost replied yes right away—it had been a while since he'd eaten anything but pasta or canned food for dinner—but caught himself in time.

I have to study through dinner. Why don't you come here after? he asked.

There was the telltale mark of indecisiveness from the appearing and vanishing bubbles before she texted a thumbs-up.

Let's say 9, he told her, not wanting her to be seen around his cabin while it was light out, either.

WHEN EMILY KNOCKED ON HIS DOOR THAT NIGHT, SHE ASKED IF THEY could hang out outside at first. He suggested the big rock by the water beyond the main house; John was away for a few days, so he didn't have to worry about being spotted.

As they started in on a couple of beers, Conor thanked her for the book and told her how much he'd liked the tennis essays. They chatted about them for a few minutes, though he didn't detail the ways he'd felt like the player in the profile.

"So," she said when the discussion petered out, "you should know ahead of time that I'm not really a booty call kind of girl."

"What makes you think that's what this is?" he asked.

"I invited you over to dinner, and you asked me to come to your place late at night."

"I told you, I have to study through dinner."

"Uh-huh. The old 'I'm busy till really late at night' move."

"You've seen me on the beach—I'm studying every waking moment."

"Have you seen yourself in the mirror lately?" she asked.

"I don't get it," he said.

"Well, if you haven't noticed this about yourself"—she let out a puff of laughter—"you're a very conventionally handsome guy, and you very much give off the impression that when you tell a girl to come over, she drops everything and does it. And don't be so pleased with yourself. You look like someone on a dating show who, I don't know, sells condos in Florida and likes jet-skiing and uses the word *badass*. Or like a guy who's running for office mostly because he looks the part. I'd be embarrassed to be seen with you. People would think I . . . paid you, or something."

"Thank you," Conor replied coolly, stifling the discomposure from her last remark. "That's very kind of you to say."

"I just mean, don't think I'm slobbering over you. I actually see it as a detriment. Usually guys who look like you never had to develop a sense of humor and have no interior life, because they're used to getting whatever they want without even trying."

The only area of his life this applied to was with girls. Everything else worthwhile he'd always had to scrape for.

"And you think I'm the kind of person who gets whatever he wants without trying?"

"Yes. You're clearly a . . . a *winner*." She spat out the word as if it were an insult. "Which is not at all my type."

"What is your type?"

Emily bit her lip in concentration. "Losers. Funny, charmingly self-loathing losers." She looked at him. "Any thoughts?"

He took a long drink to buy time for a response.

"None," he said. "Because I have no sense of humor or interior life. And I hate myself for it."

"All right," she said. "That's not bad."

"The reason I asked you to come here is because John Price made me promise not to get involved with anyone on Cutters over the summer."

"C'mon, you're kidding. Why would he care?"

Conor had prepared for this. "He said he was concerned about a #MeToo-type situation with one of the younger cousins here and that he'd be held responsible as my employer and landlord."

Emily laughed. "That's the stupidest thing I've ever heard. I'm twenty-three years old, not a teenager. I can tell him I won't hold him 'responsible' for anything."

He doubled down on his lie, which was the only plausible-sounding excuse he could come up with that would also ensure she couldn't investigate its veracity. "I think it was even mentioned in the contract I signed. Please don't say anything to him."

"So you invited me here to tell me you can't see me because *John Price* has *contractually* forbidden it?"

"No—to tell you I *do* want to see you. But that it has to be, you know . . . in secret."

"Oh, in *secret*," she said. "Of course, of course. So stupid of me to think *you'd* tolerate being seen with *me*."

"I know how it sounds. But, look—I really need this job. My mom's on unemployment now. I don't know how she'll pay the rent if I lose this."

This convinced Emily—or, more powerfully, she seemed humbled by the invocation of a money problem that wasn't about the trauma of inheriting too much of it.

"But . . . why would you want me to come to *your* place if you're worried about John finding out? Wouldn't my place be safer?"

"Don't you live with your parents?"

"Just my mom. They're divorced. Didn't I tell you that? And anyway, you saw I have my own separate house there."

"Still, if your mom saw us together, maybe she'd tell John, or she'd tell someone who'd tell him."

"She can't see my front door or into my house, and she absolutely never goes inside—she's terrified of Covid and thinks it's lurking in every room she walks into," Emily said. "Besides, I can just tell her not to say anything. She doesn't give a shit what I do."

"Don't do that—she might let it slip." If Catherine really did avoid Emily's place, though, perhaps it was a safer meeting spot than his cabin, where she could potentially make an unbidden appearance. "But I guess I could see you there sometimes. If it's late enough."

"You really know how to make a girl feel special," she said. "'As long as it's pitch black, I suppose I could deign to—'"

Conor kissed her. She kissed him back. Her mouth tasted of tooth-paste, no hint of cigarettes; she'd been ready for this.

The ocean rumbled, nearly as dark as the sky salted with stars. A cool wind blew in, followed by plunking raindrops, then the roll of distant thunder. Despite himself, he got the feeling something conse-quential was happening, a tectonic shift. There was a spasm in his chest—not just arousal, not just anticipation, but a warmth that buzzed through him and wanted to leap out of the confines of his body. He'd had countless first kisses; this was different. This, finally, was what he was supposed to feel. This was what people talked about.

This was life—life far beyond the stifling perimeter of the tennis court. Of all the girls, there had never been anyone like Emily; no one as smart, as funny, as artsy.

No one as rich.

Aside from her mother.

"I'm gonna tell John Price on you," she said. "John! Oh, John! Look what Conor's doing! He's breaking the law! Your employee's a sex offender! You've got a hardened criminal in your—"

"Shh—shut up," he said, half-jokingly, as he covered her mouth, even though John was out of town.

THEY FLED INTO HIS CABIN TO DUCK THE GATHERING STORM. SHE LOOKED around the bare-bones interior. There wasn't anywhere to sit besides the desk chair and the bed.

"I'm not sleeping with you tonight," she said. "Just FYI."

"Okay," he said.

"I mean it. You're not getting everything you want."

"What makes you think I even want that?" he asked.

He'd said it as a joke, but as they fooled around on his bed for a while, he wondered if it was good that she'd issued this early restric-tion. It felt natural to be with someone his age again. And someone who wasn't paying him for the pleasure.

"Your bed smells like vanilla," she said.

"I sprayed an air freshener before," he told her.

Emily's own mother had been on top of these very sheets twenty-four hours earlier. His college teammates would think *this* was the coolest thing ever, to get a hot mom and her daughter into his bed on successive nights. But what he was doing was sick, certainly unfair to Emily, even to Catherine, and if it had begun as a forgivable error, now he was willfully digging himself a deeper hole.

"Promise me you won't look at me when we wake up in the morning and say, 'Hey, you,'" she said at one point after Conor kissed her.

"You don't have to deflect everything with a joke, you know," he told her.

"Look, Conor," she said after a moment. "You seem like a nice guy, and despite being grossly good-looking, you're somehow not a humorless idiot. But you don't want to be with someone like me. You're a normal and successful member of society, and I'm kind of fucked-up inside."

Conor had been shot down by girls before, mostly ones with boyfriends, but he'd never been spurned quite like this.

"I'll be the judge of what I want," he said. "And you don't seem fucked-up to me."

CONOR WOKE IN THE MIDDLE OF THE NIGHT FROM A VIOLENT THUNDER-clap. Still half-clothed, Emily was sitting up in bed, resting on her bent knees in the wan moonlight coming through the window as rain pattered outside.

"Hey, you," he said. She didn't react. "Just kidding," he added. When she still didn't acknowledge him, he asked if something was wrong.

"I spent three months in a psychiatric hospital my senior year at Bard," she said.

He couldn't tell if this, too, was one of her jokes testing out his gullibility.

"Did you . . . why'd you go?" he asked when it became clear she was serious.

In an even-keeled voice, without dwelling on the details, she told him that she'd been diagnosed with "an inability to function," or what was more commonly known as a nervous breakdown. She was involuntarily committed to a "luxury depression-treatment center" in Connecticut (she couldn't hide her plain scorn for the term), where experimentation with different cocktails of drugs, plus half a dozen electroconvulsive therapy sessions, eventually restored her desire to get out of bed.

She'd graduated from college a semester late because of the time she'd missed, had worked for the woman on the Upper East Side for just two months before she was fired, and after a few weeks of lockdown, with no structure, she'd started feeling depressed again. Not knowing what else to do, she'd checked herself back into the treatment center. She didn't tell her mother about this stint, just paid for her treatment herself out of her trust. When she returned to Brooklyn in June, she was afraid she'd relapse without any structure or seeing anyone regularly; after her first time in the center, everyone at school had treated her differently, and she'd kept just one close friend, who now lived in Boston. She'd decided to come up to Cutters, where, at least, she'd be around people she'd known her whole life.

"So," she said, "do I still not seem fucked-up to you?"

She did, now, in ways with which he was unfamiliar. But whereas Georgia's middle-of-the-night confession had turned him off, Emily's drew him in. Even the electroshock treatment carried a certain mystique.

"Even if you are," he said, "something about you makes me want to take care of you."

He kissed her, running his tongue over the ridges of her perfect teeth as the rain thrummed and the western wind carried the cleansing scent of the ocean into his cabin.

He registered that he felt something momentous again, something he hadn't felt in all his time together with Ally, something normal people probably experienced all the time: that, despite the greater safety of keeping it shut tight, one of you had opened your door a crack, and you and the other person were sharing something no one else in the world was sharing right now.

"You're not an asshole who plays mind games, right?" Emily asked. "You don't just say what you think girls want to hear?"

"No," he said.

She looked out the window into the wet, black night. Then she turned back.

"Because that was pretty good, what you said," she told him.

CHAPTER 10

After she left while he was sleeping, he didn't hear from Emily all the next day. Maybe she was waiting for him to reach out to her first, after she'd opened up to him. He would have normally done so, but Catherine was coming over that night, and he now felt even more conflicted about what he was doing.

The honorable thing was to end his arrangement with Catherine. If it happened now, before he progressed further with Emily and before any harm was done, he could still feel all right about everything. She couldn't be that upset by it; he was well within his rights to quit what was essentially a job, and she'd expressed no interest in him beyond his body. No one would be hurt.

When Catherine arrived, though, opening up a bathrobe to reveal lacy black lingerie with a garter belt, he caved. No harm in one final romp. They lunged at each other with more than their usual ferocity, as if Catherine, too, knew this was their last hurrah, with fingers slipping into various openings, until she procured, from a pocket in her robe, a bottle of personal lubricant. "I don't think you need it," Conor said.

"Not there," Catherine said. "Here." She got on her knees, reached behind herself, and applied a generous dollop. "Have you done this before?"

He nodded. Ally had emphatically refused, though he'd done it a handful of times with other girls. It was overrated, in his opinion, but if she wanted to try it, especially on their parting visit, he wasn't going to say no.

"I haven't," she told him. "Go slowly."

With plenty of lubrication, he coaxed himself inside, thrusting carefully, wondering why she hadn't pursued this in the past if it was something she was interested in, then refocusing on the task at hand when that line of thinking brought him to Emily's father and then Emily. Each of her moans began building on the last until, eventually, Catherine surrendered to an orgasm so convulsive that Conor, amid his own explosive unbottling, was unsure how much was pleasure and how much pain.

She'd been right that time she whispered into his ear, saying he'd wanted to do this. He'd never had a sexual escapade more intoxicating than to be the first man to plant his flag in the landscape of Catherine Havemeyer, beautiful insurance and shipping heiress worth tens of millions of dollars.

Conor had never cheated on Ally and had no experience with this particular set of emotions. He felt like confessing to Emily; he felt like confessing to Catherine; he knew that he'd do neither. This was his punishment, the anchor of guilt he'd have to tow around, even if he were never exposed.

The other thing he knew instantly was that he couldn't give this up; it was too good. It was the sort of sex that people assumed someone who looked like him was having all the time—the sort of *life* they assumed he was leading. But he'd waited twenty-five years for this without even knowing it was out there, at the very end of Cutters Neck Road.

He'd put a stop to things with Emily, then, if her daylong silence wasn't an indication that it was already over. Whatever he'd felt for her the previous night must have been the romantic atmosphere, the rainfall, the dramatic story of her breakdown. It wasn't real. It couldn't have been—not like this.

When Catherine left, Conor disabled airplane mode on his phone, which he'd activated beforehand, to send Emily his deferred breakup text. But there were already three messages waiting from her. The first read, simply, *"Hey, you,"* in scare quotes. The second apologized for interrupting him if he was working. The last was a GIF of Glenn Close from *Fatal Attraction* with the captioned threat, *I'm not gonna be ignored, Dan.*

He'd been lying to himself. What he felt for Emily was genuine.

When you finally find the girl you want to marry, don't blow it—they don't come around often, Richard had advised him. Another Emily might not come around in his life.

But neither would another Catherine.

The hazy outlines of what he was considering were impossibly foolhardy, not to mention impossible to pull off. It was bound to combust spectacularly. And he wasn't the kind of guy who could do it, as a matter of conscience, to either woman.

Except he'd already been doing it the last couple of nights.

If they ever did find out, they could handle it, even Emily. They had more money than anyone could ever want—that cushioned nearly all of life's blows. And, he was now starting to think, there was a way to arrange it so that they wouldn't find out.

He could really do this.

I was studying, just saw these, he wrote. *Want to get together tomorrow?*

He deposited Catherine's check on his phone and, once he received the email notifying him of its receipt, ripped it into pieces and buried them in the trash under paper towels and coffee grounds, where Emily, who confirmed that tomorrow worked for her, would never see them.

III

CHAPTER 11

July's blinding glare slanted into the coppery haze of August. The days slumbered from the heat that had accumulated from all the summer's blazing afternoons like layers of dust in an untended house; the ocean warmed to a bath-like temperature; the crickets trilled in a shimmery chorus each lengthening night. It was a glorious spit of land, worthy of each extravagant dollar in the tax assessment, and it would have easily been the best summer of Conor's life were he simply giving the occasional tennis lesson, preparing for the bar, and either enjoying his burgeoning relationship with Emily or having enormously pleasurable and remunerative sex every few nights with Catherine.

Instead, over the next several weeks, he had to negotiate between the two women with vigilance and skulduggery. He soon found that his cautious temperament transferred well from tennis to infidelity. His trysts with Catherine were only at his place; when he went to Emily's, he arrived on foot after dark (the entrance was, as she said, not visible from the big house). As an antivirus measure, but also a convenient pretext for them not to talk, Emily and her mother communicated mostly by text, infrequently by phone, seldom in person outdoors, and never indoors together. This made sleeping at Emily's cottage safe, as he didn't have to worry about Catherine's barging in (though, if she ever did, he was prepared to run into a closet). Emily, in turn, was very respectful of his need to study—and to hide their relationship from John Price—and never visited his cabin unannounced. Even though she didn't come over much, he was nonetheless careful to spray down his cabin and bed with Febreze to mask her mother's perfume each time (he also purchased a vanilla-scented air freshener spray as a decoy). Whenever Catherine demanded a "lesson" on a night he had plans to see Emily—which became, in time, every night—he canceled with the latter, begging off with deficits of work and sleep. He changed their names in his phone, which he set to airplane mode before seeing both, and deleted texts from them immediately on receipt.

Because he was so conscientious and clandestine, because he never took any undue chances or committed a single unforced error, and because there was a pandemic that disrupted normal social patterns, it worked flawlessly.

HE BARELY THOUGHT ABOUT COVID ANYMORE ASIDE FROM WHEN HE talked to his mother. He supposed this was what normal life was like for people this rich: so removed from the ravages of the world that to be concerned by them would be like fretting over natural disasters on Mars.

It was pure bliss on the neck, surrounded by endless ocean in endless summer. Kids biked and scootered unsupervised without helmets, perfectly groomed dogs roamed off leash. Before the dinner hour, residents sat on their porches with wine and cheese brought out by their personal (masked) cooks. A community vegetable garden yielded cherry tomatoes that burst in your mouth as sweet as candy. Saturday mornings there was a boat race, the winner of which was announced in the neckwide email disclosing the new gate code that Conor now received with a sense of pride (and relief, as he imagined Charlie rolling up in his Buick to commit more crimes and being denied entrance). There were magical spots everywhere he turned: untouched fields where deer romped in rainbow arcs; winding paths through the woods, one of which led to a tiny cabin built right into a hillside; a salt marsh on the beach filled with crabs; and a glade of purple clover near John's house he tried to visit each evening, where the sunset bronzed the stone wall that set it off from the road and shot pole vaults of light through the clustered trees.

Being on Cutters brought to mind something a professor had said during his freshman-year sociology lecture that he remembered every time he went to the airport. The airline industry was a microcosm of American society, with each stratum marked by a corresponding level of visibility: there were the working-class masses, many of whom the passengers never saw, who slung food in the air and on the ground, serviced the planes, and so on; the sizable middle class, who sat very noticeably in coach and played a pacifying role by giving the workers the meager dream of airborne travel to aspire to; the more exclusive sliver of the upper class—subdivided between the amenities of business and the opulence of first—who were hidden mostly out of sight behind a curtain as they dined on their restaurant-quality meals; and finally the minuscule population of the .01 percent flying private out of their own airports and thus, for very different reasons, more unseen by the rest of the ecosystem than the most subterranean of baggage handlers. Air travel, the professor told them, catered to the upper class and even more so this last microclass, because that was where maximal profits lay. The rest of us were losers whose taxes subsidized the flights of the ultrarich, either laboring away to prop up the industry or reduced to begging for an entire can of soda and a second package of cookies from our cramped seats, literally unable to see how much better the people on top of the pyramid had it.

Each time Conor biked around the gate with his cargo of groceries and was greeted by a current of uncontaminated ocean air and rabbits darting across the road, he still couldn't quite believe he lived there, even temporarily: the real estate equivalent of a private jet, the kind of place that would never be glimpsed by most Americans—by, that is, the losers.

Although, of course, he had a claim only to a guesthouse and was therefore a quasiloser himself. Everyone else was to the manner—and manor—born. Someone in their deep past, as Charlie had probably accurately speculated, had committed a crime to enable their descendants to live like this; not a violent crime, likely not anything technically illegal, but cannily gaming the system so they would profit at others' expense. When you got down to it, the crime of capitalism. And their offspring now feasted in perpetuity off the capital gains.

He wondered what he'd be doing now if he'd remained with Ally. She'd landed in Manhattan after graduation, working in marketing for an ecoconscious fashion something-or-other, and had likely fled the plague for her parents' place in Albany, where he would have had to accompany her. He'd always liked his visits to their four-bedroom house, with pictures of Ally and her brother and sister lining the wall by the stairs, a small, fenced backyard where her dad would grill in the summer, a finished basement with a foosball table. They were the sort of family that went to the movies on Christmas. Very American, as Catherine would put it. Or, more bitingly, middle class.

He'd never had a problem with it in college—if anything, he'd thought it was something to aim for, even the overly cheerful extended family. But he couldn't go back to that kind of life. Not after this.

And the only permanent way into an un-American—or, in another sense, quintessentially American—place like Cutters Neck, besides being born into it, was through marriage.

IF CONOR HAD WORRIED THAT MARRYING ALLY WOULD BE RESIGNING himself to a lifetime of tepid feelings, he had no such concerns with Emily. She was funnier, worldlier, smarter than he was. Respectably unimpressed by male beauty. She would challenge him, educate him, entertain him. She did a routine that made him laugh hard every time: wearing socks on the linoleum floor of his kitchen, she'd simulate her mental state of paralyzing uncertainty off her psychiatric medications by running in one direction, sliding, then cartoonishly reversing course and sliding again.

Emily's political conscience didn't manifest itself through grandiloquent, self-serving speeches or hectoring social media posts, like his more outspoken law school classmates. When reading the news, she'd become incensed by the cruelty, stupidity, and injustice of the world, though she had little patience for liberal bromides. "These people are fucking idiots," she said one night, looking up from an article about corporate diversity training in the wake of George Floyd. "Teaching their employees not to be racist, or sexist, or whatever, it's all a bullshit Band-Aid. They know the real problem is money, and the only way to solve it is changing who gets the money. But they don't want to give up any of their own money, so nothing will really change." Even if Conor didn't share the fervor of her convictions—he didn't have the luxuries of time and resources to concern himself as she did with the suffering of others—he admired her for it and for how she walked the walk with her frequently opened pocketbook.

She told him more about her family. Her father, the "great-great-whatever-grandson" of the second governor of the Plymouth Colony, had remarried a hostess from an Upper East Side cigar lounge, producing two young half brothers Emily barely knew. After her first stay at the treatment center, Emily had decided he was a "toxic presence" in her life ("I know how overused that word is, but it applies in this case") and stopped talking to him.

Conor was careful not to display too vested an interest in Catherine, though at times he couldn't resist asking questions; Emily was his only outside perspective. She had had some boyfriends when Emily was younger but nothing that ever took, partly because "she was always paranoid guys were trying to marry her for her money." She'd trained to be a painter when she was young but had given it up when Emily was three or four. Hiding his surprise over Catherine's artistic past, Conor asked why she'd stopped.

"She says she lost interest, but I think the real reason was that she wasn't successful, even with all the opportunities and connections in the world, so there was nothing to blame except her talent, or lack of it," Emily said. "So she just gave up. Not sure if you've noticed, but people around here think having a lot of ambition and trying to get ahead is déclassé."

In lieu of working, Emily told him, her mother spent her days on the Upper East Side going to fancy lunches and black-tie charity dinners, "where the disgustingly rich delude themselves into thinking they're altruistic. When I told her I'm gonna give away the majority of our money once I control it, she made her accountant— Sorry, is this really gross? I've never talked about this stuff with anyone."

"It's not," he said. He was intrigued by all this casual tossing around of presumably life-changing amounts of money.

"She was horrified by the idea that I'd 'squander' the Havemeyer fortune, even after she's dead. She can't legally cut me out of the trust, because her parents set it up for me, but she made the accountant put all these restrictions on it. There's a set amount on how much I get each month that goes up a little each year. Most trusts, the kid gets full control at eighteen or twenty-one, but I don't until I'm thirty. And when I do, she better not have drunk herself to death yet so she has to watch me give it to people who deserve it more than she does."

Richard's theory about big shots was vindicated. Even the oldest of old money, its assets as secure as possible in low-risk bonds and treasury bills, was looking over its shoulder, anxious about losing its hold on the top rank.

"Is this the kind of thing you write about in your book?" Conor asked.

"Not the financial wheeling and dealing," she said. "I don't understand anything about that. Just the emotional repercussions. My mother's a very damaged person, and I can trace most of it to money. It's made her incapable of expressing love in a normal way."

"Like how?" he asked, a bit too eagerly.

"Well, does your mom ever hug you?"

"Hug me? Yeah, of course."

"Then you're lucky," she said. "Mine doesn't. Ever."

"*Never?*"

"I guess not 'never,' since I have pictures of her being affectionate with me when I was really little, but I don't have any memories of her touching me in a genuinely motherly way. From what I can tell, she became a different person after the divorce. Frigid and withholding and sort of . . . joyless."

"And it was all because of the divorce?"

"Maybe it would've happened anyway. My therapist says it's because she's a narcissist and she lost interest once I wasn't a baby she could fully control," she said. "I slept in the room here next to my parents, and after the divorce she moved me all the way to the other end of the hall and got rid of all my baby toys and clothes and my crib—just cleared out that room completely. It's like she didn't want to be reminded that I once was a baby she loved."

When Emily spoke about herself, it wasn't with egocentrism or self-pity. It sounded to Conor like the perceptive analysis of someone who was simply far more introspective and emotionally intelligent than he was.

It was all going well, save for one key department. The first time they had sex, after a week and a half of Emily telling him she wasn't ready yet, was lackluster despite all the anticipatory buildup. A few minutes in, she told him he should finish and not to worry about her. "But I want you to," he said.

"It's not gonna happen right now," she said. "Just take care of yourself."

He had to finish by thinking not about the silent, motionless person beneath him but the most recent (and vocal) orgasm Catherine had had in his bed.

The moment he pulled out, however, Emily began touching herself. Unsure what his role should now be, Conor watched as she deftly and quietly climaxed. It was exciting, witnessing her get off, though frustrating that he'd played no part in it.

"Am I doing something wrong?" he asked Emily after the next time they slept together, which produced the same result—worse, even, because when he'd tried fondling her breast as she rubbed herself, she'd quickly removed his hand. "Something you don't like?"

"It's not you," she said. "It doesn't really ever . . . happen for me with guys."

"Is it an issue of technique? Like no one does it the right—"

"I don't know."

"Can't you just touch yourself while we do it?"

"It doesn't work when I'm having sex. Or even while someone's touching me. I've tried, trust me. It's not the meds I'm on, either—I've always been like this. The only way I know how to describe it is there's a kind of blockage."

This was not something he had encountered before. "Do you think it's because your mom stopped touching you?" he asked.

"What?"

"Do you think you can't do it while someone's touching you because of what you told me—how your mom stopped touching you after the divorce?"

Emily was silent.

"That's a pretty fucked-up thing to say to someone," she finally said.

"I'm sorry—I thought it might be the kind of thing you talked about in therapy."

"Do *you* not like talking about your feelings because your dad dropped dead of a heart attack when you were a kid?" she asked.

Before he could answer, she said, "Sorry. That wasn't nice."

"It's okay," he said. "And sorry again, also. I just . . . wanted to help. I won't bring it up again."

HE CERTAINLY THOUGHT ABOUT IT MORE, THOUGH. IT WAS DISPIRITING having sex with someone who could enjoy it only by herself, who wouldn't even let him be in contact with her during the endgame. Like most men, he regarded female pleasure as a goal worth pursuing as much for his own psychological well-being as for her satisfaction; unlike most men, he would rather forgo his climax if it meant guaranteeing his partner's.

He still very much *wanted* to sleep with Emily, though. He continued to find her beautiful, and her sexual uninterest in him, after a decade of girls throwing themselves at him, was, if anything, an enticement. He was particularly inflamed when she stayed up all night writing, hunched over her laptop with earbuds in, immersed in her made-up world, not needing the outside one or his attention in the slightest, completely unavailable and industrious—as locked into writing as he was into each point on the tennis court. It was just that intercourse, no matter how desirable he found her, was always a letdown.

His athlete's hunger for a challenge kicked in with Emily. He treated every time they got naked as if he were being crushed by a superior opponent and needed to devise a novel strategy, find some chink in the armor, and crack her sexual code. After all, he knew it wasn't a physical thing, just a mental hang-up. Maybe it would be as simple as a maneuver or position she'd never tried, or the more complex development of intimacy and trust over time. Or something neither of them could foresee that cleared away whatever "blockage" was getting in the way. He was patient, dauntless, and, he liked to think, talented in this arena. If anyone could wring out a victory here, it was him.

By marked contrast, the momentum that might have otherwise stalled out with Catherine was preserved, even accelerated, by their arrangement's inconsistency, strangeness, and, despite the angst it induced at most other times, the perilous thrill of illicit conduct. Waiting for her to reach out at a time of her choosing, creep into his cabin late at night, fuck him, hold him on her breast for five or ten minutes, then leave a check and depart when she'd had her fill—this turned him into an addict craving an ever-bigger dopamine hit. The best sex he'd had and the best money he'd ever made, in one weapons-grade package.

Emily supplied all he could ask for except sexual contentment; her mother gave him nothing but that (plus three hundred dollars a pop). Together, they were everything he wanted.

The complicated situation would work itself out. In the meantime, he was enjoying himself in ways he never had before, and Catherine's checks were keeping him and his mother financially afloat. He had only to last till his departure at the end of the summer.

And, should his relationship with Emily continue past August and become more serious, he'd someday have to reveal it to her mother. How exactly he might accomplish that, he didn't know.

. . .

"WHAT'RE YOU THINKING ABOUT?" EMILY ASKED HIM ONE NIGHT AFTER another dismal attempt at sex. When he didn't immediately answer, she added, "I know that's the most annoying question to ask someone in bed, but you sometimes seem like you're not altogether there."

He'd been thinking, at that moment, about his previous, far more successful session with Catherine, involving tongues and orifices that didn't normally go together. He'd juggled casual sex with multiple girls in the past without compunction. But this triangle made him disgusted with himself. Each time he saw Catherine made it harder to extricate himself, and every night he was with Emily he itched with an uncomfortable combination of powerful feelings and remorse. Despite what he'd always thought about himself, despite his copious excuses for why it was sort of, kind of okay to do this, despite the fact that neither of them had any clue and therefore it was ultimately a victimless transgression, he wasn't a good person. A good person would have immediately sacrificed one, if not both, of his avenues of pleasure.

But so many people in power in the country were grabbing more than their fair share, especially lately. Was he, hardworking and scrupulous Conor O'Toole, devoted son, from a two-bedroom apartment in Yonkers, not entitled to this single indiscretion on Cutters Neck, just *one* big shot after years of unerring, steady strokes?

"Nothing," he replied. "I have no interior life."

CHAPTER 12

Conor was taking his weekly multistate performance test for the bar in his cabin early one evening. Though he might have expected that his studying would suffer from the stress of maintaining two distinct relationships, the opposite was proving true: recently his mind was sponging up everything he read and seemed to be operating in a higher gear of reasoning than before, as though it were benefiting from its extracurricular strategic training. (Or, he cynically mused, it was getting practice for becoming a shady lawyer.)

He was midway through the ninety-minute practice exam, trying to draft a persuasive brief concerning a hypothetical guardianship case, when Emily called. (He left his phone on during these practice tests in the event his mother had a medical emergency.) He ignored the call and went back to the brief.

Then she sent a one-word text: *Help.*

"I've got a plumbing emergency!" she said as soon as he called back. "Can you get over here as fast as you can?"

He sped over, relieved it wasn't anything worse, hiding his bike behind Emily's cottage. He could hear the issue before he saw it, and then he felt it when he entered the steam-choked bathroom. One of the bathtub faucets—evidently the hot one—had come off the wall, and water was spewing out horizontally from the exposed pipe as if it were an open fire hydrant. Emily, her face drenched in sweat and tears, was frantically bailing out the half-full tub with a cooking pot and dumping it into the toilet.

"The faucet shot off!" she shouted above the thunderous flooding. "It's filling up faster than it can drain!"

The detached faucet was resting on the lip of the tub. Conor attempted to clamp it over the pipe, but the water scalded his hand. He retracted it and tried again. The temperature was intolerable, and the propulsive pressure of the stream made it impossible to screw the faucet back on. Worse, the partial covering caused the pipe to spray in various directions like a hose with a finger over it, and lasers of scathing water strafed his arms.

"It's impossible!" Emily screamed. "I kept burning myself!"

Conor didn't see a water-shutoff valve or access panel anywhere. "Is there a way to shut the water off in the whole place?"

"I have no idea! It's gonna destroy the bathroom!"

She was right; the waterline was inching up, and the floor was wooden. He could join her in bailing out the tub, but that would grant them only a short reprieve from the inevitable.

"Did you call a plumber?"

"No one's picking up! I'll call my mom! Maybe she knows how to turn it off!"

"Don't! Wait!" Conor redoubled his efforts.

Emily unloaded another pointless bucket in the toilet. "It's okay," she yelled, defeated. "There are some gaps in the wood. The hot water'll run out eventually. We'll just replace the floor."

Conor got an idea. He turned on the cold-water faucet.

"What are you doing?" she asked. "Now there's even more!"

"So I can stand in the water," he explained. "Keep bailing it out."

As soon as the temperature in the tub was less torturous, he shed his flip-flops and stepped inside to get more leverage. The rising water covered his calves and was still painfully hot. He couldn't last long in there.

He pushed and twisted the faucet with both hands, the direct angle at least protecting his arms from getting burned. But every time he thought he'd finally secured it, the water repelled him once again.

"You can stop," Emily told him. "Don't kill yourself."

"Motherfucker," he grunted as he summoned strength from his shoulders and triceps down to his quads and boiling calves to push against the pipe while rotating the faucet, as if he were unscrewing an impossibly stubborn childproof cap.

As veins bulged in his sweaty forehead, there was a palpable click between the faucet and the pipe. The flood suddenly, miraculously ceased. The water in the tub, disturbed by Conor's movements, spilled a few harmless ounces over the side. After all the chaos, the bathroom was quiet and still and undamaged.

"Jesus Christ," Emily said. "You did it."

Conor stepped out of the tub. His feet and calves had turned scarlet, and his hands were lobster red. She told him to run his hands under cold water and grabbed a jar of petroleum jelly off a shelf.

"I can't believe you did it," she said as she tenderly salved his mottled skin. "You're a genius."

"I'm not sure that's the word for screwing a faucet back on with brute force."

"It *wasn't* just brute force. You didn't lose your cool and you figured out about the cold water. *And*," she said, looking at him with an astonished admiration he'd never seen from her, "even when there was no hope, you kept going. *I* gave up, and it's my bathroom."

After he recovered, she initiated sex, a rarity, which made Conor think that this time might be different, that his heroic act had jolted her out of her numbness. But it ended as it always did: with him running up against Emily's impenetrable, insoluble "blockage."

A FEW DAYS LATER, CONOR RETURNED FROM A LESSON WITH DICK GARRISON to find, on his doorstep, a box addressed to him containing a new laptop. Inside was a gift message: "For services rendered by my genius plumber—E."

"A computer is way too much for what I did," he told Emily over the phone.

"Replacing the floor would've cost a lot more," she said. "And you said your computer's really old and slowing down."

With the exception of Richard's 529 plan, no one had ever spent this much money on Conor without expecting anything in return.

"Still. It's just too expensive."

"There's always money," Emily said. "Oh my God. That's what my mom always says. I'm turning into her. Look, please just let me do this for you. It makes me happy."

Conor saw he wasn't going to convince her and thanked her profusely; along with a new phone, he did need a new computer and had been dreading plunking down the money himself. And there *was* always money, at least for her. The other day he'd seen, in an open tab on her laptop, a receipt for a donation to a New York food bank for three thousand dollars. This was like an impulse purchase at the cash register for her.

When he got off the phone he looked up the real estate listing for Emily's Brooklyn address, which was on the order slip. He'd held off doing so thus far, not wanting to taint his feelings for her with a specific monetary value.

She lived in a two-bedroom rental with a private garden in a brownstone, and it went for—Conor didn't believe it the first time he read it—seven thousand dollars a month. Eighty-four grand a year for a rental. That would be enough for a down payment in most of the country.

Her trust fund was bigger than $2.5 million. Much bigger.

THEY SAW EACH OTHER ONLY AT NIGHT (EXCEPTING THE TWO OR THREE times a week Catherine claimed him), but one morning in bed, before he left for his lesson with John, Emily asked if he wanted to swim together that afternoon. She said they could travel to the beach separately if he was nervous about someone seeing them. He reminded her that he wasn't a good swimmer.

"That's why I'm suggesting it," she said. "If you're up for it, I thought I could give you a lesson."

He was resistant, but she assured Conor she wouldn't think less of him, and he reluctantly assented. They met up later on the beach beyond the line of boulders separating Cutters from Tanners Point, the neighboring gated community, so that no one they knew could possibly see them. Emily showed him how to do the crawl stroke. When Conor floundered and nearly swallowed a mouthful of seawater, she offered to hold his body afloat as he practiced.

"Try not to get a boner in public," she said as she supported him under his midsection and chest.

Those early lessons on the tennis court with her mother. The guilt was never going away, was it? Even if he got through this unscathed, even if it was fifty years from now, with Emily out of his life and Catherine long since dead, he would still think from time to time about what he'd done that summer he was twenty-five.

By the end of the afternoon he was able to swim a few lengths without assistance before his coordination faltered and he needed to stand. They committed to a lesson every day.

CATHERINE ARRIVED ONE NIGHT WITH A SILVER FLASK IN HAND. SHE HAD never brought alcohol to his place, but Conor always smelled it on her breath under a vapor of mouthwash. Its presence went unmentioned.

Judging by her wobbly motions, she was quite drunk. When Conor kissed her, she didn't respond.

"You okay?" he asked.

"Get undressed," she said.

They went through the motions. Catherine wasn't her usual rapacious self and just lay limply on her back. This was the only time this had ever happened to them. Had she somehow discovered him and Emily?

"Is something wrong?" he asked.

When she didn't answer, he pulled out.

"What are you doing?"

"I want to stop," he told her.

"I'm paying you," she said. "Finish the job."

He was conditioned at this point to obey her. He reinserted himself, thrusting harder to get it over with as soon as possible, but the creepiness of the situation was hostile to any sort of mental pleasure.

"I'm not able to come," he said. "Let's do it tomorrow."

"No—it has to be tonight," she insisted.

"Why?"

She didn't respond as he pushed back and forth, now even more disturbed.

"Why tonight?" he asked.

Catherine's body shook beneath him. At first he thought she was having an orgasm. But she was crying.

He tried to pull out again, but she grabbed him and forced him back in.

"Why tonight?" he demanded once more.

"Davey's birthday," it sounded like she said.

"Who's Davey?"

"My baby's birthday," she said.

"Whose?"

"My baby's."

"Your . . . daughter's?" he asked, though Emily's birthday was in May.

"My baby's," she repeated.

"*What* baby?"

"Jacob," she said as she let out a wail. "It's Jacob's birthday."

Conor went cold at where he sensed this was going. This abyss seemed darker than even Georgia's childhood and Emily's depression.

He withdrew. This time she didn't stop him.

"Who's Jacob?" he asked quietly.

"My baby," Catherine said.

"Where . . . where is he now?" Conor asked.

"He died," she said.

As she continued crying, part of him suspected she was making it up to manipulate him; Emily surely would have told him about something this monumental. But from the way she was acting, with a vulnerability she'd never come close to exhibiting before, he could tell Catherine was speaking the truth.

"How did he— How did it happen?"

Catherine sniffed and cleared her throat. "In his sleep. During dinner. Thanksgiving dinner. Fourteen weeks old."

Conor didn't want to hear any more details. But there was one thing he did need to know.

"How old would he have been?"

"Twenty," she said. "Twenty years old today."

"Your daughter was alive then?" he asked, pretending not to know. She nodded.

He wanted to know why Emily had never brought this up, but he couldn't ask that. "How did she react?" was the best he could come up with.

Catherine didn't say anything for a minute as her breathing slowed and her sobs ebbed. The crickets were chirping, a background noise that had been growing louder all summer, a sound Emily said was mournful because, once it became too cold, they would die.

"We didn't talk about it," she said. "She was three. There was no need for her to know."

"But didn't she . . ." He still didn't understand why Emily, so open with him about her feelings toward her family, hadn't divulged this crucial piece of information. "Didn't she ask where he was?"

"She did, for a while."

"And then what?" he asked, though he was afraid he already knew the answer.

"And then," Catherine said, "she forgot about him."

CATHERINE LEFT SOON AFTER HER DISCLOSURE, WITHOUT FURTHER elaboration, rebuffing Conor's offer to walk her home in her shaken (and inebriated) state.

Conor wished he hadn't received this information. He couldn't tell Emily, of course. It wasn't his place, it would only cause her pain, and, moreover, once she asked her mother about it, Catherine would know that he'd been the intermediary.

He'd have to keep it to himself. Yet another thing he had to hide from her.

The next night, as he and Emily watched a documentary about the 2016 election, Conor kept peering over to study her. It seemed impossible to cut out such a consequential memory—and yet he had no reason to doubt Catherine's story, given the way it was delivered, and it didn't seem like something Emily would keep private.

"What is it?" she asked when she noticed him staring. "Is there something on my face?"

"Nothing," he said, and they resumed watching footage of the presidential debates.

While Catherine made it sound as though she and her husband had only been protecting Emily, obviously *they* hadn't wanted to confront it, and if they'd told their daughter the truth, they would have had to continue dealing with it the rest of their lives, answering questions from her about him, reliving their nightmare over and over, wondering if they'd done something wrong. Meanwhile, they'd deprived her of a chance to grieve—even to simply *know* this most meaningful part of her life.

"*What?*" Emily said, catching him looking again. "You're like Trump stalking Hillary onstage. It's like you're about to jump me from behind."

"I was thinking about something you said a while ago," Conor said. "You asked if I don't talk about my feelings because of how my dad died."

Her expression softened. "I was just being defensive. Don't listen to what I said."

"I was just wondering, in general, what your therapist says about how people react when bad things happen to them if they don't . . . process it. If that can make them eventually forget about it altogether and block it out."

She closed her laptop. "However his death affected you, you've turned out fine. More than fine. I'm sure you haven't blocked anything out." She tilted her head sympathetically. "Is there something you want to talk about?"

He hadn't meant to become the subject of the conversation.

"Conor?"

Emily was a fragile person. She'd been in a depression treatment center twice, had required electrical currents to shock her brain out of its torments. Someday, she'd inevitably find out what he'd done with her mother, and it would crush her. He'd been not simply unethical but selfish, convincing himself it would all be fine because he *wanted* it to be fine, blithely overlooking the destruction for which he would eventually be responsible.

The right thing to do was to give her an out, now. Let her move on from him before they got any deeper.

"Maybe you shouldn't be with me," he said.

"Why do you say that?"

"I'm not good for someone like you," he said. "I'm . . . a damaged person."

It occurred to him that she'd used the same term to describe her mother.

"Why do you think you're damaged?" Emily asked. When he didn't answer, she said, "Do you want to talk about your dad?"

He couldn't tell her what he needed to tell her—*that* would be selfish, to jettison his burden onto her. But she was inviting him to tell her something else. Something he hadn't blocked out but that he'd lied about for so long it was almost as if he had, until it no longer even registered as a lie, just a tweaking of the truth that he'd justified to himself, because, despite what people said, no one really wanted to hear about something like this, no one wanted to be stuck under this dark cloud with him, and it was better for everyone if he maintained the simpler fiction and they never really knew him.

But now he wanted Emily to know him, to know things about him no one else did, for their intimacy to be reciprocal, because, he was only lately coming to understand, he'd never been truly close to anyone in his life.

"My dad didn't have a heart attack," he said. "He killed himself."

Emily was too stunned to respond.

Conor slowly told her the full story. His father had had chronic back pain, and they found out later it had worsened so much that he'd been out of work for about a year without telling them. He'd leave every morning and pretend to go to a construction site, but he was probably sitting in his car somewhere. His unemployment benefits weren't enough to pay the bills, and the disbanding of his union a couple of years earlier had limited his ability to collect workman's comp, so he racked up huge credit card bills that he hid from Conor's mother. Conor theorized that he thought he was doing them a favor by killing himself and clearing his liabilities. But the credit cards were in both their names, and Conor's mother was saddled with the debt, which they were still paying off.

It took Emily a while to respond. "How did he . . . sorry, you don't have to answer that."

"He overdosed on painkillers," Conor said. "Then he got in the bath. I guess he figured in case the pills didn't do it, the water would finish the job. I'm the one who found him."

The memory was grainy at this point, though he would have spared Emily the details anyway. Coming home from school with his mother and thinking the bathroom was accidentally locked from the inside and sticking a paper clip in the doorknob to open it. Seeing his father's burly figure submerged in the tub, just his knees and thinning hair poking above the water. Bursting into tears and unsuccessfully trying to haul him out, his body already stiff with rigor mortis. Shouting through his cries for his mother, who shrieked even more hysterically at the sight and did nothing, absolutely nothing, to get her husband out of the tub. Calling on capabilities he didn't know his eleven-year-old body had and pulling his head above the surface. The pale Irish skin already bluish purple. Having the presence of mind to call 911 and, while they waited for the needless ambulance, deciding that he could either continue bawling over his dead father while his mother lost it, or do something useful, something productive amid the misery, and hold and comfort her. How he chose the latter, at that moment and for the rest of his life.

"Oh, God." Emily's hand was over her mouth. "Oh, Conor. That's awful. Why didn't you tell me?"

"I don't talk about it with anyone," he said.

"Just your mom?"

He shook his head.

"Does . . . *she* talk about it with anyone?" Emily asked.

He again shook his head. "We've always told people it was a heart attack."

Emily squinted, surely judging his mother, and him, for their secrecy. Why had he done this? He'd surrendered this piece of himself and now he couldn't get it back. If they broke up, she'd still have it in her possession, could wield it, if she chose, as a weapon, use it to explain and criticize his behavior, his dysfunctions. He should've kept it to himself. Life was easier that way.

"I honestly don't know what to say right now," Emily said. "Except that you're not a damaged person. Or so am I, and the only people who aren't are boring, and I'd never want to be with someone who was undamaged."

She threw her arms around him and hugged tightly.

Emily would never seek to turn this against him. And that was why he'd done it. Because she was the only person in the world, after fourteen years of not speaking a word of it to anyone, whom he'd ever trusted enough to tell, and he knew—had always known, underneath it all—that the alternative was no way to get through life.

EMILY EMAILED HIM THE NEXT MORNING.

"Don't feel any obligation WHATSOEVER to read this, now or ever, but I finished the first draft of my novel," she wrote, attaching the manuscript.

"Excited to read," he replied. "I could use a break from constitutional law anyway. Can probably finish it today."

He really was eager to read it, as he'd never seen any of her writing—her work in the college lit mag wasn't online—and he started. Emily had described the book's modest structure accurately: it was just a series of very short anecdotes ("vignettes," she'd called them), usually no more than three or four pages long, marking the passage of time in the life of the main character, Alice.

On a technical level, Emily was a very skilled writer, certainly better than Conor. And she had an insider's grasp of her subculture (those threadbare robes the Cutters people wore to swim were known as "towel-coats"). But as he finished the third chapter, he worried that this wasn't shaping up to be a good book, and it wasn't due to the plotlessness, though that didn't help. He was certainly no critic, not even a casual reader of fiction, but the central problem Emily herself had alluded to—that no one was interested in or sympathetic to how an excess of money had poisoned a rich white girl's family—was inescapable.

He shouldn't have promised Emily he'd read it all that day. She'd ask him what he thought, and if he told her he'd instead decided he needed to study, she'd keep pressing him to finish it. His only hope was that this was a shaky start and the book would improve as it went on.

It didn't. By the end of its two hundred and forty excruciating pages, Conor despised the teenage Alice. She was spoiled, oversensitive to any slight, the constant victim in her own mind of her absent, apathetic father and monstrously narcissistic mother. If Emily had been this bratty as an eighteen-year-old, he was glad he hadn't known her then.

All that talk about "inherited trauma," and she didn't even know about the real trauma she and her family had been through. If she did, maybe she would have written a better book.

At the outset of their relationship, he couldn't have imagined he'd care whether her novel was any good. But now he wished she'd give it up and find something practical to do with her life.

"You really know how to keep a girl in suspense," Emily said when he came over that night and didn't bring it up. "Did you read it?"

"I did," he said.

"And?"

"I was very impressed with your writing."

"Okay . . . ?"

"Yeah. You're much better than I am. I should have you edit my stuff."

"That sounds like very faint, and vague, praise to me," she said. "What'd you think about the characters? About Alice?"

"She was . . . interesting."

"Interesting?"

"I'm not a book reviewer. I don't know how to talk about these things."

"But that's all you have to say about her? That she's *interesting*?"

"I thought it was smart that you didn't try to make her likable," he said.

Emily cocked her head. "What do you mean?"

"You once told me female characters in fiction used to have to be likable, but now everyone's swung in the opposite direction and intentionally makes them really unlikable."

"Shit," she said. "I knew it. You think Alice is 'really unlikable.'"

He'd come up with the idea off the cuff, thinking it might flatter her, but he'd misjudged it. Emily was Alice and Alice was Emily; he was essentially telling her that she, Emily, was unlikable—and so was her novel.

"No, not at all," he said. "I *thought* you were going to go there, because of her money. But then you see how money has . . . traumatized everyone in the book, and by the end you like her way more *because* you didn't expect to."

Emily looked skeptical.

"It was very funny, too," he said, recalling a detail that he hadn't actually found amusing, though he could tell that was the intention. "Especially that scene where her great-aunt loses her clothes after skinny-dipping and walks down the road naked."

"I'm pretty sure you're not telling the truth," she said. "You think it's terrible. Just admit it."

"I am telling the truth. I'm just not good at explaining it." He needed to bring out the big guns. "And then the moment at the end, when the girl at school who had cancer comes back healthy, and Alice thinks about what it is to be a good person—"

"That was based on a real girl from high school. Laura Chasen, senior year."

"It made me tear up a little," he said.

It hadn't, but it was, at least, one of the few parts Conor thought was well executed, a moment when Alice had extended her endless capacity for self-absorption to the consideration of the plights of other people. It was baffling how Emily, fully capable of caring about others in the real world, seemed to shed that part of herself when she created a fictional one, or how her finely calibrated self-awareness went haywire on the page.

"You're being honest with me?" she asked. "You don't think it's masturbatory whining about how hard it is to be rich, and everyone will instantly hate it and me?"

She looked as vulnerable as he'd ever seen her—even more than when she'd told him about her psychiatric issues. Emily was just twenty-three, and this was her first novel. It was clear she had natural talent; surely she'd improve with age and experience, and she probably just had to get this bad book about her childhood out of her system. The world would eventually inform her of its inadequacies, which she herself had just accurately cataloged; he didn't need to be the one to shatter her dreams and possibly send her back to the treatment center. She needed him to support her.

"If anyone hates you," he said, "it'll be because they're jealous of how talented you are."

He couldn't tell if he'd convinced her. But then the compliment made Emily cry, and she hugged him.

People's capacity for believing what they wanted to believe was infinite.

AS THEY GATHERED BALLS AFTER A LESSON, JOHN HAD TWO QUESTIONS for Conor.

"First, are you interested in working here past Labor Day? I'm now planning to stay until October, at least, and several other residents are, including Dick and Suzanne, so you'll have a chance for some extra business. The cabin gets a little colder at night by the end of September, but I can give you blankets and a space heater."

Conor could use the money—by all appearances, Catherine would be staying on indefinitely—and, moreover, it meant additional time with Emily, who had no plans of her own to return to Brooklyn. He told John he'd be happy to extend his stay.

"The second thing is that my firm lifted its hiring freeze," John said. "I don't know if you have anything else in the works, but if you're interested, we'd love to interview you sometime in the next couple weeks. I'd recuse myself from the process, of course."

Conor was ecstatic—for a second or two. With his degree, he had no real chance at landing a job. John had pulled strings for him solely out of charity.

"I really appreciate the opportunity," he said. "But your firm gets applicants from the top law schools. I don't deserve an interview on my merits."

"Our applicants typically do have outstanding résumés, that's true," John said, laying an avuncular hand on Conor's shoulder. "But we don't often get people who've really carried themselves all the way like you have against the odds. That says more about your merits than anything else."

Conor thanked him and said he'd be honored to interview. That night, he explained to Emily that the firm was stocked with lawyers who'd attended Exeter and Harvard and Harvard Law and that, no matter what John said, he still didn't have a shot.

"Those people suck," Emily said. "Especially the ones who went to all three." She hadn't gone to Exeter but to a similarly exclusive boarding school, and she had a particular bias against Harvard, as her father and three generations of Remsen men before him were alumni, and he'd been upset when she'd been accepted to Bard early without even giving his alma mater a shot.

"I'm pretty sure multiple partners at John's firm went to all three."

"No guy from Exeter or Harvard would've fixed my bathtub like you did," she said. "They all would've given up and told me to get my mom to pay for the repairs."

Like his own mother, Emily was clueless about how these things worked. John was simply trying to give him some interview experience; that was all that would come from this.

"Don't you not really want me to work for a firm like his, anyway?" Conor asked. She'd previously encouraged him to apply to nonprofits or a government agency like the EPA.

"I understand you have to pay off your loans," she said. "It's not like you're trying to be a criminal lawyer."

"You mean you'd be upset if I were defending guilty people?"

Emily looked aghast. "*No*—the opposite: if you were a prosecutor who was part of the corrupt criminal justice system," she said. "I don't think I could be with you if you did that."

That evening was particularly warm, and she suggested they cool off with a celebratory nighttime swim. Their daily lessons had improved his crawl stroke enough that he could now swim for a good ten minutes before his still inefficient mechanics wore him out.

It was a clear evening, with enough light from the moon to see. Conor thought she just wanted to take a dip, but as they passed through the path to the beach, Emily said, "Let's swim to the yacht club and back."

That took half an hour for Emily, a strong swimmer. For him, it might be forty-five minutes—assuming he could even make it. "It's not a good idea at night," he said. "Or any time, really. I can't swim that far yet."

"You can always float or do the backstroke if you get tired." She pointed to an orange life jacket resting on the beach. "And I brought that here earlier. I can carry it while we swim. If you need it, we slip it on you."

Conor looked doubtful. She laced her fingers behind his back.

"I'm not gonna let anything bad happen to you." She looked as if she were taking his safety more seriously than her own.

"Okay," he said, his fear of drowning outstripped by the prospect of looking weak in her eyes.

They took off with the current, Emily sidestroking right by him, letting him set the slow pace. She told him if he grew tired to stop and ask for the life jacket. He continued without pausing, though, and after a while they neared the yacht club. It was the farthest he'd ever swum.

"Are you tired? You want to get out here and walk home?" she asked.

His arms were dead and his lungs felt like he'd played a three-setter. But he'd already come this far. "No, let's turn around," he said.

They made the return trip more haltingly against the current. His breathing was labored, and moving his arms through the water was like pushing wet cement. Waves sometimes found their way into his gasping mouth. He should ask her for the life jacket now. But it would be emasculating, especially because it looked like she could do this for another hour without a problem. He plowed on.

"Emily?" he called out at one point, panicked and unable to see her in the dark.

"Right behind you." She touched his back. "Do you need the jacket?"

"No," he said, and he swam forward with renewed perseverance.

A few minutes later, just when he thought he might need to admit failure and ask for help, his foot thudded against the soft ocean floor. He stood and hyperventilated.

"You okay?" Emily asked.

He nodded, and his breathing slowed as they held each other's wet, goose-bumped bodies. Behind her was the yacht club. It looked like it was across the ocean. And Conor, who could barely dog-paddle before this summer, had swum there and back, all on his own.

No, not on his own. With Emily. She'd taught him how to swim, made him believe he could do it, safeguarded his passage. So what if they might never be sexually simpatico; there was more to life than that. He still couldn't believe his luck in finding her.

"Are you cold?" she asked, stepping back to get a look at him and his shivering body. "What's wrong?"

He couldn't remember the last time he'd cried, even alone. He'd certainly never done it in the presence of a girl.

"Nothing," he said. "Nothing's wrong."

He'd said it before, to Ally, and it had always come easily, tossed off at the end of phone calls and upon heading out the door. But this wasn't that cheaply dispensed sentiment. This was real, he was sure of it, in spite of what he'd been doing with Catherine, and the possibility that Emily might not reciprocate, or that she would, but in a week or a month or a year she'd reconsider, made speaking the words terrifying.

"I think I love you," he said.

"*Think?*" asked Emily. With enough reticence to show him that this wasn't the easiest thing for her to express, either, she whispered into his ear, "I love you, too."

But even as his heart bobbed with the water and the moonlight glinted like a silver knife off the ocean while they clung together, the thought that so frequently entered his mind made another unwelcome appearance: that what had begun as something of a youthful adventure, a braided opportunity to explore a deepening emotional relationship with one woman and an addictive sexual attraction with another, had become an ever-tightening bind.

And under that anxiety, the ever-present horror that the truth would somehow find its way out: that Catherine could decide this was the night to enter Conor's cabin or Emily's cottage without warning, or Emily would mistakenly visit when her mother was with him, or any number of other missteps or unforeseen events might occur, and it would all come crashing down and destroy the best thing—the best *things*—that had ever happened to him, and he'd have no one to blame it on but his own greedy, deceitful self.

CHAPTER 13

John was hosting a party at his house and insisted Conor attend. Due to the near-certainty of seeing Catherine there, he apologetically asked Emily not to come, on the grounds that John might observe them together and pick up on their relationship. She said it was no great sacrifice to miss out on socializing with the drunk Cutters crowd, and he told her to swing by his cabin after the party ended.

Simplifying matters for him, Catherine was nowhere to be seen at the event, which sprawled out on John's lawn with scores of unmasked residents juggling drinks and paper plates of hors d'oeuvres and shellfish from a raw bar. Unlike at the pool party, staff dispensed the food and beverages. The workers all wore masks.

Every time Conor saw this double standard in practice, it struck him: they really seemed to think the virus couldn't hurt them, and maybe they were right. They could still contract it, of course—though not from these masked servants—and for the older people it remained a threat as ever, but their money was a kind of vaccine. They never had to shop in a crowded grocery store or endanger themselves by working a party for meager pay. If they were hospitalized, they'd receive the best possible treatment. As the pool party hostess had predicted, probably no one here would die from Covid, just as they surely wouldn't from serving in the military, from gunfire, even from diabetes. They seldom even entered places where such fates were commonplace. Some of them had do-gooder jobs, and for social standing it was all but mandatory to donate to charitable organizations benefiting urban youth and immigrants and refugees—but always from their sheltered perches on Cutters Neck or Fifth Avenue or in Beacon Hill.

Outside of unpreventable disease, old age, and flukes, they were safe. This was the true privilege of the untouchable rich, the steel-plated security. Money may not have made them all that much more content than regular people—Catherine was a prime example—but it removed so many of the problems that caused misery, and wasn't that its own form of happiness?

Conor chatted with the people he knew and counted the minutes until he could leave. When he was at the bar getting a third gin and tonic—he was done with studying for the day—he received a tap on the shoulder.

"Nice to see you again," Catherine said to him, for once showing restraint in public, as she proffered her wineglass to the bartender.

"You, too," he said.

The bartender gave her a new glass and they stepped away from the table.

"I'm sorry I haven't taken any lessons in a while," she said. "I've been a little busy."

No one was listening to them; they didn't need to keep up this game. "I understand," he said.

"Well," said Catherine, "how about one right now?"

His cabin was within sight of everyone at the party. "Right now?"

She took a step closer. "Right now," she said under her breath. "I want you to bend me over your bed."

Ever since she'd told him about Jacob—whom she hadn't brought up again—she had become even more sexually single-minded during their encounters, with some episodes passing wordlessly from start to finish.

He sipped his cocktail. There was no escape; if he was at the party and drinking, he couldn't rely on the excuse that he needed to study. The door to the cabin was hidden from the partygoers, so she could enter and exit without calling attention to herself. This would be fast and still turn into three hundred dollars. She'd probably even planned on it and brought her checkbook.

And the money hardly mattered. Once she'd said what she wanted him to do to her, his mind couldn't veto the decision his body had already made.

"Meet me there in five minutes," he said.

He left first. Inside his cabin he fired off a text to Emily canceling for the night, claiming John had talked to him about the interview and Conor felt he needed to prepare more. Then he turned his phone on airplane mode.

Catherine let herself in a few minutes later. She sniffed the air. "Why does it smell like cigarettes here?" she asked.

Emily had been over the previous night, and, though he normally forbade her from smoking in the cabin, he'd made an exception because she was stressed out and had allowed her to smoke right outside the door. A faint smell lingered despite his generous application of Febreze.

"Some of the kids at the party were smoking right outside earlier," he said.

He went to close his window and pull down the blinds above his bed, though no one could see inside with the lights off.

"Leave it open," Catherine said.

He was about to protest, afraid someone might hear them from afar, before he understood her thinking. The low but still potential threat of exposure riled them both up, and they clawed and bit flesh like feasting lions before she bowed over his bed with her skirt hiked up. His excitement was compounded by watching, in the distance through his window, the darkened figures of the prim, air-kissing partygoers.

When they finished, Conor didn't want to take the risk of staying there with her and having some oblivious attendee walk in on them (he'd stopped locking his door, having adapted to the safe haven of Cutters). He said he needed to return to the party, explaining that John had set up an interview for him and he couldn't afford to look rude by missing any of it. If she didn't buy his excuse, she didn't reject it, either.

"You go," she said. "I need to wash up."

Conor walked out. The self-loathing that flooded in just after seeing Catherine was more intense than usual. It was sick and perverse—*he* was sick and perverse. Why did he keep having sex with a forty-nine-year-old woman whose daughter he was in love with?

But he knew why—for the same reasons he'd just consented to that quickie. The thirty minutes or so he spent with her every few days were the most exhilarating of his life, doled out so sparingly that, more than two months in, she still held him under her spell. If being with Emily gave him unwavering safety and closeness, a joey tucked into its marsupial mother's pouch, being with Catherine was like skydiving with a parachute that threatened not to open each time, until it did at the very last moment—and he wasn't sure which sensation he ultimately preferred.

As he approached the crowd, he took his phone off airplane mode. There were several texts from Emily asking if the party was winding down or over yet and should she come now. Above them was a notification: his cancellation text to her had not gone through before he'd put it on airplane mode.

And there she was now at the raw bar, slurping from an oyster shell while talking to one of her cousins.

She waved at him, apparently forgetting their ruse. It would be more conspicuous if he completely ignored her. He just had to talk with her briefly, and the cousin's presence provided some cover.

"Oh, shit!" Emily said when he came up to them, covering her mouth with her hand. "Should I . . . go?"

"No," Conor said tersely before the boy could pick up on the tension.

"Conor, you remember my cousin Bobby?" she asked. He was the gay, shaggy-haired kid. "Bobby Nuke, we call him. He's one of four Bobbys on the neck."

"Why 'Nuke'?" Conor asked.

"For Newcomb," said Bobby.

"Is Lawrence Newcomb your dad?"

"No, he's my son. I had him when I was seven. He's big for his age."

Emily laughed as John came over to their trio. "Glad to see the youth contingent finally showed up," he said. "Where's the rest of the gang?"

"They're en route," Bobby said.

"Good. Please—eat, drink, have fun. Conor, you know these two?"

"Just a bit," he said.

"Emily's an upstanding young woman. Bobby's sort of a ne'er-do-well. A bad apple. Steer clear." He tousled Bobby's hair and moved on.

"I'm gonna grab James," Bobby said and left the two of them alone, exactly what Conor didn't want to happen. He glanced back at his cabin but didn't see Catherine.

"Sorry I'm here," Emily said. "I kept texting you if the party was over, but you didn't answer, so I thought it was done and I came over to check. And then I ran into Bobby right outside on the road and I had to pretend I was going to the party, and he basically made me come and stay with him, and I didn't see you, so I figured it was okay."

"My phone was on airplane," Conor said. "I was prepping for the interview and lost track of time."

"Well, John didn't seem to figure out we're with each other. Or he didn't care."

Conor ignored this and subtly scanned the crowd for Catherine. As his eyes roved, the exposed portion of the face of the guy manning the raw bar a few feet away looked familiar.

The townie. Charlie.

Conor hid his uncovered face. Emily grabbed the last oyster from the raw bar's bed of ice and swallowed it. "You've got to try one of these," she said.

"I'm okay," he said.

"Just have one. They're so fucking good."

"They're all out, anyway."

"There's a bucket with more behind the bar. Just ask the guy to shuck it for you." When Conor hesitated, Emily faced Charlie.

"Hi," she said. "Would it be possible for us to get a couple more oysters?"

Charlie pried open two oysters with the stubby blade of a knife. His gloved hands held out one to Emily and the other for Conor. He had to take it.

Charlie's eyes locked onto his. He'd remain quiet. Neither of them could acknowledge they knew the other or else be exposed as a thief or an abettor to a crime.

"Good, right?" Emily asked when they were done.

Conor nodded and looked around. "I should find a garbage."

"Just drop it on the ice. They'll throw it out."

Conor placed his empty half-shell on the ice without looking at Charlie.

"We should stop talking," he said quietly. "I think John was just drunk. He made his feelings very clear to me at the start. And now that I've got this interview lined up, I really can't take any chances."

"Would you like another oyster, miss?" Charlie was holding one up for her.

"Thank you." Emily went over to receive it. "You want another?" she asked Conor.

"No," he said.

"It's no problem at all," said Charlie. "Allow me to prepare it for you, sir."

Conor was sure he was smirking under his mask. As Charlie shucked more oysters and Emily ate hers, she and Conor were forced to wait in the uncomfortable silence of being served.

"You from Cutters, miss?" Charlie asked.

"Yes," she said.

"And how about you, sir?"

"No," Conor said.

"Just coming to the party with your girlfriend?"

Other than Charlie's generally being an asshole or incorrectly thinking he was unmasking Conor for having cheated on his girlfriend with Georgia, Conor couldn't believe he would try to make him sweat like this. Charlie had much more at stake; the revelation of their connection would leave only him, a cater-waiter who couldn't afford a lawyer, open to criminal charges for burglary and vandalism.

"Working here for the summer," Conor said.

Charlie set an oyster on the ice and picked up a lemon wedge and a bowl of cocktail sauce. "Lemon or cocktail sauce, sir?"

"No, thanks." Conor grabbed the oyster and stepped out of earshot before Charlie could say anything else. After he downed his oyster, he continued looking for Catherine.

"Want to get some chocolate cake with me?" Emily asked.

"No."

"You sure? It looks really good."

"I don't like chocolate cake."

"*Chaw*-colate," she repeated with a smile.

"What?"

"You say 'chaw-colate.' Like the way you say 'caw-fee.' It's your Yonkers accent."

"I don't have a Yonkers accent," he said.

"It's cute. I'm not making fun of it."

"You're the one who says *tum-ah-to*." He didn't deliver this observation with teasing affection.

"It's how I was taught to say it," she said softly. "I know it's embarrassing. I don't say it when I'm around . . . other people."

Catherine finally came into view, entering from John's main driveway.

"We should go," Conor said. "Separately."

"We could just separate without leaving the party," Emily said. "I want to get some cake."

Catherine was looking in their direction from afar as she joined the party.

"Fine, you stay," he said. "I have to do more prep for this interview."

"Should I come over later?"

"Text me first. And wait till you hear back from me." He made a show of shaking her hand. "Nice to meet you," he said loudly.

Emily walked off. Conor waited until she was lost in the crowd before returning to the raw bar. He dropped the empty oyster shell onto the ice.

"I know it was you," he said in a low voice to Charlie.

"What was me?"

"Don't fuck with me. You're lucky I didn't say anything."

"I got no clue what you're talking about, bro," Charlie said.

His denial was unpersuasive. "You come back here and pull another stunt, I won't be so lenient," Conor said before he left for his cabin.

"Enjoy your summer, sir," Charlie cheerfully called to his back. "I'll tell Georgia you said hi."

HE KEPT AN EYE ON THE PARTY THROUGH HIS CABIN WINDOW, RELIEVED to see Emily didn't talk with either her mother or Charlie. When it petered out and he was certain Catherine was gone, he texted Emily that she could come over so long as no one would see. Once she arrived, he reset his phone to airplane mode.

"Olivia and I made plans to go to this island tomorrow," she said, naming a place he had no idea how to spell. "Want to come and meet her? We're gonna have a picnic and walk around, and we'll be outside the whole time."

He had Sundays off, and he could use a change of scenery. "Sure," he said. "Sounds fun."

She lay down on the bed, removed her glasses, and rubbed her eyes. Still frazzled from nearly getting caught by Catherine, he did some dishes he'd left in the sink.

"I haven't been there since I was a kid," she said. "There's a ten o'clock ferry, so we have to leave here by nine, and we'll have dinner there and get back by about eight. You've got a check on the floor."

"I've got to check what on the floor?"

"You *have got a* check," she enunciated. "It's on the floor."

A check was facedown on the floor near the bedside table. Catherine must have put it on the table after he'd left, it had blown off from the breeze, and he hadn't noticed it earlier. Emily stretched over from the mattress to retrieve it.

"I got it," he said, walking fast to beat her to it, but he didn't get there in time. She held it up for him, and he snatched it out of her hand.

"Wait—did I read that right?" she asked.

She'd seen her mother's name on it. He had to come up with a fast excuse.

"What?"

"Was it for three hundred bucks? I thought your lessons cost one-fifty."

She had thick glasses and could barely see without them. Incredibly, she hadn't read the check beyond the dollar amount.

"They are," he said, stuffing the check in his pocket. "Suzanne Estabrook paid me for two at a time, since she sometimes forgets her checkbook."

"Oh." She stroked his leg from the bed. "It sort of turned me on, to be honest. Isn't that fucked-up? That I write about how money has made my family miserable, but when I see your paycheck, I have this visceral arousal?"

"It's fine," he said.

She pulled him by his belt loops down to her on the bed.

"I'm still viscerally aroused," she said.

They kissed while she massaged him over his fly, then unbuttoned it. In the midst of his own growing excitement—maybe *this* was what their moribund sex life needed, for him to become the breadwinner, or, to gratify his own depravity, for him to nearly get busted—he realized he hadn't washed himself since being inside her mother ninety minutes earlier. Emily was on birth control, and they'd stopped using condoms after the first couple of weeks.

"I'm dirty," he said, pushing her hand away.

"I *know* you are."

He got off the bed. "Seriously, I haven't showered yet today, and I played tennis. I should at least wash down there. It probably doesn't smell great."

"I like when you're sweaty from tennis. You smell like a red-blooded man who does real work." She leaned her head close to his crotch and inhaled deeply, her nose near both her mother's scent and pocketed check.

"I'm gonna wash up," he told her, jerking away.

"Don't take too long," she said.

He cleaned himself thoroughly at the bathroom sink, scrubbing off Catherine's musky smell and whatever fluids she'd left behind. The thought of what had nearly just happened nauseated him, though the ultimate object of revulsion was himself. He deserved to get caught. Maybe, on some level, he wanted to get caught, so he wouldn't have to make the decision himself and could end the suspense.

As he urinated, he took his phone off airplane mode. He had four texts and three voice mails from Catherine. The texts, sent in succession half an hour earlier, all said, *Lesson*. He played the voice mails quietly.

"Pick up your phone," went the first. "Answer me," she said on the second. And the last, delivered just ten minutes ago: "If you won't pick up, I'm coming over."

He'd made it the whole summer without this catastrophic occurrence, and not only was it now happening, but Emily was probably already stripped naked on his bed.

Just got texts, he wrote back. *Bad reception. I have food poisoning. I can give you lesson tomorrow if better.*

The text didn't go through despite his repeated attempts. He really did have bad reception.

She'd be there in five minutes. He had no choice but to phone her. He ran the shower and placed the call. After stalling, it went through and she answered.

"Where the fuck have you been?" she asked. The ocean roared dully in the background.

"I'm sick," he said quietly. "Maybe from the raw bar. I've been throwing up for almost an hour."

"Oh." She continued breathing heavily from the exertion of walking. "Well, I can bring you medicine."

"No, I've got some. And it's not just vomiting. I've been having . . . gastrointestinal issues." His mother had once told him that malingerers who showed up at her office often professed to have diarrhea, because it was impossible for the doctor to confirm and embarrassing enough that few people would make it up. "I'll be fine, but I don't want anyone around when I'm like this."

It sounded like she'd stopped walking. "Fine. Come over tomorrow afternoon, if you're better. My daughter'll be gone all day."

"Okay," he said. "I have to go—I'm feeling sick."

He turned his phone back to airplane and jumped in the shower. He'd averted disaster but had been far too careless; he shouldn't have been with both women on the same night, especially not after Catherine might have seen him with Emily at the party.

He came out of the bathroom with a towel around his waist. Emily was under the covers, not wearing anything on top. "Who was that?" she asked.

"Who was what?"

"On the phone. I heard you talking."

"Oh—my mom. She needed help with a disability form." He turned his back and toweled off. "I forgot I have a lesson at noon tomorrow with someone from Tanners," he said. "So I don't think I can go to the island."

"Can't you reschedule?"

"The guy said he's leaving Monday."

"Can you just cancel it?"

"I've never canceled a lesson in my life."

"I'll pay you the hundred and fifty bucks," she said. "It's nothing."

He waited a moment. "That you think you can just throw money at me and make me do what you want, it makes me feel like I'm your . . ."

"I'm sorry," said Emily.

As much as he was milking his reaction for effect, the part of him that took pride in earning every cent through hard work was genuinely offended by the cavalier ease with which she assumed that she, just like her mother, could control him with her rentier's money—and also that she considered a hundred and fifty dollars, a figure that would always seem meaningful to him, "nothing."

"I really am sorry." She put on a kittenish voice. "Connie boy, come into bed. Please?"

He knew he should be grateful that she was in the mood, if only as a peacemaking tactic, but instead he returned to the sink to clean the rest of the dishes, his back to her. Neither of them spoke as he scraped egg off a frying pan with steel wool.

"Sometimes"—she took a while to finish the sentence—"sometimes I feel like you're not really present. Like even when you're holding me in bed, your mind's elsewhere. If we weren't isolated here and I wasn't spending nearly every night with you, I'd almost wonder if you were seeing someone else."

He didn't answer.

"My dad's like that," she went on. "I'd spend these long weekends with him as a kid, and he'd barely talk to me."

Conor rinsed the pan with scalding water and dried it without speaking.

"It was obvious he didn't really want me around."

At that, Conor walked over and hugged her. "I'm here. I'm not your dad."

"You should give your lesson tomorrow," she said when they unclenched. "You know I really admire how hard you work. That's the root of me being turned on by it. How self-sufficient you are. Not the actual money you make."

He nodded.

"You *aren't* seeing someone else, right?" she asked. "You don't have a girlfriend back home or anything?"

"I am," he said. "Suzanne Estabrook. That's why she pays me so much."

She let out a conciliatory giggle. "Who's the guy from Tanners? I might know him."

"Uh . . . James or John something. I don't remember his last na—me," Conor said, the stammer brief enough that Emily didn't notice it.

THE NEXT DAY, AFTER CONFIRMING HE'D RECOVERED, CATHERINE TEX-ted Conor to come at five o'clock, well before he knew Emily was due back. Unafraid of encountering her, he biked down the main road, a much-faster trip than walking the shoreline path, hid his bicycle near the end of the neck, made sure no one was nearby, sauntered up to the front door, and rang the bell.

"Conor!"

Emily was coming out of her cottage. He froze at the door.

"My phone was dead," she said as she approached. "I was about to text you."

"What're you doing here?"

"What're *you* doing here? Why are you ringing my mom's bell?"

Catherine opened the door.

"Hi, again," Conor said to her. Without skipping a beat, he spoke to Emily: "I had a lesson from Tanners that never showed up. I was waiting on the court for him when your mother walked by, so I gave her the lesson instead. I came by for the check."

Catherine looked at them both.

"Why are you home so early?" she asked her daughter.

"The ferry's on a pandemic schedule," Emily said. "We didn't real-ize till we were there. We got the last one back of the day."

"You two know each other?" Catherine said.

"We met at John's party," Conor said. "It's . . . Emily, right?"

She nodded stiffly.

"I'll get your check," said Catherine. Before she ducked into the house, she stopped. "Why don't you two join me for a cocktail on the patio?"

Conor didn't answer, assuming her daughter would rebuff her for them both.

"I could go for a drink," Emily said.

"Conor?" Catherine asked.

Turning down the invitation might make either woman suspicious—or, worse, in his absence, Emily might heedlessly reveal their relationship. "Okay," he said.

"See you there," Catherine said and closed the door.

He was an idiot for trying to shave off a few minutes. If only he'd taken the shoreline path, this wouldn't be happening.

Conor started off for the patio then stopped. "Where is it?"

"Keep going, all the way around the garage," Emily said. "So, is my mom good?"

"What?"

"Is she any good at tennis? She's always bragging about how she was the best on her high school team."

"She was . . . on the *tennis* team?"

"Yeah, a few colleges even wanted her to play. She was on the swim and badminton teams, too. In between all her debutante cotillion bullshit. She tried to teach me when I was a kid, and I hated it. No offense. I've been trying to figure out how to break it to you."

"She wasn't bad," he said.

Catherine joined them in a few minutes on the patio with a tray of gin and tonics. If Conor had been told, that night he'd first seen this $26 million house, that before the summer was through he'd be an honored guest there, sitting next to the daughter of the owner, to whom he'd professed his love and vice versa, as they enjoyed the clink of ice cubes in gin balloons—that he would now be on familiar footing with the term *gin balloons*—amid the honeyed warmth of the afternoon sun and the ambient pounding of ocean surf, he would have thought he'd hit the jackpot.

This, however, was like driving on an icy mountain road.

"I'm sorry, Emily," she said. "I don't have any beer in the house."

"This is fine."

"Conor," said Catherine, "I've been trying to tell Emily that men don't find girls who drink beer attractive. What do *you* think?"

"I . . . don't really care either way," he said.

"It's just so . . . *lumbering.*" Dropping her voice to the oafish register of the most recent Supreme Court appointee, she added, "I like beer."

Conor studied his ice cubes.

"Emily's a writer," Catherine said. "Or she writes, that is. Do you tell people you're a writer?"

"I say I'm working on a book, if they ask."

"There was a literary agent who wanted to work with her," Catherine told Conor. "Emily turned her down."

"I didn't 'turn her down,' and she didn't want to work with me yet. You put your friend from Williams—and me—in an extremely awkward position by emailing us at the same time without warning and suggesting we work together, and purely out of politeness she said she'd be happy to read my work, and I said it wasn't ready yet. And I'm certainly not going to send it to her when it *is* ready, either."

"I was just trying to help," Catherine said. "You don't have to act like I've done you a disservice by offering a connection."

"For once in my life, I'd like to make it completely on my own. Maybe you can't understand why anyone wouldn't want to unfairly benefit from nepotism."

Conor had always felt uncomfortable around friends when they bickered with their parents, and never more so than now.

Catherine scrutinized her daughter's face.

"What?" Emily asked, touching it.

"You have a blemish."

"I'm aware, thank you."

"I'll give you some concealer."

"You know I don't wear makeup."

"You really should make an exception for this," Catherine said. "It's quite unsightly."

Emily pasted on a sarcastic smile. "So glad to be sharing this precious time with you, Mom."

"Well, I'm *sorry*," her mother said, as if she were the one who should be offended. "I'm just trying to help. A little makeup goes a long way. And you should stop smoking. It's horrid for your skin. You're very beautiful, but you make absolutely no effort. Don't you think she's beautiful, Conor?"

He avoided looking at either of them. "Of course."

"But wouldn't she be even more beautiful if she made the *slightest* attempt?"

"I don't know much about makeup," he said.

"Because men also like that, right?" Emily said. "Girls who wear makeup and don't drink beer. A woman's entire purpose in life is to attract male attention by being demure and fixated on her appearance."

"Oh, stop being hyperbolic—I didn't say that. And we're being rude to our guest. How about you, Conor? What is *your* entire purpose in life?"

"I just graduated from law school. I've been looking for a job."

"John Price's firm is interviewing him," Emily piped up proudly.

"How'd you know that?" he asked. "Oh, right, he came over when I met you and your cousin at his party."

"That's impressive," Catherine said. "His firm is very white shoe. Lots of Porcellian and Skull and Bones men. Where did you go to law school?"

"New York Law School."

"NYU's quite good, isn't it? Right up there with Harvard and Yale?"

"Not NYU," he said. "New York Law School."

"I'm sorry I misunderstood," she said, though it seemed to him that she hadn't. Without a transition, she remarked, "You must have had a lot of girlfriends in college."

"Just one serious girlfriend," he said.

"One 'serious' girlfriend?" said Catherine. "Does that mean she never smiled, like Emily?"

Emily snorted.

"And just one?" Catherine frowned. "But I'm sure you had plenty of . . . do they still say 'hookups' now?"

She was seeing what she could get away with, a cat taunting a cornered mouse. She'd surely been drinking before they arrived. With a few more gin and tonics in her, he could see her flippantly exposing their relationship to her daughter.

"Yes," he said. "I mean, people still say that."

"And did you? Hook up with lots of girls?"

"Average amount, I guess," he mumbled.

"But you're so handsome," Catherine said. "And an athlete. I'm sure you had all the sorority girls spreading their legs for you."

"*Mom*," Emily hissed. "Jesus fucking Christ."

Out of evasive answers and afraid this would spiral into a fight between the two women, Conor pretended to receive and read a text.

"Sorry, I have to call my mom back real quick," he said.

He walked onto the lawn and simulated a call, talking quietly to himself with his back turned. After a minute he came back. "I'm very sorry, but I have to log into her bank account at home and help her with something. Thank you for having me over."

"I forgot to get your check." Catherine looked at Emily. "He's very good at what he does. You should take a lesson."

He could have used the money, and though he hadn't provided a service, he deserved it for what she'd just put him through. But he couldn't last a minute longer and didn't want to be in her debt.

"It's on the house," he said as he left.

CONOR LATER TEXTED EMILY THAT HE NEEDED A NIGHT ALONE TO STUDY and prepare for his interview.

His brushes with calamity were getting closer and coming faster. This wasn't sleeping with two strangers in New York City; he was seeing a mother and daughter who lived within spitting distance of each other. At some point at least one of them would find out, ending both relationships in the most awful way imaginable. Maintaining the status quo was untenable.

He could tell John he had to look after his mother and depart the neck right away, but then he'd be reneging on his promise to a potential, if unlikely, employer in the practice of corporate law. There was only one reasonable course of action, something he should've done a long time ago: break up with one of them.

If he severed ties with Catherine, he'd lose his funding for the next month and change. But she was only a short-term cash infusion, a stimulus check that would soon be spent. Emily was the long-haul investment.

The next time he saw Catherine, he'd tell her it was over. He'd have to be stronger this time, to be willing to sacrifice his future pleasure, to break it off in one clean blow. And, if necessary, he'd have to be willing to hurt her.

HIS OPPORTUNITY ARRIVED LATER THAT SAME EVENING, WHEN CATHER-ine sent him a text. After she came over and they did their business, he forced himself to say it while he lay on her chest.

"I'm not sure I can keep doing this," he said.

"Doing what?"

"This. This whole thing."

Catherine was silent.

"You're not enjoying yourself?" she asked.

"I am."

"Am I not paying you enough?"

"You are."

"Then what, exactly, is the problem, Conor? We're both getting something out of it." She paused. "Do you have a girlfriend?"

"No," he said. "It's nothing like that. I just— I don't think it's good for me. We have to stop."

He was committed to standing his ground against any rebuttal she might make. Too much was at risk every time he saw her. And even if Emily never found out, each occasion he had earthshaking sex with her mother reminded him that he'd never come close to it with her and that an essential component of their relationship was missing. If he'd never met Catherine, maybe he wouldn't have minded as much, but it was too late for that. All he could do was eliminate her from his life and try to pretend what he'd had with her simply didn't exist.

"And maybe it's not good for you, either," he said when she didn't argue. "The other night, when you brought up your son, it seemed like maybe—"

"I don't know what you're talking about," she said coldly.

He nodded, chastened, and waited for her to speak again.

But she didn't. Instead her torso shuddered beneath him. He sat up.

"Don't," she said, tears leaking from her closed eyes. "Don't leave me."

Once again he couldn't tell if this was an act. She'd faked her ineptitude at tennis pretty well.

Whether it was real or not, her vulnerability turned him on. In this rare moment, just as when she was climaxing, she was temporarily relinquishing her power and letting him assume control.

He mounted her for the second time in a quarter hour. She clutched the hair on the back of his head.

"You'll never find anyone else who makes you feel as good as I do," she told him.

"I know," he whispered back.

He'd said it not just because that was what she wanted to hear but because it was quite possibly true. Doing this—exactly this, with her— was when he felt best in the world. Nothing could touch him, nothing else mattered when he was inside her.

"You're mine," Catherine said. "Remember that. You're all mine."

IF HE COULDN'T BRING HIMSELF TO CUT IT OFF YET WITH CATHERINE, he had to break up with Emily. Not permanently, just a pause as he entered the stretch run for the bar, postponed again by the virus to

October. Then he could string it along a few more weeks, claiming job applications were ramping up. Once they returned to New York, far away from Catherine, they'd pick up where they left off. No harm done to anyone.

The next night, before Emily was due at his cabin for his "persuasive brief" about why they should take a short break, Catherine texted him: *Lesson tomorrow 930*. He gave it a thumbs-up. Then, uncharacteristically, she immediately called before he could switch to airplane mode. He didn't answer. A minute later she called again. She knew he was near his phone, as he'd just texted her, so to preempt a repeat of last time, he went in the bathroom and picked up.

"Never mind the lesson," she said. "I have houseguests here the next few days and I won't be able to get away. But all I can think about is your cock."

"Uh-huh." He was generally wary of talk like this, but especially when Emily could arrive any minute.

"Tell me about it. Tell me what you'll do with it."

"I can't really talk," he said. "I'm with John."

"I'm *aching* for it," she said. "Send me a picture to tide me over."

He'd never sent a dick pic in his life. His college coach had strictly prohibited the practice, not that he needed any discouragement; it was stupid and pointless. "You'll see it in person once your guests leave."

"I'll pay you just for this," Catherine said. "Three hundred for a picture of your hard cock."

Her plea alone got him worked up. "Give me a minute," he said.

He snapped and sent off a picture of his unidentifiable erection in the bathroom. Three hundred dollars for a minute's work. That certainly wasn't pointless.

He deleted the picture and his texts with her.

"Whatcha been up to?" Emily asked when she showed up fifteen minutes later.

"Civil procedure." He yawned and got them two beers.

"Sorry again you had to witness the horror show that is my gin-infused mother," she said. Over texts after the encounter, she'd asked why Conor hadn't told her he'd given a tennis lesson to her mom. He'd lied that he hadn't pieced together that Catherine was her mother until he'd arrived at her address.

"It's okay," he said.

"I'm at least glad you got to see what I've been talking about with her." She held up the bottle. "Like the beer thing. And all the little undermining digs about my appearance and writing. And she does it in this polite-society, Waspy, 'It's *quite* unsightly' voice. Oh, and the way she was *flirting* with you. What a fucking . . ."

"I didn't notice," he said.

"You didn't *notice*? 'Oh, Conor, you're so handsome, I'm sure you slept with tons of sorority girls.'"

"I don't know if that's flirting, exactly."

"Of *course* it's flirting."

"But not with any real intent."

"*Ob*viously. Obviously not in a way where she thinks it would be reciprocated—she's, like, twice your age. It's just to have power over me. To show me she can still get a guy's attention in a way that she thinks I can't, because I don't exercise three hours a day and starve myself like she does and I have no plans to get the kind of work she's had done. I'm almost tempted to tell her we're together."

"Don't do th—at," Conor said.

Emily smiled gently. "Do you sometimes have a little stutter? I thought I heard it another time, too. Like a little pause in the middle of a word."

"No, I had something in my throat," he said.

Conor tried to gin up the fortitude to present his breakup plan and, this time, see it all the way through. Before he could start, Emily looked at him queerly and said, "I'm not scaring you off, am I?"

"What're you talking about?"

"When you said you didn't want to see me last night, I thought maybe seeing me with my mom made you think about me differently. Like I'm from this depressing, dysfunctional, spoiled-rich family you wouldn't want any part of."

Maybe he was Catherine's property, but the most important thing was that he cared about Emily, despite everything he was doing, and he couldn't stand to hurt her. He had to show that he wasn't her absent dad or withholding mom.

"Of course not," he said. "Seeing what you've had to deal with made me want to take care of you more."

He had no idea how to actually, successfully end it with Catherine, but he would have to, and soon, because there was no future with her and there never had been.

And because someday, he'd become more and more convinced, in that magical glade on Cutters Neck, as the sunset washed over the stone wall and purple clover and filtered through the trees, he was going to marry Emily Havemeyer Remsen.

CHAPTER 14

The next Friday night Conor was at home, readying for his interview with John's firm so that at least he wouldn't embarrass himself. Emily was writing in her cottage, and he texted her that he'd come over around nine o'clock.

There was another party on the neck, which he was decidedly not attending; nor would he go to any other social functions the remaining weeks, to preclude further interactions in the same space with both women. Once it was October and his commitment to John was satisfied, he'd return to Yonkers, where, with sex no longer on offer, he could easily cut off contact with Catherine (who would surely stay on Cutters until it was fully safe again) and continue seeing Emily (who'd now said she would come back to Brooklyn once he left). After enough time had passed that they would have to divulge their relationship to her mother, he'd get Emily to pretend that they'd run into each other in New York and begun as a couple only then. By that point—months, perhaps even years if the pandemic wore on—Catherine would not, or might not, care.

It could work. It could. He could put his mistakes behind him from this summer, his anomalous, irresponsible behavior, so long as he was characteristically prudent the rest of the way.

When he was nearing the end of his work, he heard someone approaching his door. It was Catherine, clutching a tall drink topped with a wedge of lime, apparently having come from the party.

"Hi," Conor said, alarmed by her first unannounced visit.

The sex would have to be fast; he didn't want Emily wondering why he was late.

But she wasn't there for that. Her eyes darted around the room. Then she stomped into the bathroom and looked inside.

"Where is she?" she asked.

"Where's who?" His voice and body language were calm from his desk chair, but this was the moment he had long feared, the moment that, despite his propensity for planning, he still hadn't precisely figured out how to react to beyond blanket denials.

"Emily," Catherine said. "Where the fuck is she?"

"Your daughter? How should I know?"

"How long's it been going on?"

"How long has what been going on?"

She glared at him. "How long have you been fucking my daughter?"

"What?" said Conor.

"Do you think I'm a fucking idiot?" Catherine snapped.

He'd laid on the incredulity a little too thick. But she had to be going solely by the little she'd seen of them together at John's party and whatever she'd picked up on when they were over for drinks. And she was paranoid, trying to trick him into a confession.

"I have no clue what you're talking about," he said. "I met her at John's party and then again when—"

"Stop it," Catherine said. "Stop lying to me."

He mustered a nonchalant chuckle. "I'm not lying."

Catherine downed her entire glass as though it were water. There had to be at least two cocktails' worth in there. She hadn't appeared too drunk upon arrival, but she would be soon.

"I know you're seeing her," she said, slowly and with conviction. "Break it off with her."

She knew the truth, somehow. When he'd tried to end things with her, she'd asked if he had a girlfriend; he'd raised her suspicions. There were any number of ways she could have spied on them if she'd wanted. At this point further disavowals would only anger her. If he refused and she punished him by ending their own arrangement, then she'd be doing him a favor.

"No," he said.

For a moment she didn't say anything to this, his very first act of real disobedience.

"Then I'll tell her about us," Catherine said. "I'll tell her to come over right now and see for herself."

Jealousy was making her irrational. He couldn't let her do this.

"All that would accomplish is ending your relationship with her," he said.

"What relationship," she scoffed. "She didn't even tell me she went back to the treatment center. My accountant saw the bills and told me. *That's* our relationship. My fucking accountant."

She didn't care. He was the only one with anything to lose.

Conor took a deep, coming-clean breath.

"I'm sorry. I really am. I didn't mean for things to turn out like this," he said. "I'm more attracted to you than I've ever been to anyone in my life. That's the truth. But I'm in love with your daughter. Please don't ruin this for us. She hasn't had the easiest time lately. She's entitled to some happiness. Please think about her."

Catherine considered this request for a few seconds before setting her glass down on his desk and taking her phone out of her pocket.

"I'll tell her I only did it because you were paying me," Conor said.

"You think *that* makes you look *better*?" she said. "Taking money for sex?"

She was right.

"Then call her now," Catherine said, "and break up with her. Put it on speaker."

As ever, she was ordering him around as a subordinate. When it was in service of their bedroom dynamic, he'd gotten off on it. But now she was blocking something he cared about, his opportunity for real happiness.

Enough. He'd bitten his tongue and allowed her to set the terms too many times. He didn't care anymore how good the sex was—and he couldn't go back to it now, anyway, not after this.

"Why do you even care?" Conor said. "What do you think's gonna happen? She's the only thing getting in the way of you and me? Like we have a future together?"

Catherine's mouth puckered.

"Call her," she repeated.

He could just do what he'd planned to before, tell Emily he needed to study hard and couldn't be in a relationship right now. When Catherine was gone, he'd call her back and suggest reuniting once they were in New York. The only way they could be a couple after this, though, was if he persuaded her to cut off contact with her mother, which probably meant losing her inheritance, too. So be it. They'd have her trust—Catherine couldn't take that away—and his income from whatever law job he'd find. That would be more than enough. They didn't need Catherine's tens of millions.

"Fine, whatever." He picked up his phone from the desk.

"And tell her," Catherine said, "that you've been seeing me."

She didn't merely want to ensure that there was no possibility of his and Emily's reconciliation; she wanted to wound her daughter in the worst conceivable way. It went against the natural order of things: a parent who wanted to be happier than her child—or, since she didn't seem capable of experiencing happiness, who wanted her child to be unhappier than she was.

"I'll break up with her," he said. "But I won't do that."

There was an incandescent anger in Catherine's eyes he'd never seen before. If a man on the subway looked like that, Conor would switch seats.

She entered her passcode.

"Stop," said Conor. "I'll tell her I don't love her, whatever you want. But please don't call her. It'll break her. Please, don't do this."

She continued pressing her screen.

"I'll tell her you became obsessed with me after I gave you the lesson," he said. "She's in love with me."

Catherine fixed him in another stare. This one wasn't angry so much as it was piercing, judgmental—the same way she'd looked at him that first time they met at the party, as if she were assessing him as a lower life-form.

"You're not good for my daughter," she said.

"I'm not good enough for her?" he asked. "Why? Because I didn't go to Harvard? Because my family didn't come over on the *Mayflower*? Is that all you fucking care about?"

"I didn't say 'good enough,'" Catherine said. "I said 'good.'"

Conor had no reply.

"What kind of a person *are* you," she said, "to do this to someone?"

He knew what kind of a person he was. The kind who'd started with a minor impropriety, a brief lapse in judgment, then a bigger one and a bigger one, the ligament stretching like taffy, until one day it snapped like a wishbone.

"And *you're* a good person?" he shot back. "Hiding her brother's death from her, her whole life? How about I tell her about *that*?"

He wouldn't do it, but Catherine didn't know that. She glowered at him before swiping her phone's screen.

"She hates you," Conor said. "And with good reason. She'll believe my word over yours."

She ignored him and continued swiping the screen, an action that would be unnecessary for placing a simple phone call. None of his texts would reveal anything incriminating—he'd been very careful.

Except for one.

The dick pic. It had been a trap.

Even if he somehow convinced Emily that he'd meant to text it to her and not her mother and that Catherine was fixated on him, she'd soon come to her senses.

Conor leapt up from his chair and knocked the phone out of her hand. Catherine was too stunned to react, which gave him time to grab it from the floor. He was trying to access the text messages when her teeth sank into his forearm, piercing the skin.

He cursed and dropped the phone and, as he freed his arm from her mouth, inadvertently elbowed her in the face.

Conor stopped what he was doing. He'd never hit a person in his life, much less a woman.

Catherine touched her mouth. "You asshole," she said, examining her bloody finger.

"I didn't mean to hit you," he said, putting up his hands in apology. She picked up the phone from the floor.

"Please don't call her," he pleaded. "We can work this out. I'll just see you."

"Call 911," Catherine spoke into her phone.

He instantly registered the repercussions, which were far worse than those of her telling Emily. Assault and battery. No job with John; probably no law job at all. The end of his career before it ever started.

Catherine looked at the phone's screen and cursed to herself; the call had failed. She brought the device to her mouth again.

"Call—" she said as Conor lunged.

The phone again went flying out of her hands, clattering in its case toward the door. Conor scrambled for it on his knees. He had it in his hands when something hard struck him on the back of his head. The clanging pain made him drop the phone as he shielded himself with his arms from further blows. Catherine was hitting him with a racquet that had been against the wall.

Keeping his back to her as the erratic beating continued, he picked up the only object in his vicinity with which he could defend himself. Without anticipating its projected path or what it would do, with no forethought whatsoever but only the reflexive desperation of reacting to an opponent's overhead smash—just get the racquet on the ball and hope for the best—he used both arms to swing clockwise all twenty-five pounds of the steel-constructed stringing machine.

There was a sickening thunk.

Conor stood there, paralyzed, the machine still in his hands. At his feet lay his tennis racquet and, next to it, Catherine's motionless body.

CHAPTER 15

He shouted her name between frantic curses as he tried to rouse Catherine. She was unconscious but not bleeding from the head, at least not that he could see; it had been a blunt strike with the smooth, curved base of the machine.

He picked up his phone to call 911. Then froze.

A teacher in his high school had slipped backward on ice and concussed himself, didn't go to the hospital, because there were no visible wounds, and died overnight of brain bleed. If a simple fall had killed someone, a direct blow to the side of the head with a heavy steel object powered by a half revolution of centripetal force from a strong young man could certainly do it.

Even with the claim of imperfect self-defense—she'd come to his cabin, bitten him, attacked him with the racquet—he was looking at voluntary manslaughter, at minimum. And if she survived, she'd be more determined than ever to take him down for aggravated assault. No jury would accept that a twenty-five-year-old male athlete had been in such fear for his life that he'd had to defend himself with this degree of force against a forty-nine-year-old woman.

The consequences for his elbow to her mouth were quaint by comparison. This wasn't just a misdemeanor that unofficially locked him out of a job in the law. He'd be stuck with an underqualified and overstretched public defender, and a DA would be highly motivated to convict him for the homicide, successful or attempted, of the richest woman on Cutters Neck.

No matter the medical outcome for Catherine, it meant a felony and real jail time. Years, perhaps decades. His life would be over. His mother's life would be over.

A college teammate had been clunked on the head in a match by his doubles partner's racquet and was knocked out, but just for fifteen seconds or so. In the aftermath, they'd learned that unconsciousness from concussions seldom lasted more than a few minutes.

He'd spent only about thirty seconds mulling what to do, the phone still warm in his hand. But that was enough time for an irrevocable transformation, for moving from a state of disarrayed, helpless panic into a decisiveness as clear and cold as ocean water.

CHAPTER 16

With Catherine's limp body slung over his shoulder, he stepped outside his cabin.

The thick sea fog and nearly moonless sky provided as much cover as he could hope for as he staggered beneath her slack weight to the woods. Despite her willowy frame, it was still an effort to carry her. He drew rapid sips of air while his mind, seeking affirmation for what his legs and back were doing, reconsidered all the hypotheticals at the speed of crisis.

If he called 911, the cops would take the word of the rich older woman who lived on Cutters over the cash-strapped tennis instructor from Yonkers. There'd be no she-said, he-said; it would be she-said (while showing the likely bruise on her head), and he'd be arrested on the spot.

If Catherine came to on her own and was fine, she certainly wouldn't listen to reason now.

That left this.

It would be bloodless. He wouldn't have to use a weapon or even his hands—a necessity, because he didn't have it in him to be the active agent of death. He'd just hold her head under the water. She was still out, and if she awoke from the shock she'd be in too much of a stupor to resist; it would be done with quickly. She was probably going to die from the brain bleed anyway—an injury she'd forced him to inflict. He was only speeding up the process more humanely.

He wouldn't need to bury her, either, which would take all night, require finding a shovel, and risk detection by dogs. After she was dead, he'd carry her body along the path to the end of the neck near her house and bring it into deep water, where it would be pulled out to sea and never found. If somehow it was, she had alcohol in her system and was a known lush; the assumption would be that she'd accidentally drowned while swimming.

And her drowning would ultimately be easier for Emily to absorb than discovering what had gone on between him and Catherine. The former would be a tragic but faultless mishap; his father's death, as far as she knew, was worse. As awful as it was, she'd get over it in time. The latter would annihilate her trust in her mother, in men, in the world. She would never recover.

This was the only possible action he could take to protect both Emily and himself.

He reached the part where he had to walk about ten feet in the clearing to get to the ocean path. The back porch light was on, as were some in the house, though that didn't necessarily mean John or his wife was home; they could still be at the party. But if they were in a dark room and happened to look out a western-facing window, they might glimpse, through the scrim of fog, one figure carrying another down to the ocean.

He made a break for it, walking as fast as he could manage, his heart thumping with exertion and terror.

The declined path was easy to walk down on one's own in daylight, but, encumbered as he was in the blackness, he had to be very careful not to trip. He navigated the uneven terrain until he reached the boulder he routinely sat on. Beyond it, the ocean churned at high tide. The fog was even denser here, nearly solid.

If John had seen him and decided to investigate the suspicious sight, he'd be coming down. And it had been at least a couple of minutes by now. Catherine wasn't awake yet, but she would be soon, albeit groggy. He had to do it immediately. He slipped out of his flip-flops and trudged into the waves.

The cold water had a bracing effect on his thinking. This was absolutely insane. He couldn't do it. He still had time to call an ambulance. The police might believe him: she'd left bite marks, probably some bumps on his head, it happened in his cabin. It would end his relationship with Emily, but that was better than a lifetime of—

As the water reached Catherine's dangling feet, she stirred and groaned.

His body reacted instinctively, overriding his second thoughts and squeamish aversion to direct violence, and became, in an instant, a remorseless machine, as if his actions were somehow in his muscle memory. He slammed her backward into the ocean, trying to pin her below the surface. She struggled, all her limbs flailing, saltwater splashing in his eyes, until something hard—a foot, a fist, an elbow, maybe a knee—hammered him in the balls. The pain radiated up to his abdomen and kidneys. As he protected his groin with his hands, he lost his grip on Catherine.

He couldn't see her in the foggy blackness. He groped underwater but felt only slimy seaweed. She couldn't have swallowed enough yet to drown.

Then the sound of disturbed water. Ten feet out to sea, her head lifted above the surface, its outline barely visible through the gauzy mist. She turned, saw Conor, and dived under again.

He swam after her.

After a few seconds her head reappeared, briefly checked that Conor was in pursuit, and disappeared below.

She surfaced for air intermittently, sometimes going in a new direction, each time distancing herself from land; she must have reasoned that losing him in the water was her only possible escape. The waves grew choppier, slapping his face as he swam the crawl, looking up after every few strokes to track her. Despite the blow to her head, Catherine was a strong swimmer, still more adept than Conor; Emily's lessons had made him competent, not fast. She must have kicked off whatever she'd had on her feet by now and was wearing an above-the-knee dress that wouldn't get in the way. With her unpredictable and cloaked zigzagging, she was slowly increasing the gap between them.

She was going to elude him at sea, safely return to the neck alone, and seek help.

Yet she was still recovering from being knocked unconscious, there was alcohol in her system, and she was taxing herself by periodically swimming submerged in buoyant salt water. And he was an athlete in his prime, if out of his element. After another minute, he began gaining on her and pulled just a few lengths behind.

But the effort was now wearing him out. His and Emily's trek to the yacht club and back had been at a snail's pace, and he hadn't challenged himself like that since. He couldn't keep this up for much longer; she would outlast him. And if they got out much deeper, *he* might be the one to drown.

His steady strokes were failing him; his only means of catching her would be to take a chance. He'd have to intercept her, which would require guessing her direction underwater. The next time she dived under, he turned to the left, thinking she might start returning to land and would instinctively head home to the end of the neck. If he chose wrong, she'd be even farther out of reach once she surfaced.

Something grazed his arm. He reached out, felt skin, and managed to snatch an ankle. She kicked, but he held tight and pulled her closer, cinching her around the waist from behind with his other arm. They both plunged below momentarily then bobbed back up. As she kicked and elbowed him, he got his hands around her neck.

He dunked her before she managed to lift her face just above the water, sucking in air with an asthmatic, horrific gasp.

Then he pushed her head back under and kept applying downward pressure on her shoulders as she squirmed and thrashed and fought until, suddenly, he was no longer touching her.

He jabbed all around him, connecting with nothing. She wasn't visible. He treaded water as Emily had taught him, rotating in place, ready to dart in any direction, waiting for her to pop up.

CHAPTER 17

She didn't.

CHAPTER 18

Immediately—relief, as when an opponent faltered on a fifteen-shot rally: it was finally over.

Then nausea, as the helter-skelter stilled, and he was left to contemplate, amid the white noise of the roiling ocean, what he'd done. Had she died from the head injury, that would've been one thing, a justifiable act of self-defense. But he'd carried her down to the water and drowned her. That wasn't self-defense.

He'd done it. He'd killed a person.

Fuck.

Not just a person. His girlfriend's mother. His mistress.

And not just killed. Not just manslaughter.

Fuck fuck fuck fuck fuck.

He himself might be killed if he didn't swim back now.

As he swam to shore, the physical exigencies of survival took priority and, along with the cold water, numbed him, dulling his nerves, as it had so often when fighting off set and match points. It wasn't letting him think of what he'd done, of what was at stake. It only sharpened his concentration for the next step.

IV

VI

CHAPTER 19

Conor crawled onto shore and collapsed. He heaved like a beached whale, too tired to stand, almost too tired to think.

But he did, lying there on the pebbles. Catherine was gone, by his hand, sinking to the bottom of the ocean.

In the last half hour he'd ruined his life.

But it hadn't just been the last half hour. He'd been sleeping with Catherine for more than two months, and he'd been seeing Emily for the majority of that time. He'd had dozens of opportunities to end it before it reached this point, and he'd passed them all up out of weakness and greed.

He should've let himself drown. That would've been better than living with this.

But if he hadn't done what he did, she would've ruined his and Emily's lives. His mother's, too. There was a chance, now, that only Catherine's was over.

And Conor O'Toole wasn't the kind of person who let himself drown.

He got to his feet.

FIRST HE HAD TO TAKE CARE OF THE PHYSICAL EVIDENCE.

Inside his cabin, he dried off and changed into a clean outfit. He balled up his wet clothes—no blood visible—in a shopping bag, which he tied up and hid. He'd dispose of them later.

A cursory examination revealed no blood on either the floor or the undamaged stringing machine. He could throw the machine out now, but someone might see him carrying it on the road, even stuffed in a bag, and it would eat up valuable time. He'd deal with it the next day, too.

They'd been perhaps two hundred feet from shore when Catherine had gone under—no, when the body had gone under. Even if it didn't remain submerged, they'd been in deep enough water that it would be swept out to sea. But in case it wasn't, he'd have to scout for it up and down the shore in the daytime.

Next, the data.

Her phone lay on the floor. His photo and texts were on it—and, far more dangerously, in the cloud, potentially accessible even if he threw the device into the ocean. She'd once entered the code in front of him, but he'd seen only that it ended with two zeroes. It obviously wasn't her birthday, and it couldn't be Emily's, either.

On his phone he looked up the date of Thanksgiving in 2000 and punched it in.

It worked.

Morbid, putting herself through that every time she opened her phone.

He scrolled through her texts and deleted all their exchanges and his number from her contacts (he was identified as "Pro"), then reviewed her photos. There were very few, and she hadn't saved his picture to her library. She didn't use the cloud for any backups, either.

Unless she'd emailed about him to anyone, which he very much doubted, any indefensible digital information about their relationship was now erased.

A class he'd taken on data protection and privacy law had taught him that the police's ability to track phones was more limited than the public imagined. If he remembered right, they could trace its precise location only if they possessed the device itself, to see when it connected to various Wi-Fi routers. Otherwise they had to go by pings off cell towers, which covered a wide radius.

Catherine's phone wasn't connecting to John's router extender. They'd never know she'd been to his cabin.

He could chuck it now. But if he did, it would be only a day or two until Emily or someone else on the neck tried to reach out and found their calls going straight to voice mail. If her scent lingered within and around his cabin, a police search with dogs would lead them to it, and they'd be able to detect any DNA she'd left behind.

His forearm throbbed. The bite. Her upper and lower teeth had left distinct crenellations in the skin. He'd never been bitten before like this, but he imagined it would bruise and take at least a week to heal and fade.

He had to buy as much time as possible before anyone noticed she was gone.

CHAPTER 20

Before leaving his cabin, he opened all his windows to air out Catherine's scent—her body's and her perfume's—and patched the bite marks with one of the bandages she'd given him that time he'd cut his finger.

He brought Catherine's phone with him, leaving his at home, and raced along the shoreline path to her house, entering through the patio door, which he opened with the hem of his T-shirt.

He went up to the bedroom, careful not to touch anything with his hands, and plugged her phone into the charger, still using his shirt as a glove. If she received any calls, at least the phone would now ring before sending them to voice mail.

As far as the police would know from her phone data, Catherine had left her house that evening for the party on the neck (which others would corroborate) and had now safely returned. And if they ever sought out his phone, it would show him as having been at his cabin the entire time.

He thought he heard someone coming into the house, but it was just his own feet on the floorboards. The momentary alarm jarred him. If someone saw him doing anything he shouldn't, or simply his being in an unexpected place, he was done for.

He couldn't let himself agonize over these outcomes. He had to anticipate, strategize, remain in motion.

Catherine was last seen alive at the party over an hour earlier. He needed to establish an alibi immediately.

CONOR RAN ALONG THE SHORE BACK TO HIS CABIN AND RETRIEVED HIS phone. As he passed the yacht club on the way to Emily's cottage, distant laughter sailed up to him. He strolled down the gravel driveway.

A bunch of the cousins were hanging out by the tennis court, drinking beer around a cooler. Bobby Nuke was among them.

"Hey, Bobby," Conor said.

"Hey," said Bobby. He probably didn't remember his name.

"Mind if I join you for a beer? I've been working all night and could use a break."

Bobby handed him a sweaty can. "Hey, everyone," Conor said. "We met a while ago. I'm Conor. The tennis pro."

There were six of them. Six witnesses.

He sat next to Bobby, pretending to drink his beer, as the others discussed an upcoming pickleball tournament on Cutters.

"I'm the *worst* at volleys," one of the girls said. "When someone hits it right at me, I'm like, *ahh!*"

He would have to wipe down his racquet handle to remove her fingerprints. He'd get rid of the stringing machine as soon as he could. He hadn't had sex in her bed since July; nothing from him would show up there. He'd go through her phone more carefully the next day in case she'd ever mentioned him to anyone, though he doubted she would have. If he accounted for absolutely everything, if he covered or erased every track, he could make it through this. No one would have any reason to believe the tennis pro studying for the bar had anything to do with the disappearance of Catherine Havemeyer.

"If they make me play Oscar, I'm demanding an umpire," said a boy. "His cheating is next level."

Conor had lost a match in tenth grade to a boy who'd called every close shot out, even some that were half a foot within the lines. There weren't enough adults present for him to request a line judge, so Conor had had no recourse other than to call the kid's shots out, too, though he wasn't shameless enough to do it unless it really was questionable; he was an inveterate stickler who always gave his opponent the benefit of the doubt. When he told Richard about it later, he'd been surprised by the vigor of his mentor's response.

"You *never* cheat," he nearly shouted, perhaps the only time he'd showed anger to Conor. "I don't care if your opponent's doing it. You don't stoop to his behavior. And he's cheating himself most of all, because now he knows he's not a real winner—he's a cheater."

The lecture made its intended impact: Conor had never again done it, not even when his opponent was taking advantage of him.

Richard would say he shouldn't have stooped to Catherine's level, that if she was going to expose him to Emily, then he should've let her and faced the music. And there was no question what he'd say about the stringing machine. Or the ocean.

But Richard was a small-time real estate lawyer who'd handled disputes over breaches of contract, about who owned a tree with roots and branches on opposite sides of a fence. His ironclad code of ethics didn't apply to this, an area of the deepest gray. Catherine had threatened him, bitten him, hit him with a hard object that could have seriously injured him. Conor had done what he had to do to protect himself, first physically, then legally. It was human instinct. Richard would've done the same exact thing. That was how things worked in the real world.

These rich college kids without a care in the world, laughing about a pickleball tournament, and less than an hour earlier he'd been chasing her in the ocean, holding her down—

"Did I do the thumb trick yet this summer?" Bobby asked the group as he held up an unopened can in Conor's field of vision. The rest of the crew said he hadn't and egged him on.

"Take a video," he said to a girl. Others illuminated him with their phone flashlights as he pressed his thumb hard against the side of the can near the base until he punctured the aluminum, generating a geyser of beer to rowdy cheers. Conor leaned into the frame of the video, cheering along with them, as Bobby chugged it, the foam bearding him.

That time after the first lesson when Catherine had streaked water from a bottle onto her neck and chest.

He had to shut out these thoughts.

"Send it to the cousin text," someone told the girl.

"Could you send me that video, too?" Conor asked Bobby when he was done with the beer. "I want to show my friends in New York."

Bobby beamed with pride as he texted him the video. When no one was looking, Conor dumped out his beer. "I gotta get to sleep," he said. "Thanks for the beer."

He went back up the driveway and reviewed the video on his phone. He was visible, for a few seconds, at the end.

HE NEARED EMILY'S COTTAGE AS IF UNDER THE INFLUENCE OF MAGNETIC repulsion. He couldn't go in, couldn't face her and act like nothing had happened, like this was just another normal day in their normal summer.

But he—and his phone, connecting to her Wi-Fi—needed to be there, to be able to document that he'd spent the entire night with her the evening her mother was last seen.

"I thought you were coming over at nine," she said through a yawn when she greeted him at the door.

"Sorry," he said. "Your cousins were drinking at the yacht club. I stopped by and had a beer with them."

"You hung out . . . with my *cousins*? Why?"

"Desperation, I guess," he said as he plopped onto her couch. "I was working nonstop all night."

Emily hummed a tune as she busied herself in the kitchen.

The way he'd rationalized it before, that this was preferable to her learning the truth—he'd been deluding himself. He was right. She should have stayed away from him.

What kind of a person are *you to do this to someone?*

He was a damaged person. A damaged person who damaged other people.

"You okay?" Emily asked. She was holding out a beer for him, which he hadn't noticed.

"Just wiped out from studying," he said.

"What happened to your arm?" She pointed at the bandage.

He put a hand over his forearm from her even though the wound was covered. "Scraped it on something. It's fine."

Emily sniffed him. "You smell like the ocean. You went swimming?"

"No," he said. "A while ago, I mean. Before dinner. I didn't shower after."

"You want to watch something before bed?" she asked.

"I'm pretty tired," he said. "Maybe let's just go to sleep."

With nothing to occupy him in the dark, his mind compulsively replayed the night's events. The collision of the stringing machine with Catherine's head, the solidity of the blow. Crumpling to the floor like a knocked-out boxer. Her underwater fight. Hunting her down in the ocean. Then that death rattle for oxygen before he'd pushed her below one final time and flooded her lungs.

Why had he even gone for her phone when she'd tried to call the police? If he'd succeeded in stopping her, she only would've called later. He should've just allowed her to summon them, told his side of the story. He was studying for the bar at his home while sober; Catherine had visited him inebriated and uninvited. She probably wouldn't have pressed charges in the end. Maybe she was willing to burn bridges with her daughter over Conor—or, as she'd claimed at the end, to save her from him—but evidence or even rumors of a dalliance with him would have embarrassed her far more than him. And if she did take him to court over a piddling elbow to her lip from a tussle, a jury would have found a diligent law school graduate who'd pulled himself up by his bootstraps more sympathetic than a multimillionaire heiress with a drinking problem; he'd have been acquitted. It would have terminated his relationship with Emily, but *this* wouldn't have happened.

It won't hurt, will it? Catherine had asked him that time in the car, playing a freshman. *You won't hurt me, will you?*

He had, in ways she never could have anticipated, in ways he hadn't thought he'd ever be capable of. But she'd tried to hurt him, physically and emotionally, and Emily, too. And once he'd involuntarily defended himself the way any person would, she was going to die anyway. She'd hurt herself.

He hadn't been the greedy one, or at least the greediest one. She was, trying to keep him all for herself—her concern for Emily was disingenuous—and if she couldn't get what she wanted, no one could.

In his haste to return the phone to Catherine's house, he'd overlooked something obvious: if he kept it by her bed for the coming week, the continuous hits to the internet router would make it look as though she never left the house. She'd also receive calls and texts that would go unanswered. The calls he couldn't do anything about, but he could reenter the house surreptitiously, respond to any important texts as Catherine would, then take her phone outside for a little while, away from her internet router, before returning the device to her bedroom; simply turning it off in the house wouldn't simulate normal activity, and although he could deactivate the Wi-Fi and stay put, he shouldn't remain in her house any longer than he had to.

He could do this every day until his bite marks faded. Eventually he'd bring her phone out at night with a bottle of wine to the private pier by her house, making it appear she'd drowned while drunkenly swimming.

It was good, once again, to be consumed with logistics.

CHAPTER 21

He awoke for his tennis lesson with John after barely any sleep, under the black cloud of having escaped the narrative of a nightmare but not its lingering disquietude.

Except he couldn't remember any dreams, only the macabre facts of the previous night. What had happened was real, it was still there, and it would always be there. He couldn't erase or undo it.

But he could, gradually, cover it under enough layers of sedimentary rock that it never poked through the surface. He was capable of this. Mental toughness. He hadn't told a soul about his father for fourteen years, hadn't even talked about it with his own mom, and, over that time, he'd thought about him less and less, until both his life and death had narrowed to a pinhole in his mind. That parable about the oak and the reed was bullshit, truly a fable. If you had a strong foundation and thick bark, you could weather any storm.

He left the cottage before Emily was up, saving himself from conversation with her. He and John rallied without much talk. Conor played with the racquet Catherine had used, to cover her prints. When it was over, John asked, "All set for your interrogation?"

Conor stopped picking up balls. "What?"

"The interview's this week, isn't it?"

"Right," Conor said. "Yes. Monday."

"Little nervous?"

"A little, I guess."

"Whenever I get nervous before something big," John said, "I think, 'What's the absolute worst thing that can happen to me if I screw this up and everything goes wrong?' And it's never really that bad."

Only a guy with the kind of money John had could think that way. Conor couldn't afford any complacency. He had to conceive of worst-case scenarios, to imagine it all going wrong, and to counter them pre-emptively. He'd have to consider and account for any vulnerabilities based on what had happened earlier in the summer, in the days before, the night of, and now everything he did in the aftermath.

"So what do you think?" John asked.

"About what?"

"The cocktail cruise. You want to come tonight, take your mind off the interview?"

"Oh. Sorry, I didn't hear you."

His imagination reformulated the ingredients of the two of them alone on a boat in the ocean into his garroting John with string from his machine, anchoring him to it, and dumping him into a marsh.

"Thank you, but I think it's better if I stay in tonight and prepare," he said.

When he returned home, his first order of business was disappearing the stringing machine. Not the murder weapon, by definition, but a weapon nonetheless. He carried it in a trash bag to the neck's dump, concealing it under garbage in one of the dumpsters, and did the same with the clothes he'd worn in the ocean and the glass Catherine had drunk from.

Back in his cabin, he turned off his phone to circumvent any interference from Emily, donned a pair of dishwashing gloves, took the shoreline route, and entered Catherine's house through the patio. Her phone was where he'd left it. She'd received a call from an 800 number and one text from a friend in New York: a selfie in a mask and an evening gown. The woman and Catherine texted frequently enough that he'd have to respond in some form. The fewer words he impersonated her with the better, so he combed through their old messages to see whether Catherine ever "liked" texts in response, and if not, what her texting style looked like. As he scrolled back into the archive, an exchange stood out.

"Thank you for talking to Margo about her miscarriage," the woman wrote. "She told me it helped a lot."

"Anything for my beloved goddaughter," Catherine had replied, with a heart emoji.

He wished he hadn't read that.

She'd given a thumbs-up to several other texts, so he added one for the selfie, left the house with the phone, and walked back along the shoreline, eyeing the ocean and the shoreline for the body. He was afraid to search for his name in her texts and emails, lest a future forensic data analysis reveal he'd done it, so he instead did quick visual scans for it in a few recent text threads and some emails. There was nothing about him or her romantic life. He considered deleting all her texts, but if she'd mentioned him to a friend, the person would have the messages anyway, and it would mean he wouldn't be able to study her verbal mannerisms again. When he neared the path to John's house he doubled back and plugged the phone in by her bedside table, wiping it down with a hand towel first.

That wasn't too hard.

IN HIS CABIN, HE EXAMINED THE HARDWOOD FLOOR OF THE LIVING AREA more carefully with the assistance of his phone's flashlight. Even if the stringing machine hadn't gashed her head, his elbow had bloodied her lip.

He didn't see anything in the dark wood and was about to stop when his eye caught three spots of what had to have been blood clustered near one another. He wiped the area with cleaning spray, but no matter how hard he scrubbed, he couldn't get rid of the stain; the wood had absorbed it overnight. He feared that using bleach would discolor the floor and draw more attention to any blood that remained. In an evidence class, his professor had told them about a case in which a man was convicted of murdering his mistress in part because an application of the chemical over blood spatter hadn't degraded the victim's DNA as much as expected. He could buy sandpaper and try to strip the wood in that area, but his tampering would be conspicuous and still potentially leave behind traces of DNA he couldn't see.

The absolute worst thing that could happen to him would be if a crime scene search were ever conducted there. An investigation with the chemical luminol would certainly detect it, lighting up the faintest splatter like bioluminescence, and they'd match Catherine's DNA with Emily's.

It was midmorning, and he hadn't eaten yet. He cracked two eggs in a bowl, whisking them with a splash of milk until he had a smooth blend, which he poured into the hot skillet and scrambled.

He set down his spatula and texted Emily to come over that night.

AFTER GRABBING A BEER IN HIS CABIN AND PLAYING MUSIC ON CONOR'S new laptop, Emily talked animatedly about a spat she'd had that day with her friend Olivia. He nodded along affirmatively.

One time, before they'd shifted their meetings to his cabin, they'd fucked in her jetted tub. Another time she'd sat on his face as they'd sixty-nined, ground down on him hard, and stroked him off as he nearly suffocated.

And all the times lying on her breast in the dark above the gentle tide of her rib cage, her fingers combing his hair, sometimes clenching the roots as if she didn't want to let him go, and he didn't want her to, either, just wanted to be tethered to her for as long as he could before she left.

It wasn't just about lust or money. He'd loved her, too. A sick love, a fucked-up love between two damaged people, but that didn't mean it wasn't real.

"Don't you think so?" she asked.

"Don't I think what?"

"That Olivia's re-creating the power dynamic of her relationship with her sister with me?"

"Yeah, for sure," he said.

He walked barefoot to the kitchenette for a glass. When Emily wasn't looking, he dropped it hard on the linoleum section of the floor. It shattered.

"Careful!" she said from his bed. "There's pieces everywhere."

Conor took a step and intentionally landed on a jagged shard. He swore as it lacerated the sole of his foot.

"Baby!" she said. "You okay?"

His foot was bleeding. He didn't let Emily see it yet. The wound was deep enough that it would leave a scar for at least a little while—hopefully weeks.

"I'm okay. I should put on flip-flops before I clean this up."

He walked around the area where Catherine's body had been and stepped several times over and around the bloody spots before continuing to the door, leaving a trail of crimson blots.

"You're tracking blood," Emily warned him, putting on her own sandals and retrieving paper towels from the kitchenette.

"Shit," he said, examining his foot for show. "Can you deal with the glass? I'll get to the blood after I cover up this cut."

After he bandaged himself, he brought the cleaning spray over to the mess. When Emily's attention was diverted, he smeared his blood all over Catherine's. Much more of his was present than hers. He rubbed it hard into the wood and spread it around into a wide oval, then lacquered it with more fresh blood from a paper towel and left it untouched.

"I can't get all the stains out," he said after a few minutes of purposely ineffectual cleaning. "I've got to tell John. I hope he doesn't charge me for this."

He texted several photos to John of the bloodstains and the glass, apologizing and offering to pay for a professional cleaner and the broken glass. John said not to worry; you could barely see the stains in the dark wood, and it was just a measly glass.

"If you promise you won't tell anyone, you want to hear some juicy Cutters gossip?" Emily asked as she swept glass. "So that burglary at the Bakers' house—you know who it was? I'll give you a hint. You were talking to him at John Price's party."

When Conor still didn't answer, his heartbeat in sync with the uptempo song from his laptop, she said, "At the raw bar."

Charlie had finally been apprehended. Something else to worry about. But if Emily was acting like it was a secret, that meant he hadn't ratted out Conor yet. Maybe he could get away with pretending he didn't know him. Or he could tell the truth that he'd met him at that bar in town, but lie that he hadn't given him the gate code or invited him onto the neck, and therefore he wasn't responsible for anything he'd done. Except he'd already told Lawrence it was law school friends.

This was small potatoes compared with what else he was hiding, but if he were discovered to be untruthful regarding the burglary, it would hurt his credibility otherwise.

"How'd they know it was him?"

"His dad was rooting through his drawers, thinking he was hiding drugs, and he found some diamond earrings, and they turned out to be Margie Baker's."

Conor was confused. "But . . . how would he know they were Margie Baker's?"

"He obviously put two and two together and figured out they were the earrings that were stolen."

"But how would his *dad* ever know that?"

"Anytime there's any wrongdoing on the neck, Lawrence makes it his business to know everything about it," she said.

It took Conor a moment to adjust to this information, to the relief that he had nothing to do with it, and to the unexpected, even traitorous, guilt he felt over his threatening accusation of Charlie.

"It was . . . your cousin? Bobby Nuke?"

"Yeah. Wait, who'd you think I was talking about?"

"No one," he said. "I just can't believe it. How'd you find out?"

"I saw him on the road a couple hours ago, and he told me. He and a friend from off the neck snuck into the Bakers' to raid the liquor cabinet, and they got drunk and found jewelry and made a really dumb mistake."

"And *he's* the one who wrote 'BLM' on their walls? Why would he do that?"

"You know that Black Lives Matter sign on the Newcombs' house?" Emily said.

"*That's* Lawrence Newcomb's house?"

Emily nodded. "So, the Bakers made some disapproving comment about it at an association meeting because they think people shouldn't put up political signs on the neck. Even though *they've* got that obnoxiously huge American flag on their porch, which is like a step away from a MAGA hat. Bobby heard about what they said, and that's what motivated him to break in in the first place, to take their liquor, and once they got drunk he took the jewelry and vandalized the place."

All that sleep he'd lost, thinking he was to blame and Lawrence Newcomb was going to expel him from the neck, and it was the lead investigator's son the whole time, with what could even be considered a reverse hate crime of sorts.

"So his dad knows the full story?"

"As of last night, yeah."

"What's he going to do to Bobby?"

"He made him give the earrings back to Margie Baker and apologize, obviously. Bobby wasn't going to pawn them or anything, but he was afraid if he returned them he'd get caught. And they're reimbursing them for painting over the graffiti."

Off Conor's appalled expression she said, "The whole thing's crazy, right? You promised you wouldn't tell anyone."

"That's *it?*" he asked. "Nothing else?"

"I mean, she's not pressing charges or anything. She's known him since he was a baby, and he was really remorseful."

"But they're not telling anyone else on the neck?"

"No. Bobby swore me to secrecy. He's not even telling the other cousins."

Conor snorted.

"What?"

"His dad had no problems grilling me when it happened, acting like the sheriff of the neck and more or less accusing me of doing it because I'd had some law school friends over that night to swim," he said. "Then when it turns out to be his son, he sweeps it under the rug."

"Yeah, but Bobby's never going to do anything like this again. He was actually crying today when he told me about it. He's a sweet kid and there's no way he would've done it if he wasn't drunk. It was a really dumb mistake, just a one-time thing. They're all completely mortified."

Conor paced the room, his blooming outrage supplanting his self-incriminating thoughts. The egregious hypocrisy and double standards and lack of accountability and tribalism. The rich granting pardons to their own, wiping the slate clean with crocodile tears and an apology. Lawrence was probably even the one paying for the paint job.

"If I *had* been the one to do it, I wouldn't get a second chance like that," he said.

"Well, yeah, of course."

"Why 'of course'?"

"Because you . . . aren't from here. I mean, they don't know you. They wouldn't be inclined to forgive you."

"Good to know where I stand," he said.

"I didn't mean it like that."

"Would *you* defend me? If I made a 'dumb mistake' like that?"

"You're a twenty-five-year-old lawyer," she said. "You'd never do it in the first place. Bobby's a twenty-year-old idiot who went into someone's house looking for alcohol and made a bad decision while he was drunk. It wasn't premeditated or anything. It's the kind of thing guys used to do all the time around here. My dad told me he did shit like this all the time when he was a teenager."

"So it's just part of life here," Conor said. "Rich boys will be boys, breaking into houses for alcohol, and sometimes they get a little tipsy and make a dumb mistake and steal diamond earrings and vandalize the place and don't confess until they get caught, and then all of a sudden they cry and show remorse. I wouldn't know, because when I was twenty I was working my ass off to get into law school and practicing tennis three hours a day so I wouldn't lose my scholarship."

Emily didn't have a response.

"You know, you talk about how everyone else here is a product of this culture," he said. "But when it comes down to it, you're from here, too."

CHAPTER 22

He slept poorly again. The fight with Emily hadn't helped, and every time he stirred awake he was bombarded with images and sounds of Catherine in the ocean. Also the worries, springing out like water from a punctured balloon, that he must have overlooked something in his cover-up. The most carefully planned murders were often discovered, and everything he'd done had been improvised and hastily acted on. There were a thousand ways he could be caught, through sloppiness or ignorance or simply bad luck. A thousand ways he *would* be caught.

What he'd done was all in self-defense of one kind or another. Maybe he could confess to just that, self-defense: he'd killed her, yes, but accidentally, with the stringing machine, and only after she'd attacked him in a drunken rage, irrationally jealous that he was in a relationship with her daughter. Understandably frightened that no one would believe him, he'd carried her corpse into the ocean.

After his lesson with Suzanne Estabrook, he asked if he could borrow her phone for a minute to look up an address, as he'd left his at home. In a private browser, he searched for Massachusetts sentencing guidelines for voluntary manslaughter. Three to twenty years in state prison plus victim restitution. And no one would believe it was just voluntary manslaughter after what he'd done not to be caught.

So he would have to remain not caught.

HE RETURNED TO CATHERINE'S HOUSE IN THE AFTERNOON. SHE HAD A few more texts from friends, all of which he reasoned he could ignore or like. He took the phone out for its daily walk, again scoping out the water for Catherine's body.

At home later, his mother FaceTimed him from the living room couch. "I haven't heard from you in a while," she said.

"I've been busy," he said. "Studying and preparing for this interview."

"Just working? You're not having any fun?"

He wouldn't be in this position if she'd found another job, if she'd made more money, if she'd remarried someone to help with the bills, if she didn't have health problems. Maybe even if she'd just been fucking open about the fact that her husband had killed himself and she hadn't made Conor keep it a secret all these years.

"I've been seeing a girl here." He'd decided a while ago that he wouldn't tell her about Emily until the summer ended and he was certain he'd be with her.

"I thought that might be the case," she said with a smile. For the past three years she'd lobbied, with decreasing subtlety, for Conor to reduce his workload and find a girlfriend.

She asked about her. After rattling off Emily's qualities—her intelligence, sensitivity, sense of humor—he added, "Her family's got a place here."

"I figured."

"I mean, she . . . comes from money. A lot. Even compared to the people here."

His mother paused. "Is she a good person?"

"Yes, of course."

"And she makes you happy?"

"Yes."

"Well, that's all that matters, Conor."

"I know that, Mom," he said defensively.

His mother got up with a grunt from the couch. He'd never thought much about their décor before, but, seeing it on his phone's screen, he was aware, for the first time, of the place's shabbiness. No, that was the wrong word; if anything, the furniture in Catherine's house and Emily's cottage was shabby to the untrained eye—frayed ends of rugs, sun-faded sofa cushions, cracked benches. But his eye had been trained over the summer and could now tell that their stuff was generations old, bought with old money, built to last decades, centuries, and that they disdained the shiny new crap destined for landfills that new money purchased. His mother's belongings weren't dirt cheap or falling apart. It was that they were *trying* to look fancy but weren't nearly up to snuff—faux materials, shoddily crafted, mass-manufactured in a country with no labor laws. In their failed ambitions, déclassé.

The place got awful light, too, and had low ceilings he could easily touch. He'd never been that bothered by it, but now that he was used to the cinematic sunsets and wide-open spaces of Cutters, it looked like a prison.

With raspier breaths than should have been necessary, his mother toddled into the kitchen and took a jar of olives out of the cupboard. "Have you met her parents?"

"They're divorced," he said. "Her dad doesn't come here anymore."

"What about her mother?"

"She's here."

"What's she like?

He scratched his nose. "I've only met her briefly a couple times."

She struggled to open the jar and wheezed as she labored.

"You all right, Mom?"

She nodded and ran the jar under hot water. She looked significantly older than she had when he'd left—heavier, less mobile. Someday she'd need a cane, then a walker, then a wheelchair. He wouldn't be able to attend to her at that point, so they'd have to hire an aide, assuming they could afford one. Maybe she'd qualify for Medicaid the next year, though that would augur poorly for her employment status. Until that happened or she found a full-time job, they would need to pay for overpriced, subpar insurance, skipping doctors' appointments because of the punitive copays and deductibles.

Not that many years from now, from diabetes or Covid or something else, his mother was going to die alone in that coffin of an apartment.

It was deeply unfair—no, un*just*—the more he thought about it, as she attempted to open the olive jar in their harshly lit, laminate-countertop kitchen. His mom—a woman who had been given little, worked hard for decades without much to show for it, raised a boy mostly by herself, and uncomplainingly shouldered setbacks that would embitter or demoralize most people—should be the kind of person who inherited millions of dollars, not someone whose poor health was either going to bankrupt her or lead to her early demise.

He had to get her out of there. She deserved a longer life, a better life, the kind every person on Cutters, young and old, took for granted. A life he couldn't provide for her even on a lawyer's salary.

"HOW'S YOUR FOOT?" EMILY ASKED WHEN HE CAME OVER. THEY'D EVEN-tually patched things up a little after their argument over Bobby, but their interactions the rest of the night had been stilted. It had exposed a chasm between them that they'd both always known was there but had mostly managed to bridge, or at least detour around.

"Still a little tender," he said.

She handed him a beer and pointed to his bandage. "And your scrape?"

"It's okay."

"You know it heals better if you expose it to the air overnight."

"No," he said. "I don't want to risk any infection."

"So," she said as they settled onto her couch, "I'm really sorry again about what I said last night, about Bobby. I've been thinking about it more, and for the record, if you did somehow do something dumb like he did—which you wouldn't, but for the sake of argument, if you did—I'd absolutely be on your side."

"You don't have to apologize," he said. "I got worked up over nothing."

"No, you had a point. I'm from here, as much as I try to deny it. An insider. And you're an outsider. But—and I know this sounds corny . . ." She looked embarrassed. "I only want to be an insider with you. Not with anyone else. Even Olivia. You've kind of become it for me."

He'd been a fool all along to think anything mattered but Emily. He should have known better than to chase the erotic magnetism of Catherine. Beauty fades, as Richard said, and sex fades even faster. This was lasting: being an insider with someone else, the two of you becoming it for each other.

"Me, too," he said, embracing her.

But he couldn't allow her to get too far inside now. No matter how intimate he got with anyone, with Emily—assuming they managed to remain together after what he'd done—this stayed secret forever. It was a kind of solitary confinement in lieu of criminal punishment, a loneliness he'd have forever.

Were Bobby in his position, Lawrence Newcomb would help him wriggle out of the consequences. Conor's dad wasn't even around to be useless. He had to fend for himself, as he'd always done.

He could do it. All of it, now and in the future. He was used to lonely secrecy.

"I think I saw your mom out on your pier late the other night, through the window," he said, laying the groundwork for the drowning. "Does she ever go there at night?"

"Not that I know of."

"Well, I saw someone coming back from there. I assumed it was her."

"People sometimes use our pier, even though they're not supposed to. Could've been anyone."

Before they went to bed, she asked if he could fix a nail protruding from a wall in the back room that she'd snagged her shirt on earlier.

"You have a hammer?"

"No," she said. "There's a tool kit in my mom's house. I could ask her to leave it out for me tomorrow."

"Don't bother," he said. "I'll figure something out."

The nail was popping out half an inch from the wood, likely caused by the permanent moisture in the air. Conor went outside and found a flat stone from the nearby woods.

"Can I watch?" Emily asked when he returned. "It's sexy when you work like this."

He shrugged and bludgeoned the nailhead with the stone. It wasn't as effective as a hammer, but after several bashes he drove the nail into the wood. The clean, strong contact felt like a forehand on the sweet spot that hurdled the net and kissed the baseline—the joy of exerting mastery over an obstacle in the physical world.

There'd been a split second upon impact when he'd had that same pleasurable feeling of connecting with the stringing machine.

He went to the back door and threw the stone as far as he could into the woods.

CHAPTER 23

He'd reached the final phase of his plan.

When he took Catherine's phone out for its morning walk, there were a couple of texts he couldn't easily ignore or swat away with likes, including one from a woman on the neck confirming Catherine's attendance at an outdoor dinner party for that night.

"So sorry for the late notice but I had a terrible night's sleep and am not feeling up for it," he texted, in what he thought was a passable imitation of Catherine's somewhat formal writing with this particular friend. "Could I take a rain check?"

The second message was from Emily. She'd forgotten that her Brooklyn rent had gone up five hundred dollars, and she now owed two months' back rent plus next month's; could Catherine authorize her accountant to raise the monthly withdrawal from her trust into the rent account?

He was slightly befuddled by the request (did she really have an entire account dedicated solely to rent? And who *forgot* that their rent was raised by that much?) and irritated that her reckless spending had created this problem for him to solve. Emily had new clothes delivered to her cottage weekly, and a pair of glasses had recently arrived with the same prescription as her perfectly good old ones. Conor thought he'd misread it when he first saw the receipt: they cost nearly a *thousand* dollars, and she hadn't even bothered to use health insurance.

"Yes," he replied. Emily would notice verbal anomalies more than a friend of Catherine's would, and the two of them seemed to have terser communications. If she followed up before they "discovered" the drowning, he'd protract the process with excuses.

When Conor returned the phone to the house, he noticed a grocery delivery app on its home screen. The fridge was nearly empty. According to her purchase history on the app, she received grocery deliveries about twice a week and had last ordered them three days before her death. He'd need to put in at least one delivery immediately to maintain the appearance that she was still alive.

Catherine's past orders all had the same strict instructions for the deliveryperson to ring the bell and leave the groceries outside the front door. He couldn't hazard Emily's seeing him bring them inside. He turned on his phone and called her.

"I've got an upset stomach from nerves over the interview," he said. "Would you do me a huge favor and drive into town later to get me something from the pharmacy?"

Emily said of course, asking what he wanted and how soon he needed it. In the app, the fastest he could get an order delivered was for shortly after noon.

"I don't want to interrupt your morning work, and my interview's not till four. If you left around noon, that'd be enough time for the medicine to kick in."

She said she'd do it and wouldn't dawdle at his door in case John was around. Conor repeated Catherine's last order in the app. He had to stay in the house to keep an eye on Emily's garage or else he wouldn't know if she'd left.

Her Prius drove off at around noon, and five minutes later the doorbell rang with the groceries. Conor waited until the courier departed, made sure no neighbors were walking within sight on the road, and brought in the shopping bags. He stored most of the food in the fridge and cupboards, opened a few containers of perishables, and took a bag with him to throw out later to account for Catherine's consumption. (Even as a necessary act of survival, wasting edible—and expensive— food made him wince.) He raced back to his cabin before Emily arrived.

"You feeling okay enough for the interview?" Emily asked as she handed him the medicine at his door. "You look kind of sweaty."

"I'll feel better when this is all over," he said.

• • •

JOHN HAD LENT HIM A NAVY BLAZER, A WHITE DRESS SHIRT, AND A NAVY tie, all from Brooks Brothers. Fifteen minutes before the interview was to start, Conor was unable find the tie despite the paucity of hiding spots in his cabin. He was already a subpar candidate; now he'd look like he couldn't be bothered to dress up, too. He had to acknowledge it at the top.

"I seem to have misplaced the tie John lent me," he told the lawyer conducting the interview over Zoom. "I suppose the pandemic is the new casual Fridays."

"Don't worry about it," said his interviewer. "First-round interviews are pretty relaxed."

His utter indifference confirmed Conor's suspicions: this was merely a favor to John. He had neither the CV nor the connections (aside from being John's tennis pro, which was somehow worse). The position was destined to go to someone from Harvard or Yale—or to a nepotistic brat whose uncle was a partner.

After the questioning, the lawyer told him they'd be in touch "if we go to a second round," and part of him welcomed the certain rejection. At least he wouldn't have to be anxious about it anymore.

THAT NIGHT, CONOR STOLE INTO CATHERINE'S HOUSE, RINSED A GOLD-rimmed wineglass—better odds Emily would recognize it as theirs over a standard glass—and brought it out to the private pier on her property.

Over beers in the cottage, Conor told Emily the interview had been a bust. She asked if he wanted to watch something light to take his mind off it.

"I've been looking at screens and reading all day," he said. "Let's go sit outside somewhere."

Once they were out of the cottage, he pointed to the pier. "Want to sit there?"

"Aren't you worried my mom will see us?" she asked.

"I forgot to tell you, John said something the other day that made me realize whatever he said about not seeing anyone here was a joke that I was too nervous to get at the time," he said. "There wasn't anything about it in our contract, after all."

"Are you serious? All this time we've been hiding in the shadows because you didn't get a joke?"

"I guess so."

"Well," she said, "you're lucky, then. I'd have never gone for a chump like you if it wasn't against the rules."

They reached the pier and sat on a bench. An end-of-summer nip had begun to settle into the night air. The ocean was placid under a crescent moon. Far out in the water was a gargantuan boat.

"Look, the party yacht's here," Emily said.

Every year around this time, she explained, the same mysterious superyacht dropped anchor off the neck for about a week. No one knew who the owner was or ever saw who was on board, but the cousins had heard that the yacht cost around $25 million.

"*Twenty-five?*" Conor asked. "That's what your mom's house is worth."

Emily wrinkled her forehead at him.

"I assume it's around that," he said. "But, seriously, who needs a boat that costs that much?"

"This is profoundly shameful to admit, but my dad owns a yacht that's not quite as big, so not as expensive, but it's not far off."

"Well, he probably really likes sailing, if he grew up around here."

She shook her head. "It's not just for fun. He has—Jesus, this is embarrassing—he has a captain on retainer who's on emergency call for him and his family, and it's got supplies to last a year. He thinks there's going to be an apocalypse, and the yacht's his escape hatch. He even has a plan for how to deal with pirates."

"What kind of apocalypse?"

"He's convinced that everyone but the superrich will die in the next few decades from a nuclear attack, or another pandemic, or societal collapse, or something we haven't even thought of," she said. "He sounds a little cuckoo when he talks about it. But he's also pretty smart about these kinds of things, and he talks to high-level people in government all the time who must be giving him the inside scoop, and I know he left for his place in the Hamptons way before anyone else started to freak out about Covid. So I'm not sure what to think."

It did sound cuckoo to Conor—yet, a year earlier, so would have talk of a novel virus that nearly brought the world to a standstill. Already it had become clear that the pandemic's worst comorbidity was poverty, and future catastrophes would only widen the gulf between the haves and have-nots. If he wasn't going to be aboard Thomas Remsen's luxury yacht, or even John Price's one-third share of his sloop, then he and his mother needed their own escape hatch of some kind.

"Is there room on the boat for us?" Conor asked, not really joking.

"He'd actually be way into you," Emily said. "He's self-loathing about being born on third base. It's like his one redeeming quality. He once told me the only men he really respects in business are the rare ones who didn't grow up with money and who're motivated by beating guys like him. The rich boys." She smiled. "Probably why I'm into you, too."

"That yours?" Conor asked, pointing in the darkness to the wineglass he'd planted on the opposite bench. He picked it up to justify any of his fingerprints on it and handed it to Emily.

"One of my mom's," she said.

"Told you I saw her out here."

Emily rotated it by the stem. "It's not like her to leave a wineglass out. Especially one of these heirloom ones. She's not sloppy like that."

"I'm sure she just didn't see it in the dark."

"Maybe," she said. "I'll bring it to the house later."

He paused an appropriate beat. "Actually, you should keep it for the cottage," he said with a half laugh. "She's got— I'm sure she's got a million of them, and you don't have any."

"Because I never drink wine," Emily said, and switched to the goon's voice her mother had used: "'I like beer.'"

"Well, *I* might like to drink wine once in a while, and it'd be nice to have a wineglass for it."

"Oh! Pardon me! I didn't realize your tastes had become so refined, my good sir. Can you only quaff from a vintage wineglass now?"

"It seems reasonable to want to drink wine from a wineglass once in a while," he said without laughing along.

"Just making a joke," she said. "Don't get so testy."

As they walked back to the cottage, Emily glanced at the big house. "That's weird. All her lights are off."

They'd been off for days, but the view from her cottage captured only the front of the house, whose darkness wouldn't have caught her attention, and he'd worried that leaving some on perpetually would have looked odd.

"She's asleep. Or she's at someone's house."

"She'd be back by now if she had dinner somewhere. And it's not even ten thirty—she's usually up later." She stopped, looked at the wineglass in her hand, then back at the house. "Maybe I should check on her."

"I bet she had some wine and went to bed early," Conor said, looping his arm around Emily's waist and steering her toward the cottage. "Let's watch something funny. I want to forget about today."

CHAPTER 24

When Conor picked up Catherine's phone the next day around noon, there were several texts and missed calls from Emily that morning asking whether her mother had gotten the accountant to raise the withdrawal limit from the trust, with the last few texts demanding to know why she wasn't responding.

Afraid she might sound an alarm if he continued to delay, Conor texted from the bedroom. *Sorry. Went to bed early last night and didn't see these until now*, he wrote. *I'll reach out to accountant soon.*

Emily wrote back right away: *Can you do it ASAP? Or at least write me a check? Landlord demanding money by Friday.*

He couldn't say no, but if he told her that Catherine would do it, then Emily would pester her until she received confirmation, and he wanted to keep the exchanges with her to a minimum. While he stood there deciding how to thread this verbal needle, Emily called Catherine's phone. He let it go to voice mail.

A minute later, the front door opened.

"Mom?" Emily said downstairs. "Hello?"

Conor didn't move.

"I'm coming in!" she yelled. "I'm wearing a mask!"

He heard her enter the house and, it sounded like, go into the kitchen.

She'd eventually come up to Catherine's bedroom, maybe poke around in the closet. Lacking any better options, he made a break for one of the bedrooms down the hall, walking as gingerly as possible, but a floorboard groaned.

"Anyone home?" Emily's voice called up.

He veered into the first room he passed, which had been shut. All the other doors on the hall were at least partially open, though, so closing it again would draw her attention and might make a sound. The room was completely empty, without even a closet to hide in. He flattened himself against the wall behind the door.

Emily's old room. Probably where Jacob had briefly slept, too.

She called out again for her mother downstairs. Then he heard her start up the stairs.

If she found him, he'd have to lie and say he was looking for her mother, that he'd been worried about her after their conversation last night, and the reason he was in this room was he'd come upstairs and heard her phone buzzing in there.

He heard her go into the bedroom. "Mom?" she said. "You in here?"

Catherine's phone buzzed with a call in his pocket. Emily's name was on the screen. He moved fast to quell the vibrations then turned the phone off altogether.

There were no sounds of movement from the adjacent room. Either she was figuring out what to do next or she'd heard the buzzing and was calling again in an attempt to locate the phone. It was too late to use his cockamamie story of searching for Catherine and hearing the phone. And once she was declared missing, this would nail him as a suspect.

"Hello?" Emily said loudly out in the hall.

Her footsteps stopped right outside his room.

"Someone there?"

He held his breath and didn't move, paranoid she could hear the internal sounds his body was generating: a humming in his own ears, the tackiness of his dry mouth, his heart's percussive rhythm.

Then her steps retreated and descended the stairs, and the front door opened and closed.

It was only a matter of time until she searched more thoroughly for her mother and determined she was missing. The bite marks remained, and Catherine's scent might still be detectable in his cabin, but he couldn't wait any longer.

He waited until she was long gone, made certain she wasn't outside, and turned on the phone once he was back on the shoreline path. Emily had sent another text requesting Catherine call or talk to her in person.

Accountant may be on vacation, he wrote. *Can't find checkbook now. But there's always money. I'll get it to you by Friday.*

Where are you now? Emily texted. *Can we talk?*

There was only one way to justify a refusal to verbally communicate with her.

Out for a walk now for fresh air, he replied. *Woke up with sore throat. It's my only symptom but hurts to talk and don't think I should be near anyone else.*

After Emily texted that she hoped she was okay and would check up on her later, he returned to Catherine's house and hid the phone under the kitchen sink, wrapped in soundproofing rags, in case Emily came looking for her again. He'd be back for it that night, when he would fake her drowning.

HE TOLD EMILY HE NEEDED TO STUDY THROUGH DINNER. AT NIGHTFALL, wearing his dishwashing gloves, he retrieved Catherine's phone from under the kitchen sink and replaced it in her bedroom, writing Emily that she still had a mild sore throat but no other symptoms. He took a towel from the bathroom, found a summer dress and casual sandals in the closet, and grabbed a pair of underpants from the wicker laundry hamper in there.

The underpants were silky and black. He'd probably rolled this exact pair down her thighs half a dozen times.

Back in the kitchen, he opened a bottle of chardonnay from the fridge, dumped it down the drain, overflowed a wineglass with water and left it in the sink to remove any trace of potential fingerprints and lip smudges, and placed the bottle and cork on the counter.

He brought the clothing and towel to the pier and arranged everything on the bench to appear as though Catherine had gone for a wine-drenched nighttime skinny-dip, a Cutters pastime. Then he booked it home, returned the dishwashing gloves, and came back to Emily's cottage.

No more chicanery was required of him. Everything could unfold as it naturally would have had Catherine really drowned on her own.

"What do you want to do?" Emily asked him.

"Whatever," he said. "We can watch a movie."

"It's been a long time since we, you know . . ." she said.

They hadn't had sex since Catherine's death. It was the last thing he'd wanted to do.

"I'm kind of beat. Maybe another time."

She looked hurt. "You've never turned down sex. Ever."

It was true; he'd leapt at every opportunity, hoping each occasion might be the one that finally broke through her "blockage." Down the road, if a police officer asked her if Conor had been acting unusual at all around the time of her mother's disappearance, he didn't want her remembering this.

"Well, maybe I just got a second wind," he said. "Yeah, there it is."

They fooled around, but this time the blockage was Conor's.

"This has never happened to me before," he said.

"Is it something about . . . me?" Emily asked.

"Of course not," he said, again not wanting her to think anything was off. "Let's keep trying."

As they kissed and grappled in the nude, Conor fantasized about sexual experiences that would take him far from this one, far from this place. Ally, girls in New York, the Halloween party sophomore year of college when he'd had a threesome with two seniors from the women's team. Nothing worked.

Without inviting it in, he thought of the first time Catherine had brazenly bumped her ass against him on the tennis court.

Not only did this give him an instant erection, but before he could transition to intercourse, before he even knew what was happening, he came, as if his body were trying to expel a toxin.

"Sorry," he said. "I don't know what happened."

"I'll take it as a compliment," Emily said. "Let me get some paper towels. These sheets are new."

He lay there, soaked in embarrassment, until something worse occurred to him: the only other time this had happened to him.

That was what he'd overlooked, the enormous crater in his planning. He'd last had sex in Catherine's bed in July, so his DNA was surely gone from there by now. But it was all over her Mercedes.

CHAPTER 25

The next morning, he smuggled rags and a spray bottle with white vinegar and water into Catherine's house, found her car key in her bag in the bedroom, and let himself into the dark garage. With the aid of the roof lights and his phone's flashlight, he examined the interior of the car.

A constellation of faint white discolorations speckled the roof and the leather upholstery of the back seat; they'd had sex there, too, after his premature episode. He tested the spray on a small area of the back seat but failed to remove the stain completely. He could try a harsher cleaning agent or bleach, but it would noticeably damage the leather, and, as with the floor of his cabin, might not remove all the DNA. Time would likely flake off all the dried, microscopic spots of semen, but he didn't have time.

The musty air of the garage tickled his nose, and before he could think to cover his face, he sneezed three times in succession, powerful blasts that shotgunned the car interior.

Fuck. Only a professional detailing could adequately remove his traces, and that was obviously out of the question.

Once Catherine was discovered to be missing, especially under presumption of drowning, the first place they'd search for clues after her house would be her car. Simulating a swimming accident was no longer an option.

It took him the rest of the day to come up with another plan.

WHEN IT WAS DARK, HE RETRIEVED ALL OF CATHERINE'S POSSESSIONS from the pier. Before going over to Emily's, he stashed his backpack in some bushes on the periphery of Catherine's property.

At Emily's cottage, he checked his email, as much to avoid conversation as for any interest in his inbox. Then he saw the first few words of the message from John's firm: "Dear Mr. O'Toole, we are pleased to invite you . . ."

He'd made it to the second round of interviews in September.

His heart jumped at the news then crashed just as fast. This was exactly what he'd wanted, professionally, all spring and summer—all three years of law school—and now it seemed pointless. He'd not only wrecked his life, he'd wrecked a potentially great life.

"What's wrong?" Emily asked.

He told her what the email said.

"That's amazing! Why don't you look happy?"

"I'm sure it's just another favor to John."

"Stop being so self-effacing," she said. "Remember, you always get whatever you want. You're a condo salesman. You're a *badass*."

He grew antsier as bedtime neared. Up to then he'd simply had to do things, and to do them immediately, to turn into a being of pure, present-tense action. Now he had to think ahead of the complicated mission he had mapped out for the next several hours, and premeditation invited countless doubts.

"I'm feeling a little wired," he said when they were getting ready for bed. "Maybe it's the interview news. Can I have one of your sleeping pills?"

Emily was a fitful sleeper who often woke in the middle of the night, except when she took her prescription sleeping pills, which she restricted herself to using twice a week for fear of becoming dependent on yet another medication. "You sure? They're pretty intense."

"Yeah, I've been sleeping badly."

She handed him a pill from the bottle in her bedside table. "You're not taking one, too?" he asked.

"I'm ready to pass out. And I've already had two this week."

"Would you take one, so I'm not doing it by myself?"

"Oh, Conow's a widdle scaywed to take a sweeping piw awone? All right, fine." Emily popped a pill into her mouth and swallowed it with her beer, which she offered to him.

"I don't want to mix it directly with alcohol the first time I take it," he said. He went to the bathroom, turned the faucet on and off, dropped the pill into the toilet, peed, and flushed. When he came back, he set his phone on "Do Not Disturb," not airplane mode, and placed it under Emily's bed.

Once she was asleep, he crept out of bed without waking her, carried his clothes and sneakers to the front door, and quietly left. He was trembling, his nerves acting up in a way they never had on the tennis court. He dressed outside, found his backpack, and returned to the patio of Catherine's house.

He could go back to Emily's and leave well enough alone. Maybe they wouldn't search the car that carefully, or he could try cleaning it again—this might be further incriminating himself unnecessarily. It wasn't just getting hit and hitting back harder, his dad might say.

Well, fuck his dad. His dad just gave up. No mental toughness. If it were him, he'd probably run straight to the cops and write out his confession.

He stopped shaking and went inside.

Upstairs, with the dishwashing gloves on, he collected Catherine's phone, laptop, and bag, which contained her wallet and the car key. From her bathroom he took her electric toothbrush and its charger, then rifled through the medicine cabinet for any prescriptions she'd bring with her. One name stood out: lorazepam, the same medication Emily had just taken and which he'd pretended to ingest for insomnia. Catherine's bottle was half full. He quickly calculated, based on his estimate of how many pills were left and when it had been prescribed, that she took the full dosage each day.

He flushed the remaining pills down the toilet and dropped the empty bottle into the bathroom wastebasket.

Conor brought everything downstairs to the garage. There was no way to lift the door manually. The clicker was in the messy console, hidden under the cord of the phone charger. When he clicked the button, the garage door retracted with a screech so piercing he was certain it would wake Emily inside the cottage. If her light turned on, he'd hightail it out through the patio door and claim that he hadn't been able to sleep and had gone for a walk.

He waited two minutes. The sleeping pill was evidently potent enough. He backed the car out, closed the garage door behind him, and cruised down the road at a regal pace to avoid attracting attention. If someone saw him in her Mercedes, that would be the end.

Halfway to the gate, two of the college kids were walking in his direction on the driver's side of the road. It was dark out, and they were probably drunk or high. But they still might see his face.

He flicked on his brights. They shielded their eyes from the beams and stepped aside as he passed. Only after they were out of sight did he realize he could've been wearing his mask, somewhat reasonably, to conceal himself. He put it on.

He made it off the neck without further incident, entered a distant Cape Cod town into the map on Catherine's phone, pulled onto I-195, and drove east.

CHAPTER 26

He'd been driving for half an hour, hovering just below the speed limit. He'd safely researched that there were no tollbooths on his route, but the farther he went, the greater the risk of encountering a highway camera (though it was dark and he was well hidden in his mask) or of something else disastrous, most of all an interaction with a patrolman.

He pulled onto the shoulder of the highway, ripped the E-ZPass tollbooth transponder off the windshield and threw it out the window, and yanked off the right dishwashing glove. On Catherine's phone he sent a text to Emily, who had written asking her mother how she was feeling. She habitually turned her phone off before bed and wouldn't see it until morning—provided she slept through the night.

Making it appear Catherine was heading back to New York would be a mistake; she surely had a doorman building, and her absence would be readily noticed. An arbitrary trip would raise red flags. He'd had to pick someplace relatively nearby in Catherine's milieu but to keep the destination vague, and there was only one area he could think of that fit that description.

· *Over my sore throat*, he wrote. *Was feeling stir crazy, decided to go to the cape. Will stay in motels to avoid covid. Calling accountant soon.* That also covered her health and the suddenness of her departure, and bought a few more days before Emily inquired about the accountant.

He continued east for another fifteen minutes, turned Catherine's phone off, exited the highway, and got back on in the opposite direction.

It was two in the morning when he arrived in Providence, an easy journey along I-195. He crossed over the Providence River and parked near the water. After confirming that there was nothing in the trunk of the Mercedes identifying its owner, he set out on foot with Catherine's laptop, bag, phone, and the car's registration from the glove compartment.

In a full trash can on the street, he buried Catherine's credit cards, her driver's license, and anything else that had her name on it. He ripped up the registration and peeled the labels off her prescription bottles and threw them out, too—better to get rid of everything in one place than scatter her possessions and multiply the chances of an item's discovery. He discarded the wallet, but not before taking its eighty-three dollars in cash; this mundane theft, strangely, felt in some ways like the most criminal act he'd perpetrated.

Then he walked to the middle of a nearby pedestrian bridge. No one was in the vicinity, and the water appeared deep. After wiping down her phone for fingerprints yet again and removing the SIM card with a paper clip he'd brought, he tossed it into the river along with Catherine's laptop.

The last known location of her phone would be somewhere on the highway going to Cape Cod.

HE STOPPED AT A RED LIGHT, ROLLED DOWN HIS WINDOW, AND, OBSCUR-ing his dishwashing glove–clad hands, asked a pedestrian for directions to the bus station now that he was mapless. Once he was within walking distance of the station, Conor roamed around for an unsafe-looking side street that wouldn't attract the notice of a police cruiser. It took him a while to find one that met both criteria, on a block with a number of boarded-up houses.

Déclassé entered his head.

He parked and got to work with the bleach and rags he'd brought in his backpack, dousing all the semen stains he found and dabbing the roof, doing what he could to get the DNA degradation process started; it no longer mattered if the bleach stood out. He wiped down anything else he might have touched without his gloves on, too.

When he was satisfied, he rolled down the driver's side window all the way and left the key in a visible spot on the dashboard.

THERE WERE A FEW TAXIS LINED UP OUTSIDE THE BUS STATION AT THIS hour, but they were all app-based services. Conor asked the first driver if he could pay his fare to the village near Cutters in cash, to cut out the middleman, but was refused. The second agreed. Conor paid in advance, kept his mask on and didn't speak, and upon arrival tipped 20 percent so that nothing about the ride would be memorable. From there he walked back to the neck.

The sun was just breaching the horizon when he reached Emily's cottage. He opened the door and tiptoed into the bedroom as she slept. He removed his clothes and was taking off his socks when she stirred.

"Conor?" she murmured. "Are you getting dressed?"

"Shh," he said, sliding into bed and spooning her. "Go back to sleep."

Within a minute she was lightly snoring.

Catherine's Mercedes would almost certainly be stolen from the spot he'd left it in, and even if it wasn't, he'd done a decent job getting rid of his DNA. Her phone had been traveling toward Cape Cod, with her last text to her daughter corroborating her destination. His own phone had been connected to the router in the cottage the whole night.

As far as anyone would know, he'd been in Emily's bed the entire time Catherine Havemeyer had taken off in the middle of the night for a trip and disappeared, either of her own volition or somebody else's.

CHAPTER 27

After Conor's lesson with John in the morning, Emily called to report on her mother's late-night text. "It's weird," she said. "She doesn't even *like* Cape Cod."

"Does she have friends there?" he asked.

"Not that I know of. And she said she's staying in motels, which is also strange. I don't think my mom's stayed in a motel in her life. I'm not sure she completely knows what a motel *is*."

"It's to avoid Covid," he reminded her.

"I know, but— Wait, how'd you know that was why?"

"That's what people are doing now instead of hotels."

"Oh," she said. "By the way, did you get undressed when you got into bed last night?"

"When I got into bed? Of course I undressed."

"Not the first time you got into bed. Later in the night."

"No," Conor said. "But I remember when I came back from the bathroom, you woke up and rambled incoherently about my clothes. It must have been from the sleeping pill."

He spent the day apart from Emily. He couldn't make even another small mistake like the one about the motel.

WHEN HE ARRIVED AT HER PLACE AT NIGHT, EMILY WAS STILL ON THE subject of her mother's abrupt departure.

"She didn't respond to my texts today," she said. "I feel like she's been avoiding me for a while now. She wasn't answering my calls or texts before this trip, and then she told me she missed them because she was going for a walk. She *never* goes for walks."

"Everyone's taking walks now during the pandemic," Conor said. "And it's not like the two of you ever hang out or talk on the phone much, anyway. She's on vacation and probably not in a rush to get back to you."

"Yeah, but she's supposed to . . . it's awkward telling you this, but she's supposed to raise my withdrawal limit from my trust because my rent's going up. And my landlord keeps hassling me about getting him the money."

"How much is it going up?"

"Five hundred, but I owe for three months."

"Can't you call the accountant yourself?"

"I'm not authorized to make any changes without her permission."

"And you don't have fifteen hundred bucks anywhere?"

"I'm really bad with money," she said.

Conor took out his phone.

"What're you doing?"

"I just Venmoed it to you."

"No!" she said. "Absolutely not! Take it back!"

"Don't worry about it. I've got enough."

Emily continued to threaten to return the money to him, but he insisted. "God, I don't know what I'd do without you," she said. "I mean it. I'll pay you back the second I get it from my mom. I'll text her right now that I had to borrow the money from a friend. That'll make her act faster."

"Don't bother," he said. "Let her enjoy her vacation. I'm sure she wants to be left alone."

She gave him an accusatory look. "*You're* not avoiding me, are you?"

"How am I avoiding you? I'm here now."

"Not physically. You've just been really distant lately."

"You keep saying that. I'm not."

He'd meant to be reassuring, but it came out as aggravated. She was silent for a moment before her eyes welled up. "I'm sorry," she said.

"For what?"

"For being so needy."

"You're fine," he told her, but it again sounded like he'd had his fill of her, and her crying amplified.

"You can break up with me," she said. "It's okay. I understand."

"I'm not gonna break up with you, Emily."

"You *should*." She wiped her nose with her arm. "For your own good. I've thought about this a lot. I'm holding you back. Maybe not now, but eventually. I'm like a wounded bird who can barely leave the nest. And you're a rocket ship, flying to all these places on your own power. You could be, like, a senator or something if you wanted. You've already got your mom to look out for. You don't want another person to take care of who doesn't have her shit together."

He didn't know what to say to pacify her. Beyond not wanting to break up with Emily—he'd already decided she was his whole future—he needed to be with her to keep her calm over her mother's disappearance. But as it had with Catherine, her sobbing did something to him physically. He kissed away her salty tears. Within a minute they were taking each other's clothes off more urgently than they ever had.

She was wetter than usual when he slid inside her. Emily pulled him in deeper.

"That feels good," she said softly, the first time she'd spoken during sex.

He sensed a difference in her. After she began making quiet grunts of pleasure, he took a chance, twined his fingers in hers, and slowly brought them over to where their bodies joined. Then he raised his torso to clear room and let go of her hand. Her fingers crept down her abdomen.

"Little slower," she instructed him.

He reduced his pace, listening to her signals until he reached the ideal rhythm, a rocket ship launching himself into her. Her panting grew faster and louder, her stomach contracting with each breath.

"Oh my God," Emily whispered, not so much out of ecstasy as incredulity. "Oh my God."

Her mouth open wide, she sucked in a sharp lungful of air and quaked below him.

As Emily Remsen achieved an orgasm during intercourse for the first time in her life, Conor imagined her birth control failing and spreading his seed within the English-blooded great-great-whatever-granddaughter of the second governor of the Plymouth Colony and, with the fertile gush that immediately arrived, spawning a child who would someday stamp the name of the low-born O'Tooles of County Offaly on the deed to the palace crowning Cutters Neck.

"I can't believe it," Emily said in the afterglow, their limbs in a hot pretzel. "I can't fucking believe it. Don't worry, I'm not gonna require crying as foreplay from now on. And it wasn't from that, anyway. I could just feel the blockage was . . . gone. Oh my God. This changes everything." She laughed in shocked disbelief, kissed him, and went to the bathroom.

She was right—it did change everything. This was the one nagging defect in their relationship, which had appeared as though it were never going to be remedied. But they'd gotten over it. He could have a good sex life with her. Maybe even as good as it had been with Catherine.

Her mouth at the end, open, gasping for air. Like Catherine's in the water.

"Conor?" Emily asked when she climbed back into bed. "What's wrong? Are you . . . crying?"

What had been building up inside him for months without relief and for days without sleep was finally expressing itself against his will. The facts were plain and indefensible. He'd been having sex with Emily's mother for money while also sleeping with her. Rather than own up to his behavior, he'd attacked Catherine. And then he'd stalked her in the water and savagely drowned her.

He couldn't tell her all of this. But he could partially unburden himself. He'd say Catherine had enlisted him for tennis lessons over the summer, commanded him not to inform Emily, developed an obsession, and ordered him to break up with her daughter or else she'd find some legal means of cutting off her trust fund payments. He'd refused, she'd hit him with the racquet, and the rest played out as it had in his previous hypothetical confession of self-defense in which, after the accidental death, he'd gotten rid of her body. Emily hated her mother and knew she was jealous; she would believe him, and might even understand it had happened because he'd had no choice, and she'd keep it a secret with him. It wouldn't be so lonely if she also knew, and he wouldn't feel so guilty if she believed that he'd done it to protect her—which he had, in part.

"Conor?" she asked. "Whatever it is, you can tell me."

No. Of course he couldn't tell her. Ever. She wouldn't understand. There was nothing to understand. No matter how much she'd loathed her mother, no matter how convincing he made it sound that his hand had been forced, that he was only defending himself and her, she was still her blood, and Conor would always remain an outsider who wouldn't be forgiven for something this atrocious.

There was only one thing he could do to make things, if not right, then less wrong: atoning. Not by confessing, but by committing himself to service to Emily. He'd devote himself to her in a way her parents never had, make her feel safe and loved, redress her loss.

That was the solution. He'd dedicate his life to taking care of her to make up for the life he'd taken away.

And, as a bonus, what he was about to suggest would further postpone her reaching out to the police.

"*What?*" she said after he'd popped the question.

"Will you marry me?" he repeated.

She looked quizzical. "I can't tell if you're joking."

He wiped away some tears and sniffed. "It's not a joke. I'm asking if you'll marry me."

"But, Conor . . . now? After two months together?" She'd gone from tender to sensible in the span of a minute. "We haven't even really talked about what we're doing after this summer."

"Not right now," he said. "But when we're ready. You've never thought about it at all?"

"Of course," she said. "Of course I have. But I thought it'd be a while till we had to make a decision. I'm twenty-three, you're twenty-five. We have plenty of time."

Richard would agree with her. And, given all the information, he'd also say that they were doomed from the start, no marriage could work after what had happened, and if Conor wasn't principled enough to turn himself in, the least he could do was spare Emily a lifetime of living with her mother's rent boy and murderer.

But if she remained ignorant, and if Conor, too, learned to operate as if it had never happened, then that was something. Unions predicated on worse mutual delusions existed.

"The pandemic has made me see that the world can be a lonely place," he said. "And that I've been lonely my whole life. I've told you before I want to take care of you. But I also want you to take care of me. I'm not always a rocket ship, you know."

He really did mean it. The two of them provided something for each other no one else in their lives had, maybe that no one else would. And certainly not now, not after this. He was tainted, even if no one ever found out. Only by marrying and tending to Emily could he remove that rot.

She didn't say anything for a long time. Then she laughed to herself.

"This is crazy," she said. "But fuck it. Yes."

"Really?"

"I mean, you *did* just give me my first orgasm during sex, so I can't say no to a lifetime of that," she said. "But, for real, you're the one I want to be with, so why not now? And it's sort of cool to get married so absurdly young. What's the worst that can happen? We get divorced? So does everyone. Might as well find out way before we have kids. You *do* want kids someday, right?"

He nodded—he really did; he'd do a better job of providing and being there for his children than his dad had for him—and they kissed, and she laughed again with incredulous giddiness. "Not to put the cart before the horse, but since we've never discussed any of this stuff, I want two. Not for a long time, don't freak out. One of each, preferably."

"That sounds good."

"And then . . ." She gave an embarrassed smile. "Could you maybe ask me in the traditional way?"

"Yes," he said. "Is it okay that I don't have a ring?"

She opened the top drawer of her bureau and removed a small box lined with emerald velvet. Inside was a diamond ring. "This was Gramily's," she said, her paternal grandmother. "She gave it to me when I was nine, just before she died."

She handed it to him. Conor didn't know from rings, but this one looked stratospherically beyond his means. He touched the diamond briefly, then bent to a knee and, like a courtly gentleman in an old novel, asked for her hand in marriage.

After she formally accepted, she said, "We don't have to start planning right away or anything, but even though I have complicated feelings about this place, when I was a little girl I always thought I'd have my wedding here. Once it's safe to have gatherings. Would you be up for that?"

"Of course," he said.

"Olivia's gonna be shocked when she finds out. I always thought I'd be the last of anyone I knew to be married." She smirked. "My *mom*'ll have an aneurysm when I tell her. I want to take your last name, too—she'll flip out when she realizes our branch of the Havemeyers is gonna die out."

"I was thinking maybe we should keep this to ourselves for a little bit," Conor said. "Just, you know, something for us to think about privately before we share the news."

"You mean you *don't* want to me to post it on Instagram with a picture of my ring finger seconds after your proposal?"

"So let's wait, I don't know, at least three days before we tell anyone," Conor said. "I won't even call my mom, just to make sure I don't let it slip."

CHAPTER 28

Each morning Conor woke up, he braced for news of the Providence police's either finding the abandoned Mercedes or arresting someone in connection with its theft. But no word arrived, and Emily seemed distracted enough by their engagement that she didn't bring up Catherine's silent absence.

After three days, Emily FaceTimed Conor at his cabin and proposed they jointly tell their mothers their big news over the phone.

His bite marks remained quite visible under the bandage, though to speed up healing he'd taken Emily's advice and exposed them to the air when he was alone. "I've got a lot of studying to do right now," he said.

"It won't take long to call them," she said.

"Don't you not even really care about telling your mom?"

"I'm kind of excited to see her reaction. Especially since she's met you. I know she's always thought I'd end up with some pathetic clown."

"Let's just hold off another day," he said. "When I can focus on it."

Emily screwed up her mouth guiltily. "I just texted my mom that I had something important I wanted to tell her over the phone soon. Sorry. I couldn't hold off."

"Just tell her never mind."

A few hours later Emily called back and said her mother hadn't replied yet.

"You told her never mind," Conor said. "And she's on vacation."

"I still feel like she's upset with me about something, but I can't think what."

"You always think you did something to make a person mad at you if they don't respond to you," he reminded her. "I thought you were working on it with your therapist."

"I am."

"So this is a good time to . . . what's the phrase you use, when you're supposed to stand back and look at what you're doing as if it was someone else?"

"The observing self."

"Try it out," he advised. "Imagine what you'd tell me if I was freaking out because my mom didn't reply right away."

Emily agreed to let it go. But when they reconvened that night in her cottage, she confessed that she'd called her mother several times. "It kept going straight to voice mail," she said. "And I texted that I needed to talk to her immediately, and still nothing."

"Maybe she's sleeping."

"At eight p.m.?"

"Or she's got bad reception on the Cape. I miss calls all the time here. I'm sure it's worse there."

Emily picked the label off her beer bottle. It looked like she might stop worrying about it.

"Something's weird about all this," she said.

Conor didn't answer.

"I could almost see her hiding out in the house and pretending to be gone," she said. "Can you come with me to look for her there? I'm scared to go alone."

It would be a good opportunity to explain why his scent, fingerprints, and DNA were in the house. They left the cottage, masked up, and rang Catherine's bell. After a few more unanswered rings, Emily opened the door and called out for her mother. They entered each room on the ground floor.

"Let's go to her room," Conor suggested. They went upstairs together, Conor in front. He started off toward Catherine's room before pretending he didn't know which one it was and deferring to Emily. They looked inside, and Conor examined the bathroom and closet.

"You check the other rooms up here, I'll go to the bowling alley and basement and garage," Emily said.

"There's a bowling alley?" he asked, raising his eyebrows. Emily shrugged.

"Her car's gone," she said when they reunited downstairs. "I called her doorman, and they haven't seen her."

"So she's on the Cape, like she said."

Emily pursed her lips in concentration.

"The mail," she said.

Conor trailed her outside to the mailbox. He'd completely forgotten about this, even with all the debate over mail-in ballots that summer. A thick stack of envelopes had accumulated.

"A bunch of things were postmarked way before she left," Emily said after thumbing through them. "As far back as the seventeenth."

"The mail's been slow all summer," Conor said. "It probably arrived after she left."

"And took, like, *ten* days?" Emily said. "I'm gonna take the golf cart and ask if anyone's heard from her."

He couldn't stop her now. He had to hope that the mail had been his only remaining oversight.

"I can go with you," he said.

"It's okay," she said.

"Well, then I'll go through the house once more, in case we overlooked anything." If his fingerprints remained anywhere else from his visits earlier in the summer, this would cover him, and it appeared Emily was getting close to contacting the authorities.

"I talked to people from around half the houses," Emily said when she returned from her expedition down the neck. "No one's seen her since the Beresfords' big party, which was over a week ago, or even really heard from her. Except for Celia Sturges, who says my mom canceled dinner plans with what sounds like a bullshit excuse."

"Huh," Conor said.

"Lawrence Newcomb's going to email the whole neck asking if anyone else has heard from her."

"Well, nothing else we can do now," he said. "Let's see if anyone responds. Might take a few days for everyone to see the email."

"I WANT TO CALL THE POLICE," EMILY SAID THE NEXT MORNING WHEN Conor returned from his lesson with John.

Further resistance from him would, at this point, look questionable and was mostly unnecessary. Catherine's car had almost certainly been stolen in Providence; if it had been impounded or otherwise wound up in the hands of the police, they would have heard by now. The bite marks were faint and still required use of a bandage, but it was cooler now and he could get away with wearing long sleeves.

"Okay," he said. "I'm sure you have to file something like this at the station in person. I think they'll take it more seriously if I go, as a lawyer, and a man, than if you do. They'll just think you're a daughter who's overreacting."

Emily acquiesced to his reasoning, and Conor prepared to leave. He'd downplay Catherine's absence, telling the police that his girlfriend's mother hadn't been seen for a little over a week, which didn't concern him, as she seemed like the kind of person who'd take off on a trip without being in touch with anyone, but Emily thought it was prudent to notify them anyway. He was certain that they would open a file but do little to nothing else immediately, and being the one to come to them first would be beneficial once the investigation deepened.

Just before he set out, Emily stopped him. "I want to come with you," she said.

"You don't have to," he told her. "It's just a formality, to open a case."

"I want to make sure they have all the info they need."

"I can call you if there's something I don't know."

"I looked up everything they can do." She spoke with a steely competence at odds with her checkered history as a personal assistant.

"They can search for her car and get her phone's location and her phone records and look up her credit card activity. But if they're lazy, they might not do it unless I force them to."

Conor nodded. He had to worry about more than just the police now. Emily was also on the case.

CHAPTER 29

The police station was a quaint brick-and-stone building out of a Norman Rockwell painting; it looked like the worst cases they handled in this sleepy township were for disorderly conduct at bars.

Partly due to its modesty, Conor felt no nervousness as he walked in. But he'd also taken care of the physical and digital evidence, created alibis when necessary, thought of everything big that could come back to bite him. These small-town cops would barely investigate Catherine's disappearance, let alone pin a murder on him.

Conor and Emily were the only civilians present, and when she explained why they were there, an officer at the front desk sent them into an unoccupied room. They sat in two chairs at a desk, and a few minutes later a gray-haired man wearing wire-rimmed glasses above his mask joined them.

"Good morning. I'm Detective Clark," he said, his mild New England accent pronouncing it closer to *Clahk*.

Emily recounted the pertinent details as the detective took notes on his computer. He appeared even more blasé than Conor had hoped.

"A few people got texts from her after that party, but no one else on the neck has seen her since the twenty-first," she said.

"The neck?" Clark asked. Emily had so far only told him that they had a summer house nearby.

"Cutters Neck."

The detective perked up. "Okay," he said. "I'll need you to give me a recent picture of her face so I can create a flier for any Jane Doe DOAs at nearby hospitals."

"DOAs?" Emily asked.

"Dead on arrival."

"You think she's . . . dead?"

Conor put his hand on Emily's leg. In lieu of his preferred solo role, he'd have to play the part of the supportive partner comforting his easily upset girlfriend—now fiancée—who jumped to ghastly conclusions.

"No, no," Clark said, likely regretting his blunt cop-speak. "It's just a first step to rule out anything else. Does her car have a navigation system? Even if it's not turned on, it makes our job a lot easier."

Emily squinted as she thought. Conor's heartbeat stuttered. He hadn't even thought to investigate the computer dashboard on the Mercedes. They'd find it, and whatever remnants of his DNA he hadn't been able to bleach out, within an hour.

"I don't think so," Emily said.

"You're positive?"

She nodded. "Both our phones weren't getting a signal once in Vermont, and her car didn't have anything we could use."

The tightness in Conor's body eased—but only a little. He may have made other mistakes that were beyond his technical knowledge.

Clark asked for Catherine's full name and birthday and typed on his keyboard. "No police contact so far with her plates," he reported. "Are there any distinguishing features on the car? Roof rack, dents, parking permit decals?"

Emily shook her head. "Nothing I can think of."

"No bumper stickers, nothing like that?"

"She'd never put a— No, nothing."

"If you can find a picture, send it to me. I'll put a BOLO on it— that's 'be on the lookout'—in a national database. If an officer anywhere runs its plates for anything, it'll come through the computer that it's wanted in connection with a missing-persons case."

"What about her phone?" Emily asked.

The detective's frame straightened with interest. "You've got her phone?"

"No. I didn't see it in the house, but I can look again."

"If you find it, bring it here. There's a lot we can find out if we have access to the device."

"Like what?"

"Texts, emails. When it hit different Wi-Fi routers, which would give us her exact locations before she left."

"Can't you call her phone company and find out all that stuff?"

"We can get CDRs—call detail records—in a day or two. That'll show us who her calls and texts are with, but not what's in the texts. We can issue a subpoena to her carrier to turn over the texts, but it'll be hard at this point to convince a judge to sign off on a warrant, and a lot of times the texts are lost, anyway. Emails are even harder to get. And you can only see the router data if you have the phone. Everything's a lot easier if we have it, even if we don't know the password."

"Can't you just ask her phone company to tell you where her phone is right now?"

"To go up on a phone immediately, you need an exigent circumstances exception. Would you be willing to swear to a judge that your mother is a danger to herself or others?" He phrased it in a way that suggested he knew, from experience, that most people would balk at the prospect of going through with this in a court of law.

"I guess she's not," she said. "There's nothing else you can do with her phone?"

"I apologize for putting it like this, but since your mother has a place on Cutters and owns a Mercedes"—*mothah, Cuttahs, Muh-cedes*—"does that mean she . . . has a good amount of money?"

"Well . . . yes," Emily said.

Clark nodded. "Good. Good. That'll make it easier to get a warrant for her cell tower info. It's imprecise, but it'll give us the general location."

It was hard to miss this suggestion that a rich person's life was considered worthier of law enforcement protection.

"Can you put out an alert for the police to stop cars that look like hers or anything?" Emily asked.

"Your mother isn't a child or elderly or mentally impaired," the detective explained. "There are no suspicious circumstances here. Odds are she went on a trip, just like she told you—her phone isn't working or she's not getting reception, and she's not checking or responding to her email. It's a free country, and people are entitled to go where they want without being in contact with anyone. We can't call in the cavalry every time this happens. This is all we can really do until we have cause to believe your mother's in danger."

Another reassuring response. The detective had no reason to think this was anything beyond a wealthy woman taking a trip on a whim without alerting anyone to her whereabouts.

"One more question," Clark said. "No one's seen her since the twenty-first. Between then and now, was there any moment something seemed amiss? Maybe you noticed her car was gone, anything like that."

"There was that one night all her lights were off," Emily said, glancing at Conor for confirmation. "It was the night we saw her wineglass on the pier, maybe a week ago. Though it's not that strange, I guess."

"Anything else?"

"Not really. I didn't think anything was off until I texted her that I had something important to tell her, and she didn't respond at all. That's when I started to get worried."

"What was the important thing?"

"That we got engaged," Emily said.

Clark again looked quite curious about this new piece of information, and Conor wished she hadn't revealed it. He'd been able to recede into the background thus far, but a shotgun engagement to the daughter of a missing woman from Cutters Neck would certainly arouse suspicion. Maybe he shouldn't have proposed to Emily at all. But she would have kept trying to reach her mother if he hadn't imposed a news embargo. And if he hadn't asked her now, if he hadn't locked it down, she might not ever have agreed once her mother was missing and presumed dead—in which case, everything he'd done would have been for naught.

"You got engaged? When?"

"When did you propose?" Emily asked Conor. "Four days ago?"

"I think so," Conor said. "Before we knew her mom was gone, of course."

"So the twenty-seventh?" Clark confirmed.

"That sounds right. Yeah."

"I thought"—the detective consulted his notes—"I thought you knew she was gone by the morning of the twenty-seventh. So you proposed *after* that?"

"Right," Conor said. "We knew she was traveling. Just not that she was . . . ignoring texts."

"I'm a little confused," Clark said. "If she didn't respond when you said you were engaged, and if that worried you, why'd you wait four days after that to come to the police?"

"Well, Conor—" Emily began.

"We both decided we wouldn't tell anyone about the engagement right away, including both our moms," Conor interrupted. "So we got engaged on the twenty-seventh, but we didn't actually reach out to Emily's mom till yesterday. So it was just one day. And, as we told you, we spent the whole day looking for her."

Clark added to his notes.

"So we can't do anything until you get those records?" Emily asked.

"Actually," the detective said, "me and my partner can swing by your mother's house later today and take a look around."

Emily might not have understood why he was suddenly up for a search, but Conor did. Thanks to her blurting out the news of their engagement the day after her mother left Cutters on an impromptu trip in the middle of the night, Clark had cause to believe that Catherine Havemeyer was in danger.

"I THINK THAT WENT WELL," CONOR SAID AS HE DROVE THEM AWAY from the station. "He sounded more competent than I expected."

Emily was quiet.

"Don't you?" he asked.

She was crying silently. He pulled over on a commercial street.

"I have a really bad feeling," she said. "Something's not right. This isn't like her at all."

"It's gonna be okay," he said. "It's like the detective said, she's somewhere on the Cape and she's just not checking her phone. Or she's not getting service." He hugged her and delivered more reassurances, but it wasn't working.

"Do you want to take a break from Cutters?" he asked. "Maybe go see Olivia?"

"She's camping in Australia with her boyfriend. I can't even call her."

"Someone else, then?"

Emily looked down. "I don't really have anyone else," she said.

"Do you want to call your dad?"

"I texted him. He said, 'Keep me posted.'"

Out her window was an upscale-looking coffee shop. "You haven't eaten yet today," he said. "Let's get you something in there."

They put on their masks and went into the coffee shop. Conor ordered a coffee from the barista, whose back was to him as she fiddled with the espresso machine. "What do you want, Em?" he asked.

As Emily stooped to survey the pastries under the glass, the masked barista turned around.

"Well," a familiar voice said to Conor. "Didn't think I'd see you again."

He was grateful to be wearing a mask. "Hi, there," he said cheerily. "How are you?"

"I'll get your coffee," Georgia said icily.

After Emily selected a croissant, he paid and left a large tip, stuffing the singles into the jar so that Georgia would see.

"Thanks so much," Georgia said. "*Really* nice of you."

"Who was that girl with the purple hair?" Emily asked when they were back in the car. "How does she know you?"

"I met her and some of her friends from around here at a bar at the very start of the summer, before I met you, and I invited them all to swim at Cutters that night," he said. "We ended up hooking up, to be honest. I sent her a polite text the next day saying I didn't think we should do it again. I guess she didn't think it was so polite."

Emily nibbled her croissant.

"I thought it was law school friends," she said after a minute.

"Hmm?"

"You told me you invited law school friends to swim. I remember because I'd wanted to ask you who they were, because I was insecurely thinking there was a girl involved, so I didn't end up asking. You didn't say it was strangers from town."

"Oh," he said. "Yeah. I told that to Lawrence so he wouldn't freak out. I knew they hadn't done anything, but if I said it was townies, he would've gotten the FBI involved."

"But why'd you tell *me* it was law school friends?"

"I guess I just . . . didn't want to tell you about a one-night stand, and saying it was strangers from town seemed like it would point to that. Sorry."

Conor sipped his coffee, and they didn't speak for the rest of the drive.

CHAPTER 30

Detective Clark arrived in a black Chevy that afternoon with his younger and stouter partner, Detective Sousa, whose biceps strained against his short sleeves. Both men's faces were exposed as they waited on the driveway, but they put on masks when Emily and Conor joined them.

"Shit—should I not be touching anything?" Emily asked when she opened Catherine's front door. "Because of fingerprints?"

"It's fine," Clark said. His cavalier attitude was comforting to Conor. Despite the detective's suspicions over the proposal, this visit was just ticking a box.

She showed them through the house and the garage, the pool, the pier, and the end of the neck. The search was cursory enough that the detectives didn't even notice the empty bottle of lorazepam in the bathroom wastebasket. They ventured out onto the dry boulders and peered in the crevices, then gave Emily's cottage a perfunctory examination.

"You been living here all summer?" Clark asked Conor.

"No, I'm in a cabin down the road. It belongs to the resident I'm giving tennis lessons to."

Even with his own additions, the bloodstains remained barely visible to the naked eye, and only if you were looking in the right spot for them. Volunteering it for a speedy appraisal by detectives eager to get on with their day would further suggest he was being helpful and might put off a future search.

"You want to see it?" he asked. "I mostly just use it as a base during the days."

"That's all right," Clark said. "Just keep calling Miss Havemeyer's phone every few hours and check in on her house. We'll be in touch."

CONOR HAD BEEN PUTTING OFF TELLING HIS MOTHER ABOUT THE ENgagement. But, no longer fearing an unexpected message from Catherine, he'd left his phone on a table when he went to get a glass of water in Emily's cottage, and she handed it to him as it buzzed. "It's your mom," she said.

He picked up and said hello as Emily watched him. "So, I should tell you something," he said. "It's good news. I got—Emily, the girl I was telling you about—we got engaged. I proposed to her a few days ago."

There was no response.

"Mom? You still there?"

"I'm here," she said. "I'm just . . . You've been together all of two months and you want to get married?"

Emily continued observing him.

"I know it's fast," he said. "But we didn't see any point in waiting." He gave her an opportunity to speak, but she didn't. "Normally this is when you say something like 'Congratulations.'"

"I haven't even talked to her yet," his mother said. "And you told me she's twenty-three? Are her parents okay with this?"

He took the phone into another room and shut the door.

"We haven't gotten the chance to tell them yet," he said. "She doesn't really have a relationship with her dad."

"Doesn't her mother live there?"

Conor moved to the far end of the room and spoke more quietly. "She's . . . not available."

"Not available? What does that mean?"

"Well, no one's heard from her in a few days."

"How many is a few?"

"Ten or so."

"*Ten* days? Is this normal behavior for her?"

"I guess? I don't really know her. I'm sure it's nothing," he said. "She texted Emily that she was going to the Cape—Cape Cod—but we haven't been able to get in touch. Emily's very upset about it, so I'd rather not discuss it now. The police say there's not much they can do at this—"

"The *police*? The police are involved?"

"Yes. We spoke to them today, and they searched the house."

"*Searched the house*? Conor, what's going on? You tell me you proposed to a girl I've never even *spoken* to, then her mother goes missing—"

"It's nothing, Mom. She's probably just not getting reception on the Cape."

His mother didn't say anything.

"You'll meet Emily soon," he said. "Once it's safe, and once this thing with her mom is resolved."

"HE WANTS ME TO COME DOWN TO THE STATION," EMILY SAID THE NEXT day after she got off the phone with Detective Clark. "You, too."

"Why both of us?" Conor asked.

She shrugged. He was fine with tagging along for moral support, but his requested attendance, especially after the disclosure of the engagement, made him uneasy. He told himself that perhaps the detectives needed him to run interference if Emily became distraught.

At the station, Clark met with them in his office and reviewed his computer screen as he told them that they'd secured a warrant for the cell tower data. Catherine's phone hit the tower closest to Cutters nearly continuously after the party she was last seen at, up through August 26. Then, at 12:25 a.m. the morning of the twenty-seventh, the signal went in and out for a few minutes, getting patchy service as it left the neck, and resumed pinging towers along I-195, heading east, and at 1:08 a.m. it pinged close to Wareham.

Walking the phone away from her house's Wi-Fi signal daily had been unnecessary, as they no longer had access to the device itself, but his more daring decoy had worked: it looked like Catherine had driven—or been driven—off the neck.

"Can we do the thing where I tell a judge she's a danger to herself?" Emily asked. "To find out where her phone is? I'll say whatever I need to."

"It won't do any good," Clark explained. "The phone's been off since Wareham. That's the last known location."

"So she's in Wareham? Did you call the police there?"

"They don't have anything, and no hospitals within a seventy-five-mile radius do, either. But it means that's where her *phone* was last on. Not necessarily where her person was, or was last, or even where her car was or still is. Now, it's within the realm of possibility that her phone died while she was on the highway and she just hasn't gotten a new one yet, and she hasn't checked her emails on her computer, either. Possible, but unlikely, especially since the last activity on her credit cards was a grocery order on the twenty-fourth, which would be odd if she's gone on a long trip."

"Aren't there cameras at tollbooths?"

Clark explained that the route the phone took didn't pass through any tollbooths or by any license plate–recognition cameras. They'd requested surveillance camera footage from gas stations near the Wareham exit, but nothing so far was proving useful. Her E-ZPass transponder hadn't been read at any tolls since then, either, and if someone stole the car, he said, the first thing they probably did was rip it off and throw it away.

Conor had been concerned about all this, but for all the furor about America as a surveillance state, it sounded like it was easier than people thought to drive a car undetected along the country's highways.

"Now, you said she's single," Clark said. "You're absolutely certain about that?"

"Pretty certain. Unless they drove in late at night and parked in her garage, I'd've seen anyone coming in to visit her this summer."

"What about someone living on Cutters, who wouldn't need a car?"

Conor's foot jittered under the desk. Clark was just asking standard questions, he reminded himself, and no one would ever think he was romantically involved with Catherine.

"No, definitely not. I mean, there are men around her age, but they're all married, and I just can't see her with any of them."

"What about the community next to it, Tanners Point?"

"No, Tanners is all new—" She caught herself. "She wouldn't be with someone from there."

"How about from around here?"

"You mean from . . . town?" Emily asked, nearly channeling her mother's hypothetical snobbery at the prospect. "No."

"We're still working on getting her call records, but you think there's zero chance she might be visiting someone on the Cape?" Clark asked. "Maybe someone she met online? That could explain why she might not want to be in contact, if she doesn't want you to know about them for any reason. And unless she's carrying a lot of money on her and is paying for everything in cash, it would explain how she hasn't used her credit cards in a while, if the person's paying for her."

"I guess it's possible, but she never goes to Cape Cod, and it just doesn't make—" Emily looked like she had an idea and reviewed her phone. "She wrote 'the Cape.' My mom never calls it 'the Cape.' She always says 'Cape Cod.'"

"Prolly just texted it like that to save time," said Clark. "Especially if she was driving."

"No, she makes fun of people who— She thinks her kind of people don't say it. She'd never use it."

"Maybe it was a joke? Like, she knows you know she wouldn't call it that?"

"We don't have that kind of relationship," Emily said.

"Okay," Clark said. "Would it be possible for me and my partner to talk with you a little longer?"

"Of course," she said.

Clark opened the door and called for Sousa to join him. "Conor, you mind stepping out for a bit while we talk to Emily first?" he asked. "Then you'll come in after?"

Conor hadn't realized they wanted to interrogate him—and separately.

"No problem," he said.

OUTSIDE THE STATION, CONOR RAN THROUGH HIS STORY, REVIEWING EV-erything from Emily's perspective to ensure that there were no contra-dictions in their separate narratives.

The detective had previously said they'd be able to get Cath-erine's text records. He'd always deleted Catherine's (and Emily's) messages immediately, but a void comprising just the two of them would look odd. He erased the majority of his texts from other people, taking care to permanently clean them out of the "recently deleted" folder.

An hour later Sousa retrieved him. Instead of going to Clark's of-fice, he led Conor into a small, windowless room with only a table, two office chairs on one side of it, and on the other a chair bolted to the floor, which he gestured for Conor to sit in.

"Can you remember everything you did the night Miss Havemeyer was last seen—Friday, August twenty-first?" Clark asked, a pen poised over a legal pad.

Conor pretended to have to think hard. "I'm almost positive I was studying for the bar in my cabin at night, since I do that basically ev-ery night. When I finished, I'm sure I would've gone over to Emily's cottage. I'm there most nights."

"Can you remember what time that was?" Sousa asked.

"No. Sometime after dinner, though."

"You have any texts with her from that night that might tell you?"

He scrolled through his texts. "Not with her. Let me see if I texted anyone else that night." He pretended to review his other texts and found the message from Bobby. "Oh, yeah. I stopped at the yacht club on the way over to her place and had a beer."

"The yacht club? Is that a country club?"

"No, it's not an actual club. It's the nickname for the clubhouse by the swimming dock on the neck. One of Emily's cousins texted me a video they took that night, at nine fifty-one p.m."

He played them the video of Bobby doing the trick with the beer can, pausing it on his appearance at the end.

"He's underage—he won't get in trouble for that, right?" Conor asked, playing up his solicitousness.

"No," said Sousa.

"Okay, good," Conor said. "Since he'd been caught for that break-in on the neck earlier in the summer, I wasn't sure."

"Break-in?"

Conor reminded them of the details of the case.

"So they found out that this kid did it?" Sousa asked.

"Yeah. They didn't tell you?"

Sousa shook his head.

"Huh," Conor said. "Anyway, I think I left soon after this. So I'd guess I got to Emily's place around ten."

"Then what?"

"It's possible we watched a show or something before going to sleep. I can't really remember anything about it. Just a normal night."

"How about the night Miss Havemeyer's phone left the neck, Wednesday, August twenty-sixth?" Clark asked.

"Probably the same thing. Working in my cabin, coming to Emily's at night, sleeping there. The days are pretty similar here."

"Does Miss Havemeyer taking off in the middle of the night strike you as strange behavior, given what you know about her?"

"I only really know about her from what Emily's told me," Conor said. "According to her, her mom's a pretty unhappy person who drinks a lot. Maybe she's the kind of person who makes impulsive decisions like that—I don't know."

"Anything else at all that stood out to you around this time?"

"Nothing I can think of."

"Other than you got engaged," Sousa said.

"Yeah," Conor said with a restrained chuckle. As fishy as his proposal looked, it would be far worse if he tried to avoid the topic. "It's been sort of a whirlwind romance, and we got a little carried away. We haven't set a date or anything yet. Especially not now."

"Would you mind if we took your phone for a day?" Clark asked. "You could come back for it anytime tomorrow."

He could refuse and force them to get a subpoena. But being uncooperative would look like he had something to hide. And now that he'd scrubbed his phone of the texts, there was nothing incriminating on it. He was a clean-cut law school graduate; as long as he was helpful, he'd be above real suspicion.

"No problem," Conor said. "And I'll give you my email, in case you have any other questions."

CHAPTER 31

After their lesson the next morning, John asked Conor if he'd by any chance heard from or seen Catherine Havemeyer, the woman who lived at the end of the neck.

"I haven't," Conor said. "But I've heard no one can find her."

"You're friendly with Emily, aren't you? Her daughter?"

"Yes." Reticence would only look strange. "We've actually been together as a couple most of the summer."

"Have you," John said, breaking into a you-devil-you grin. "I haven't seen her much the last few years, but I've always been very fond of her."

"I am, too. So much so, in fact, that we're more than just a couple. As of a few days ago, we're engaged."

John's bushy gray eyebrows rose. Before he could ask any questions, Conor said, "It happened before we knew about this situation with her mom. So planning for the wedding isn't at all a priority, but I hope you'll be able to come to it, whenever we do have it. If it weren't for you, it never would have happened."

"I'd be delighted to." John was still clearly adjusting to the news. "Well, congratulations. I hope this whole thing isn't casting too much of a pall over it for Emily."

"I'm sure it'll all work out. Catherine— Her mom texted her that she was going to the Cape. Cape Cod. My guess is she lost her phone and hasn't been checking email."

He'd have to train himself not to speak about Cape Cod anymore, because he instinctively called it "the Cape"—shorthand learned, he realized, from Charlie. Not what Catherine's kind of people said, indeed.

"That sounds about right to me," John said. "People don't just up and vanish. Not people from here, at least."

"THE DETECTIVE TOLD US WE CAN GET OUR PHONES AT THE STATION," Emily said when she checked her email. She'd relinquished hers, too.

"Would you mind going on your own?" Conor asked. "I'm in crunch mode over here." His second-round interview was in two days and served as an entirely reasonable excuse to skip another trip to the police station.

"He asked us both to come and clear a couple hours."

He was no longer just the boyfriend-turned-fiancé of whom they were obligated to ask a few questions. If they still wanted to speak to him now, it meant they'd found something of interest—and that he was a person of interest. They'd likely obtained her call and text records—maybe his, too—so they knew he and Catherine had communicated numerous times. Not a big deal; she took tennis lessons from him, which they'd ask Emily about also. Other than that, he'd erased everything on his phone connected to her. But he had to prepare for them to ask him something that they might already know the answer to, and which he therefore couldn't flatly lie about. He'd have to be ready to come up with responses on the spot and anticipate their questions before they knew what they were going to be.

At the station, the detectives asked to speak to Conor first in the interrogation room. It was very warm in there, especially since Conor wore long sleeves again to cover his bite marks, nearly faded but still observable to the suspicious eye.

"How are you today, Conor?" Clark asked as he pried open a laptop.

"I'm okay, considering," he said. "I've got a big interview in a couple days with a law firm that I've been preparing for. But it's been hard to concentrate on it with all this."

"Sorry it's so hot in here," Sousa said. "AC's on the fritz. I'll get us all drinks." He left and returned in less than a minute with three cold, unopened bottles of Coke, handing Conor one. "This okay? Or you want something else? Water, coffee, iced tea?"

Conor had seen enough crime shows to know they wanted his DNA from his saliva—and if they weren't asking him directly for a sample, it was so as not to tip him off about their suspicions. They did know something he wasn't aware of. He shouldn't refuse the bottle, but he wouldn't drink from it, either, nor would he touch anything. They could request a DNA sample, and he'd have to comply or else look guilty, but there was no need to do so seemingly unwittingly. If they were going to target him as a suspect, he wanted them to be compelled to state it more or less openly—to know that he knew, and if they ever closed in on him, to give him an unquestionable reason to ask for a lawyer.

Steady strokes, no big shots.

Conor gestured at the bottle without touching it. "This is fine, thanks."

"We asked about that kid from Cutters who did the break-in," Sousa said. "He's got a pretty solid alibi. But thanks for your help."

"Oh, good," Conor said, disappointed in his red herring. "Glad to help."

"So let's jump in," Sousa said. "Did you ever text or call with Miss Havemeyer prior to her disappearance?"

"Sure." He'd determined that he would never refer to Catherine by name if he could avoid it to lessen any appearance of familiarity. "She was one of the residents I gave tennis lessons to. She took several a week, starting sometime in June. She was a serious player when she was younger and was trying to get her game back. So we texted a fair amount to make or change appointments. Probably a few quick calls, too, though it was usually texts."

"We didn't see any of your texts with her in your phone."

"I delete most of my texts after I read them, to be organized and save space. It's a really old phone. I need to get a new one."

"How much did you charge her for lessons?"

At some point they'd be able to subpoena his and her bank records. "Three hundred dollars."

"Three hundred sounds like an awful lot for a tennis lesson," Sousa said.

"It is. I normally charge one-fifty, and I charged her that at first, too. But she insisted on paying me three hundred."

"She tipped a hundred percent? Why?"

"From what Emily tells me, the people around here have a lot of guilt about their money. I guess they sometimes overpay to make up for it."

"Did you ever go to her house?"

He was about to answer that he'd gone just once, when he and Emily had had that drink with Catherine. But if they were asking this, it was because they'd gleaned something else from his phone. He furrowed his brow, both trying to imagine what they knew and to simulate an attempt at recalling a trivial event that had slipped his mind.

The only phone data that would reveal his precise location at her house would be a Wi-Fi router hit. That second time they'd had drinks on her patio, she had given him her Wi-Fi password when he'd pretended he needed to check his email, and he'd entered it into his phone. Every single visit of Conor's during their liaison had therefore been logged. Her ban on pillow talk had, thankfully, kept his total time there brief.

"Yes," he said after about fifteen seconds. "Sorry, it was a while ago—I'd completely forgotten. She invited me over for drinks after the lessons the first couple weeks. I can't remember how many times."

"Right after the lesson was over?" Sousa asked.

"Maybe early on. Then it was always later at night. I think she was lonely, because of Covid, and wanted company. I felt bad saying no, so I'd come and stay for a drink or two after I'd finished studying for the night."

"I thought you said you only really knew about who she was

through Emily," Sousa said. "But you had drinks with her half a dozen or so times."

"Yeah," Conor said. "It was mostly pleasantries, or her asking about me. I wouldn't say I got to know her well. Emily told me her mom studied to be a painter when she was young, for instance, and her mom never even mentioned it to me."

"How long did this continue?"

"Once I started seeing Emily, I thought it would be strange to keep coming over."

"Why?"

Conor adopted a sheepish expression and voice. "Well, to be honest, and I feel bad about saying this, I was worried Emily's mom wanted to . . . maybe sleep with me. She didn't outright say it, but that was the impression I got. It made me pretty uncomfortable. I also had the feeling I wasn't the first young guy, or the first guy from Cutters, she'd tried it with. She married into the place, so she's not related to anyone there. Please don't tell Emily this. I could be misreading it, and I don't want her to think this about her mom."

This half truth was a big gamble, but it made him look honest and forthcoming, would help explain why she had texted him so much, and might even spread suspicion elsewhere.

"Why'd you keep giving her lessons, if it made you uncomfortable?" Sousa asked.

"She was my best client," Conor said. "I couldn't cut her off."

"How'd she feel about you dating her daughter?"

"I didn't tell her, for that reason. I was keeping my relationship with Emily quiet anyway, because I thought maybe my employer might not like it if I was seeing someone here."

"But you were about to tell her you proposed to Emily?" Sousa asked. "You weren't worried about her reaction?"

"We had to tell her at some point," Conor said with a shrug. "It's not like she was going to put a stop to it or anything."

"And how'd Emily feel about you giving her mother lessons?"

"I didn't tell her, either. They have such a strained relationship, it was best not to say anything. Though it wouldn't have been a huge deal if she found out. She did find out later, actually, and it was fine."

"Is Emily her mother's only heir?" Clark asked.

"I don't know. You'd have to ask whoever handles her money."

"Did Miss Havemeyer ever suggest she might cut Emily out of her will?"

"I wouldn't be privy to that kind of information. And it doesn't really matter, since Emily has a trust fund that can't be taken away from her."

"But her trust is smaller than what she'd inherit, right?"

"Again, I have no idea about any of this stuff," he said. "But if you think that— If you're suggesting that she . . ."

"We're not suggesting anything. Just asking questions."

"Emily knows she has more than enough money, and she plans to give the majority of it away to charity. She and her mom may not have the greatest relationship, but she's extremely upset by all this. And she'd *never* . . . the idea that Emily could somehow . . ."

"We understand," Sousa said. "Let's change the subject. What are your living arrangements in Yonkers?"

"I live with my mother."

"Your father's not around?" Clark asked.

"He died when I was eleven," Conor said. "Suicide."

Clark paused at the superfluous disclosure. "I'm sorry," he said. "I lost an uncle that way."

An awkward silence fell between the two men. Conor had told them in an attempt to garner sympathy, but now he wished he hadn't said it.

"You and Emily have been together about two months," Sousa said. "That's pretty fast to propose, no?"

"I guess a little," Conor said.

"What made you decide to ask her?"

"I wasn't planning to for a while, even though I knew she was the one," he said. "But my mom's got pretty bad diabetes, and I don't know when this thing'll be over, and if she gets Covid, she . . . I wanted to make sure she knew I was on the road to getting married. I'm her only kid."

Clark was taking a lot of notes.

"Have you and Emily ever discussed the idea of a prenuptial agreement?" Sousa asked.

"No."

"But you were aware before you proposed that Emily has a trust fund, and she was aware that you knew?"

"Yes," Conor said. "But if you're insinuating that I don't want to sign a prenup because of that, a trust is considered money made before a marriage, so in the event of a divorce, she'd keep all of it. If anyone stands to lose money from a divorce, it's me. I'll make much more in the future as a lawyer than she will as a writer."

"How about an inheritance?" Sousa asked.

The detectives had either not yet looked up this exonerating fact or believed Conor was ignorant of it.

"I'd have to review my bar exam books, but I'm ninety-nine percent certain that inheritance is treated as a premarital asset and therefore also not subject to division after a dissolution of marriage," Conor said. "And since you seem so interested in my proposal, if you're thinking I got engaged to Emily because I thought I'd be covered by spousal immunity, you and I both know that it doesn't cover matters predating the marriage, and that it would only be invoked if we got married before prosecution, and that either spouse can waive the privilege if they want. I'd have to be an idiot to propose to her and bring this kind of attention to myself for no legal gain. I did it for love, and no other reason, and I wanted to do it near the end of the summer, which turned out to be very unfortunate timing. We're obviously not making any plans for a wedding until her mom is home safe."

He'd debunked their stated and unsaid theories with such collected, articulate authority that they couldn't hide their disappointment behind their masks. If he'd just married her for her own money, then her mother's disappearance wouldn't factor into it. Emily would be the only direct beneficiary of Catherine's estate, and she was so guilelessly distressed by what had happened that they'd never really believe her capable of any wrongdoing on her own. They might hypothesize that Conor had talked her into murdering her mother to get her inheritance early (or in case Catherine had threatened to take it away), but that was a major risk to take when she was already living quite comfortably off her trust in a seven-grand-a-month apartment. And he'd shot down any link between the timing of his proposal and Catherine's disappearance.

Rational, responsible adults didn't murder randomly. They almost always have a motive, and the police had hinged whatever case they appeared to be building against Conor on the inheritance as the primary motive. That was now gone.

"Did you ever visit Catherine again?" Sousa asked. "After those first few weeks?"

"Emily and I had a drink with her once, when I went to her house to get money for a lesson and Emily happened to be outside at the same time," he said.

"That's it?"

"That's all I can think of."

"Did you see her during the daytime on Monday, August twenty-fourth?"

If they were asking, it was because they knew he'd been there. But he'd been very careful to turn his phone off each time he'd gone to Catherine's house after the murder, to ensure that Emily didn't call or text while he was there.

Except that day he'd ordered groceries and had called Emily, from his phone, asking her to go to the drugstore for him. He'd left his phone on the entire time he was waiting for her to leave, to make sure she didn't reach out with a change of plans.

"I did go one day, I can't remember when," he said. "It could've been then."

"Why'd you go?"

He'd arrived there in the late morning; a casual drinks invitation was implausible. He needed a more significant excuse for why he'd been at his tennis client's house than a mundane social visit.

"She'd somehow figured out I was dating her daughter," Conor said. "Once she knew we were together, she wanted to talk to me about something private concerning Emily."

"What was it?"

He felt guilty for the pain that this would cause Emily—they'd have to share this information with her—but it was the only explanation he could come up with that was exculpatory enough, and the story also planted more seeds of doubt about Catherine's mental health at the time of her disappearance.

And fuck her parents, both of them. They'd kept Emily in the dark too long. She deserved to know, too.

"She said that she'd been keeping a secret from Emily her whole life, and she wanted my opinion on whether she should tell her. She always struck me as a little unstable, so I can't be sure if she was telling me the truth, but it seemed like she was."

He related the few details he knew about Jacob. Neither Clark nor Sousa appeared all that perturbed by it, likely being accustomed to tragic family histories.

"Why'd she tell *you* this?" Sousa asked. "Why not just tell Emily directly?"

Conor took a deep breath. "Emily was—I think she'll be okay with me telling you this—she was involuntarily committed to a mental health center her senior year of college, with a nervous breakdown. And she checked herself back in in the spring. She kept the second stay secret from her parents, but her mom told me she found out about it from her accountant. She was concerned the breakdowns were some-how the result of what had happened to her brother—she said be-cause Emily was never allowed to process it—and she wanted to know if I thought Emily was emotionally strong enough to handle hearing about it now."

"Who else knows about her brother that could corroborate it?" Sousa asked.

"I imagine the adults on Cutters knew about it but kept it under wraps all these years, so you could ask them. Or Emily's dad, of course."

"And Emily has *no* idea about it? Her brother died when she was three, all these people around her knew, and she never found out or remembered him?"

"She's never mentioned it to me, and she tells me everything. So either it isn't true—and the way her mom was talking about it, I don't think that's the case—or she really did wipe out the memory."

Clark and Sousa glanced at each other. They were dubious, just as Conor had been.

"If you have to ask her, I hope you'll handle it with as much sensitivity as possible," Conor said. "Learning she had a brother who died, and that everyone hid it from her, will be very traumatic for her, and she was just starting to get back on her feet again before all this happened."

"Understood." Clark took a paper out of a folder and pushed it toward Conor. "I think that's all we have for now. Before you go, would you mind signing this consent-to-search form?"

"Consent to search wh—" Conor's lips moved wordlessly behind his mask with a loud insuck of air. "—ut?"

The eyes of both detectives registered his stammer. He couldn't let it happen again. No verbal tic was a clearer sign of guilt, and his issue didn't even sound like a normal stutter.

"Your cabin," Clark said.

They had declined an informal search on their visit to the neck, when they'd had no reason to suspect him. This wouldn't be the two of them poking around; it meant a full crime scene search. If he refused, they'd be able to secure a warrant, and it would only make him look evasive. A request for a lawyer at this point would also be damning.

"Sure," he said. "I'm staying there for free, if you need the owner's signature, too."

Clark nodded and waited for Conor to sign the form. "We'd also like to fingerprint you, to rule out your prints," he said. "And do a quick cheek swab."

They'd seen he hadn't drunk from his soda, and he couldn't reasonably fend off the DNA test any longer. He gave his consent.

After they returned his phone, they fingerprinted him and swabbed the inside of his cheek, his second such swab within a few months: the first at the beginning of his affair with Catherine; this one marking, with forensic precision, its termination.

CHAPTER 32

How'd it go?" he asked Emily in the car when she emerged from the station a solid hour later. She shrugged. Judging from her neutral face, it was obvious they hadn't asked yet about her brother.

"It sounds like they're going to search my cabin," he said. "As a precaution."

"My cottage, too. And they're getting a warrant to search my mom's house."

"Good," Conor said. "They're doing their job."

They didn't speak as he drove over the drawbridge out of the village and back to Cutters. Maybe he hadn't gone far enough by just covering and mixing the blood. He didn't know how accurate the analysis would be—whether they took just a few small samples and catching her three drops would be like finding a needle in a haystack, or if they were somehow able to survey the entirety of the bloodstain—and he'd been afraid to research it on the internet and leave behind a trail. It was too late to buy sandpaper, and he'd rejected that idea for a reason, anyway.

If they were going to get him, it would be from this. At least dried semen from over two months ago was hard to see. Bloodstains were impossible to overlook.

As they entered the gate to Cutters, she asked, "Did you give my mom tennis lessons? Beyond that one time?"

"Yeah," he said. "We started before you and I met. Sorry I didn't tell you."

"Why didn't you?"

"When I realized you were her daughter, I thought it might be weird if you knew I was giving her lessons. Like maybe you'd stop me or her from doing it, and I needed the money badly. And she also asked me not to tell you. I don't know why."

"And you came to her *house*? For drinks?"

"Only before I met you. Once we were together, I stopped."

"Why'd you go in the first place?"

"It's common to get a drink with someone you give a lesson to," he said. "I used to do it all the time with students in New York."

"But at nine, ten at night?"

"I can't study after I've had a drink, so I agreed to come over after I finished work for the day," he said. "She seemed like a lonely, kind of sad woman. I thought if my mom was in the same position, I'd want someone to visit her."

"And then you saw her *after* the Beresfords' party?"

"Yes," he said. "Not right after. A few days later."

"So you were the *last* person to see her here?"

"I don't know. Maybe someone else saw her, too, and they just don't realize when it was."

"Why'd you visit her then? It was in the morning—it couldn't have been after a lesson."

"She'd figured out we were together, probably from when we all had cocktails together that time. She wanted to talk about all of that."

"All of *what*?"

"I don't know." He didn't want to be the one to tell her about Jacob if he could avoid it. "Just . . . stuff. You said she never met any of the guys you were with at Bard, so maybe she was just curious."

"Well, that's really fucking weird," she said. "Conor—Jesus. Why didn't you *say* you were the last person who saw her?"

"I had no idea what date I came over, or that I was the last person. The days all blur into each other here. The police told me just now myself."

"My mother disappears off the face of the earth, and you don't *remember* that you saw her just a few days before, at her *house*?"

"You know what?" he said as he parked by her cottage. "I've got a lot on my mind these days. I've got a mom with diabetes who could die any day if she breathes in the wrong air. I'm studying for the bar exam and applying to jobs every free minute of the day so I can buy her insulin to keep her alive and pay off a hundred and forty-four grand in loans, plus my dead dad's credit card debt. Sorry if I don't remember the *exact* date of every social call I make."

"The police think it's weird, too," she said.

"Jesus fucking Christ, Em," he said, banging the steering wheel. "You *do* understand what they're doing, right? We learned about this in law school. When these small-town cops don't have any real leads, they need to pin the blame on someone so they're not accused of incompetence or negligence. So I guess they're going after me. What a coincidence, that they'd pick the *one* person on Cutters who's not from here and doesn't come from money and therefore looks the part of a criminal. And, as a bonus, who wouldn't be able to pay for a good lawyer if they charged him. I'm really glad to learn you're siding with them. You, of all people, who says the criminal justice system is corrupt."

"I'm not *siding* with them. I'm only saying they thought it was—"

"And by the way, when they were talking to *me*, they were making all sorts of nasty allegations about *you*."

"What?"

"They were suggesting you were after your mom's money. Trying to get your inheritance early."

She looked horrified. "What'd you tell them?"

"I got pissed off and told them you'd never do anything like that in a million years. So either they think you have something to do with this on your own, or we're in cahoots and they were hoping I'd slip up covering for you or sell you out. And apparently they were doing the same thing when they talked to you. It's a classic interrogation technique. Split up the suspects and use the prisoner's dilemma to get them to turn on each other, even when they're both innocent. But the difference between you and me is that *I* defend you."

Emily looked at her lap. He'd never come close to expressing this level of anger at her. He let her silence linger for a while, though he was feeling the same self-loathing she must have been. But he'd had no choice. If Emily told the detectives that she, too, suspected him and pointed to moments that suggested guilt or a motive, it wouldn't matter to a jury how well he'd covered it up—a fiancée's accusations held too much water.

"This is just like Lawrence Newcomb blaming the burglary on me when it was his own entitled, fuck-up son," he said. "I thought you were different."

"I *am* different," she said. "I'm different, Conor. I'm sorry. You're right. I'm out of my mind now and I'm not thinking straight. I didn't know police really do that. Can you forgive me for this? Please?"

He brooded through the windshield at the ocean in the distance, chewing his thumb. "It makes me think you don't know me at all."

"Please, Conor." She touched his forearm, over the bandage hidden by his sleeve. "I'm so sorry."

After a drawn-out moment, he nodded grudgingly.

"Should you get a lawyer?" she asked. "Or should we get one together? If they're trying to blame us?"

"Of course not," he said. "We have nothing to hide, and we want to cooperate and do everything we can to help find your mom. I think they're just throwing everything at the wall right now to see what sticks. Even crazy ideas."

Emily nodded. But after another silence, she asked, "What exactly *did* my mom want to talk about with you? The last time you saw her?"

He'd been evasive on the subject too many times. And the detectives would ask her about it soon enough, once her father confirmed it; it was better for her if she heard it from him.

He still didn't want to have this conversation.

EMILY HAD CRIED SEVERAL TIMES THAT WEEK OVER HER MOTHER'S DISAP-pearance. But, aside from the expected shock and disbelief, she was otherwise strangely composed as Conor, still in the parked Prius, repeated what he'd told the detectives about her infant brother. When he was done, they sat in silence for a few minutes.

"Why didn't you tell me about this?" she finally asked.

"She made me swear not to say anything," he said. "Since she told me, I assumed she was going to tell you soon."

"But if not, you were just going to keep it to yourself forever? We're married and live to a hundred, you still wouldn't tell me?"

"It was a heavy thing to learn about, and I didn't know what to do. And after she— I would've said something eventually. I'm sorry."

"I'm gonna go for a walk," Emily said. She left the car, and he waited inside the cottage for her.

She could have easily gone the rest of her days without being aware of this, if he hadn't needed an excuse for the detectives. There was no benefit to knowing a torturous truth when you could be living a painless lie in ignorance. He'd not only killed her mother but now he'd also, in a sense, killed her brother.

Emily returned after an hour, reeking of cigarettes. She didn't look as though she'd been crying. When she went to the kitchen sink, Conor followed.

"Maybe I shouldn't've told you," he said as she scrubbed her hands. "It wasn't mine to know, and it wasn't my place to say."

She rinsed.

"I wish I hadn't gone to her house that day." He could feel the radiant heat from the sink. "I wish I'd never— I wish none of this had—"

Her hands were turning lobster red. He yanked them away from the scorching water. They were limp and burning in his grip. He ran the cold tap over them.

The dam finally broke in her. Unlike the times her and Catherine's crying had had an aphrodisiac effect on him, this was only painful to watch.

"I'm sorry, Em," he said as he held her and stroked her head. "I'm sorry this is all happening at once. But she'll turn up. And you can talk about all this with her then, too."

BY NOW THE ENTIRE NECK HAD BEEN INFORMED OF THE INVESTIGATION into Catherine's disappearance, though they'd been asked to keep it quiet and not speak to the media. The detectives had interviewed

Emily's father over the phone, and his alibi was unassailable: he'd been on his yacht with his family for the past three weeks in the Caribbean.

The next day, a crime scene team conducted a search of Catherine's house, Emily's cottage, and, with John Price's sign-off, Conor's cabin. Emily and Conor were ordered to remain off the premises during the investigation, which would take most of the day.

They set up camp at the yacht club. Conor attempted to prepare for his interview but was too anxious about what was happening out of sight.

In the late afternoon, the detectives summoned Conor and Emily to meet them in Catherine's driveway.

"Did you find anything?" Emily asked.

"We have to wait for the labs to process any samples," Clark said. "You're free to return to your house here. We're sealing up your mother's house for now and also Conor's cabin. If you need anything from there, you should tell us now so we can get it for you."

"You're sealing up his cabin?" Emily asked, glancing over at Conor. "Why?"

He should have scuffed the floor with sandpaper. Calling attention to the spot was preferable to the alternative. They were going to process the samples, identify Catherine's DNA beneath his, and arrest him.

"Just standard procedure," Clark told her.

FORCED TO DEAL WITH A COMPLETELY DIFFERENT AND GRUELING assignment—seven hours of Zoom interviews with John's firm—Conor managed to shift gears and acquitted himself well. He capably handled the generic softballs and did even better answering concrete queries about his internship experience.

But each new person concluded by asking him why their firm made sense for him, and, having come up with no more original answers in his preparation, he reverted to the same stodgy, jargon-clotted response he'd employed in the first round. After citing two of the firm's recent litigation cases that suited his skills and interests, he said, "I'm also drawn to the altruistic values you embody, as demonstrated by your lawyers' average of over eighty hours of pro bono work per year, and its culture of inclusivity." In his final interview, the two senior-most partners, even more patrician-looking than John, appeared as uninspired as all his other interlocutors.

He wasn't going to win the job over his secret society Ivy League counterparts with this pro forma mission statement that may as well have been copy-and-pasted from the internet. Richard would tell him to keep up his steady strokes, that he'd gotten this far with prudence. But he recalled John's advice about playing aggressively when you were down forty-love.

"On the topic of inclusivity," Conor continued, "as you know, I didn't go to an Ivy League or comparable school, for either law or undergraduate, as just about all of your lawyers did. I certainly don't expect any special treatment regarding that—quite the opposite. I bring it up because I'm used to competing against people with an advantage over me. In tennis, my opponents were usually better and more experienced, because tennis is a rich sport, and they were rich. My only chance of defeating them was to play very conservatively. The word for that kind of player is a 'pusher.' If you win, it's by waiting for the other person to beat himself. No one wants to be known as a pusher."

He couldn't get a read, from the small boxes on his screen, on how the lawyers were receiving what was turning into an improvised and extended sports metaphor.

"But even though I was a pusher, I couldn't be pushed around," he said. "What I lacked in training and talent, I made up for in patience, in perseverance, and most of all, in ruthlessness. And I never enjoyed winning against anyone more than someone who thought he was better than me because he'd started playing when he was younger and went to tennis camps and had a fancier racquet. To put it bluntly, because he was a rich boy. If I work for you, against other Ivy League lawyers, that's who I'll dedicate myself to beating—the rich boys. Ruthlessly."

The partners appeared rattled by this final pronouncement, and neither one reacted immediately. Then one coughed, thanked Conor for his time, and, before he knew it, the Zoom session had ended.

What a fool. He'd blown it, and he'd probably miscalculated the score before the final question, too; if he'd just kept to the rote answers they expected, he might still be in the running—if he'd ever actually been in the running to begin with. But now no one at a white-shoe, blue-blooded firm would hire someone who spoke in a job interview about his class-based grudge against people who were exactly like them.

It hardly mattered anyway, not compared with what was happening, as he spoke, in a crime lab somewhere.

"Sorry," was all Emily said when he told her he didn't think it had gone well.

"I know you're worried, but everything's going to work out with your mom," he said. "Just try not to think about it for now."

THE NEXT TIME CLARK ASKED THEM BOTH TO COME TO THE STATION, Conor knew it must mean they'd finished processing the blood samples on the floor of his cabin. They would question him about it but might not tell him yet if they'd identified Catherine's blood, to see how he initially responded and potentially use his false answers against him later.

Conor was called in first. "We found some blood in your cabin," Clark said after a few preliminaries. "Any idea where it came from?"

"Blood?" Conor manufactured an expression of concerned confusion. "Where?"

"You tell us. Anyone bleed there recently?"

He pretended to try to remember. "The only thing I can think of is I cut my foot on broken glass a while ago. Was it on the floor? Here." He pulled off his sneaker and sock and showed off his scar. As he held up his foot, Clark looked intently—not just at his foot, it appeared, but at all exposed skin, likely for defensive wounds sustained in a fight. The bite marks on his arm were finally gone, and Conor had worn short sleeves to show he had nothing to hide.

"When did it happen?" Sousa asked.

"Maybe . . . two weeks ago." Left unspoken was that this was right around when Catherine was last seen by others. "I remember I texted John Price about it, because I was worried it would stain the wood and I asked if he wanted me to pay for a cleaner." He checked his texts with John, which he'd erased in keeping with his supposed purging practices, knowing John would surely have kept the messages. "I deleted my old texts with him, but you can ask him when it happened."

"Did you get a cleaner?"

"No, he said he didn't care."

"Anyone else see you step on the glass?"

"Emily might've been there. I can't remember."

"You mind waiting in the station while we talk to her and Mr. Price?" Clark asked. Conor acceded, and Sousa brought him to an unoccupied office and left.

Conor sat in a chair, staring out the window at the parking lot. Previous times he'd had to wait for Emily they had let him go outside, but now they'd asked him to remain in the station. These might be his last minutes of complete freedom. Emily and John would back up his story, but if they'd found Catherine's DNA, it was immaterial: they'd arrest him right away.

Half an hour later, Clark opened the door.

"All right," he said. "You can go. We'll be unsealing both properties."

Conor had to restrain himself from smiling on his way out of the station. His blood had successfully masked Catherine's. There was nothing to tie her to his cabin, or him to her house. And even if Catherine's Mercedes turned up anytime soon, by this point his DNA would be gone, and all the suspicion would turn to whoever had stolen the car.

He'd done it.

CHAPTER 33

Each morning without news meant another day that Catherine's body remained missing, that someone had almost certainly stolen her car and removed its plates, and that her phone, laptop, and ID cards were still in a junkyard or at the bottom of the Providence River. Even if they found his explanations dubious, the police hadn't mustered nearly enough hard evidence with which to charge Conor. Neither Emily's inheritance nor her trust was a plausible motive for Conor to commit murder, and the story about Jacob, the fundamental facts of which were confirmed by Emily's father, had apparently justified his presence at Catherine's house after she'd last been seen. And Emily was either sufficiently chastened by his reaction to her initial mistrust or too dazed by everything that had transpired that she didn't question his narrative again.

Catherine's estate lawyer notified Emily that she was the sole beneficiary of her mother's will, but a missing person couldn't be presumed dead for seven years, so her assets wouldn't transfer before then unless Emily mounted a legal challenge. Catherine's accountant had taken measures to quadruple her monthly withdrawals from the trust for now, to ensure she was taken care of. As she could stay for free in the house on Cutters, the property taxes, utilities, and upkeep of which would continue to be paid for by the accountant out of Catherine's assets, there was no practical reason to pursue the inheritance. (The accountant had also usefully corroborated Conor's claim that he'd been the one to inform Catherine of her daughter's stay in the treatment center. His testimony that Catherine had never reached out to him about Emily's increased rent didn't raise any red flags, as Emily said her mother was often "flaky" when it came to fulfilling these kinds of requests.)

Conor stayed mum on the subject. Persuading her to gain early control of Catherine's fortune might be viewed, at best, as gauche; at worst, as a motive in her disappearance. Seven years wasn't that long.

JOHN OFFERED TO DISCONTINUE HIS LESSONS, UNDERSTANDING THAT Conor would need to tend to Emily, but he insisted he hold up his end of the bargain, so the two men continued meeting mornings at the tennis court, with John politely but discreetly asking after any developments with Catherine.

One afternoon, John knocked on Conor's door. "I'm afraid I'm going to need you to vacate the cabin immediately," he told Conor with a serious expression. "And we'll have to end our tennis lessons. I'm in legal jeopardy if I continue associating with you."

The police had teased out Catherine's blood in his cabin, after all. They'd told John. They were coming after him.

He'd brought his passport with him to Cutters. Emily kept the keys to her Prius on a hook by the door.

He couldn't do that. He should surrender himself now. It would almost be a relief.

"I'm sorry, I shouldn't be kidding you," John said, chuckling at Conor's expression. "We're offering you a job. Starting after the election."

Conor took a moment to process the news.

"Are you serious?"

"Completely serious," said John. "My partners were very impressed. They said this was the first time they've ever interviewed someone who wasn't just telling them what they wanted to hear the whole time. Or, to use language they would never use, who wasn't bullshitting them."

After years of mumbling that, actually, it was New York Law School, not NYU, Conor O'Toole would soon be able to announce to the world that he was an associate at one of the best firms in New York

City—for his area of focus, arguably *the* best. His gambit had, improbably, paid off. They'd hired him specifically because he'd said things no one else would in a job interview, statements that were borderline offensive. On the verge of defeat, he'd gone for a big shot—and *acted* something like a big shot—and ended up winning the whole goddamn tournament.

John told him that Conor did, unfortunately, have to move out of the cabin; human resources had informed him that he wasn't permitted to demand goods and services from an employee, paid or in kind, and his lodging was initially provided under that arrangement. Conor said he'd move out right away and offered to continue playing informally with John as friendly colleagues rather than as instructor and student.

"Much as I'd like to, you're a professional lawyer now," John said. "Probably best if we both play it completely by the rules." Before he left, he said, "Oh—I busted a string in a game yesterday. Could I squeeze one last stringing in before you sign your contract?"

"Wish I could," Conor said, "but my machine broke."

"Want me to drive it into town to the sporting goods store? I bet they could repair it."

"I just threw it out. It was really old and barely functioning before it broke down."

"You talking about the stringing machine or my body?" John joked. "Well, I guess it doesn't matter now. Your tennis pro days are over." He smiled broadly. "Go west, young man."

MOST OF THE RESIDENTS WHO HAD STUCK AROUND AFTER LABOR DAY trickled out as winds buffeted the neck with ghostly moans. The trees crackled and inflamed with oranges and reds. The air, scented with woodsmoke from chimneys, was autumn-crisp during the day but still moist at night, leaving their sheets cold and sodden by morning. The ocean went from unpleasant to nearly unswimmable.

Emily spoke little, swallowing her greetings when she and Conor crossed paths, half-listening to the brief recapitulation of his day at dinner, and retreating to a small room in the cottage soon after. They barely touched, and certainly didn't come close to any sexual intimacy.

The cottage wasn't winterized and became too chilly to stay in for a New England fall, even with blankets and a space heater. Though she'd been avoiding Catherine's house, they were forced to move into it.

They took a guest room and kept the door to the master bedroom closed. Conor maintained his swimming regimen in the heated pool, doing laps for half an hour a day. The house had an outdoor shower, but the one in their suite had a marble bench on which he could sit as he lathered himself. There were three living rooms, two dining rooms, a wine cellar, a barroom, a gym, and, as promised, a belowground two-lane bowling alley, though he used it just once by himself. He had to avoid any appearance that he was enjoying their new digs too much.

With Emily's blessing, Conor invited his mother to stay with them. She turned him down.

"You can go for walks. You don't have to worry about Covid at all here," he said over the phone. "The place is huge, so you won't get in our way, if that's what you're worried about."

"I like it fine here," she said, ever a provincial creature of habit.

"Look at this," he said, panning the phone's camera around the living room from which he'd placed the call, lingering on a curved stone wall that surrounded a fireplace. "You really want to keep living in a small, dingy apartment in Yonkers when you could be breathing fresh ocean air? You know how much this place is worth?"

She was silent for a moment.

"You didn't used to care about how much things are worth, Conor."

"Well," he shot back, "one of us has to, or we'd be out on the streets."

EMILY WOULD STAY UP THROUGH THE NIGHT ON THE INTERNET RE-searching missing persons before sleeping it off in a separate room till the afternoon. She ramped up her Zoom therapy sessions to five times a week but hardly talked to Conor about her mother and said nothing regarding her brother. She lost interest in the presidential race and was apathetic even when the president she despised contracted Covid and, for a few tantalizing days, it appeared he might die in the most just way possible.

It hurt Conor to see her like this. She was depressed, but unlike the previous times he hadn't witnessed, this was for a very concrete reason, and she dismissed his idea of her returning to the treatment center. But it would pass, eventually. People mourned, and even if they never got over it fully, even if a part of them was forever broken, they became functional again, learned how to get through the day. He and his mother had. They'd had no alternative.

He took the long-delayed bar remotely and felt confident about the results, which would come later in the winter. With his plum job lined up, for the first time in his life he had no mountain of textbooks to scale, no tennis practice under the flaying sun, no fretting about money. Whereas slacking off used to make him anxious that he was compromising his future, the future was now taken care of, and he found his new state of indolence pleasurable. So this was life as a rentier.

Once in a while he reflected that, had he not gone to the pool party and talked to Catherine, he would have still met Emily and snared this job from John's firm. Everything would have worked out more or less as it was now, just without this having happened and weighing on his conscience.

But it wasn't actually weighing on him as much anymore. No longer was it the first thing he thought of upon waking, nor did it haunt him when he fell asleep. The times it did slip under his mind's wall— when an image flashed on the black canvas of his eyelids of Catherine's head sinking underwater, when he remembered in his bones the wallop of steel against skull, or each time he toweled off his feet and saw the scar from the broken glass, a wispy red seam, perhaps a permanent reminder on his sole—he pushed it out fast, like antibodies repelling a virus. She'd accosted him in his home, blackmailed him, bitten and attacked him with a blunt weapon, and been prepared to destroy him—and her own daughter—out of malice. He'd meant only to fend her off, not knock her unconscious. Was he supposed to bear her blows unflinchingly with a tennis racquet, then accept an unjust prison sentence that would annihilate not only his life but also Emily's and his mother's? Break up with the girl he was in love with and submit to sex like a well-paid concubine? He'd worked tirelessly since he was a child, had overcome a family tragedy, taken care of his sick mother, struck hundreds of thousands of tennis balls against a wall by himself for long, lonely hours to earn a college scholarship, and, against all reasonable expectations, become a self-made man about to embark on an elite law career. Everything in Catherine's life had been built for her by someone else, prepared on a silver platter alongside her healthy servings of passive income, and all she'd done was fritter away her days with liquor and socializing and sardonic remarks. And she had planned to hoard her money, too, until the day she died. Once Emily inherited it in seven years, she'd spread most of it around. The world would be a better place because of this.

He'd not only done what he had to do, he'd done the right thing.

CONOR SIPPED $130-A-BOTTLE SCOTCH AND WATCHED THE FINAL PRESI-dential debate on his new computer one night in the barroom. He didn't particularly like scotch and wasn't into political theater, but the novelty of having an entire bar in their house hadn't yet worn off.

Emily came in. "Can I talk to you about something?" she asked.

"Sure." He muted the debate and looked at her.

"You mind turning that off?"

He shut the laptop. She took some time before she spoke.

"When you proposed to me, it made me really happy," she said. "And I said yes without thinking it all the way through. And then by the time I really started thinking about it, my mom was gone. Even Olivia, who's the most impulsive person I know, thinks this was way too fast and that I don't know you well enough to get married."

There was an anxious pang in his chest from where she was going with this. If they were no longer together, she'd reassess everything—especially that he'd given her mother tennis lessons without telling her and that he'd gone to her house late at night several times and been the last one to see her. She might well call to the attention of the detectives details she'd previously overlooked, such as Catherine's flirtatious behavior that time they'd all had cocktails.

Then another pang, of rejection, one he fully deserved. Emily was through with him. And once she got over the end of their relationship and the disappearance of her mother, she'd pair up with some Brooklyn writer in skinny jeans who went to therapy and couldn't hurt her. Or, worse, a Wasp with his own family's summer house and a job at a cousin's company and a drawerful of pink shorts.

And, though he'd be exiled back to Yonkers with his mother, he'd be alone again. More alone than ever.

He took a drink of scotch to give himself time to formulate a response, to build some armor around himself, and because the taste—peaty, smoky, almost medicinal—was growing on him.

"Well," he said slowly, "what do you want to do? Call off the engagement?"

"I don't know," she said. "This has been a fucking nightmare. I know I'm not being a good girlfriend, or fiancée or whatever, right now. This isn't what you signed up for, either. I'm a mess. I'm barely eating. We don't sleep in the same room. I hardly even talk anymore. You can't tell me you're happy being with me."

If he didn't feel the same ardor he used to, if his heart didn't catch in his chest upon seeing her anymore, then circumstances were to blame; no one could possibly pass through the brambles of recent events and emerge with the unscratched love he'd had before all this. But he hoped that, at some point, she would return to a version of her old self, to doing that slipping-in-socks routine on the kitchen floor again, and his occasional thoughts about what had happened would cease, and they could find their way back to being the couple they'd once been. He was even confident that, in time, they'd pick up where they left off with sex, too. But only if he could convince her to stay with him.

"It sounds like you *do* want to call it off."

"Well, maybe it'd be good if we spent a little time apart. I could stay here, in case the detectives need me, and you could go home and take care of your mom for a while."

He tapped his fingers on the marble bar top. The base was solid burnished wood, shaped in a graceful crescent. The cost of this structure alone was probably a few years' worth of his mother's insulin.

"It seems to me that you're reenacting your parents' divorce," he said, playing shrink. "A tragedy happens, and your instinct is to leave."

"You have no idea what they went through. Or even what I'm going through now."

"No? I have no idea what it's like to lose a parent unexpectedly?"

She looked down at the bar.

"What you're going through now is horrible," he said. "But I would've thought having me around, someone who knows at least a little about what you're feeling, would be a comfort to you. That's what I thought relationships are about. Especially a marriage. Finding someone who takes care of you when you need it. I assume I'll need it from you someday, too. But the way you're reacting makes me think that's not in your DNA. That you're the kind of person who cuts bait when things get hard. So maybe you're right. We should just end things now, permanently, before anyone gets hurt more. I'll leave in the morning."

Conor stalked out of the bar, then the house, shutting the door loudly. He walked down the neck to the community vegetable garden, ignoring several calls from Emily.

He returned after an hour. She was waiting for him outside the front door.

"I love you," she said immediately. "And I need you now. You're all I have. Please don't go."

He hugged her.

"I'm staying right here," he told her.

. . .

THEY RESUMED SLEEPING IN THE SAME BED THAT NIGHT.

Conor continued to avoid suspicious internet searches, but he'd confirmed in a bar exam book that inheritances were considered pre-marital assets, as he'd told the detectives. It was a moot point for now, anyway. Unsure about whether inherited *property* was treated the same as money, he called a former classmate working at a divorce and family law firm. Conor pretended that a friend of his was expecting to inherit a valuable house soon and was worried his girlfriend was pressuring him to get married so that she could lay a claim to it.

"First of all, I'd advise your friend not to marry someone he's wor-ried is after his inheritance," the lawyer said. "But an inherited house is the same as inherited money. It belongs solely to the heir—unless, once she's his wife, she can prove she's financially responsible for some of it. And cohabitation won't cut it. She's got to be paying part of the mortgage or taxes or bills. If they pay it from a joint bank account, that would be enough for her."

"What if the property taxes and bills are paid out of just his ac-count?" Conor asked.

"Then the only other way is if she pays, completely on her own, for maintenance or renovations that raise the house's value. If she's the one who writes a check to remodel the kitchen, for instance, that would convince a court she's owed a portion of the resale value. The more she pays for, the bigger the portion."

"And what if she pays for some of these things before they get le-gally married?"

"I'd have to think that would still count," the lawyer said. "But I wouldn't worry about it. No woman in history has ever paid to reno-vate her boyfriend's house before they're married."

THE LOCAL PAPER HAD FINALLY CAUGHT WIND OF CATHERINE'S DISAP-pearance and written a short article on it. Due to the ambiguous circumstances, however, it hadn't yet generated any other media attention.

While Conor was eating dinner with Emily a few nights later, she received a call from a number she didn't recognize. She picked up, as she now did with every unidentified number in the hopes that it was her mother or connected to her case.

"From the *New York Times*?" she asked the caller. "How'd you get my number?"

She listened to what sounded like a series of questions from a male voice. "Yes, he's my dad, but they've been divorced a long time," she said. "No, he was in the Caribbean when it happened . . . I'm not sure . . . Can we not—"

The reporter said more things inaudible to Conor. He walked around the table.

"I-I don't know," Emily stammered. "Can you please just talk to the police if you have questions? I don't want to say anything that—"

Conor grabbed her phone. "This is Emily's husband . . . Yes, her husband. This entire conversation is off the record. Mine and hers. We're issuing no comment. Don't fucking call my wife again. Ever."

He hung up.

"Fucking asshole." He looked at Emily, whose face was frozen in shock. "It's easier to help you with these things as your husband than just as your boyfriend."

Emily's eyes were moist. From her chair, she stared up at him in gratitude and crumpled against his sturdy body.

AND SO THEY PASSED THE DAYS LIKE THIS, IN GREAT MATERIAL IF SCANT emotional comfort, until a windy afternoon at the end of October when Detective Clark called Emily for the first time in weeks. She put it on speakerphone with Conor in the room, afraid to hear what he had to tell her alone.

"We found a body," he said.

CHAPTER 34

A passerby had spotted a fully skeletonized body in a marshy spot under a bridge about two miles off the neck. DNA analysis, compared against a sample previously taken from Emily, confirmed it was Catherine.

The local department was coordinating with the state police to shore up the investigation. Given the high stakes of the outcome, they were bringing in a veteran medical examiner from Boston. Waiting for him, along with a toxicology report they were trying to expedite, meant the exam would take several more days to finish.

After bawling over the news, Emily became catatonic again with grief, camping out in one of the guest rooms during the days and sleeping there alone.

"I guess this is better than not knowing where she is," she said to Conor one night. "If I never found out what happened to her, if I was wondering where she was or if she'd ever show up, it's all I'd be thinking about the rest of my life."

Insufficient evidence had hamstrung the investigation thus far, but the discovery of Catherine's remains changed everything. If the examiner ruled her death a homicide, it might result in a more sophisticated reappraisal of the blood from his cabin floor, or at least more cops looking for her Mercedes. And Conor was the only real suspect. He knew nothing about autopsies and wasn't going to take any chances researching them now, but if the examiner could pinpoint a time of death at odds with his testimony about when he'd last seen Catherine, the police would have probable cause to arrest him. They might do it with a homicide ruling, anyway, on the basis of circumstantial evidence—

people had been arrested for much less. Or if that was a bridge too far, they could use the ruling to turn Emily against him and parlay her testimony into a charge. She hadn't yet seemed to remember his climbing back into bed the night he'd returned from Providence, among other suspicious behavior. With some prodding, she might—or, worse, some coaching, convincing her that Conor had done it and all they needed was her word against his to lock up her mother's murderer, and she might invent something damning that hadn't even happened.

No matter whether he eventually beat the charges, a mere arrest for homicide would kill his relationship with Emily, kill his career. A death sentence rendered by the court of public opinion.

WITH THE IDENTIFICATION OF THE BODY, THE ESTATE LAWYER INFORMED Emily that the distribution of Catherine's estate would now commence, though it would take several months before any assets transferred to her. The restrictions on her trust fund would remain in place until she turned thirty, but that hardly mattered, as she would soon assume control over her mother's enormous reserves of cash and portfolio of investments.

Emily didn't want to hold a memorial service and was emotionally incapable of handling the staggering volume of paperwork that came her way. She asked Conor to review it all and just tell her what to sign, especially everything related to the Fifth Avenue apartment and the Cutters house.

"I'll take care of it," Conor promised. "Is there anything else I can do to make things better for you these next few months?"

She shook her head.

"Well," he said, "would you feel safer, until we figure out what happened to your mom, with some kind of alarm system here?"

"Maybe," she said. "I can't think about anything like that now."

CONOR WATCHED ELECTION-NIGHT COVERAGE BY HIMSELF AFTER EMILY went to bed early with a sleeping pill. As the tight race unfolded and the probability of victory swung like a pendulum, he was more convinced than ever that the outcome would have no effect on his life. Regardless of who was president, he'd either be so rich that politics couldn't touch him or he'd languish, for the rest of his days, in a Massachusetts state prison.

CHAPTER 35

On a gray, drizzly Saturday morning two days before Conor was to start his new job, as the nation awaited confirmation of Biden's apparent but disputed victory, Detective Clark asked Emily to come to the station to discuss the medical examiner's report. He said Conor should join her.

"I ended up calling an alarm company and made an appointment here at eleven," Conor said. "I'll push it back," he added, projecting confidence that this wouldn't take long.

But he was far less assured as he drove them through the light rain. If he was being arrested for homicide, the police could have come to their house. Maybe this was a way to avoid a scene on Cutters, where a few residents remained, to spare Emily the embarrassment. Or were they going to interrogate him again in a casual manner, hoping he'd make one last blunder they could exploit with whatever new information they'd found? Was it possible they'd found the photo he'd sent, or other messages with Catherine that were more incriminating than he remembered?

When they arrived at the station, both detectives welcomed them into Clark's office. "Emily, would you prefer to be alone or to have Mr. O'Toole present?" Clark asked.

They'd never called him Mr. O'Toole before. The formality was disconcerting. It sounded like what they'd call him before making an arrest.

"I want him here," she said.

"Very well," said Clark. "Because your mother's body was found, the subpoenas for the emails and texts were approved. We're still combing through her emails, but we haven't found anything notable yet going back six months. And, as we feared, the texts are all gone."

Conor's calves, thighs, and buttocks unclenched.

The toxicology report, Clark said, showed the presence of ethanol in her bone marrow, though absent any blood or tissue to correlate it with, they couldn't make a confident prediction as to what her blood alcohol level was at the time of death. During the search of her house they found an empty bottle of lorazepam in her bathroom trash can that had been discarded well ahead of her renewal date, which raised the possibility that she either habitually abused it or had overdosed on the night of her death. There were traces in her bones of some of the prescription drugs she took, including the lorazepam, but it was difficult to determine how much was present at the time of death. Likewise, the bones couldn't give them an accurate postmortem interval, or the time since death.

This was all very good news for Conor.

The detective cleared his throat and read from a paper on his desk. "'The medical examiner found evidence of blunt-force trauma to the head. The subject's parietal bone . . .'" He glanced at Emily and adjusted his language. "There was a linear fracture on the right side of your mother's skull. That's a hairline crack. If we didn't suspect foul play, we might conjecture that she was standing on one of the boulders by the ocean, maybe she'd had a few drinks or took too much lorazepam—or both—and she slipped and knocked her head and fell unconscious in the water. Because of the stolen car and phone, however, our inclination would be to view this as not accidental."

Clark resumed reading: "'The examiner concluded that the fracture could have resulted from the skull hitting a rock, on either a single occasion or multiple occasions, while the body was submerged in the water. Alternatively, it could have resulted from a single blow or multiple blows from an object manipulated by an assailant.'" He looked up. "Like a heavy rock used to bludgeon. In which case we would treat this as a homicide."

Emily's gasp was audible. Conor drew a slow, deep breath inside his mask.

"So . . . you're treating it as a homicide?" Emily asked.

"Due to the examiner's uncertainty," Clark said, "he's made this a CUPPI for now."

"What's a CUPPI?" Emily asked.

Conor had never heard of this, either.

"'Cause undetermined pending police investigation,'" Clark explained. "It means we can't make a determination on the case."

"I . . . I don't understand," Emily said. "What does this mean?"

"With the information we have now, we can't conclusively establish what happened to your mother," Clark said.

"But she showed up dead with a . . . a broken skull. Isn't it obvious someone did this to her? That's not enough?"

"In order for it to be classified as a homicide, the examiner has to be able to prove the cause and manner of death," Clark said. "Right now it's too vague. He doesn't know if the injuries were pre- or postmortem. He doesn't know if your mother drowned, was assaulted, or had a heart attack on land and fell or was pushed in the water. He doesn't know if she took a bunch of benzos with a bottle of wine just before it all happened or not. He doesn't even know when it happened. He couldn't testify in court that this is definitely a homicide. So he won't make a final determination without further investigation that sways him one way or the other."

"But her car and the phone were stolen and driven far away, and she showed up dead around here," Emily said. "The two things are obviously connected. Doesn't that prove that someone did this to her? That it was an assailant?"

"I agree, someone else is involved, but we still can't hundred percent rule out the possibility that your mother drowned in an accident, and the person she was with got spooked and drove the car away to make it look like she took a trip. Unless we get a death certificate that says it's a homicide, we can't charge homicide."

"But you're saying the only other possibility is that someone covered up a drowning. Can't you charge someone with *that*, at least?"

"You need sufficient evidence or a motive to charge a specific individual."

"And you don't have that?" she asked.

"No," Clark admitted, and his eyes alighted for a moment on Conor.

Not only were they not charging him with homicide, they didn't even *know* if it was a homicide.

Emily was silent. Conor put his arm around her.

"Does that mean you're closing the case?" she asked in a small voice.

"No," Clark said. "Absolutely not. We're going to reinterview people on the neck and we're recanvassing her route in case there's anything we didn't catch the first time. In the meantime, you might be able to help us. I want you to really think about the days before and after your mother went missing and let me know if you can remember anything that seems off—anything at all, no matter how insignificant you might think it is. Very often it's the little things people overlook that end up being crucial."

"But that's all *you're* doing?" she asked. "Reinterviewing people and going over her route?"

"Well, we still have all the police in the state looking for her car," Clark said. "Which could potentially give us the evidence to charge someone."

"Because the . . . person's fingerprints will be in there?"

"Not at this point, no. Whoever took it likely abandoned it and it's been stolen, or they flipped it on the street themselves, and any biological evidence linked to them is long gone by now. And if they took it to a chop shop, the car doesn't even physically exist anymore in one piece. But modern cars have something called an infotainment system. It's the menu and screen on your dashboard. Your mother's Mercedes has one, even though it doesn't have GPS. When you plug your phone into the car, it automatically downloads all the data from the phone and keeps it there permanently. That means texts, pictures, contacts, everything. It's like we have the phone itself. It's possible we'd find something useful then."

Conor's terror resurged. If Catherine had plugged her phone in before he'd deleted the picture of his penis, then it would be there.

He'd have to use the excuse he'd come up with earlier when Catherine had threatened him with the picture: he'd meant to send it to Emily but had mistakenly addressed it to her mother instead.

But no one would believe that now, not on top of everything else. A picture of his penis on her phone wasn't evidence of a murder, but the cover-up of an affair would give the police what they needed for a homicide charge: a strong motive.

"How would you even find the car, if it hasn't shown up yet and if it wasn't taken to a chop shop?" Emily asked. "You told me the license plates would've been taken off already and it would be a new color."

Clark explained the process by which the police discover that a car has been stolen: if it's been abandoned, or if an officer ever makes a traffic stop, runs its plates, and discovers it doesn't match up, it's impounded. Then, through the confidential Vehicle Identification Number hidden in a place on the car that only the manufacturer and law enforcement know about, they can trace it to the rightful owner.

"What are the chances of finding it?" Emily asked.

"If it happened yesterday, I'd say we'd be more likely than not to recover it," Clark said. "But this happened over two months ago, and it was stolen in conjunction with a homicide or a drowning, so the thief would be very prudent—this isn't some teenager taking it out for a joyride and leaving it on the side of a highway. And it's a 2016 Mercedes C-Class, not a junker. They'd be careful with it."

"So what are the chances?" she asked again.

"Hard to say, but based on those variables, I'd say you're looking at around a fifteen percent chance of recovery."

"Fifteen percent isn't great," Emily said.

"No," Clark said. "But it's not zero."

There was a nonzero chance of the police finding Catherine's car and, with it, all her data.

"She had all her stuff delivered when the pandemic started," Emily suddenly announced. "Groceries and everything."

"What do you mean?" Clark asked.

"She never drove, once she got to Cutters. She didn't leave the neck, not a single time. And anywhere she went on the neck, she used her golf cart. If she didn't get in her car for months, would the . . . the info thing still work?"

"It would only have the data since the last time she plugged it in," Clark said. "You're certain she never drove?"

"She made a point of telling me she hadn't touched the car since March, because she was annoyed I shopped for my own groceries and was putting myself at risk for Covid."

"Well, it's still possible the car would give us something useful if we find it," Clark said, though it was clear he, too, was disappointed. "People leave all sorts of evidence behind."

But not Conor. Catherine's outrageous entitlement, her bottomless reservoir of money, her ability to pay other people to come serve her rather than inconvenience or endanger herself by going to them, had saved him. The police had nothing, and they never would.

"There's nothing else you can do?" Emily asked.

Clark leaned forward and spoke conspiratorially. "Here's the thing. Me and my partner don't actually think it was a homicide. We believe the most likely explanation is your mother had a . . . an intimate partner that you weren't aware of. Maybe from New York, maybe the Cape, maybe from the internet, maybe from around here. Maybe even someone on Cutters. Or she could've just been with a friend. They could've been swimming or on a boat, they had a few drinks, and she drowned. And even though it wasn't anyone's fault, the person she was with panicked and tried to cover it up, like I said before, and made it look like she went on a trip. Happens all the time. Moving the phone and the car after an accidental drowning isn't really even a crime. If he makes a confession, a judge and jury would look very favorably upon him. It's possible it doesn't even go to court."

"Why would someone confess now, if they haven't already?" Emily asked.

"Well, the DA's pissed off that we spent all this time on it and created a scandal," Clark said. "He's given us till the end of this week.

After that, the FBI will get involved. They've got powers we don't have access to. We might choose to get word out in the press about that, and if we do, the guy could realize he's in way over his head and come to us. And the sooner he does it, the better the outcome for him. Especially because the medical examiner is skeptical that it was an accident. He hasn't made the death certificate official yet. If we don't find anything soon that strongly points in the direction of an accident, he might change it to homicide."

Clark wasn't a subtle actor. He was baiting Conor into a simpleton's confession. Moving the phone and the car absolutely were crimes, and confessing two and a half months after the "accident" would not be viewed favorably by anyone and would result, thanks to changing his story all of a sudden, in a quick homicide charge. And it seemed counterintuitive that a medical examiner would ever change his determination because of a lack of new evidence—only if new evidence came to light, exactly what the CUPPI outcome stood for.

The detectives couldn't charge him, but they knew he'd done it—and that the cover-up was almost certainly of a homicide, not an accidental drowning. Anyone taking objective stock of the available evidence, as they had, would deduce that Conor was the most likely "intimate partner," or that he'd had some other reason to murder Catherine, such as her forbidding him to marry her daughter (which, in effect, she had). He'd visited her house numerous times late at night and had kept those meetings and his entire business relationship with her secret from her daughter and his girlfriend; he'd proposed to that daughter, the sole heir to her mother's carefully controlled fortune, shortly after Catherine went missing; he'd bled over his cabin floor the night after she was last seen by anyone else; and, the most prejudicial fact of all, he was the last person to see Catherine alive and hadn't told anyone about it until it had been discovered.

Emily's thinking, however, had been far from objective, clouded by shock, grief, and the sheer impossibility of imagining a scenario in which her boyfriend turned fiancé, her hardworking, straight-

and-narrow caretaker, had been sleeping with her mother, violently killed her, and expertly concealed her murder. Her former suspicions that he'd quashed would someday revive. Once enough time passed, she would perceive things more clearly, recognize that his alibis had too many holes and coincidences, think of all the times Conor had been "distant," and eventually come to believe he had something to do with Catherine's death, even if those holes and coincidences weren't quite big enough for a criminal charge. And if she continued to communicate with the detectives, they could decide to tell her their theory, either out of a desire to protect her, if they feared Conor might someday attempt to off her for her inheritance, or merely for the satisfaction of poisoning his relationship if they couldn't arrest him.

He was safe legally, but not matrimonially. This wasn't the time for steady strokes. He had to go for the big shot and act, once more, as the lone protector of his delicate, defenseless fiancée.

"Absolutely unacceptable," Conor said.

"What's that?" Sousa asked.

"It's absolutely unacceptable. The only hope we have of finding out who killed her mother is if a press conference scares the murderer into *confessing*? Is that a joke? You're not doing anything else?"

"As we explained," Sousa said in an unperturbed voice, "we're re-interviewing people from Cutters and we're—"

"Fucking unacceptable," said Conor, striking the desk with his fist.

"Conor. It's okay." Emily touched his forearm. He crossed his arms.

"It's not okay," he said. "What about interrogating everyone who's stolen a car recently?"

"In all of New England?" Sousa scoffed. "You want us to ask each felon if he also happened to murder and drown a woman before he stole it?"

"There's plenty of other shit you guys could've done differently," Conor said. "You could've done a real search of her house right away instead of waiting, what, four or five days? And you should've had a dive team out looking for her in the water. You would've found her right away and had a better chance of figuring out what really happened."

"We don't bring out divers every time someone who lives near the ocean goes missing," Sousa said.

"How about police dogs? I didn't see any."

"Our department doesn't own one. They're expensive."

"But you could've brought one in, and you didn't."

"We don't call up another county to get their dog for missing-persons cases that get reported by relatives who, at the time, are pretty blasé about what they think is going on," Sousa said.

"And you've looked through *all* the surveillance video you could find?"

"We've gone over this. There's nothing useful there. As we told you, most of these places erase their footage after a week, which makes it very difficult when people get reported kinda-sorta missing a while after they were last seen by one of the very people making the report."

Sousa was getting testy, stepping up to the line of speaking aloud what he and Clark privately thought.

Conor couldn't show fear. He needed to keep playing aggressively.

"So now you're just throwing your hands up," he said, charging past the insinuation. "Maybe we should hire a private investigator to do your job for you."

"That's entirely your prerogative." Sousa stood. "I think we're done here."

"Hold on," Conor said, lowering his voice, as he shook his finger at the detectives. "I'm not ruling out suing your department, either. This is not a game to me. I'm about to start working at a major law firm in New York. Things can get ugly."

They were all silent. Conor was certain the detectives saw through his motive, but he sensed his performance had convinced Emily. And a police department that couldn't afford a dog wouldn't want to piss off a lawyer at a powerful New York firm who'd just threatened to sue them. He doubted they'd ever share their theories with Emily. The fallout wasn't worth it to them.

"You're free to pursue any legal options you like, Mr. O'Toole,"

Clark said. "Emily, you can call me anytime if you have other thoughts about the case that might be pertinent. Or if you have any questions. Anything at all."

She thanked him, and she and Conor stood to leave.

Clark's gaze found Conor one more time. "I want to assure you that I won't give up on this case," he said. "Ever."

"Good," Conor said. "Neither will I."

IT WAS RAINING HARDER AS CONOR DROVE THEM HOME THROUGH THE village.

"You really want to sue them?" Emily asked. "And hire a private investigator?"

"I mostly said all that to push them to do more, and I think it worked," he said. "What Clark said at the end, about not giving up on the case, made me think he's going to take it more seriously. They're not going to be negligent now that they know I'm pissed off."

"So you *don't* actually want to sue or hire one?"

"Well, we don't need the money from a lawsuit, and I'm ninety-nine percent sure it would just bring more media attention to the case. And a classmate who does criminal law told me a PI wouldn't come up with anything the police wouldn't find. Less, even, because he can't coordinate with the authorities. You'll have to be more involved instead. Your dad, too, probably. He'll interview you a lot about your mom and dredge up things from your entire life. But we can look into it, if you want."

She traced a fingernail over the condensation in the window, etching thin lines on the glass.

"No," she said.

They drove in silence. When they crossed the drawbridge out of town, Emily started crying.

"Em?" he asked.

"I keep thinking . . ." she said.

He waited for her to finish, but her tears got in the way. He pulled over to the side of the road. "You keep thinking what?"

"Of someone hitting her on the head with a rock. And that word," she said. "*Bludgeon.*" The word seemed to echo within the chassis of her Prius. "I knew the world was violent, but I didn't . . . I didn't really know."

He hugged her closely enough that she couldn't see his face.

"It might not have been," he said. "You have to remember that. The examiner said it's undetermined. It could've been from boulders in the wat—er."

"I don't care what the examiner said," Emily replied. "We all know someone did this to her. An assailant. And now I'll be picturing it for the rest of my fucking life."

"You won't," he said, stroking her head. "You think that now, but it'll go away with time."

Once she seemed stable enough, he drove on. A white van with a logo for Radion Home Security Systems turned onto the road behind him. Emily powered on her phone, which she'd shut off at the police station. It shook with a slew of notifications.

"The Associated Press called it," she said quietly. "Biden won."

"Good," Conor said, calibrating his reaction to the somber atmosphere. "That's a big relief."

"Yeah," she said, barely audible.

She plugged the phone into the charger. A song automatically blared from the car's speakers with assaultive percussion.

"Sorry," she sniffled as she turned off the music. "It does that now whenever I plug it into the car."

The Cars.

Catherine's car.

Catherine hadn't connected to the infotainment system—*he* had.

All his phone's data was permanently stored in her Mercedes, nearly as damning as the biological data he'd bleached away.

This was more than enough to charge him with homicide.

Fifteen percent, Clark had pegged the odds of finding the car. Better than a one-in-seven chance of going to prison.

But a nearly six-in-seven chance of never getting caught. If you were at a casino and had a six-in-seven chance of winning a game, you'd be stupid not to bet all your chips.

He'd just have to put the alternative, the one-in-seven prospect of losing everything, out of his mind.

He looked back at the van in the rearview mirror.

"So what do you think?" Emily asked.

"What?"

"What I just asked you."

"Sorry, I was distracted." The van was close behind him. "This guy's right on my tail."

"Do you think they've got a chance of finding out who did it?"

"Well," Conor said, "like he said, the odds are against i—"

He couldn't finish the word, his mouth opening and closing silently like a fish's. Though he badly wanted to let it go, a more powerful force, perhaps the same trait that led him never to give up on anything, impelled him to complete the sentence.

"—it," he finally eked out.

A feeling of dread coursed inside him, pooling in every hollow. Twice in a row. He'd resume his enunciation exercises that night, in private.

Or maybe it would go away on its own if he ignored it.

He reached the turnoff for Cutters and coasted downhill to the gate. The van followed. It was a downpour now, the rain bouncing off the road like oil sizzling in a frying pan.

He stopped by the gate box and punched in the code, soaking his hand and forearm.

The gate didn't open. He reentered the digits, but it remained shut.

"You know the new code?" he asked.

"No. Lawrence emails it to everyone on Saturdays. They probably just changed it."

He took out his phone to search his inbox. The van honked.

"But there's still a chance, right?" Emily asked.

His email wasn't loading. "My phone's not getting a signal. Is yours?"

She checked her phone and shook her head. The white van honked. Conor held up his index finger out the window to request patience and moved his phone around the interior of the car, trying to catch a few stray radio frequency waves.

If only he hadn't been self-conscious about his old phone's damaged speaker, or if he'd had the money to replace it earlier, he'd have nothing to worry about. Though if he'd had enough money, he wouldn't have slept with Catherine for it, or even taken this job in the first place.

It sounded like a gaggle of angry geese in back of him. A delivery truck was now behind the white van, and both drivers were leaning on their horns over the delay.

Finally his email refreshed. He found the message with the new code and entered it into the box. The gate groaned to life.

"Conor?" Emily said as the barrier yielded with agonizing slowness. "Do you think there's any chance?"

But what was done was done. Weak people dwelled on the past, wallowed in their losses, leaned on the crutch of psychobabble to justify their defects. The strong forged ahead, forged themselves into whomever they wanted to be, and he was nothing if not strong. Mentally tough. Not a pusher; a rocket ship.

Look where he was now. Look where he was going. He could be a senator if he wanted.

Why stop there.

"Conor?" she asked again.

One in seven. Almost nothing.

"There's always a chance," Conor said, and he sped through the gate, past the notice deterring trespassers, past the controversial sign on Lawrence Newcomb's house, past the waterlogged American flag drooping from the Bakers' porch, past John Price's guest cabin and its bloodstained floor, until they reached the dead end of the road.

He opened his door and stepped out. Emily stayed put.

"Coming?" he asked.

"In a minute," she said. "Go without me."

He started to say something, but thought better of it and shut the door.

Then Conor hustled through the rain and waited for the driver of the white van under the porch of their house, whose deed was in the process of transferring to Emily Havemeyer Remsen—someday O'Toole—and whose value, already the highest by far on Cutters Neck, would soon, with the modern security system he'd install once his first paycheck cleared, rise even more.

ACKNOWLEDGMENTS

Thank you, once again, to my agent, Jim Rutman. On the West Coast, the collective efforts of Will Watkins, Andrew Murphy, and Michael Wilson have been life-changing.

It has been a joy to reunite with my editor, Millicent Bennett; as usual, she left this novel in far better shape than she found it. I am also grateful to Liz Velez for all their diligent work. Douglas Johnson returned an uncommonly sensitive copyedit. Thank you to Maya Baran, Katie O'Callaghan, Robin Bilardello, Jonathan Burnham, and everyone else at Harper for their support.

Sarah Bruni, Elizabeth Graver, Robert Kuhn, Daniel Loedel, Diana Spechler, and John Warner gave me thoughtful and generous feedback on early drafts.

Joshua Gradinger not only answered my numerous questions about criminal law and vetted the manuscript but also offered ideas I couldn't have conceived of on my own. So did members of the New York City Police Department Detective Bureau concerning police work. Any errors are mine.

Thank you to the late Robert M. Pennoyer for providing a home during part of the writing of this book, and many other times, too.

Finally: Phoebe, Angus, and Kate Greathead—anchors without which I'd be at sea. I love you.

ABOUT THE AUTHOR

TEDDY WAYNE is the author of six novels and a winner of a Whiting Award and an NEA Creative Writing Fellowship as well as a finalist for the Young Lions Fiction Award, the PEN/Bingham Prize, and the Dayton Literary Peace Prize. A frequent contributor to *The New Yorker* and a former columnist for the *New York Times*, he has taught at Columbia University and Washington University in St. Louis. He lives in Brooklyn with his family.